Advance Praise for *West of Sin*

"*West of Sin* blazes with page-turning tension, wit, exceptional dialogue, and affable characters."
— *Foreword Reviews*

"Fans of zippy, high-tension thrillers with romantic and humorous elements will be enthralled by this fresh and original novel."
— *BookLife Reviews* (editor's pick)

"An explosive adventure that pays off repeatedly with nail-biting scenes that often manage to surprise." — BestThrillers.com

"Mr. Lewis has displayed a superb writing talent equal to that of a young James Patterson."
— *Affaire de Coeur* (reviewer's choice)

"A very impressive first novel...Lewis knows how to deliver plot twists, things most astute readers will not see coming...A rousing, well-researched thriller." — *Kirkus Reviews*

WEST OF SIN

A Thriller

Wesley S. Lewis

Red Granite Press
LLC
AUSTIN, TX

Red Granite Press LLC
4301 W. William Cannon Dr.
Ste. B-150-222
Austin, TX 78749-1487
www.redgranitepress.com

Publisher's Note: This is a work of fiction. Names, characters, places, and incidents are a product of the author's imagination. Locales and public names are sometimes used for atmospheric purposes. Any resemblance to actual people, living or dead, or to businesses, companies, events, institutions, or locales is completely coincidental unless otherwise stated in the Author's Note & Acknowledgments on page 335.

WEST OF SIN / Wesley S. Lewis — 2nd ed.

PUBLISHER'S CATALOGING-IN-PUBLICATION DATA
Names: Lewis, Wesley Scott, 1980- author.
Title: West of sin: a thriller / Wesley S. Lewis.
Description: Austin, TX : Red Granite Press, 2020.
Identifiers: LCCN 2019950130 | ISBN 978-1-7340157-0-6 (hardcover) |
    ISBN 978-1-7340157-1-3 (paperback) | ISBN 978-1-7340157-2-0 (ebook) |
    ISBN 978-1-7340157-3-7 (audiobook)
Subjects: LCSH: Robbery--Fiction. | Kidnapping--Fiction. | Human trafficking--
    Fiction. | Organized crime--Russia (Federation)--Fiction. | Skydiving--Fiction.
    | Suspense fiction. | BISAC: FICTION / Thrillers / Suspense. | FICTION /
    Thrillers / Crime. | FICTION / Romance / Suspense. | FICTION / Women. |
    GSAFD: Suspense fiction.
Classification: LCCPS3612.E9879 W47 2020 (print) | LCCPS3612.E9879 (ebook) |
    DDC 813/.6--dc23.

For Terry and Gale, my biggest fans.

"[Las Vegas] may not be the end of the world per se, but you can certainly see it from there."

—Robin Williams

WEST OF SIN

CHAPTER ONE

Jennifer Williams's tears had turned to anger about twenty miles back. She had no plan and no destination, just a basic need to keep putting miles between herself and that hotel room thick with the stench of sweat and betrayal.

The past hour was a blur. She vaguely recalled running for the elevator and stumbling through the lobby. Her wits had returned to find her speeding through the Nevada desert in a stolen Chevy Traverse.

Jennifer had forgotten to give Bryan the valet ticket after using his rental car to pick up the extra marketing flyers he'd insisted on ordering, but she'd remembered it when making her escape. For the first thirty miles or so, she simply drove, not considering where she was going, just trying her best to keep the shimmering lights of the Las Vegas Strip in her rearview mirror. When the city disappeared behind a mountain, she dried her eyes and started seeing red.

One year had passed since their conversation in the lounge atop the Stratosphere Tower, one year since he'd confided in her that he thought his marriage was ending, twelve long months since she'd privately decided to wait for him.

Jennifer wasn't so naïve as to think Bryan had left his wife for her, but she had presumed his marriage was the only thing keeping them apart. In the four months since his separation, they had walked a fine line between friendship and something more, enjoying the occasional movie or dinner together but keeping things platonic so as to avert office gossip and avoid complicating his already sticky divorce.

Now that the divorce was final, Jennifer had expected this trip to end—or preferably begin—with something a bit more intimate than the prolonged embraces they sometimes shared after a night out. What she'd gotten instead was the crushing realization that her hopes for the coming months—being in a real relationship by fall, introducing him to her family over the holidays, going someplace tropical for her fortieth birthday—were never going to come true.

From some dark corner of her mind came the terrible thought that maybe he'd never wanted more, that he'd used her as an emotional placeholder.

She pushed the thought away. This was not the time to question things she knew—or, at the very least, things she'd known an hour ago—to be true. She was buzzed from four rounds of drinks and punchy from ten hours spent pitching retail properties to bored tenant reps who cared more about the real estate beneath her skirt than about anything in New Wave's portfolio. She was tired, she was lost, and to top it all off, the lace pattern on her expensive French panties—the kind made to be seen, not worn—had imprinted itself painfully on her backside. Comfort had not been her top priority when selecting her attire for the evening, and nothing she'd chosen was well suited to a long drive.

For the first time since leaving the hotel, she took note of her surroundings, looking for any clue as to where she might be.

Her rearview mirror reflected nothing but a black sea of desert. To the left and right, she saw more of the same. A couple of miles ahead, a single cluster of lights beckoned from the left side of the road.

◆ ◆ ◆

The conspicuous *click-clack* of her high heels on the tile floor made Jennifer wish she'd left the overpriced stilettos in the car and walked barefoot. Wearing a slinky black dress into a remote truck stop was uncomfortable enough without her shoes announcing her entrance.

A quick glance at her surroundings eased her mind. The truck stop had only one customer, and he seemed oblivious to anything beyond the contents of the beverage case. She approached the front counter.

The leather-skinned woman behind the register gave an uneasy smile, revealing two missing front teeth.

Jennifer forced a smile of her own. "Excuse me, I seem to be a bit lost. Where are we in relation to Las Vegas?"

The clerk sighed and, in a voice that suggested a pack-a-day habit, said, "You're about an hour west of Vegas. Head east on 160 till you hit the interstate." When Jennifer didn't immediately respond, the woman added, "Just turn right out of the parking lot."

"Thanks." Jennifer glanced around the store. "Where is your restroom?"

"Restroom's for customers only."

Jennifer took a deep breath and forced another smile. "I'm going to buy a cup of coffee."

"We're out of coffee."

"Okay, I'll buy something else."

"It's out of order."

"What?"

"We only got the one restroom," said the clerk, "and it's all plugged up."

Jennifer exhaled slowly. "Is there another gas station around here somewhere?"

"Lots of 'em up the road in Pahrump."

"How far is that?"

"About ten miles west. Just turn—"

"Left out of the parking lot, I got it." She turned away from the cashier. "Thanks."

Jennifer didn't need to pee so badly as to drive another ten miles in the wrong direction, but there was no way she could make it back to Las Vegas without caffeine. She worked her way to the back of the store, where the lone customer—a well-built man in a pair of khaki shorts and a blue polo shirt—was still studying the beverage case.

She spotted a row of iced coffees and reached for the cooler door.

The man in the blue shirt pivoted toward her. "Can I help you?"

She hesitated. "Uh, no. Just getting a drink."

"What do you want?" He opened the case. "I'll grab it for you."

Jennifer was tiring of these socially awkward desert dwellers. "Thanks," she said, reaching into the case, "but I can manage."

As her hand came to rest on the glass bottle, she froze. Either the day's stress was getting to her or something on the other side of the case had just moved. She peered between the shelves, trying to see into the unlit stockroom.

Behind the row of beverages, a pair of eyes stared out of the darkness. She released the bottle and took a quick step back.

She struggled to make sense of the eyes, which seemed to float in the darkness. Then she saw the gun barrel wedged between two rows of sodas, and the missing piece fell into place.

In the dark stockroom behind the drinks, someone in a black ski mask was pointing a shotgun at her.

CHAPTER TWO

Jennifer screamed and stumbled backward, trying to put as much distance as possible between herself and the gunman inside the cooler.

Twenty feet to her right, a door swung open, and another man in a ski mask stepped out of a small restroom, carrying a chrome-plated pistol.

Still reeling, Jennifer tried to turn toward the front of the store. Her high heels skidded on the tile floor. She lost her footing and fell hard.

Ignoring the pain in her tailbone, she used her hands and feet to scoot backward across the tile, not thinking about anything but escape. She kept kicking and pushing for a couple of seconds before realizing she'd backed into a row of shelves.

The masked man from the restroom stopped at her feet and raised his pistol. Jennifer closed her eyes and waited for the bullet that would end it all.

When the bullet didn't come, she looked up at the man and waited for him to say something. He just stared at her. She followed his gaze down to her lap and saw that her dress had ridden up to her waist.

Her expensive French underwear was meant to be seen, but not by him. She grabbed the hem of her dress and slid it down over her hips. With her modesty restored, she crossed her ankles and placed her hands in her lap. The man in the mask looked on without a word.

From somewhere near the front of the store, a male voice bellowed, "Well, that worked for shit."

Jennifer looked in that direction, saw a masked man pointing a pistol at the back of the clerk's head, and shuddered at the realization that he must have been hiding behind the counter the whole time.

Somewhere on the other side of the shelves, a heavy door opened with a thud. A moment later, the man in the blue shirt rounded the end of the aisle with his hands raised, followed closely by the barrel of a shotgun—the one Jennifer had seen inside the beverage case—and the masked man who'd almost scared her to death.

Without taking his eyes off Jennifer, the man holding her at gunpoint said, "I told you we should have grabbed her when she walked in."

"Fuck you, Al," responded the man with the shotgun. "How was I supposed to know she'd look in the cooler?"

The man guarding Jennifer turned and pointed his chrome pistol at the man with the shotgun. "Do I have to shoot you in the face? Is that what it's going to take to get you to stop saying my name?"

The man in the blue shirt took a slow step to the side, out of the potential line of fire.

"Let it go," called the man guarding the cashier. "I'm pretty sure everyone knows your name by now."

"I'm sorry," said the man with the shotgun. "It just slipped out."

"Well, it's been slipping out too goddamn much," replied Al, turning his unsettling gaze back toward Jennifer. "And this is taking too goddamn long, and we've got too many goddamn witnesses."

"Maybe we ought to just bail," said the man with the shotgun.

"Maybe you shouldn't have told us you know how to break into an ATM when you clearly don't," said Al.

"All I said was that I'd broken into slot machines. Then you guys said that slot machines don't hold enough cash. Then I said, 'What about an ATM machine?' and you guys got all excited. But this thing ain't like no slot machine. It's like a fucking safe."

"We don't have time for your excuses. Just figure out a way to get the money out of the machine."

"Al's right," said the man behind the counter. "We need to get that money and get the hell out of here before anyone else shows up."

"Can I make a suggestion?" asked the man in the blue shirt.

Al turned and pointed his gun at the man's forehead. "If you're going to suggest that we shouldn't leave any witnesses, I'm starting to agree with you."

Jennifer was beginning to dislike the man in the blue shirt.

"No," said the man, unfazed, "I was going to suggest that, rather than focusing on getting the money out of the machine, you should focus on getting the machine out of the store."

"It's bolted to the floor," responded the man with the shotgun.

"No it's not," said a raspy voice.

All eyes turned toward the clerk.

"I know," she continued, "because they've moved it twice since I've been here."

Al glared at the man with the shotgun. "You didn't even check to see if it was secured?"

"What's it matter? It ain't gonna fit in the car."

"He's right," said the man guarding the cashier. "We can't exactly strap it to the hood."

"Take my truck," said the man in the blue shirt.

Al's eyes narrowed. "Truck?"

"The white half-ton Ford parked out at the pump. It could carry at least six of those machines."

If this were a real estate transaction, thought Jennifer, *these robbers would owe him a facilitator's fee.*

"Where are the keys?" asked Al.

The man glanced down at his khaki shorts. "Front right pocket."

Al stepped forward and, without breaking eye contact with the man, reached slowly into the pocket and pulled out a set of keys.

He took a step back and glanced at his partner holding the shotgun. "Watch these two, and don't do anything stupid."

Without waiting for a reply, he turned and ran to the front of the store. He paused at the door just long enough to scan the parking lot and tuck the chrome pistol into his waistband before sprinting outside.

The man with the shotgun looked down at Jennifer, then back up at the man in the blue shirt, then down at Jennifer again.

"Okay," he said, "you two move up to the front of the store. And don't try anything funny."

Jennifer wondered if he actually thought they might try something *funny* or if he'd said that because it felt like something a masked robber should say in such a situation. She had no intention of trying anything *funny*, and the man in the blue shirt clearly intended to cooperate.

She pulled her feet under her, wincing at the pain in her bruised tailbone.

The man in the blue shirt offered his hand. "Let me help you."

She accepted and the man hoisted her to her feet.

His mouth formed a faint smile. "I bet now you wish you'd let me grab that drink for you, huh?"

"Now I wish I'd driven on to the next gas station," she replied, not seeing any humor in it.

The man with the shotgun motioned them forward with the barrel of the gun. "Get moving."

"Watch where you're pointing that thing," said the man in the blue shirt.

"Just move."

The three of them walked to the front counter.

"Okay," said the man with the shotgun, "both of you get back there with—"

Jennifer was pretty sure he was about to say the name of the man guarding the clerk, but he was interrupted by the tail end of a white pickup crashing through the glass doors at the front of the store.

The tires squealed as the truck skidded across the tile floor. Jennifer turned away from the careening vehicle and closed her eyes, certain she was about to be crushed against the row of celebrity gossip magazines lining the front counter.

As she braced for the truck's fatal impact, she instead felt a pair of hands grab her by the waist and hoist her into the air. Suddenly she was hurtling headlong across the counter. She opened her eyes just in time to see the clerk and the other masked man jump back as she landed at their feet.

She sat up and realized that the commotion had stopped. Peeking over the counter, she saw that the truck's rear bumper had stopped less than a foot from the man in the blue shirt and the man with the shotgun. Al forced open the driver-side door and hopped out.

"Are you fucking nuts?" screamed the man with the shotgun.

"Shut up and go get the ATM," said Al. "Both of you go. I'll watch them."

The third robber hurried from behind the counter and headed for the far end of the store.

The man with the shotgun raised his left hand and flipped Al the bird before turning and chasing after their partner.

Al turned to the man in the blue shirt. "You go too."

"Why?"

"Because that thing's too heavy for them to carry themselves."

The man glanced at the women, then back at Al. Without a word, he turned and followed the two masked men.

Al opened the tailgate of the pickup and sat on it. "You two come around here where I can see you."

Jennifer and the clerk inched around to the front of the counter.

Al pointed at the ground. "Have a seat."

Jennifer kicked aside a few shards of glass and lowered herself to the floor, minding her bumps and bruises, careful not to let her dress ride up again. Al watched, not saying a word. Jennifer found his gaze more disconcerting than his gun.

From her spot on the floor, she could hear but not see the three men struggling with the ATM. One of them instructed the other two to grip it from the bottom. That was followed by a loud crash, followed by a lot of cursing, followed by someone—she was pretty sure it was the man in the blue shirt—suggesting they turn it on its side.

How lucky for them he's here to help.

Another loud crash preceded a yelp of pain from one of Al's accomplices. This robbery had all the subtlety of a Three Stooges routine.

Al glared at Jennifer. "Does this amuse you?"

"No, of course not."

"Then why the stupid grin?"

She hadn't realized she was grinning. She swallowed the smile and said, "Just imagining I'm someplace else."

"Oh yeah?" He rose to his feet. "Where?"

"Anywhere but here."

"Yeah," he said, walking toward her, "you look like you were planning on being someplace else." He stopped at her feet. "You're way too dressed up for a shithole like Pahrump. What happened? Get lost on your way to Sin City?"

Jennifer stared up at the masked man. "I was out for a drive and got a little turned around."

"A little turned around, huh?"

"That's right." She tried to read his eyes, wondering what thoughts were dancing around inside that ski mask.

"Stand up."

"Why don't you leave her alone?" asked the clerk.

"Why don't you shut up before I bash your head in with the butt of my gun?"

"It's okay." Jennifer rose to her feet.

Al looked her up and down, then pointed his gun at her chest. "Turn around."

"Why?" Her gaze darted between his gun and his eyes.

"I forgot to frisk you. You could be carrying a concealed weapon."

"You didn't frisk me either," said the clerk.

Al pointed his gun at her. "This is your last warning."

The clerk didn't respond.

Al turned his attention back to Jennifer. "I said turn around."

"I can assure you I'm not carrying any weapons." She tried to suppress the note of fear creeping into her voice. "Where would I be hiding them?"

"That's for me to find out." With the gun still in his right hand, he grabbed her by the waist and spun her around. "Put your hands on the counter."

Shaking, she complied.

She felt his body brush past as he knelt behind her and heard him set the gun on the ground. He placed his hands gently around her left calf and slid them slowly upward. They reached the hem of her dress with no indication of slowing.

"Can we get some help here?" asked someone behind them.

Al removed his hands from her thigh. She heard the gun being picked up and felt his body brush by again as he stood. She risked a glance over her shoulder and saw the other three men straining to hold a small, heavily damaged ATM with a shotgun perched atop it.

"Can we get some help?" repeated the man in the blue shirt. "This thing is really heavy."

"Jesus Christ!" Al walked to the men and grabbed the shotgun off the machine. "Why don't you just give this guy a gun?"

Jennifer half sat, half collapsed onto the ground and tried to assure herself that the danger had passed.

"Okay, I can't hold it any longer," said one of the masked men. "Set it down."

With a collective grunt, the three load bearers lowered the machine to the ground.

When they'd righted themselves, Al tossed the shotgun to the one who'd just spoken. "Be more goddamn careful where you leave that."

Jennifer saw that the other robber had tucked his pistol into the waistband of his pants.

"Are you going to help us load this?" asked the man with the shotgun.

"Get that old bag to help you," said Al, pointing to the clerk. "I've got something to take care of."

He turned and walked toward Jennifer. She tried to scoot away but once again found herself backed into a shelf.

"Come on." He grabbed her by the wrist.

She struggled to free her arm, but his grip was too strong. He yanked her to her feet.

"If you need me," he said to his cohorts, "I'll be in the stockroom."

CHAPTER THREE

Terrified, Jennifer strained against Al's pull as he dragged her away from the counter.

"Make it quick," said the man with the pistol in his belt. "We can't afford to wait around after this thing is loaded."

"I'll be quick," said Al.

"How's it that you always manage to avoid the hard work?" asked the man with the shotgun.

Al paused for a moment, apparently considering the question.

Jennifer felt her last strands of rational thought slipping away. She scanned the room for any sign of hope. Helpless, she locked eyes with the man in the blue shirt, knowing that even if he wanted to help—and she was pretty sure he was more concerned with saving his own skin—there was nothing he could do. He stood with his hands on his hips, watching her fate play out before his eyes.

"It's like this," said Al, clearly impressed with the answer he'd constructed. "There are two types of people in this world—"

Jennifer didn't get to hear Al's philosophical explanation of the categorical dichotomy of mankind because at that moment the man in the blue shirt pulled something from beneath the tail of that blue polo. He moved with such speed that Jennifer had no idea what he was holding until she saw the muzzle flashes and heard the first two shots echoing off the walls.

Al released Jennifer's hand and stumbled sideways before collapsing to the ground.

The other two men, who hadn't been watching the man in the blue shirt, were slow to register what had just happened. The man with the pistol in his belt was turning toward the smashed doorway, perhaps thinking they were being ambushed from outside, when the next shot tore through his ribs.

As the man with the pistol fell to the ground, the man with the shotgun finally identified the source of the gunfire. He was in the process of raising his weapon when the last two shots caught him square in the chest. He tumbled face-first onto the tile floor.

Jennifer placed her hands over her ears but couldn't block out the painful ringing.

The man in the blue shirt approached and circled the bodies. When he seemed satisfied, he turned to Jennifer and the clerk.

The clerk sat on the ground, her knees tucked up to her chest. Jennifer leaned against the counter, not trusting her legs to support her.

The man said something Jennifer couldn't make out. She removed her hands from her ears.

"Are you okay?" he asked again.

She nodded, unable to speak.

"Good." He surveyed the carnage. "I'll secure their guns. You..." He seemed to lose his train of thought. "You call—" He staggered to the right and braced his free hand against a rack of audiobooks.

"Are you all right?" Jennifer managed to ask.

"Just a little sleep deprived.... Maybe I should—" He tumbled forward, pulling the rack down with him and sending CD boxes skidding across the floor.

The clerk screamed in surprise.

The man lay motionless among a few dozen abridged readings of twenty-year-old bestsellers.

Jennifer rushed forward and knelt beside him.

The clerk stood to get a better view. "He having a heart attack?"

Jennifer watched the man's chest rise and fall. "I think he just fainted."

"Lucky him." The clerk took a seat on the tailgate of the crashed pickup and glanced around the store. "How am I going to explain this to my boss?"

Jennifer looked from the damaged truck to the bodies of the three robbers and thought, *How am I going to explain it to* mine?

CHAPTER FOUR

EARLIER THAT DAY

The casino was surprisingly crowded for a Wednesday night. The crowd was only a fraction of what it would be in three days, when weekend warriors from Southern California and Phoenix would occupy most of the tables and slot machines, but the floor was alive with the voices of dealers and cocktail waitresses and with the constant ringing of electronic games.

Fortunately, Jennifer knew where the rest of her team would be—at the center of the casino floor, where the gaming tables gave way to the open-air cocktail lounge. This delicate merging of vices allowed those who'd sworn off gambling to mingle with those who'd sworn off drinking.

Cutting across the gaming floor, she turned just enough heads to reassure her that the slinky black dress was doing its job. She'd cursed herself for a full week after buying it, but every time she'd considered returning it, she'd pictured herself walking up to Bryan—the wispy fabric clinging to her body in all the right places, the almost dangerously short hem dancing with every sway of her hips—and that image had quelled any lingering doubts.

"Jen!" a woman called from somewhere inside the lounge.

A waving hand beckoned beneath a Riviera-themed banner advertising something called Le Tournoi at La Condamine. Jennifer could just make out the bare shoulder and golden locks of the firm's newest hire.

Ashley Thomas was a year out of college, blond, and attractive enough to spark rumors that she'd gotten the job on the merits of something other than her résumé. Jennifer was quick to quash such gossip, not just because she'd once inspired similar rumors herself but also because Ashley was competent. While most of the women envied Ashley's natural beauty, Jennifer envied her natural ability to navigate even the most tedious of deals.

As Jennifer neared the row of small cocktail tables, each occupied by two or three of her colleagues, she scanned the group, hoping to spot a pair of piercing green eyes framed by a thick head of salt-and-pepper hair. With considerable disappointment, she realized that her entrance had been lost on the one person who mattered. Her boss and soon-to-be lover was not among the dozen or so New Wave employees.

"Hey, roomie." Ashley rose from her seat and gave Jennifer a hug. "I think I owe you an apology."

"For what?"

The young woman released her embrace. "For doubting you when you said this conference would make me question my career choice. My feet are blistered, my throat is sore, and I'm going to gouge the eyes out of the next guy I catch staring at my ass while pretending to read a marketing flyer."

Jennifer laughed. "Just staring? Nobody has propositioned you?"

"Not yet." Ashley slipped back into her chair. "But the night is still young, and this guy is three sheets to the wind"—she motioned to the young man sharing her table—"so we'll see what happens."

Jennifer choked back another laugh. Around the office, it was an open secret that Tom Blackwell was smitten with Ashley. If he'd had his wits about him, he likely would have lost them at the mere suggestion, joking or not, that she might be open to such a liaison.

Jennifer took the seat next to him. "Tom, you'd better pace yourself. You have to make it through two more days."

"Four more," he said, speaking somewhat slower than normal. "I'm staying through the weekend."

"Good lord. Three days isn't enough for you?"

"Careful," said Ashley. "It's a sore subject. The airline lost one of his bags and ruined his plans for the weekend."

"Really?" Jennifer turned to Tom, intrigued. "Do tell."

"Yes," said Ashley with a smirk, "I'm still waiting to hear about this big money you were going to win."

"See," said Tom, "this is why I don't talk about my personal life at the office. I mentioned one little detail, and you're already using it to tease me."

"Who's teasing?" asked Ashley. "You said you had a chance to win big money, so I'm curious."

"I said 'real money,' not 'big money,' and it's not going to happen now, so just forget it."

Ashley rolled her eyes.

"Well," said Jennifer, "I guess there are worse things than spending a weekend sipping Coronas by the pool."

Tom drained the last of his drink. "I don't think the Blue Parrot has a pool."

"The Blue Parrot?"

"It's on the north end of the Strip, across the street from the Stratosphere. That's where I'll be rubbing fanny packs with the rest of the Priceline shoppers."

Jennifer winced. In her eagerness to move the conversation in a more cheerful direction, she'd inadvertently drawn attention to the fact that Tom was the one person in the group who almost certainly couldn't afford two extra nights at La Condamine Hotel and Casino.

Tom was one of two team members, along with Bryan's elderly assistant, Grace, who worked on salary rather than commission. He'd given up a presumably less-than-lucrative career producing Internet videos of young daredevils performing all manner of death-defying and sometimes illegal stunts and taken a position producing marketing presentations for New Wave. He never complained about his job, but Jennifer got the impression that commercial real estate didn't quite live up to whatever expectations he'd had for his late twenties.

"Tom," she said, "my advice is to find some sweet young gal to help take your mind off your troubles until the airline finds your bag."

"Oh, they know exactly where it is—in a locker in the TSA office. They found it three hours after they lost it, but now they're holding it pending, as they put it, 'verification.'"

"Verification?"

"Yep." He shook his glass as if looking for any stray drops of alcohol hiding between the ice cubes. "My tax dollars hard at work fucking me over." Before Ashley or Jennifer could respond, he slammed his empty glass on the table and rose to his feet, almost knocking over his bar stool in the process. "We need another round. Jennifer, what are you drinking?"

Although she wasn't sure she wanted to start drinking yet—she planned on needing her energy later—Jennifer reasoned that Tom was a man in need of a mission.

"Martini," she replied. "Two olives."

"Okay, one martini, one appletini, and one Seven and Seven coming up." He turned and disappeared into the crowd between the tables and the bar.

For a moment, neither woman said anything. Finally, Ashley let out a stifled laugh.

"What?" asked Jennifer.

"That poor boy needs to lighten up."

"If you ask me," said Jennifer, "that poor boy needs to get laid."

Ashley's expression grew serious. "A lot. He needs to get laid *a lot*."

Both women erupted in laughter.

When they regained their composure, Jennifer asked, as casually as she could, "Have you seen Bryan?"

"Yeah, you just missed him. Tammy needed help drawing up a letter of intent."

"Oh, for the love of God. Now she can't draft her own LOIs? Someone needs to tell her she's about two decades too old for that helpless-schoolgirl shit."

Ashley giggled. "If I didn't know any better, Miss Williams, I'd say you're jealous."

CHAPTER FIVE

After two hours and four rounds, Jennifer, Ashley, and Tom were all in much better spirits. Tom had seemingly forgotten about his thwarted plans, Ashley had apparently decided that Tom wasn't so uptight after all, and Jennifer was only mildly distraught that Bryan hadn't yet returned.

Had Tom acquiesced to Ashley's repeated pleas to let her get the next round, the three of them might have gone on like that for another hour. However, he insisted on getting it, only to encounter an unexpected protest from his feet. He stood, took one step forward, stumbled, and nose-dived toward the tropical-themed carpet, knocking an empty tray from the hand of a passing waitress as he fell.

Both Ashley and Jennifer leapt from their chairs and, working to contain a mutual case of the giggles, helped Tom to his feet.

"Tom," said Jennifer, "I think it's time we put you to bed."

"Maybe so," he muttered, struggling to regain his composure.

"I'll take him if you want," said Ashley. "Hang out and visit."

Jennifer thought of Bryan, probably just then wrapping up Tammy's letter of intent, possibly already headed back to the bar.

"Are you sure you don't mind?"

"Nah, I'm beat anyway. If I'm going to survive tomorrow, I should get some sleep."

"All right. I'll try not to wake you when I come in."

"You won't."

Jennifer cast a stern look at the inebriated young man. "Tom, don't give her any trouble."

Tom grinned. "I don't know the meaning of the word."

Ashley laughed. "I'll keep him in line."

With Tom's arm over her shoulder, she led him through the crowd, in the general direction of the elevator bank.

◆ ◆ ◆

For what felt like at least an hour, Jennifer caught up on the life of every coworker she could even remotely stand to be around. Still there was no sign of Bryan.

She knew it had to be after eleven, but, like every casino, La Condamine had no clocks on the gaming floor. She reached for her bag, then remembered that her cell phone was upstairs in her room. After weeks of planning and an hour of primping, she'd discovered that her little box clutch, which complemented her little black dress, was capable of holding either her cell phone or her makeup kit but not both.

Unfortunately, all her planning and primping now seemed to have been in vain. With tomorrow's first round of meetings not much more than eight hours away, she had little hope that Bryan might still make his way back downstairs for a couple of drinks.

Across the table, Meredith Higgins and Steve Howard argued about their differing interpretations of a popular reality TV show. Jennifer reluctantly accepted that the evening was not likely to improve.

Hoping to avoid a round of obligatory good-night wishes, she stood and walked toward the bar, allowing her coworkers to assume she'd gone in search of another drink. Once out of sight, she cut through the crowd, toward the elevator bank. Five minutes later she was inside an express elevator whizzing toward the thirty-second floor.

Away from the excitement of the gaming floor, she felt the first pangs of exhaustion. For most of the day, anticipation had held fatigue at bay. In the past few minutes, that barrier had fallen.

She studied her reflection in the mirrored walls of the elevator. From the neck down, she was the beacon of feminine sensuality she'd aspired to be. The view from the neck up, however, told a different story. Her eyes hung heavy with weariness and disappointment. And age.

She took a step to the left, allowing her face to disappear behind a framed advertisement with the headline LE TOURNOI AT LA CONDAMINE: THE STRIP'S PREMIER POKER TOURNAMENT.

I bet that explains the crowd downstairs.

She slid a finger along the smooth gold frame and let her mind wander to Bryan. Would he be asleep yet? Would he be receptive to being awakened? Her finger wandered to the panel of buttons and made slow circles around the number forty-one.

Maybe he's just watching TV. Or reading.

She pictured him lying in bed, a paperback in his hands, reading glasses perched on his nose, a glass of scotch beside him, his salt-and-pepper hair still wet from his evening shower. Would he be glad to see her?

Maybe she could say she needed advice on a deal.

And I waited until almost midnight to ask?

She could say that Ashley's snoring was keeping her awake.

So I threw on my cocktail dress and heels and went for a walk?

With a loud ding, the elevator slowed to a stop on thirty-two. The doors opened.

Her finger continued to circle the button for the forty-first floor. She stared into the empty corridor, searching for a plausible excuse. After a moment, the doors began to close.

She abandoned the well-fondled button and extended her arm to stop the doors.

Patience, she thought, stepping into the empty hallway.

Outside her suite, she swiped her card key—one of the few things that fit inside her tiny clutch bag—and eased open the door, hoping not to wake Ashley.

Ashley was not asleep. Nor was she alone.

Trapped in a momentary state of shock, Jennifer stared and thought, *Well done, Tom.*

Her eyes took in the images faster than her mind could process them—Ashley's toned, arched back; Ashley's blond curls brushing against the hummingbird tattoo on her right shoulder blade; the strong, masculine hands gripping Ashley's perfectly round ass—until she realized she was witnessing something she wasn't meant to see. She took a slow step back, hoping to escape without causing the couple any embarrassment.

Sorry to stop by so late, Bryan, but my roommate is fucking the multimedia guy.

She almost had the door closed when, through Ashley's rhythmic bouncing, she glimpsed the owner of those strong, masculine hands. Her mind struggled to make sense of it.

Tom doesn't have salt-and-pepper hair.

CHAPTER SIX

Matt Crocker wasn't sure where he was, but he was sure the hard surface under him wasn't his bed. He opened his eyes to find a woman smiling down at him.

Dear God, he thought as he stared up at the gap-toothed grin, *how much did I have to drink?*

"I think he's okay," said the woman in a raspy smoker's voice.

One look at his surroundings unleashed a flood of memory. He bolted upright.

"Take it easy," said a much softer voice.

He turned and saw the woman in the black dress holding a chrome Beretta at arm's length, dangling it between her thumb and forefinger like a soiled diaper.

"You took a pretty good fall," she continued as she added the pistol to a small collection of firearms on the front counter.

He staggered to his feet, tested his legs, and walked to the counter. He could feel the women's cautious eyes on him as he plucked his .40-caliber Glock from the bunch, checked both the chamber and the magazine, and slipped it back into the holster concealed beneath his shirttail.

When the gun was once again hidden from sight, the woman in the black dress said, "The police may want to take that as evidence."

"They will." He turned toward her. "Have you called them?"

She gestured toward the clerk. "Maddi did."

He nodded appreciatively.

The woman added, "I'm Jennifer, by the way."

"Crocker."

"Is that your first name?"

"Last, but it's what people call me." He surveyed the aftermath of the shooting. To his left, a banner advertising some sort of lime-flavored beer covered the bodies of the three robbers. "How long was I out?"

"Less than five minutes. Maddi got that banner out of the back. I couldn't stand looking at them."

"Sorry. If I'd thought there was any alternative…"

"Don't apologize. It's good you were here."

"Not good for my truck, though." He stared at his pickup's damaged rear end just a few feet away.

"I don't get it," said Maddi. "If you had a gun, why give 'em your truck?"

Crocker sighed. "I survived more than four decades without having to shoot anybody. I was hoping to keep that streak alive." He hesitated. "Plus, I had to wait until they weren't pointing guns at any of us."

In the distance, the faint sound of police sirens cut through the predawn silence.

Here we go, he thought. *I am never going to live this down.*

He'd finally been involved in a real shooting, and he'd fainted. He could try explaining to the officers that he was sleep deprived and overcaffeinated and that the sudden rush of adrenaline had overloaded his system, but it wouldn't matter. He was going to be a laughingstock.

◆ ◆ ◆

Beneath the large pylon sign for the Placer Gold truck stop, a haphazardly parked fleet of emergency vehicles crowded the previously deserted parking lot. For at least fifteen minutes after the first patrol car arrived on the scene, the lot had been a surreal discothèque of flashing red and blue lights, the disorienting effect of which had given Jennifer a splitting headache. To her relief, the sheriff's first act upon arriving had been to order the first responders to *"shut off those goddamn lights."* Only the two Nevada Highway Patrol cars stationed near the street still flashed red and blue.

Near the truck stop entrance, two paramedics sat on the bumper of an ambulance marked PAHRUMP VALLEY FIRE-RESCUE, chatting with two highway patrolmen who'd just finished stringing yellow crime-scene tape.

Jennifer sat in the open back door of a Nye County Sheriff's Office squad car, wrapped in a blanket given to her by one of the paramedics. The blanket was almost unbearably scratchy, but it was her only protection against the night air, which, despite the fact that June was only days away, was surprisingly chilly.

She waited for her two interrogators—a sheriff's deputy who looked to be right out of high school and a highway patrolman of perhaps thirty—to stop laughing. Their just-the-facts-ma'am demeanor had crumbled when she told them how Crocker, the man in the blue shirt, had collapsed after the shooting. She was about to ask what they found so funny when the sheriff emerged through the demolished front entrance of the truck stop. Upon seeing him, the two officers quickly regained their composure.

The sheriff was a short, stocky man at the tail end of middle age. Based on the heavy shadow of stubble on his face, Jennifer guessed he'd been called out of bed on short notice.

"Parker," he called, "have you and Trooper Haley finished taking her statement?"

"Yes, sir," replied the deputy. "I think I got it all."

"Was it the same story we got from the other two?"

"Pretty much."

"Don't tell me 'pretty much.' Was it or wasn't it?"

"Well, sir," said the deputy, stifling a laugh, "she says that after Crocker shot the perps, he fainted."

"Yeah," said the sheriff, unamused, "I saw it on the tape. Anything else?"

"No, sir." The deputy tried unsuccessfully not to smile. "I guess Crocker just forgot to mention that in his statement."

The sheriff gave the deputy a hard look. "Son, are you finding some humor in this situation? Because if so, please don't hold back. Share it with the rest of us."

"Sorry, sir. I didn't—"

"Just keep the shit-eating grins to yourself, and go let the poor man out of the backseat of my car."

Every trace of amusement left the deputy's face. "Yes, sir." He ran off in the direction of the sheriff's squad car.

The sheriff turned to the highway patrolman. "Haley, let Sergeant Menendez know we're releasing Crocker pending further investigation. I'll have Becky send over copies of our reports plus Metro's forensic analysis, assuming they eventually decide to grace us with their presence."

"Thanks, Sheriff," said the trooper. "We appreciate being kept in the loop." He turned and strolled toward a highway patrol cruiser parked alone near the gas pumps.

Over by the sheriff's car, the young deputy was removing a pair of handcuffs from Crocker's wrists.

"Excuse me," said Jennifer, "but is he with you?"

"Ma'am?" asked the sheriff.

"I mean, is Mr. Crocker with the sheriff's department or the highway patrol or what?"

"Oh, Crocker's no cop. That would be an unforgivable waste of talent."

Talent? thought Jennifer.

She leaned around the sheriff to get a better look at the man in the blue shirt. "Is he...like...a CIA special forces assassin or something?"

The sheriff chuckled. "He's a First Shot instructor."

Jennifer wondered if that was supposed to mean something to her.

Her confusion must have been apparent because the sheriff added, "First Shot Shooting Academy—it's a firearms school a few miles east of here."

"And that's how you all know him?"

The sheriff nodded. "Most everyone here has trained under him at one point or another."

Jennifer watched the young deputy shake hands with Crocker and point to where she and the sheriff were waiting.

"So he teaches police officers to...to do what he did in there?"

"Matt Crocker is kind of a minor celebrity among shooting enthusiasts. Everyone from Boy Scouts to SWAT officers comes here to train with him."

Jennifer tried to imagine what a class full of Boy Scouts and SWAT officers would look like and concluded that that probably wasn't how it worked.

She watched Crocker approach and considered how much likelier it would have been for the man in the blue shirt to be a plumber or an accountant. "I guess I got lucky."

"Ma'am," said the sheriff, "you couldn't've been any luckier if you'd been choking and found yourself seated next to Dr. Heimlich."

A couple of steps away, Crocker said, "You're not giving Dr. Heimlich enough credit. He probably would have remained conscious afterward."

"Never know," said the sheriff. "Adrenaline does weird things to a body. I once knew an officer who stepped out of his cruiser after a high-speed pursuit and found his pants sopping wet. He'd pissed himself without realizing it."

"Can you come tell that story to my fellow instructors? They're going to be merciless."

"Spare me the self-pity. This little incident will probably double First Shot's attendance next season."

Crocker didn't respond.

"Anyway," said the sheriff, taking a more serious tone, "I'll be at the Pahrump station all day tomorrow. If you need somebody to talk to, stop by."

"I'll be working, but I appreciate the offer." He hesitated. "Does that mean I'm free to go?"

"I have two witnesses and a surveillance tape that corroborate your story. If the DA wants anything more from you, she can get it on her own time."

Crocker extended a hand. "Thanks, Bill."

The sheriff shook Crocker's hand. "Get some sleep. You look like hell."

"Maybe at lunch. My class musters on the firing line in less than two and a half hours." He glanced back at the demolished front entrance of the Placer Gold truck stop. "And unless you're going to let me drive my truck out of your crime scene, I'm going to have to wake somebody to come get me."

"Sorry," said the sheriff, "but we can't move it until the lab rats from Vegas Metro are done with it."

"Can I get my phone out of the console?"

"If it were up to me, I'd say yes, but those crime lab boys are pretty up-tight about anybody disturbing their scene. Ever since someone got the idea to make a TV show about them, they've taken themselves way too damn serious."

Crocker sighed. "In that case, can I use your phone to call for a ride?"

"Sure. Or I can have one of my deputies drive you home once the CSI team takes possession of the crime scene."

Before she realized what she was saying, Jennifer blurted out, "I can give you a ride."

Both men turned toward her, visibly surprised.

"Unless," she added, "I'm not allowed to take my car either."

The sheriff arched his eyebrows at Crocker—Jennifer wasn't sure if he was amused or concerned—then turned to her and said, "As long as you think you're okay to drive, your car can go. It's not part of the crime scene."

Crocker looked skeptical. "Are you sure? I don't want to put you out."

Jennifer nodded toward the bustling crime scene and said, "I think I owe you a lift home."

◆ ◆ ◆

Jennifer had experienced some awkward silences in her life, but driving through the predawn desert with Matt Crocker made every bad first date and uncomfortable family dinner seem downright jovial by comparison. She'd made the offer on impulse, but now she hadn't an inkling of what she was supposed to say to this stranger who, only a few hours before, had gunned down a trio of armed robbers in front of her.

Nice shooting?

She stole a glance at her passenger. In his khaki shorts and polo shirt, he would have looked at home at her firm's annual golf scramble. Nothing about his appearance suggested he was capable of killing three men in less time than it would have taken to greet them by name.

I wonder if I'll ever know their names.

She supposed the cops would send her some sort of final report.

Was Al short for Albert?

She didn't really want to know.

She glanced again at the pistolero riding shotgun. He looked harmless. She knew he was no longer armed—she'd watched a deputy take possession of his gun—but she doubted she would have felt threatened either way. He looked no more dangerous than most of the brokers she'd encountered the day before. In fact, he looked like he might do pretty well as a broker. At the very least, he'd do well at the after-hours receptions where conference attendees were known to tender offers unrelated to real estate.

His full head of hair put him one up on many of her male peers, and he lacked the telltale beer gut that so many of them tried to hide beneath expensive suits. She couldn't think of a word to say to him, but under different circumstances, she would have let him buy her a drink.

He glanced in her direction. Jennifer tensed, waiting for him to speak.

He returned his gaze to the road. Jennifer relaxed.

"I hope you're not as uncomfortable as you look," he said, still staring straight ahead.

Her hands tightened around the steering wheel, causing the car to rock. "Uncomfortable? Do I look uncomfortable?"

"Maybe I'm just being self-conscious, but you look like you're ready to open the door and jump."

"Oh. No, I—"

"You don't need to explain. I should have let one of the deputies drive me home."

"No, really," Jennifer insisted, "it's not you. I just...I can't decide if I should say something or not say something or..." She took a deep breath.

"Trust me, I get it. I seem to have learned everything about how to survive a shooting except how to act normal afterward."

The tension in Jennifer's forearms eased up just a bit. "So this was your first? Shooting, I mean."

"Yeah."

"Is that why—" She caught herself, but it was too late. The embarrassment in his eyes said he knew what she'd intended to ask. She tried to cover. "Is that why they handcuffed you?"

"Why they handcuffed you"? she thought. *What the fuck is that supposed to mean?*

Crocker's face softened into a smile. "No, that's standard procedure."

Jennifer returned his smile, grateful to have been let off the hook but unsure of what to say next.

Just as the silence threatened to turn awkward again, he asked, "Did you have big plans in Vegas?"

The question was so unexpectedly benign that she took a couple of seconds to recognize it as small talk.

"Or," he added, "did you get this dressed up for a night out in Pahrump?"

"No, I was definitely not planning on spending my evening in Pahrump."

If he detected the melancholy in her voice, he didn't show it. Instead, he grinned and said, "I'm going to guess..." He looked her up and down. "Bachelorette party?"

She shook her head. "Not even close."

"Huh. I'm usually pretty good at this." He rubbed his chin. "Quickie wedding?"

"What? No."

"Quickie divorce?"

She rolled her eyes. "You're not even trying."

He watched her for a moment. "Celebrating the end of finals with your sorority sisters?"

This time she managed a smile. "Wrong again, but thanks."

"Am I getting close?"

"Not even remotely. How about I just tell you?"

Crocker shrugged. "Have it your way."

"I work for a commercial real estate firm out of Dallas. Our entire office is in town for a conference."

"The one for retail developers?"

"That's right," she said, impressed. "You're familiar with it?"

"Only vaguely. I was asked to work a party tonight for some of the attendees."

"Work?" She watched him out of the corner of her eye. "I'm afraid to ask, but how does a firearms instructor work a party?"

He half grinned. "Security. I do private security in my spare time."

The empty desert had given way to a steady stream of RV dealerships, gas stations, and manufactured homes. Ahead of her, Jennifer saw the first cars she'd seen since leaving the truck stop. In her rearview mirror, she saw the first hint of daylight in the eastern sky.

"And you're working security at one of the conference receptions?"

"No, I had to turn it down. They wanted me at eight, but my last class doesn't get out until ten."

"*Ten?* You have to be at work at seven in the morning, and you don't get off until ten at night? That's a fifteen-hour day!"

Crocker chuckled. "It's not as bad as it sounds. The academy is only open September through May. We hold class four days a week, ten hours a day. During the first and last month of the season, the desert heat can get pretty oppressive, so we hold classes in the morning and in the evening and take a five-hour break during the heat of the day."

"So you get an afternoon siesta?"

"That's the idea. But I usually spend the time giving private lessons."

A neon-adorned monstrosity of a casino beckoned from the right side of the road. Based on the number of recreational vehicles in the parking lot, a person could easily have mistaken it for another RV dealership.

"By the way," he said, "you're going to want to take the first right after the casino."

"Thanks." Jennifer took note of the approaching traffic light. "So let me ask you a question: Between private lessons, private security, and your day job, when do you find time to sleep?"

"Summer."

"You're off all summer?"

"Just like a schoolteacher."

She turned onto the side street beside the casino. "And that's why you work all the extra jobs?"

"I could probably get by without the extra work, but it helps make the house payments and lets me put something away for retirement."

She saw his gaze drift to the dashboard clock, which now read 5:02.

"Speaking of work," he said, "I need to find a way to get there. Could I borrow your phone to call a coworker?"

"I'm sorry, but I don't have one."

Even in the dimly lit car, she could see the skepticism in his eyes.

"I mean, I have one," she continued, "but it's back at my hotel." She glanced away as she recalled her hasty retreat from La Condamine. "I left in a bit of a hurry."

"That's okay. I'll grab a quick shower and walk down to the Chevron station and use the pay phone. I can grab a cup of coffee and wake myself up a bit while I wait for someone to come get me."

"I know it's none of my business, but wouldn't your boss understand if you took the day off?"

"Oh, I know Jeff would understand. But I'm not sure the students who paid twenty-five hundred apiece to take our four-day combat handgun course would be quite so understanding about the head instructor playing hooky on the last day."

"Oh," she said, still thinking that any right-minded person would understand the need to take a day off after shooting it out with three armed robbers.

"Besides," he said, "today is the last day of the season. Come Monday, I'm on summer vacation."

Jennifer didn't respond. She was lost in thought, trying to decide what she was going to do about her own work situation. Would she tell her co-workers what had happened at the truck stop?

She wasn't sure she was up for reliving the incident right away, and she knew she wasn't up for the inevitable questions: *"What were you doing so far outside of town?"* *"Whose car did you take?"* But if she didn't tell them what had happened, they'd expect her to be on the convention center floor, bright eyed and bushy tailed, at seven thirty sharp.

"It's the first driveway on your right," said Crocker as they left the gaudy casino behind.

Jennifer decided to put off thinking about work for just a little longer. "I have an idea. Why don't I wait for you to shower; then I'll drop you off at work before I head back to Vegas?"

"Do you have time? The academy is a ways off the main road."

"I'll make time." She slowed and signaled the approaching turn. "It's the least I can do."

"Okay," he said, "I'll accept on one condition—you have to let me make you breakfast."

For the first time since starting the drive, she smiled without effort. "You've got yourself a deal."

She was about to make a joke about his offer of breakfast sounding like a pickup line when she saw the driveway he'd told her to turn in to.

Did he say, "Helps make the house payments"?

CHAPTER SEVEN

Crocker felt the cobwebs clearing from his brain as the hot water washed over his body. For the first time since he'd regained consciousness on the truck stop floor, all cylinders were firing. Every inch of his body screamed with exhaustion, but the return of his cognitive abilities made the physical strain more bearable.

Now that the fog had lifted, he wanted to pistol-whip himself for the way he'd handled the aftermath of the shooting. Every student who attended one of First Shot's self-defense courses heard a speech titled "After the Smoke Clears: Your Rights and Responsibilities Following a Self-Defense Shooting." The speech offered a few small pieces of legal advice and one big one: *Always* ask for a lawyer. Even though Sheriff Cargill was an old friend, Crocker's peers would no doubt view the waiving of counsel as more egregious than the fainting spell that preceded it.

He'd also exhibited terrible judgment in accepting a ride from a woman still reeling from a traumatic event. Fortunately, there had been no arrest at the scene and no fiery car crash on the way home, just casual conversation with an attractive woman.

Of all the things Crocker should have done differently in those early morning hours, the one that kept gnawing at the back of his mind was his failure to warn Jennifer Williams about his current living arrangements. She wasn't the first woman to see the ancient Argosy travel trailer parked in slot forty-seven of the Rangoon Harbor RV Park—one of the classier amenities offered by the Rangoon Harbor Casino—but in the past he'd always been careful to explain the situation beforehand.

He turned off the water and opened the shower curtain. As he reached for his towel, he noticed his sweat-soaked shirt lying beneath the rack and realized that in his sleep-deprived state, he'd made one other miscalculation: He'd forgotten to bring a change of clothes into the bathroom.

◆ ◆ ◆

Jennifer caught herself nodding off and jerked her head upright. The adrenaline surge from the truck stop had dissipated; now she could only postpone the inevitable crash. She longed for sleep, but she wasn't about to let herself doze off inside this time capsule from 1976.

The trailer's interior was a kaleidoscope of fake wood paneling and muddy yellow-orange hues that reminded her of childhood. The only part of the interior that appeared to have been updated was the linoleum flooring, which looked to be fifteen to twenty years newer than the rest of the trailer.

I guess the shag carpeting wore out.

From her seat on the built-in sofa, she could see straight down the single corridor that led from the front sitting area to the small sleeping quarters at the back. Though dated and unimpressive, the place was at least well kept. She wasn't sure what to make of Matt Crocker, who seemed intelligent and hardworking but who apparently lived like a vagabond.

Before retreating into the bathroom, he had put on a pot of coffee to brew, and the strong aroma now taunted her. She wanted a cup, but her enigmatic host had neglected to set out any mugs, and she wasn't sure if she should search for them herself or wait for him to finish his shower.

She occupied her mind by surveying his few personal possessions. On a small shelf to her right sat two framed photographs. She guessed that the first, a faded picture of a man and woman standing in front of Mount Rushmore, was of Crocker's parents. The second showed Crocker, perhaps ten years younger, standing next to a woman with freckled skin and dark brown hair. Both he and the woman were smiling and holding up paper targets riddled with holes.

The only other photograph in sight was a framed eight-by-ten hanging above the stove. It looked like a landscape, maybe a sunset, but she couldn't tell for sure from where she sat. She was about to stand for a closer look when the bathroom door opened and Crocker stepped into the narrow hallway, wearing only a bath towel, which he'd wrapped so tightly around his waist that it looked as if it might give out under the strain.

"Good," he said. "You're still here. I was afraid my humble digs might have scared you off."

Jennifer searched for a polite response, but her sleep-deprived mind stopped short of anything even tangential to polite and backtracked to her host's well-toned chest.

He opened the door to the small closet across from the bathroom and reached inside. "Did you have some coffee?"

"Oh, no," she replied. "I, uh...I thought I'd wait for you."

He turned back from the closet. "I hope I'm not embarrassing you." He glanced down at the towel. "I should have thought to take a change of clothes into the bathroom with me."

"Not at all!" The words came out more forcefully than she'd intended. She jumped to her feet and made a beeline for the coffeepot. "Would you like me to pour you a cup? I know I could use one."

"Sure." He rounded the corner from the hallway. "Let me grab a couple of mugs."

As he reached into the cabinet above the sink, Jennifer noticed the corner of the towel coming untucked at his waist. She opened her mouth to voice a warning but hesitated, unsure of the most polite way to phrase it.

She was still thinking when the corner freed itself. Before she could will herself to look away, his left hand swooped in, grabbed the stray bit of towel, and tucked it back into place.

"I'd better go put on something a little safer." He held out two coffee cups in his right hand.

She took the cups. "I'm sure your students would appreciate that."

As Crocker turned back to the closet, Jennifer noticed a tattoo on his left shoulder blade—an amalgam of a bird, a globe, and a boat anchor. She couldn't place the symbol, but she recognized the two words below it: SEMPER FIDELIS.

Crocker took a handful of clothes from the closet and walked into the small sleeping quarters at the far end of the trailer. He turned back toward Jennifer and drew a curtain across the doorway, blocking her view.

"I don't have any cream," he said from behind the curtain, "but there is milk in the fridge and sugar in the pantry."

"That's fine," she said as she poured the coffee. "At this point I'd chew the raw grounds to get the caffeine."

When she'd finished pouring the first cup, she took a moment to inspect the picture hanging above the stove. It showed a mountain range silhouetted against an orange sky. Only the peaks of the mountains were visible—a red-hued cloud bank covered the rest.

"Where was this photograph taken?" she asked as she poured the second cup.

"The sunrise?"

"Yes. It's very picturesque."

"That's the view from my porch."

"Really?" She leaned across the sink, lifted the blinds covering the small window, and peered out into the twilight. "You have a porch?"

Crocker laughed, pulled back the curtain, and emerged from the sleeping quarters dressed exactly as he had been when they arrived, in khaki shorts and a blue polo shirt.

Jennifer let the blinds fall back into place. "What did I say?"

He grinned. "Nothing. I just realized you must be trying to figure out which side of this trailer has the magnificent mountain view." He glanced up at the photo. "This was taken at my home in Colorado."

"Colorado? So this..."

"This is what you might call my winter home. I'm here nine months and home three."

"You have a home you only see three months out of the year?"

"I used to have a house here in town, but I hardly saw it while I was working, and I didn't care much for spending my summers in the desert. So I sold it and got a place in the Rockies."

"A place you rarely see."

"I know it sounds a little strange"—he reached for one of the steaming cups—"but it works for me. And it ended up being the best financial move I ever made."

"How so?"

He took a long sip of coffee. "When I bought my place here, Pahrump was just a one-horse town that limped by on nickel slots and legalized prostitution. Then Las Vegas real estate prices spiked, and this little one-horse town turned into a thriving bedroom community. By the time I sold my house, local housing prices were higher than anybody could have predicted."

She reached for the remaining cup. "It sounds like you cashed out at the height of the real estate bubble."

She wasn't accustomed to drinking her coffee black, but she was intrigued by the conversation's sudden turn toward real estate and didn't want to interrupt Crocker's story.

"I wish I could claim some keen economic insight," he said, "but in all honesty, it was just dumb luck."

"But didn't you buy right back into the same bubble, in Colorado?"

"Like I said, dumb luck. Because my house hunting was limited to the summer months, it was almost two years later when I finally found what I was looking for."

She nodded that she understood. "And by then the bubble had burst, and for anyone with cash to spend, it was a buyer's market."

"Exactly. I found my dream home at a foreclosure auction."

"One man's misery is another man's opportunity."

"Perhaps," he said, "but it's not like somebody lost their home. The place was pretty much unlivable when I bought it. I ended up parking this trailer on the property for the rest of that first summer and sleeping in it while I started the renovations."

"Is the rest of the property as nice as the view?"

"It will be when I'm through. I still have six bedrooms left to renovate, but—"

"*Six?* How many does it have?"

"Ten. Why? Is that a lot?"

Jennifer tried to decide whether he was joking.

He grinned. "It was an old bed-and-breakfast that had fallen into disrepair. Some developers bought it before the bubble burst, hoping to use the land for a housing development."

"How much land?"

"It sits on sixty-four acres that butt up to San Juan National Forest."

Jennifer chuckled.

"Did I say something funny?" he asked.

"Before we got here, you made a comment about how you work extra jobs to help make the house payments. Then I saw this place and..."

Crocker laughed. "And you thought I must have seriously overpaid."

"Something like that."

"The security jobs fund the renovations and pay the property taxes. And I save enough that I won't have to spend my golden years waking up to a *photograph* of my perfect view."

Jennifer smiled at the realization that Crocker's good fortune would annoy Bryan to no end.

"What did I say now?" he asked.

"Nothing. I was just thinking that your home-buying story would really piss off my boss. He hates it when people luck into great real estate deals."

"Why?"

"He says stories like yours make people think our job is easy."

"Seems like a lame reason to begrudge someone a little good luck."

Jennifer nodded. "He even has a label for people like you: 'conveniently ignorant.'"

Crocker swallowed a long sip of coffee and wiped his mouth. "Is it possible your boss was created in a lab by grafting together discarded foreskins?"

Jennifer choked on her coffee. "*What?*"

"He sounds like a huge dick."

Jennifer giggled. The giggle grew into laughter.

Crocker watched her with a bemused grin.

Still laughing, she set her coffee cup on the stove so as not to spill it.

"I can't tell if you're humoring me or mocking me," he said, "but I know it wasn't that funny."

Jennifer shook her head and forced herself to stop laughing. "I'm not humoring or mocking you." She picked up her cup. "I just really needed to hear someone call Bryan a dick."

Crocker seemed amused. "Are there any other names you'd like me to call him? After the night we've had, I'm game for anything that eases the tension."

Staring across her coffee cup, Jennifer arched her eyebrows and asked, "Anything?"

Crocker cocked his head like a curious puppy.

Did I really just say that? She waited for Crocker to blush or look away, which would be her cue to apologize.

Instead, he smiled and said, "Not exactly what I had in mind, but I suppose it wouldn't be fair to try to qualify the offer after I've made it."

She couldn't tell if he was serious or just playing along. Worse yet, she didn't know which she preferred. She was pretty sure she'd meant the innuendo as a joke, but the prospect of redeeming the worst evening of her life was not altogether unappealing.

God knows I'm dressed for it.

"What time did you say you have to be at work?" she asked, still testing the water.

Crocker set his coffee cup on the counter and said, "You're my ride. I'm at your mercy."

And just like that, it was real.

Jennifer stared at her well-toned gunslinger, wondering if she should wait for him to make the first move or if she, as the initiator, was obligated to act first.

A sudden rapping on the trailer door so startled her that her free hand shot out defensively and knocked Crocker's cup into the sink.

In less time than it took for the coffee to spill from the tipped cup, Crocker grabbed Jennifer and spun her around him so that he stood between her and the door. Though he had no weapon at hand, something about his posture told Jennifer he was a real threat to whoever stood on the other side of that door.

"Who's there?" demanded Crocker.

A gravelly male voice replied, "Crocker, it's Jim Birdwell."

Crocker's posture relaxed a little. "Jim, what the hell are you doing out there at this hour?"

"I have a message from Bill."

Crocker cast a concerned glance at Jennifer, then stepped forward to unlock the dead bolt.

The door swung open, and in stepped a stout man of perhaps fifty-five, wearing a dark gray suit. He had a semicircle of white hair around his mostly bald head and a thick horseshoe mustache that made Jennifer think of Hollywood westerns.

"Have a seat," said Crocker as he shut the door. "Can I get you a cup of coffee?"

Jennifer noted that Crocker was a surprisingly courteous host under the circumstances.

"No, thanks," replied the man as he sat.

"Jim, this is Jennifer Williams. Jennifer, this is Jim Birdwell. Jim is head of security here at the Rangoon Harbor Casino. He's also Sheriff Cargill's partner."

"Oh," replied Jennifer. "I didn't realize sheriffs had partners."

Jim's expression didn't change. "Not that kind of partner."

"Oh!" she exclaimed. "I'm sorry, I—"

Jim waved off the apology. "You're not the first to make that mistake." He watched her for a moment. "I assume you're the young lady who was at the truck stop? The one who gave Crocker a ride home?"

"That's right."

Jim nodded as if this told him everything he needed to know.

"What's going on?" asked Crocker.

Jim took a deep breath and exhaled slowly. "About fifteen minutes ago, I got a call from Bill. He told me about your altercation at the Placer Gold and asked if I could run out here and give you an urgent message. At first I told him it would have to wait until I was done supervising the loading of the night's take onto the Brinks truck. But once he told me the message... Well, this can't wait."

"Okay," said Crocker, "hit me with it." His voice was calm, but something about his tone made Jennifer uneasy.

"Apparently," said Jim, "the CSI guys going through the perps' car found just under eight hundred thousand dollars in cash, bundled into seventy-some-odd envelopes."

Jennifer turned to Crocker. "What does that mean?"

His eyes remained fixed on Jim. "So the guys I shot were—"

"Bill obviously can't be certain," said Jim, "but each envelope contained exactly ten thousand dollars, so it sure looks that way."

Crocker spun to face Jennifer. "Move."

"What?" She made no effort to hide the fear she now felt.

"Move," he repeated.

Before she could reply, he reached out with his left hand and nudged her gently but firmly to the side. When she was out of the way, he knelt by the kitchen counter and opened the bottom drawer. Inside was a metal box with an electronic keypad on top.

He entered a five-digit combination, and the lid popped open with a loud click, revealing a handgun in a leather holster. He pulled the holstered weapon from the box and slipped it into the waistband of his shorts, on his right hip. He then removed a small holster full of ammunition and slipped it into his waistband, on the opposite hip.

He shut the drawer and stood, facing Jim. "Did Bill say anything about her?" He nodded toward Jennifer. "Does he think she's in any danger?"

"I can't imagine why anyone would come after her. *She* didn't shoot anybody."

Jennifer did not find that particularly reassuring.

Jim continued, "Bill thinks that the odds of them coming after you are slim at best. If those indeed were Dudka's men, they were off the reservation. Dudka didn't authorize them to hold up a truck stop, so blaming you for what happened would be a stretch."

"But if he wants someone to blame," said Crocker, "I'm the only one left."

"That's how Bill sees it."

At that, Crocker turned to Jennifer and said, "I'll get a ride from Jim. You need to get back to Vegas right now. Drive straight to your hotel, no stops."

She raised her hands to stop him. "I'm not going anywhere until somebody tells me what the hell is going on."

Crocker glanced at Jim, who didn't appear to have any advice, then back at Jennifer. "The short version is that the three men I shot are tied to some very dangerous people. And they were carrying a lot of money for those people—money that is now in the hands of the police, thanks to me."

"Okay," said Jennifer, far from satisfied. "What's the long version?"

Crocker looked again to Jim Birdwell, who still had nothing to offer. He turned back to Jennifer and said, "The men work for Vladimir Dudka, a Russian expat with rumored ties to organized crime. He owns a casino called the Winter Palace, on the west side of Pahrump."

Jennifer stared at him, waiting for him to continue.

Crocker took a deep breath. "Shortly after the Winter Palace opened, the locals noticed a pattern. Most of the time, the Palace seemed to struggle with the usual problems—a bad economy and stiff competition from California tribal casinos—but on the last weekend of each month, it thrived. Armored truck couriers reported seeing deposits that were double that of any other weekend. Local brothels reported a surge of customers coming from the Palace. Everybody knew that something was up, but nobody knew what."

"So why—"

"Two summers ago, a California highway patrolman pulled over an old station wagon heading east through Shoshone, just west of the Nevada border. The officer thought the driver and his two passengers were acting suspicious, so he called for a K-9 unit. And when the dogs got there, they hit on something."

"Drugs?"

"Yeah, but it was just a small amount of marijuana one of the passengers was carrying, nothing significant. What *was* significant was the ninety-three envelopes the officers found in the trunk, each of which contained exactly ten thousand dollars in cash."

"What was the money for?"

"They never found out—not officially, at least. The driver and the two passengers got out on bail and were never heard from again."

"They disappeared?"

"Not exactly. Six months later, a couple of hikers in Death Valley stumbled on three bodies that matched the physical descriptions of the suspects. The bodies were never officially identified."

"Why couldn't they be identified?"

"Because," said Jim, "they didn't have any heads. Or hands. Or feet."

Suddenly light-headed, Jennifer grabbed the edge of the sofa and lowered herself onto the seat beside him.

Jim continued, "At that time, California wasn't taking DNA from suspects arrested for nonviolent crimes, so the authorities had no way to positively determine whether the three bodies were in fact the same men arrested with nearly a million dollars in cash."

"But wait," said Jennifer. "If the men disappeared or turned up dead or whatever, how do you know there's a connection to the Winter Palace and this Dudka guy?"

"People talk," said Crocker. "Once word got around that the Winter Palace hadn't seen its usual end-of-the-month boom, the pieces kind of fell into place."

Jim added, "It's no coincidence that each envelope contained exactly ten thousand dollars. For tax purposes, the law requires casinos to report any gambler whose cash transactions exceed ten thousand in one day. The consensus is that those three men were supposed to distribute those ninety-three envelopes to a number of coconspirators who were supposed to lose the money at the Winter Palace."

Jennifer thought about it for a moment. "Money laundering?"

Crocker nodded. "If the rumors about Dudka's ties to organized crime are true, it's conceivable that he's using low-level hoods to gamble away his ill-gotten gains at his own casino so that he can declare the money as legitimate income."

"Okay," said Jennifer, "then why doesn't the sheriff go down to the Winter Palace and arrest this Dudka guy and all his bogus high rollers?"

"Because," said Jim, "it's all hearsay and circumstantial evidence. There's nothing that will stand up in court. Both the FBI and the IRS sniffed around for a while after the three couriers disappeared, but after a year or so of running down false leads, they packed up and went home."

"So what am I supposed to do if these gangsters come after me?"

"I think that's highly unlikely," replied Jim.

"You think or you know?"

"To Dudka, this is just business. Going after a bystander like you doesn't make good business sense—he'd have nothing to gain and everything to lose."

The slight tremble in Jennifer's voice masked the anger lurking there. "And what if you're wrong?"

Crocker sighed. "We're not helping ourselves by sitting around talking about it. By now someone could have tipped off Dudka that his money was seized. His people could be on their way here as we speak." He glanced out the window. "Jennifer, if it'll make you feel better, you can stick with me until we get more information from the sheriff, but I'm not hanging around here to find out if Dudka wants me dead."

At that moment, Jennifer didn't feel particularly safe, but when she considered her options, she felt safest with Crocker. She nodded in agreement.

"Fine then. We go *now*." He opened the door, stepped outside, and held it open for Jennifer and Jim.

Jennifer grabbed her purse and stepped out into the breaking dawn. Jim followed.

As Crocker locked the trailer door, Jim asked, "If Bill calls back, should I tell him he can reach you at First Shot?"

"No."

"You're not headed out to the academy? It's practically an armed encampment; Dudka would be nuts to try to come after you out there."

"We might be safe at the academy itself, but the roads to and from it are far too remote and far too obvious a place to look for me. I need to be someplace where I can come and go, someplace where I can get lost if I need to."

"What options does that leave us?" asked Jennifer.

"Don't worry," said Crocker. "I have a place in mind."

CHAPTER EIGHT

Jennifer was pretty sure she'd located the missing shag carpeting from Crocker's trailer. It was pink and thick and arguably the least tacky thing in the lobby of the Prickly Pear Ranch.

The décor was a nonsensical hodgepodge of Far East, Southwest, and disco. The decorator seemed to have operated on the lone criterion that every piece of furniture and art be indicative of some culture somewhere.

Jennifer had let Crocker drive Bryan's nonconsensually borrowed rental car. During the ten-minute drive from the trailer park, he'd said only five words: As they were pulling into the parking lot, he'd mumbled, *"Don't get the wrong idea."*

When, on the way into the lobby, he'd stopped to exchange pleasantries with the bouncer, Jennifer had tried to convince herself that perhaps the Prickly Pear Ranch wasn't what it appeared. But now, staring up at a velvet painting of two disrobed women being especially friendly toward one another, she was certain that the Prickly Pear was exactly what it appeared. Even though she hadn't yet touched anything, she longed for hand sanitizer.

The lobby was empty except for an elderly woman running a vacuum on the far end of the room.

You'd probably make more headway with a lawn mower, thought Jennifer as she watched the woman struggle to maneuver the vacuum over the thick carpet.

Behind the front desk a beaded curtain parted, and out stepped a plump woman with big hair and bigger breasts. She was several years past middle age and wore a conservative blue dress, but something about the sway of her hips made Jennifer suspect she had a long history at the Prickly Pear Ranch.

The moment the woman saw Crocker, her face lit up. "Matt!"

"She calls you Matt?" whispered Jennifer.

Crocker ignored the question. "How are you, Dottie?"

"Ready to go to bed. But seeing you always lifts my spirits. What can I do for you?" She glanced at Jennifer, then back at Crocker. "Are you interested in a couple's package?"

"No," he said, "not today."

His voice was steady, but Jennifer thought she detected a sudden flush to his face.

"You're not bringing me new talent, are you?" She turned to Jennifer. "Because we're always hiring, and I'm sure you'd do quite well."

It was Jennifer's turn to blush.

"Actually," said Crocker, "I'm in a bit of a bind and was hoping you might let us have a room for the day."

The woman hesitated. "We normally only rent rooms as part of a package deal—we're not a hotel." She smiled. "But you know I can't say no to you. I'll put the two of you in the Champagne Suite. I assume you remember where it is?"

"I do."

The woman retrieved a key from under the counter and set it on top. "Nobody used it last night, so the sheets are clean. But you'll need to be out of there by six—we're expecting a huge weekend crowd, and we'll need time to clean the bathroom and change the bedding."

Crocker scooped up the key. "That shouldn't be a problem."

"Is there anything else you need before I turn in?"

"Just one thing. If anyone should ask, I'm not here, okay?"

"Oh, honey," said the woman with a grin, "we haven't stayed in business this long by having loose lips."

Crocker smiled. "Thanks. I owe you one."

He waved to Jennifer to follow him and headed past the reception desk, toward a wide hallway lined with doors.

The woman turned to Jennifer and said, "Y'all enjoy yourselves."

Jennifer gave a polite but slightly embarrassed smile and followed Crocker past the desk.

Just inside the hallway, she stopped to inspect a wall of bookshelves to her right. The shelves were filled not with books but with a collection of the most uncomfortable-looking stiletto heels she'd ever seen.

"What is this?"

Crocker turned to see what had grabbed her attention. "That's the shoe wall."

Jennifer studied the shelves. "Clearly."

Crocker chuckled. "When Dottie rings the bell to signal that a customer is waiting, the girls who aren't with a client have to come running to join the lineup."

"The lineup?"

"Where the customers pick which—"

"Got it. Go on."

"The girls can't exactly run in those shoes, so when they get to right here, they change out of their street shoes and into their…" He pointed to the wall.

"Hooker pumps?" asked Jennifer.

"Exactly."

"You know, Mr. Crocker, if I didn't know any better, I might think you've spent a bit of time here."

As if on cue, two female voices squealed in unison, "Matt!"

Two unnaturally proportioned young women in skimpy negligees round-ed the corner from the reception area, ran past Jennifer, and threw their arms around Crocker, trapping him in a two-sided bear hug. The platinum blonde on his right kissed him on the cheek, and the redhead gripping him from the left followed suit.

Crocker looked more than a little embarrassed, but the women didn't seem to notice.

"Ladies," boomed a male voice.

Jennifer looked back to see a hulk of a man approaching from the same direction. He looked to be at least sixty but carried his large frame with the ease of a much younger man. At more than six feet tall and with a head of long gray hair, he looked like an over-the-hill professional wrestler.

"Give the poor man some room," he continued. "Can't you see he has a guest?"

"Sorry," said the redhead as she took a step back.

"Sorry," echoed the blonde as she too stepped away from the target of their affections.

"Jennifer," said Crocker, "I'd like you to meet two of my best students—Scarlett and Vegas."

Jennifer almost laughed out loud at the on-the-nose monikers. "Students?"

Crocker nodded. "We put together a complimentary class for some of the girls."

"And you still haven't let us pay you back," pouted the descriptively named Scarlett.

"Yeah," said Vegas. "When are you going to take us up on our offer?"

This time Crocker was definitely blushing.

"Ladies," he said, "I genuinely appreciate the offer, but as I said before, the class was complimentary. No payment necessary."

The two women uttered simultaneous whines of disappointment.

"Okay," said the large man, "you gals run along and let Crocker get on with his date. I think you've embarrassed him enough for one day."

The way he said the word *date* brought another flush to Jennifer's cheeks.

Scarlett and Vegas each made childlike sounds of protest, leaned in to give Crocker a final kiss on the cheek, then scurried off down the hall before they could be scolded again.

"Sorry about that," said the man.

"Oh," said Jennifer, realizing he was looking at her, "don't worry about it."

"Jennifer," said Crocker, "this is Larry Chappell. Larry is the proprietor of this establishment."

Jennifer extended her hand. "Nice to meet you."

Larry took her hand, leaned down, and brushed his lips across the back of it. "The pleasure is all mine."

The greeting was either chivalrous or creepy, but Jennifer was too tired to decide which.

Larry turned to Crocker and said, "Sorry for the interruption, but Dottie came back to the office and told us you were here. I wanted to say hi."

"No problem," said Crocker. "As long as you're just saying hi and not buttonholing me about this weekend."

Larry frowned. "What if I upped my offer to a thousand a day? That has to be at least double your best offer from anyone else."

"I committed to the tournament six months ago. How is it going to look if I back out now?"

"I'm desperate, pal. It's not just about the crowd from Le Tournoi—there's also a motocross race up at Amargosa and a big skydiving competition over at the lake bed."

Crocker was already shaking his head.

Larry continued, undeterred. "It's a perfect storm of horny adrenaline junkies. You know how I always say nobody likes working girls more than gamblers? Well, that holds true whether they're gambling with their money or gambling with their lives."

"I wish I could," said Crocker, "but just like your girls, us security guys are in high demand on these busy weekends."

Larry ran a hand through his stringy gray hair. "I can't understand why you'd rather babysit suitcases full of other people's money than hang out with the girls and toss a few drunks, but hey, you can only lead a horse to water."

Crocker smiled. "No hard feelings, I hope."

"Nah," said Larry, "no hard feelings." He grinned. "Of course, if you didn't have this beautiful young woman with you, I might send Vegas and Scarlett back here to try to persuade you, but—" He glanced at Jennifer and changed his tone. "But pencil me in for next year."

"Consider it done," said Crocker. "Now, if you'll excuse me, my date is waiting."

♦ ♦ ♦

Jennifer had assumed that *Champagne Suite* was a title, like *Presidential Suite* or *Honeymoon Suite*. She now realized it was actually a theme.

In the middle of the room stood a giant champagne glass at least six feet high. Beside the glass a small spiral staircase wound its way to the brim.

"It's a hot tub," explained Crocker as he closed the door behind them.

Jennifer shook her head and muttered, "Just when I thought this place couldn't get any tackier."

He latched the door. "You haven't seen anything yet. Let me see if I can figure out which..."

She heard the flip of a switch. Instantly the walls were awash in giant champagne-colored bubbles. She looked for the source and found a projector mounted to the mirrored ceiling.

A few feet beyond the projector hung a knot of straps and ropes that resembled a medieval torture device. To her left sat a round bed dressed in gold satin sheets and two large pillows.

Crocker stepped past her and took a seat on the edge of the bed. "If you want to get some rest, you can have the bed." He pulled at one of his shoelaces. "I'll find someplace else to sleep."

Jennifer surveyed the room. "Where? In the sex swing?"

He glanced at the straps dangling from the ceiling and grinned. "The first time I was here, I had to ask what that was."

For the third time since arriving at the Prickly Pear, Jennifer blushed. "I've seen ads in magazines."

"I'm not judging. Anyway, I was actually thinking I'd prop myself up against the love pillow and sleep there." He pointed to a wedge-shaped cushion resting in one corner of the room.

Jennifer took a seat on the bed. "Is this your usual room?"

"On busy weekends the staff rooms are all occupied by working girls, so I've stayed in most of the guest rooms at one point or another."

She fiddled with the buckle on one of her stilettos. "You don't make social visits?"

Crocker shot her a sideways glance. "I occasionally work security when they're expecting a big crowd. That's it." He kicked off a shoe.

"And you teach free classes to the girls."

"That was a one-time thing." He kicked off the other shoe. "Larry was concerned that some of the girls were buying handguns for protection, so I put together a half-day class."

"But do you ever come here for"—she searched for the right word—"*recreational* purposes?"

He reclined on the bed, his socked feet still on the floor, and closed his eyes. "I don't mix work and play."

"So you've never—"

"I don't mix work and play. Let's leave it at that."

Jennifer finished removing her shoes and sat up straight. "Sorry. Didn't mean to pry."

He opened his eyes and smirked. "Yes, you did. But I get it—this is a little out of the ordinary."

"A little?"

He shrugged, wrinkling the satin sheets beneath his shoulders.

"Last question," she said. "Why do all the women here call you Matt?"

"Dottie says it's only polite to call a man by his surname if you preface it with 'Mr.' She insists on calling me Matt. I guess the girls picked up on it."

Jennifer nodded. "Probably safer not to confuse them. Their cute little heads might explode."

Crocker smiled again. "Don't let the dumb-girl act fool you. They may not be angels, but they're not bimbos."

"I'll take your word for it." She stood. "If you don't need the bathroom right now, I'm going to take a shower."

"Do you want to call your people first?" He pointed to the hotel-style phone on the nightstand.

She shook her head and kept walking. "I still have to figure out what the hell I'm going to tell my boss."

♦ ♦ ♦

Jennifer was contaminated with a grime that wouldn't wash off with soap and water. The stench of death and betrayal lingered as she tried to simultaneously wash her body and scrub certain images from her mind.

Any time she closed her eyes, she saw either a dead body lying on the floor of the truck stop or a naked body straddling the man she'd hoped to marry. Sometimes the two images blurred together so that Ashley's naked body was among the corpses on the truck stop floor. Exhaustion was taking its toll.

The tears came intermittently, in quiet streams rather than violent sobs, and were quickly washed away. She knew the real torrent would come later, after she'd had time to process all that had happened.

When the shower finally ran out of hot water, she turned it off and grabbed two towels from the rack. She wrapped her hair in one and her torso in the other and walked to the sink. On the counter sat an array of complimentary toiletries. She tore open a packet containing a cheap plastic toothbrush and a single-use pouch of toothpaste.

She worked up a mouthful of suds before realizing that her bothersome French lace panties were still soaking in the sink. She took a step to the left, spit into the shower, then wiped her mouth on the hand towel hanging beside the sink.

She looked down at the uncomfortably ornate panties and decided that trendy boutiques were an okay source for little black dresses but that all future lingerie purchases would be made at Victoria's Secret.

She hated the idea of waking up and putting on the dirty clothes she'd been wearing on the worst day of her life, but washing out the sadistically designed underwear was the best she could do under the circumstances. There was no way her slinky black dress would survive a sink full of lukewarm water and shampoo.

She glanced at the dress hanging on the back of the bathroom door and took solace in the fact that it wasn't splattered with blood.

She pulled the lace torture device from the sink, wrung out the excess water, and hung it on the towel rack to dry. Looking at the rack, now bare except for the soggy lace thong, she felt a twinge of guilt for using both bath towels. Normally she would have used just one towel to dry off her body and wrap up her hair, but she currently had nothing else to wear.

She hadn't forgotten the brief moment she and Crocker had shared in his trailer, but she was pretty sure that walking out of the bathroom wearing nothing but a makeshift turban wasn't the way to reignite that flame.

She leaned over the sink and wiped a swath of condensation from the mirror. What she saw made her stomach sink. Her body might not have been naked, but her face was.

She grabbed her small purse from the counter and pulled out the only item other than her wallet and room key that she'd managed to fit inside. There wasn't much to work with, but for the first time since leaving La Condamine, she was glad she'd chosen the makeup kit over her cell phone.

◆ ◆ ◆

By the time she opened the bathroom door, Jennifer was confident her face wasn't about to confess either her lack of sleep or her true age.

She stood in the doorway, toweling her hair, and studied Crocker, who lay on the bed with the room phone sitting next to him.

"Hey," she said. "Do you think one of your friends here at the best little whorehouse might have a bathrobe or a T-shirt or something I can sleep in?"

He didn't reply.

"You awake?"

Still no reply.

She stopped toweling her hair, took a step toward the bed, and half shouted, "Crocker!"

Still, he didn't stir.

A deep sense of dread settled over her. She balled up the damp towel and flung it at his head. The towel landed on his face with a wet slap.

She waited, breathless.

Crocker reached up, pulled the towel from his face, flung it to the floor, and rolled onto his side.

Jennifer breathed a sigh of relief. She felt a little silly, but after the night she'd just experienced, she was primed to expect the worst.

She walked to the side of the bed and stood close enough to hear his rhythmic breathing. "Are you going to wake up, or did I just put on makeup for nothing?"

No reply.

Great, she thought, *my safety depends on a gunslinger who could sleep through a train wreck.*

She glanced around the room.

And I have no place to sleep and nothing to wear but a wet towel.

She walked to the closet on the far end of the room and opened the door, hoping to find a bathrobe or anything that might double as pajamas. Instead, she found an assortment of cleaning supplies, a couple dozen changes of sheets, and a shelf containing what she perceived to be the essential tools of the trade: condoms, wet wipes, and K-Y Jelly.

She grabbed one of the individually wrapped wet wipes from the economy-size box, opened it, and began scrubbing the fresh makeup from her face. When she was confident that the bulk of her makeup was now on the wet wipe, she dropped it into the small trash can on the floor of the closet and unwrapped the towel from around her body.

She lacked the energy to worry that Crocker, who'd proved himself to be a very sound sleeper, might choose this moment to wake up. She used the towel to dry her face, then dropped it in the laundry hamper beside the trash can.

A few minutes later, she sat on the side of the bed, wearing a satin sheet as a toga and waiting for the switchboard operator at La Condamine to connect her to Tom's room. She would have preferred to call his cell phone, but like everyone else in the age of smartphones, she'd long since given up memorizing phone numbers.

She knew that Tom would leave for the convention center no later than seven, which meant she was cutting it pretty close. The clock beside the bed read 6:49.

The phone rang without answer. After a moment, an automated voice-mail system picked up.

Crap.

If he was already gone, nobody would know where she was until some-time that evening. She considered trying to reach another coworker, but Tom was the only one she trusted not to ask too many questions. She decided to gamble that he was still in the shower.

The voicemail system beeped.

"Tom," she said, "this is Jennifer. Listen, I need you to tell Bryan that I'm dealing with a family emergency and won't be able to make it to my meetings today. He's going to need to find people to cover for me.

"If, God forbid, you don't get this message until the end of the day, just make sure he understands that my absence was completely unavoidable. Thanks, pal."

She looked at the number printed on the base of the phone. "If you need to reach me, you can call me back at 775-684-4368." She hesitated, then added, "Ask for the Champagne Suite. I can't really explain right now, but I'll be here for most of the day."

She hung up the phone and glanced over at Crocker, whose deep slumber seemed unfazed by her conversation.

"Okay, Matt Crocker, I'm trusting you to be a gentleman."

She held her toga together with one hand as she slid between the bed-sheets. Five minutes later, she was sound asleep.

◆ ◆ ◆

The phone rang three times before Jennifer registered what it was. By then Crocker was already leaning across her to answer it.

"Hello?"

According to the clock on the nightstand, it was one thirty in the afternoon. Jennifer fiddled under the sheet to refasten her makeshift toga, which had come loose while she slept.

"Hang on," said Crocker. He handed her the receiver.

"Hello?"

"Jennifer?" replied Tom's familiar voice. "Where the hell are you? Who answered the phone?"

"Relax, Tom. I'm fine."

"You sound like you just woke up. What the hell is going on?" He sounded more panicked than angry.

"Tom, what is with you? Is everything all right?"

"Just tell me, is Ashley with you?"

"What? No, I haven't seen her since last night. But I bet Bryan knows where she is."

"Jennifer," said Tom, "Bryan is dead."

CHAPTER NINE

Crocker's nostrils burned with the acrid stench of melted plastic, burnt upholstery, and charred plywood. He watched from a short distance as Sheriff Cargill and Jim Birdwell conferred with the two arson investigators sifting through the pile of smoldering debris occupying slot forty-seven of the Rangoon Harbor RV Park.

Staring at what remained of his winter home, he pondered how much better his day might have gone if the pretty woman in the slinky black dress had let him reach into the Placer Gold beverage case for her.

He pushed the thought from his mind. Jennifer had lost a lot more than a run-down travel trailer.

The unrelenting glare of the midafternoon sun made him miss the cheap pair of sunglasses he'd left in the center console of his truck. For the time being, the sum total of his assets in the great state of Nevada had been reduced to the clothes on his back, the gun in his waistband, whatever was still at the dry cleaner's, and a receipt from the Nye County impound lot.

He heard a car door slam behind him, followed by the unmistakable sound of Larry Chappell's heavy footsteps. His temporary chauffeur had apparently finished making phone calls and decided to join the party.

"Yep," said the longhaired hulk as he reached Crocker's side, "you have definitely made Dudka's shit list."

"You don't say." Crocker nodded toward the black pile of rubble where his trailer had stood. "Did your friends offer any other useful insights?"

Larry grinned. "They said that if you owe me money, I should collect now, while I still can."

"Funny."

The grin faded. "I know it's not much consolation, but you're welcome to stay at the Pear for as long as you want."

What Crocker wanted was to leave the Prickly Pear Ranch and Vladimir Dudka and all of Pahrump in his dust and hightail it back to his half-finished home in the foothills of the Rocky Mountains. But that would have to wait.

"Thanks," he said, "but aren't you worried that Dudka's men might come looking for me again?"

"That Russki bastard isn't going to send his thugs anywhere near my place. He knows that if he crosses me, he crosses my friends in Chicago."

Crocker didn't share Larry's confidence, but he didn't want to say anything to make his host rethink the offer. Despite his strong desire to leave town, Crocker had one very compelling reason to stay in Pahrump, and it wasn't his impounded pickup truck. It was the beautiful woman who, when he'd last seen her, had been crying into a satin pillow on the Champagne Suite's big round bed.

Less than ninety minutes had passed since a ringing telephone had roused him from a pleasant dream about cooler temperatures and higher altitudes. He'd handed the phone to Jennifer, expecting to hear one side of a conversation about missed real estate appointments. Instead, he'd heard an overture to a nightmare.

Apparently, Jennifer hadn't been the only no-show at the real estate conference that morning. Both her boss and the woman she was rooming with had also missed their first appointments.

When the boss's assistant wasn't able to reach the three missing Realtors by phone, she returned to the hotel and persuaded a member of the housekeeping staff to check their rooms. The housekeeper found the boss's room empty but wasn't so lucky when she checked the room shared by Jennifer and the other woman.

According to Jennifer's thirdhand account, her boss's naked body had been found tied to a chair, his face badly beaten, a balled-up sock stuffed in his mouth. Pending an autopsy, the probable cause of death was listed as asphyxiation due to a broken nose and a gagged mouth.

The police were still piecing together the chain of events, but Crocker was pretty sure he knew what had happened: Vladimir Dudka's goons had come looking for him and Jennifer and found two people who more or less fit their description.

Crocker had immediately called Sheriff Cargill's office, only to learn that the sheriff was already trying to reach him regarding a fire at the Rangoon Harbor RV Park. As he'd waited for the deputy to transfer the call to the sheriff's cell phone, Crocker had sat on the big round bed, thinking, *I really stepped in it this time*.

"Here they come," said Larry, jolting Crocker back to the present.

Jim Birdwell and Sheriff Cargill approached.

Before anyone could say hello, Crocker asked, "Which did they hit first?"

"First?" asked the sheriff.

"Did they torch my place before or after they attacked the couple at La Condamine?"

"Neither. They carried out both attacks simultaneously."

"Simultaneously?"

"At approximately the same time Jim called in the fire—"

"One of my patrols spotted the flames not more than twenty minutes after you and your friend left," said Jim.

"As I was saying," continued the sheriff, "at approximately that same time, the front desk at La Condamine got a call from the victims' room, asking to have a luggage cart sent up. Fifteen minutes later, security cameras recorded three men in suits bringing a cart full of luggage down to the lobby."

"No bellhop?"

"The hotel sent one, but the man who answered the door sent him away. The three men pushed the bags out to the front curb, loaded them into a white van, and drove away."

"And the girl?"

"Almost certainly in one of the bags."

"Just one?"

The sheriff raised an eyebrow. "We have no way of knowing if she was still alive, but the footage shows the men struggling to lift the largest bag into the van, so we're pretty sure she was still in one piece."

For a moment, nobody spoke. Crocker suspected that his companions were pondering the same unpleasant thought as him: If the girl was still alive when Dudka's men took her, her dead boss might be the lucky one.

He couldn't hold back any longer. "Jesus Christ, Bill, how the hell did they find us?"

Sheriff Cargill didn't answer.

"I've been thinking about it for the past hour," continued Crocker, "and the one answer I keep coming back to is that someone in your department leaked the information to Dudka's people."

"Hold on now," said the sheriff. "You don't know the leak came from my department—there were two other agencies working that crime scene."

"Tell me this: After Jennifer and I left the truck stop, how much time passed before the CSI team discovered the cash?"

The sheriff stared into the distance, rubbing his chin. "The Vegas Metro vans arrived about five minutes after you left, and it was maybe twenty minutes later that they popped the trunk on the suspects' vehicle. Why?"

"Because forty-five minutes after Metro popped that trunk, my trailer was on fire, and Jennifer's boss was having the life beaten out of him. These people are clearly good at what they do, but there is no way they coordinated and carried out simultaneous attacks with only forty-five minutes' notice."

Again, the sheriff didn't reply.

Crocker stared at him. "Dudka knew before you did."

"You may be right."

"You know I am. And since the leak had to have happened before Metro arrived on the scene, it had to have come from either your department or the highway patrol."

"Not necessarily. We shared information with Vegas Metro from the beginning. We even asked them to confirm that Ms. Williams was staying at La Condamine."

"Great," said Crocker. "So what you're saying is that there's nobody I can trust."

"You can trust Jim and me."

"And me," added Larry.

"Listen," said the sheriff, "if the missing girl isn't found by tomorrow morning, the feds will almost certainly take over the case. In the meantime, I'll put in a request for immediate FBI assistance. Between the evidence of police corruption, the possible links to organized crime, and the violence against interstate travelers, I think they'll bite."

"Good," said Crocker. "Tell the FBI that both Ms. Williams and I want federal protection. Until that's arranged, I'd prefer that nobody in your department or the highway patrol or Vegas Metro"—he glanced at Jim—"or the Rangoon Harbor security staff knows where we're staying. For now, I think the safest thing for Jennifer and me is to stay off everyone's radar."

"If you're sure that's what you want," said the sheriff. "I'd try to talk you into letting me take both of you into protective custody right now, but I know I'd be wasting my breath."

"You would be."

"I'll make the necessary calls and phone Larry when everything is arranged."

"Just be sure you make that call yourself. I don't want any of your deputies figuring out where we are."

"I still say you're wrong about my deputies, but you have my word."

"Thanks." Crocker stared at the wreckage for a moment. "I'd better get back to Jennifer. She shouldn't be alone right now." The words surprised him. It was strange to feel so protective of someone he'd just met.

"I'll take care of your trailer," said Jim, "or what's left of it. As soon as the investigators are done, I'll send a couple of my boys out here to sift through the debris and see what they can salvage."

"Thanks."

"Is there anything you want me to ask them to look for?"

Crocker thought for a moment. "There was a framed picture of Courtney and me—we're at the range, holding up a couple of targets. If by any chance that survived, I'd really like to have it back."

"I'll tell the guys to keep an eye out for it."

"I appreciate it." He cast a final glance at the smoldering debris. "Larry, let's get out of here before these fumes make us sick."

"Aye aye, Captain." Larry trotted toward the short row of parking spaces.

Crocker turned to follow, then stopped and turned back to Sheriff Cargill. "What the hell were three mob couriers doing trying to steal an ATM machine from a truck stop?"

The sheriff sighed. "They made the classic Las Vegas mistake."

"Which is?"

"They forgot that the house always wins."

"I don't follow."

"We found out they spent most of yesterday in the high rollers' pit at Mandalay Bay. They dropped close to ten grand at the blackjack tables."

"You mean they gambled away one of the envelopes they were supposed to deliver? That's why they were trying to get the cash from the ATM?"

"That's our working theory."

Crocker shook his head. "They were afraid of what might happen if they were short by one percent; now I'm stuck with the tab for the full amount."

"I don't suppose you want to reconsider my offer of protection, do you?"

"I don't suppose you want to let me have the remaining cash so that I can try to bargain for my life, do you?"

The sheriff gave a nervous laugh and shook his head. "That I can't do. But if you need anything else—anything at all—don't hesitate to give me a call."

Crocker nodded, turned, and walked toward Larry's yellow Corvette.

◆ ◆ ◆

Over the course of his life, Crocker had spent more than ten thousand hours engaging opponents armed with guns modified to fire paint pellets, navigating live-fire shoot houses populated with both paper terrorists and paper bystanders, and disarming sparring partners wielding rubber pistols. But not one of those mock bad guys, human or paper, had been connected to the Russian mob.

He gazed out the passenger window but didn't see the road or the desert. His mind was too busy estimating how much he could get for his unfinished Colorado dream home if he had to sell everything and go into witness protection.

The sudden tightening of his seat belt brought his train of thought to a screeching halt. A cloud of dust caught up with the Corvette as it came to rest on the sandy shoulder of the two-lane road.

He scanned the horizon. "Did you see something?"

"Nah," said Larry, shifting his massive frame to better face his passenger. "Something is bugging me." He hesitated as if searching for the right words. "You know I respect Sheriff Cargill. He's always been good to me and my crew at the Pear, and I'm sure he intends to do right by you and Ms. Williams, but calling in the feds is just going to get that poor woman killed."

"You think he's going to get Jennifer killed?"

"Not Jennifer, her friend."

"Her friend?" Crocker had more or less written off Jennifer's missing friend, Ashley. He didn't want to think about the particulars, but he suspected that Dudka's people had long since finished with her and dumped her body in the desert. "You think she might still be alive?"

Larry checked the road behind them. "I'm sure she is." He accelerated into a hard turn, heading back in the direction they'd come.

Crocker placed a hand on the door to keep from falling into it. "Where are we going?"

"Walmart."

"Why?"

"You need to make a phone call."

♦ ♦ ♦

Jennifer sat in the middle of the large round bed, her arms crossed tightly in front of her, her fingers clutching the edges of the extra sheet, which had long since come untucked and lost any resemblance to a toga. Tufts of unkempt hair hung in front of her face, crisscrossing the tracks of dried tears.

Just twenty-four hours before, she, Bryan, and Ashley had been wheeling and dealing on the convention center floor. Now Bryan was dead, Ashley was missing, and she was the reason.

She thought about Ashley jumping up to give her a hug in the casino bar.

She remembered Bryan, one year before, staring out at the Las Vegas skyline and trying to put on a brave face as he confided that his marriage was ending. Jennifer had tried to lift his spirits by raising her glass and toasting to better days to come. Now he had no more days to come.

Fresh tears trickled down her cheeks.

She had walked into the wrong place at the wrong time and inadvertently offended the wrong people, and those people had taken out their anger on a man and woman who probably never even knew why.

The story she'd heard from Tom played on a loop in her mind. She imagined poor Grace and an unsuspecting housekeeper finding Bryan's naked, beaten body tied to a chair in the middle of a trashed hotel room—*her* hotel room. She pictured her colleagues on the convention center floor, asking prospective tenants and buyers to excuse them as they checked their vibrating phones. She saw their carefully groomed smiles fading into grim expressions of disbelief as they learned of the horrors that had befallen two of their own.

What kind of nightmare have I stumbled into?

A knock at the door made her jump.

"Miss," said a woman on the other side, "it's Vegas. We met last night."

Jennifer recalled the two women who'd practically assaulted Crocker in the hallway.

"Can you come to the door?" asked the woman.

If she tells me they need this room, I'm going to slug her.

Jennifer crawled to the edge of the bed, placed her feet on the floor, and stood slowly, not trusting her legs to support her. When she was confident she wasn't going to collapse, she wrapped the sheet more securely around her breasts and walked to the door.

The woman standing in the hallway bore little resemblance to the tarted-up trollop Jennifer had seen the night before. Dressed in a tank top and a pair of workout shorts, her platinum hair tied back in a ponytail, the young woman—who Jennifer guessed was barely old enough to drink—looked more like a college coed than a Las Vegas prostitute.

She held a tray containing a couple of sandwiches on paper plates and two glass bottles of Mexican Coca-Cola. "Dottie thought you might be hungry."

Although Jennifer hadn't eaten in almost twenty hours, food held no appeal. "I'm not hungry. But maybe Crocker will be when he gets back. You can bring it in if you want."

"You really should try to eat a little something," said Vegas as she stepped past Jennifer into the room. "You're going to start feeling weak if you don't." She set the tray on the edge of the bed.

"Thanks, but I—"

"Knock-knock," interrupted another woman's voice.

Scarlett, the redheaded half of the duo that had ambushed Crocker, stood in the doorway, wearing a black negligee and high heels.

"I thought you had an appointment," said Vegas.

Scarlett stepped into the room. "I do, but Dottie wanted me to tell Matt's friend that she has a visitor."

Jennifer's blood ran cold. "A visitor?"

"Some guy—young, cute, says he works with you."

Relief washed over her. "Tom."

"Should I tell him to come on back or what? I have a client waiting."

"Yes." Jennifer was already backing toward the bathroom. "I just need a couple of minutes to get dressed."

Scarlett eyed the sheet hanging loosely from Jennifer's body, then glanced at the bed. "Did you and Matt actually fuck or just sleep together?"

"Inappropriate!" shouted Vegas. She shoved Scarlett back into the hallway.

"Oh, lighten up," said Scarlett as Vegas shut the door in her face.

"What's that about?" asked Jennifer.

Vegas looked embarrassed. "Matt won't sleep with her, so she thinks he's gay."

"Sorry I asked." She turned toward the bathroom.

Vegas quickly added, "I can assure you he's not."

Jennifer stopped just inside the bathroom and turned around. "Have you and he…"

"No." There was a hint of disappointment in her voice. "But unlike Scarlett, I don't mind having a conversation that doesn't lead to sex. Matt says he doesn't party with any of the girls here because he doesn't like to get his meat where he gets his bread and butter. If you ask me, I think he's still not over Courtney."

Courtney?

As if reading Jennifer's mind, Vegas added, "The woman he was engaged to."

The mention of an ex-fiancée filled Jennifer's mind with follow-up questions that would have to wait. "Tell Tom I'll only be a minute."

She closed the bathroom door, dropped the bedsheet beside the sink, and turned her attention to the bathroom mirror. Having Tom meet her in a whorehouse was awkward enough without looking like she'd just worked a double shift there.

She brushed her teeth, gave her face a once-over with her bare-bones makeup kit, and was in the process of running the cheap complimentary comb through her hair when a knock at the bathroom door made her jump.

From the other side of the door, Tom asked, "Jennifer, are you in there?" His voice was shaky.

"I'm here." She dropped the comb and grabbed the complimentary stick of deodorant from the counter. It was a men's brand, but at the moment, that was pretty low on her list of concerns. "I'll be right out."

"Okay," he said, still shaky. "I hope you don't mind, but the girl up front told me to come on in."

"That's fine." She finished applying the deodorant and turned to look for her clothes.

She grabbed the sadistic pair of lace panties from the towel rack and realized, more relieved than dismayed, that they were still damp. She dropped them into the wastebasket.

Good riddance.

She removed her little black dress from the hook on the back of the door, slipped it on, and emerged from the bathroom looking presentable enough for a woman who had survived a shootout, spent the night in a whorehouse, and awakened to the news that her boss and quasi-boyfriend was dead.

Tom, on the other hand, did not look so well. When Jennifer opened the door, he was standing in the middle of the room, nervously rocking the sex swing with one hand. His normally well-groomed hair was a mess, and his flushed face suggested he'd spent a good portion of the drive to Pahrump crying.

When he saw Jennifer, he took two quick steps toward her—she was certain he would have broken into a sprint if he'd had more ground to cover—and wrapped his arms around her.

"I'm so glad you're okay," he said.

Jennifer felt an odd mixture of relief and guilt. She'd half expected him to blame her for what had happened to Ashley. Now she half wished he would.

"Thanks." She pulled back to take a better look at him. "How are you?"

Tears began streaming down his face. "It's all my fault."

"*Your* fault?" She led him toward the bed. "How could it be *your* fault?" She seated him on the edge of the bed and sat beside him.

After a moment, he regained enough composure to speak. "Last night, when she took me back to my room, Ashley asked if I wanted her to come in and mix us a couple of nightcaps from the honor bar. At that point my head was swimming, and I told her that I couldn't possibly drink another drop. Then she asked if I needed to be tucked into bed, and I gave some stupid reply about how I would probably spend the night hugging the toilet."

Jennifer saw the genuine pain in his eyes. "She was asking you to invite her in?"

"She was practically begging me to. But I'd had myself a nice little pity party over my lost bag, and I was too drunk to accept or even understand her offer. If I hadn't behaved like such a total ass, she would have spent the night in my room, and she'd still be..." He choked back a sob.

Jennifer placed a hand on his shoulder. "The police are looking for her, Tom. They'll find her."

"After what those men did to Bryan, I..." His words faded into sobs.

Jennifer knew she needed to be delicate, but there was something she had to ask. "Tom, do you know how Bryan and Ashley...how they ended up...spending the night together?"

Tom shook his head. "All I know is that none of this would have happened if she'd spent the night with me."

Jennifer wanted to reassure him that it wasn't his fault, but a small part of her wanted to believe that it was, if only to assuage her own feelings of guilt.

She was still searching for the right words when the door to the room swung open and Crocker stepped inside.

Before Jennifer could greet him, he said, "Good, you're dressed. We're meeting in Larry's cabin in twenty minutes."

"Sure, okay," she replied, despite having no idea what he was talking about. "Crocker, this is Tom."

"Great. Bring him with you. We're going to need all the help we can get."

CHAPTER TEN

Larry's was the largest of a half-dozen modest cabins located behind the Prickly Pear's main building. Unlike the others, Larry's had no room number on the door, leading Jennifer to infer that it was the only cabin not for rent. In sharp contrast to the rest of the Prickly Pear Ranch, the cabin's interior was surprisingly tasteful, looking less like the tacky Champagne Suite than like a photo spread from *Country Living* magazine.

Jennifer sat beside Tom on Larry's big leather couch and struggled against the anxiety and curiosity pulling at her from every direction. Crocker still hadn't hinted at his reason for calling this meeting, but in light of all that had happened and all that was at stake, she suspected that her world was about to be shaken yet again.

To her left, Crocker sat on the stone fireplace hearth, scribbling something on a small notepad. In the adjoining kitchen, ice clinked into glasses as Larry prepared a round of drinks.

Across the room, the front door swung open, giving Jennifer a start.

"Hello? Anybody here?" called Vegas as she stepped inside.

Whereas the pleasant décor in Larry's cabin had almost let Jennifer forget where she was, Vegas's attire made that impossible. The curvy blonde had changed into a black satin bustier and a ruffle-covered pair of red panties. On her feet she wore a pair of orange flip-flops that clashed with the rest of the ensemble. Jennifer suspected that somewhere on the shoe wall was a pair of stiletto heels that complemented the outfit.

Vegas crossed to the couch and pointed to the empty spot beside Jennifer. "Is this seat taken?"

Jennifer hesitated, half expecting Crocker to tell the young woman that this wasn't a good time and that she should come back later. But Crocker said nothing, and after a moment Jennifer replied, "It's all yours."

Vegas sat just as Larry emerged from the kitchen carrying a tray of brimming margarita glasses. He set the tray on the coffee table and said, "I'm afraid it's only lemonade. When this is all over, we'll celebrate with something a bit stronger."

"When *what* is all over?" asked Tom, echoing Jennifer's own thoughts.

Without looking up from his notes, Crocker said, "We're still waiting on one more."

Larry walked across the room and pressed a button on the intercom box beside the front door. "Dottie, is Scarlett done with her customer yet?"

A moment later, Dottie's voice squawked back, "When I talked to her a minute ago, she was about to shower and head your way."

"Thanks." He walked back to the coffee table, picked up one of the lemonades, and settled into the overstuffed armchair across from the couch. "As soon as Scarlett gets here, we can begin."

Jennifer opened her mouth to ask why they needed to wait on Scarlett, but a loud chime preempted the question.

Tom checked his phone.

Jennifer leaned over to peek at the screen. "Any news on Ashley?"

"No," he replied, clearly disappointed. "Grace is looking for anyone who knows the San Antonio development well enough to give Bryan's presentation tomorrow."

"She's not going to find anyone. Of the three people who worked that project, one is dead, one is missing, and one is hiding out at a whorehouse in the middle of the desert."

Both Tom and Crocker shifted uncomfortably in their seats, and Jennifer immediately regretted her choice of words. To her relief, both Larry and Vegas seemed unfazed.

Crocker looked like he was about to say something when the front door swung open again. Scarlett entered, wearing a comically short silk kimono and Japanese slippers.

Inspecting the outfit, Jennifer imagined Vegas and Scarlett as slutty versions of Tweedledum and Tweedledee. In spite of everything, she had to stifle a giggle.

"Sorry to keep you waiting," said Scarlett, "but I had to shower. Ted, my Thursday regular, sweats a lot. He's quick as a jackrabbit, but sometimes the big guys—"

"That's okay," interrupted Larry. "Just come have a seat."

She squeezed past the coffee table and, much to Jennifer's surprise, settled onto Larry's lap. Without a word, she took the glass from his hand and took a long sip of lemonade.

Marking her territory, thought Jennifer.

"All right," said Crocker, taking one last look at his notes before standing. "It's time to get down to business."

His voice was somewhat deeper and slower. Jennifer wondered if this was the voice he used with his students.

"The reason for this meeting," he continued, "is that Larry and I are pretty sure we know where Jennifer's friend Ashley is."

"You know where she is?" blurted Tom. "Have you told the police?"

Larry raised a quieting hand. "Take it easy, sport. It's a bit more complicated than that."

"As I was saying," said Crocker, "we know where she is, but if we're to have any chance of getting her back, we have to act fast."

"Act how?" asked Jennifer.

"That's what we're here to figure out."

"No offense," said Scarlett, "but what does this have to do with Vegas and me?"

Good question, thought Jennifer.

"You're here to help Crocker and his friends understand what they're up against," said Larry.

"How are we supposed to do that?"

"By telling them about the last time you saw your friend Stinky."

"How is that going to help?" asked Vegas.

Scarlett sighed. "Seriously, Vegas? You can't see where they're going with this?"

Vegas looked both confused and hurt, reminding Jennifer of a puppy that doesn't understand why it's being scolded.

"It's okay." Crocker gave the young woman a reassuring smile. "It'll all make sense in a minute. Just tell us about Stinky."

The hurt expression faded from Vegas's face. "Stinky was our hookup."

"Pot?" asked Tom.

"Coke," she replied. "He was a good hookup too—we could usually count on him even when the rest of the dealers were dry. But there were a couple of weeks last summer when nobody was holding, not even Stinky.

"After the third or fourth time he told us he was dry, Scarlett told him that she was tired of wasting her time with him and that she and I were going to drive down to Tijuana and score on our own. That kind of freaked him out because he thought for sure we'd either get raped and murdered by the cartels or get pinched on our way back.

"He told us he was expecting a shipment in two days, and he promised that we'd be his first call when it arrived. That sounded good to me, but Scarlett didn't trust him."

"I didn't trust him," interjected Scarlett, "because he was a goddamned drug dealer. He'd probably made that same promise to thirty other people."

"Anyway," said Vegas, "Scarlett cut a deal with him to let us come to the buy."

"What kind of deal?" asked Crocker.

"Umm..." Vegas blushed. "She, uh, promised that we'd give him some special attention if he let us tag along."

Crocker nodded. "Tell us about the buy."

"It was really scary. We drove out into the desert, where there were these three guys waiting with this big white van."

"These were Dudka's men?"

"Well, I don't know for sure, but they're some of the same guys who come into the Pear each month after the Winter Palace has its big payday."

Crocker jotted something on his notepad.

"Anyway," she continued, "things got ugly almost as soon as we got out of Stinky's car."

"How do you mean?"

"The guys with the van weren't at all happy that Stinky had brought us along. The one in charge started yelling at him. And like an idiot, Stinky told the guy to chill out. That really pissed him off, and next thing we knew, he was pointing a gun in Stinky's face."

"What happened then?"

"I really thought they were going to kill all three of us, but Stinky was all like, 'Come on, Al, you know me. Be cool.'"

Jennifer locked eyes with Crocker. "Al?"

"I think that was his name," said Vegas. "Anyway, when Stinky said that, the guy kind of relaxed, like maybe he realized he'd overreacted. Then, all of a sudden, he swung his gun and hit Stinky so hard that Stinky fell to the ground and looked like he might not get back up.

"At this point, I was getting really scared because this Al guy was clearly nuts, and Stinky had clearly lost control of the situation. Scarlett and I just wanted to score some blow, and now it looked like we were about to die."

"But you didn't die," said Crocker.

"No." Her voice was timid. "Scarlett talked to the guys and calmed them down."

"How did she do that?"

Vegas looked away, and though she didn't appear to be blushing this time, she looked to Jennifer like she might be trying to blink away tears.

"More special attention," answered Scarlett, clearly less self-conscious than Vegas about her willingness to utilize the assets at her disposal.

"And after the special attention?" asked Crocker.

Vegas stared at the floor. "Then they sold us the coke, and we left. A few days later, Stinky disappeared. We don't know if he got scared and left town or if those guys came after him or what, but we never heard from him again."

"Tell them," said Larry, "what you saw when the guy gave you the drugs."

"Oh yeah!" She looked up. "We walked around to the back of the van to get the coke, and when the guy opened the door, I saw that there were four women sitting inside."

"Women?" asked Jennifer.

"Yeah, they were just sitting there like they were along for the ride, except there weren't any seats; they were just sitting on the floor with the drugs. I kind of smiled at them, just to be friendly, but none of them reacted. They all looked really strung out on something."

"Can you describe them?" asked Crocker.

"Well, they all looked to be about my age or younger—one looked like she might still be in high school—and they looked like they'd be really pretty except that their faces were really dirty, and their hair was a mess, and they were all wearing really unflattering gray sweat suits. To be honest, they looked like escapees from a women's prison."

"More like prisoners from some Third World country," said Crocker.

"Prisoners?" asked Tom.

"Larry believes, and I concur, that those women were being smuggled right along with the drugs."

"Human trafficking?" asked Jennifer.

"Yep," said Larry. "Sex slaves."

Jennifer cast a quick glance at Tom, who seemed to be processing this revelation.

Larry continued, "My money says that's why your friend Ashley was taken alive—Dudka is hoping to recoup some of the money you cost him."

"You think they're going to make her a *sex slave*?" shouted Tom.

Larry nodded. "It's rare for sex traffickers to kidnap an American, but it does happen. Most sex trafficking is in one direction, from poor countries to rich, and it typically involves women being recruited under false pretenses, not kidnapped. They take young women from places like Siberia and South

America, hook them on drugs so that they're too strung out to put up a fight and too dependent to run away, and then smuggle them to wealthy metropolitan areas like Moscow and Las Vegas. The women are kept as drug-addicted prisoners and forced to work as unpaid prostitutes. It's a blight on all of us involved in the legitimate sex trade."

"What happens," asked Jennifer, working to keep her voice steady, "on those rare occasions when an American *is* kidnapped?"

"Those incidents typically involve tourists traveling in countries where law enforcement can be paid to look the other way. That's not the case here, so I'm guessing Dudka will try to get your friend out of the country as soon as possible. She's too valuable to risk holding here."

"What makes her so valuable?"

"Women from Third World countries are considered depreciating assets. They're bought cheap, and when they're used up, they're disposed of."

Jennifer cringed at Larry's choice of words.

"But," he continued, "women from Western countries, particularly the U.S., are considered a valuable commodity."

"Why?" asked Tom.

"In the basest terms, they're considered a higher grade of meat. They're thought to be more hygienic, they have better teeth, and they're typically free of disease."

"That's barbaric," muttered Jennifer.

Larry nodded. "Blondes are particularly desirable because fair hair is so scarce in so many parts of the world. A private buyer in the Mideast or China might view an American blonde as an exotic purchase worthy of a premium, the same way you or I might view an authentic Persian rug."

Tom's eyes widened. "Ashley has blond hair."

"I figured as much. And I'm guessing she's young and pretty?"

"She's twenty-three and very pretty."

Larry nodded again. "She'd probably fetch quite a price at auction."

"At *auction*?"

"That's how it's done. A photo is circulated. Offers are made. It's like an underworld eBay. I'm no expert, but based on what I know, I'm guessing she could bring as much as a quarter of a million dollars."

"A quarter of a million dollars!" exclaimed Tom. "That's all a beautiful, intelligent woman like Ashley is worth?"

"No," said Crocker, "that's all she's worth to the scumbags who buy kidnapped women at auction. And therein lies our chance to get her back."

"How?"

"Dudka lost nearly eight hundred thousand dollars when I shot his couriers at the truck stop. If he sells Ashley for a quarter of a million, he takes a loss of more than half a million dollars."

"What are you getting at?" asked Jennifer.

"We're going to make him a better offer—the full amount he lost, just under eight hundred thousand dollars—for Ashley."

"That's absurd," said Tom. "We're only speculating that Dudka has her, and even if we knew for sure, I doubt anybody here has eight hundred thousand dollars."

"You're wrong on the first count." Crocker pulled a cheap-looking cell phone from his pocket.

"You got your phone back?" asked Jennifer.

"This isn't the phone I left in my truck; it's a burner Larry bought me an hour ago. Immediately after he bought it, I placed a call to the Winter Palace and asked to be connected to Mr. Vladimir Dudka.

"When his secretary answered, I told her I was calling about an eight-hundred-thousand-dollar marker I took out last night. I said that Mr. Dudka had agreed to personally carry the marker and that I wanted to make arrangements to repay my debt and reclaim my collateral. She promised to look into it and call me back."

"And?" asked Tom.

"And fifteen minutes later, I got this voicemail."

He pressed a button on the phone. There was a loud beep followed by a woman's voice: "Mr. Crocker, this is Jaclyn Goldberg following up on your inquiry about your marker with Mr. Dudka. Mr. Dudka wanted me to relay that, as is casino policy, you have until midnight tonight to pay off the balance of your debt if you wish to reclaim your collateral. He also said that any further inquiries into this matter should be directed to his associate Mr. Black at 702—"

Crocker pressed the button again, cutting off the message. "That's it."

"What did she mean by 'as is casino policy'?" asked Vegas. "They do this often enough that they have a policy about it?"

"She was establishing plausible deniability," replied Larry. "In case we take her message to the FBI, she wants to be able to say, 'Oh, I had him confused with someone else. I certainly didn't mean to imply we'd kidnapped his friend.'"

"That's exactly what we should do," said Tom. "We should take the recording to the FBI. Let them bring the wrath of God and J. Edgar Hoover down on Dudka and the rest of the Winter Palace."

"Come on," said Larry. "You don't think Dudka is holding your friend there in the casino vault, do you?"

"Maybe not, but the FBI can put in wiretaps, set up roadblocks, call in SWAT teams—do all the stuff the FBI does."

"Under normal circumstances," said Crocker, "I'd agree with you. But the only way the FBI could possibly pull together enough resources to find Ashley by midnight tonight is to involve local police, and we already know that Dudka has a mole somewhere in one of the local departments. If Dudka gets word that the FBI is onto him, Ashley will disappear faster than you can say 'shallow grave.'"

Jennifer imagined a pair of hikers finding Ashley's naked body with no head or hands or feet, like a macabre department-store mannequin.

Just a torso with a hummingbird tattoo.

She felt the hot sting of bile in the back of her throat and grabbed Tom's hand to steady herself.

He glanced at her, squeezed her hand in return, and turned back to Crocker. "So what do you suggest?"

"Like I said, we're going to offer to repay the money."

"And when Dudka and his goons realize we don't have it?"

"One step at a time. The first step is convincing them we have the money. That should be enough to get me in the same room as Ashley, which is a lot closer than we are right now. Once we have that figured out, we'll work on step two, a getaway plan for Ashley and me."

Tom sighed. "No offense, chief, but step two is kind of a big step."

Scarlett rose from Larry's lap. "It sounds like you all have a lot to talk over. Vegas and I should get out of your hair."

"Speak for yourself," said Vegas. "I want to help."

Scarlett rolled her eyes. "Do you have eight hundred large?"

Larry frowned. "Hon..."

Scarlett settled back onto his lap. "I'm just saying."

"We're not actually going to give Dudka eight hundred grand," said Crocker. "At least I assume we're not." He turned to Jennifer. "You don't have access to that kind of money, do you?"

"Hardly." She thought for a moment. "I mean, maybe if I had a week to meet with each of the firm's senior partners and explain the situation..."

Crocker shook his head. "If we had that kind of time, we'd have other options. Even an extra day or two would give the FBI time to put something together."

"Hell," said Larry, "just a few more hours would give you time to swipe the money from Le Tournoi and pay the ransom outright."

Crocker turned back to his notes. "I'm going to pretend I didn't hear that."

Larry laughed. "Like you've never thought about walking out of there with a suitcase full of cash."

"What cash?" asked Jennifer. "From the poker tournament?"

Crocker seemed annoyed. "Remember what Jim Birdwell said about casinos being required to report cash transactions over ten thousand dollars?"

She nodded. "That's why the envelopes each contained exactly ten thousand dollars."

"And that's why the entry fee for Le Tournoi is exactly ten thousand dollars. A lot of the rounders—the professional poker players—prefer to stay off the IRS's radar. They pay the fee in cash, and I and the other private patrol officers guard that cash and transport it to the vault. We also protect the prize money, which is on display during the tournament."

Scarlett leaned forward, almost falling off Larry's lap. "You couldn't really steal eight hundred grand, could you?"

Crocker shrugged. "Five hundred players checking in over the course of five hours, a tournament room located nowhere near the vault, and a million dollars sitting in a glass safe in the center of the gaming floor—it's theoretically possible. But I'm not interested in spending the next twenty years in prison, so..."

"So no asking Dudka to extend the deadline," said Larry.

Crocker shook his head. "Even if we had a realistic plan for coming up with the money, asking to extend the deadline would completely destroy our credibility with Dudka. The only way we pull this off is if we make him believe we already have the cash. If we so much as call and say we're stuck in traffic, he'll cut and run."

Larry grinned. "And so ends my dream of an *Ocean's Eleven*–style casino heist."

Tom's cell phone chimed again.

"Any news?" asked Jennifer.

Tom checked the phone. "No, just a message from Meredith Higgins, suggesting that New Wave associates forgo attending tonight's receptions"—his voice assumed a high, preachy tone—"'lest we appear callous in the face of New Wave's recent loss.'"

"Typical," said Jennifer. "Meredith never misses an opportunity to act like a self-righteous bitch."

"Returning to the topic at hand," said Crocker, "are there any other suggestions for convincing Dudka we have the money?"

"Could we fake it?" asked Jennifer.

"How do you mean?"

"Well, could we take stacks of one-dollar bills and place hundreds on the top and bottom so that they look like stacks of hundred-dollar bills and show that to Dudka's people and tell them they can have it as soon as we have Ashley?"

"Wouldn't that still be a lot of money?" asked Vegas.

"It would be a far cry from eight hundred thousand dollars. A ten-thousand-dollar stack could be replicated with"—Jennifer did the calculations in her head—"less than three hundred dollars. That means we'd need"—more quick math—"just under twenty-four thousand dollars in all."

"I'm skeptical that such a simple ruse would work," said Larry, "but I probably have that much on hand here at the Pear. Crocker, if you want to call it a personal loan, I'll spot you the cash."

"This could work," said Jennifer. "We could get one of the local casinos to convert it into the denominations we need and have it ready to go in a couple of hours."

"Hang on," said Larry. "We're talking about eighty stacks of a hundred bills each. How big is that? Can one person carry it by hand?"

"It's big," said Scarlett, "but it would probably fit inside a large shopping bag."

"I'm afraid to ask how you know that."

She punched him playfully in the arm. "I was a bank teller, you paranoid old man."

Jennifer turned to Crocker. "What do you think?"

"I think a bunch of guys who deal in drugs and kidnapped women are going to be looking for that sort of double-cross from the moment I walk in." He sighed. "But we're not coming up with a lot of other options, so let's assume that maybe—and I stress 'maybe'—flashing a bag full of cash is enough to get me face-to-face with Ashley. What then?"

"Step two?" asked Tom.

"Exactly. I walk in, show them the cash, and tell them they can count it after I see Ashley. They bring in Ashley, I hand them twenty-four thousand dollars, and..."

"You shoot them?" asked Vegas. "Like the robbers at the truck stop?"

Crocker shook his head. "Those were couriers. For this, Dudka will send soldiers. We need a plan that doesn't hinge on me being quicker on the draw."

The young woman in the bustier and ruffled panties seemed to consider this. "Then why not do the exchange someplace where there aren't any guns, like at the airport?"

Jennifer cast a hopeful look at Crocker. "What do you think? Would Dudka go for that?"

"I like the idea of trying to disarm Dudka's men," he replied, "but they're not going to meet us at any location they suspect we've scoped out in advance, especially not a location secured by federal agents."

"That's true," said Larry. "I dealt a little pot in college, and I could always count on my supplier to call a few minutes before we were scheduled to meet and change the location. When you operate entirely outside the law, paranoia becomes a survival skill."

"I've never dealt drugs," said Crocker, "but I used to be pretty tight with an undercover narcotics officer, and she said that if a trafficker meets you where he said he would, you're in trouble."

"So where does that leave us?" asked Jennifer.

"As I see it," replied Crocker, "any workable plan must meet three criteria. First, Dudka and his men must believe we have the money. If they get even a hint that we don't, you'll never see Ashley again.

"Second, Dudka and his men must believe they have the upper hand. They're not going to show unless they think they're one step ahead of us.

"Finally, Dudka and his men cannot, under any circumstances, actually be allowed to gain the upper hand. If we don't stay at least three steps ahead of them at all times, Ashley won't make it out alive, and neither will I."

"All right," said Jennifer, "so how do you propose we do that?"

"I'm not sure. Maybe we can trick them into selecting a location we control. Then we could run the show but let them think they're in charge."

Larry snorted. "How about we just tell them we'd be happy to meet anywhere except for 'that there briar patch'?"

"The Briar Patch?" asked Scarlett. "Is that the old strip club in Carson City?"

"No, hon, it's an old story about—"

"Hang on," said Crocker. "Tom, your coworker Meredith may have given me an idea."

"What?" asked Tom.

"You're invited to a bunch of receptions tonight, right?"

"Well, not me personally, but—"

"Is one of them hosted by a group called LCR?"

"Sure," said Tom. "The LCR reception is one of the big ones. All the senior staff are invited. Why?"

"Senior staff—does that include you, Jennifer?"

"Yes," she said. "Why? Is that the reception you were asked to work?"

"Yep. And if I call in a favor, I think I can still get on the security team."

"How is that going to help us?" asked Larry.

"Because," said Crocker, "the reception is taking place in the most secure building on the Strip, the Stratosphere Tower."

"I'm sorry," interrupted Vegas, "but I'm completely lost."

"It's the edge we've been looking for. After 9/11, the Stratosphere put in airport-style security at the entrance to the tower. They won't let you onto the elevators with so much as a pair of scissors unless—"

"Unless," said Jennifer with a smile, "you happen to be on the security team for a private event hosted in the tower."

"Exactly."

"Okay," said Larry. "I can see how that might give us a pretty nice advantage, but how do we get Dudka and his men to pick the tower as the site of the exchange? If we suggest it, they'll just change the location at the last minute."

"There isn't any way to guarantee they'll pick the Stratosphere," said Crocker, "but we can make it a whole lot harder for them to pick anyplace else."

"How?" asked Tom.

"We'll do exactly what Vegas suggested—we'll insist that the exchange take place at the airport."

"I don't get it," said Vegas.

"The LCR reception is from eight until eleven, so we'll schedule the exchange to take place around nine thirty. We'll tell Dudka's men that we have one condition—we'll only do the exchange if it takes place at the airport. We'll be adamant that we're not going to go through with the exchange unless we know that everyone has passed through metal detectors.

"Dudka's men will naturally look for another location with metal detectors, a location they'll assume we haven't had a chance to scout."

"And you think they'll pick the Stratosphere?" asked Jennifer.

"I know of only two places in Southern Nevada that have functioning metal detectors at nine thirty on a Thursday night—the airport and the Stratosphere Tower."

"And if they pooh-pooh your insistence on metal detectors?" asked Larry.

"I don't think they will, not if we convince them that we have the money and that the metal detectors are a real sticking point."

"And if they somehow locate another venue with functioning metal detectors?" asked Jennifer.

"Then we go with plan B."

"Which is?"

"We make a last-minute call to the FBI and pray we're able to get Ashley back before Dudka's moles alert him that it's a setup."

"So what happens if everything goes according to plan?" asked Jennifer. "You and the other guards lay a trap for Dudka's men?"

Crocker shook his head. "As soon as I alert the other guards, they'll lock down the tower and call for police backup. We can't risk involving them until we have eyes on Ashley."

"Well, at least we know you'll be armed and Dudka's men won't. That should give us a significant advantage."

"Hopefully."

"What do you mean 'hopefully'?" asked Tom.

"The reality of the situation," said Crocker, "is that we have no way of knowing the limits of Dudka's reach. I'm not one hundred percent sure he couldn't get guns into the airport. I know that sounds crazy, but after seeing the precision with which his people torched my trailer, killed Bryan, and abducted Ashley, I'm not taking anything for granted."

"And if they do have guns?" asked Jennifer, wishing Crocker would offer a bit of reassurance to counter her growing list of concerns.

"Then we'll just have to hope they're smart enough to realize they have no chance of escape if they shoot me on top of a nine-hundred-foot tower with only one exit."

"If that's your plan," said Larry, "I hope you really are quicker on the draw than they are, because the Russian mob isn't known for discretion and sound judgment. They're known for being single-mindedly ruthless and having more balls than brains."

This was not the reassurance Jennifer had been hoping for.

"I don't like it," she said. "We need to think of something else."

Crocker's eyes were sympathetic. "I think this is the best plan we're going to come up with."

"Then we scrap the whole thing and call the FBI."

"No," said Tom, "it'll work."

The defiance in his voice caught Jennifer by surprise.

"It's too dangerous," she said. "If Dudka's men figure out a way to get guns into the Stratosphere, the whole thing could turn into a bloodbath."

"It's not going to be a bloodbath," said Tom. "We just need to make a couple of changes to the plan."

Jennifer wanted to protest, but Tom's sudden confidence made her hesitate.

"What kind of changes do you have in mind?" asked Crocker.

"There is a safer way to do this—a way that doesn't involve robbing a casino or relying on crooked cops or risking a shootout at a crowded tourist attraction."

"I'm listening," said Crocker. "What do we need to do?"

"We need to get my bag from the TSA."

CHAPTER ELEVEN

Jennifer surveyed the selection of provocative minidresses laid out on the large round bed. Only one or two had real potential. Most were as gaudy as everything else in the Champagne Suite, which now served as a de facto staging area.

Even after an hour of hammering out various details and discussing various contingencies, Jennifer still had doubts about Tom and Crocker's plan. It was complicated and dangerous, and there was no wiggle room. If one part didn't go according to plan, the whole thing would collapse like a house of cards.

In the end, it was the conviction in Tom's and Crocker's voices that persuaded her to give the plan her blessing. Both men were committed to doing whatever was necessary to save Ashley.

Tom's motivation was easy to understand. He'd been in love with Ashley since the moment they met, and he was haunted by the realization that her kidnapping might have been avoided if he hadn't gotten so drunk.

Crocker's motivation was harder to pinpoint. Jennifer wanted to believe he was doing it for her, but the determination in his eyes made her suspect a motivation deeper than a simple attraction to a woman he'd just met. She wondered if something in Matt Crocker's DNA prohibited him from leaving another person in harm's way.

What she wanted at that moment was for Tom and Crocker to hurry and get back from their supply run so that she and Crocker could talk privately before, as Larry now insisted on calling it, *the big show*.

Two loud knocks shook the door behind her, followed almost immediately by the slow creak of the hinges. She turned, hopeful that her gunslinger had returned. Instead, she saw Vegas carrying a hatbox and another dress.

The young hooker had changed into a pink corset and matching thong, leading Jennifer to suspect that the black bustier and ruffle-covered red panties of two hours before had since played a part in some lonely guy's fantasy.

Vegas set the hatbox on the bed. "How's it going? Found any you like?"

"Umm…" Jennifer wanted to choose her words carefully. "I'm just not sure any of these are going to fit."

"You obviously underestimate my sewing abilities. Here"—she handed Jennifer the dress she was carrying—"hold this one up so I can see what it looks like on you."

Eyeing the gold sequined dress, Jennifer resisted the urge to ask where the batteries went and held it up over her black cocktail dress.

"Oh," exclaimed Vegas, "that one would look great on you!"

Jennifer turned to face the mirror at the foot of the bed. She studied the garment and noted that at the very least, its halter top would be reasonably secure and not too revealing.

As horrible as the gold dress was, it was the best of the lot. It was as scandalously short as the others, but the neckline didn't plunge all the way to the naval, there weren't any cutouts in weird places, and most significantly, it wasn't made of vinyl.

"I suppose this could work," she said.

Vegas stepped between Jennifer and the mirror and inspected the dress. "The sequins are going to make alterations a pain, but I think we can get away with just taking it in a little in the bust."

Jennifer eyed Vegas's chest. "Yes, you have a bit more real estate up top than I do."

Vegas smiled and, in a whisper that suggested a state secret, said, "Between you and me, they're not real."

"No!" exclaimed Jennifer, feigning genuine surprise.

Vegas winked and took the dress. She inspected the halter top and said, "I'll have to pick off one or two rows of sequins before I can alter it. Do you want to try it on so that I can see how much I need to take in?"

Jennifer looked at the dress, which was at least four inches shorter than the black one she was wearing. "Do we have to do it right now?"

"I think we should. The alterations may take a little while."

Jennifer sighed. "Okay."

"If you prefer, you can wear the red dress. It's stretchy enough that it probably won't need to be altered."

Jennifer eyed the shiny red spandex dress lying atop the pile. "No, we need to save that one."

She walked to the bathroom and reached into the trash can.

"What are you doing?" asked Vegas.

"Retrieving these." She pulled the discarded pair of uncomfortable lace panties from the wastebasket. "I was hoping to avoid ever seeing them again, but I'm not about to try on that shiny gold cocktail napkin without wearing something underneath."

Vegas laid the dress on the bed and inspected the frilly underwear dangling from Jennifer's finger. "Those are awesome. Why don't you like them?"

"Because they're like a medieval torture device. It feels like they're made of barbed wire and sandpaper."

"How long did you wear them?"

"I don't know," said Jennifer. "No longer than usual."

"Well, that's your problem. Panties like this are good for a couple of hours, tops."

"So I've learned."

"See," said Vegas, pointing to the crotch, "they don't have a gusset lining."

"A what?"

"It's that little cotton pocket sewn into the crotch of most panties. It makes the panties a lot more comfortable, but on a sheer pair like this, it would show through the lace and make them a lot less sexy."

"I guess that's why they look great but feel terrible."

Vegas smiled. "I made the same mistake during my first week here. On my second or third day, I wore a pair kind of like that as part of my outfit. After working the lobby for three hours, waiting for a customer to pick me, I ended up offering some guy the deal of a lifetime, just to have an excuse to take the damn things off."

Jennifer laughed out loud, imagining some lucky fellow being propositioned by a prostitute who was literally itching to get out of her panties. It was the first good laugh she'd enjoyed since fleeing La Condamine.

Vegas seemed to relish Jennifer's enjoyment of the anecdote. She offered a coquettish smile and said, "Panties like this should be worn just long enough to let someone else take them off."

Jennifer stopped laughing, her mirth replaced by thoughts of Bryan. "That was the plan when I put them on."

Vegas appeared not to notice the change in tone. "At least you got your money's worth out of them."

"What?"

"I mean, even if you never wear them again, at least Matt got to see them, right?"

"Oh," said Jennifer, a little embarrassed. "Crocker didn't see them."

"No? You and he didn't...?"

"No, it's not like that between us. Not yet, anyway."

"Don't worry," said Vegas, "it will be. I've seen the way he looks at you."

"Really?"

"I've seen him around a lot of girls, but I've never seen him look at any of them the way he looks at you."

"Oh." Jennifer wasn't sure what else to say.

"He's certainly never looked at me that way."

"Oh." Now she was afraid to say anything else.

"I know it's silly. I know he's like twice my age. But sometimes when he and I talk, I kind of start hoping that maybe the reason he's never accepted a freebie from me is because he's working up the courage to ask me out on a real date."

"Oh." *Crap.*

"I'm sorry," said Vegas. "Please don't hate me. I'm really not trying to steal your guy."

"No, I don't—"

"I'm smart enough to know that girls like me don't end up with guys like Matt. But sometimes he's so sweet that I forget. You know what I mean?"

"I do," said Jennifer. "But you shouldn't assume that any guy is too good for you."

Vegas smiled. "It's all right. I'd like to see him end up with someone like you. You're really nice."

Jennifer wiped her eyes before tears could form. "Thank you." She returned the young woman's smile.

"Anyway," said Vegas, pointing to the underwear still hanging from Jennifer's finger, "either put those on or don't—it doesn't make any difference to me—but you need to try on this dress if I'm going to have it ready in time for the big show."

"Don't you start calling it that too," said Jennifer as she slid the panties on under her dress.

"I like it. It makes the whole thing sound like it's just a big pageant instead of..."

A suicide mission? thought Jennifer.

"Instead of something dangerous," finished Vegas.

Jennifer reached for the gold dress and noticed the hatbox sitting beside it. "What's this?"

Vegas picked up the box. "These are my babies. If something happens to the dresses, I will eventually find it in my heart to forgive you. But if something happens to these, Vladimir Dudka won't be the only person after you." She giggled and removed the box lid.

The box appeared to be full of hair.

"What on earth?" asked Jennifer.

"Wigs." Vegas reached into the box and pulled a bright red one from the top of the pile. "It's really not good for them to be stuffed in a box like this, but I wanted you to have as many options as possible." She held out the red wig for Jennifer. "Personally, I think this one would look great on you."

Jennifer took the wig and inspected it. "Will Scarlett think I'm encroaching on her territory as the resident redhead?"

Vegas laughed and set the box on the bed. "It wouldn't surprise me. She can be a bit of a bitch sometimes."

Before Jennifer could respond, the suite door swung open and Tom entered carrying a suit bag and the type of cheap canvas backpack Jennifer always associated with her first year of college.

"Hey!" she exclaimed. "Don't you knock? I was about thirty seconds from stripping down to try on one of these dresses."

"Sorry," said Tom as he laid the suit bag beside the pile of dresses. "But right now my mind is jam-packed with logistics and contingencies, and there is no room for manners or modesty."

"Well, make room."

Tom hesitated. "Sorry. I should have knocked."

"Did you get everything we need?"

"Everything except my lost bag. Crocker is still working on that." He turned to Vegas. "You said you know how to sew, right?"

"Sure," she replied. "Do you need your suit altered?"

"Not my suit. This." He held up the backpack, which still had the price tag hanging from it.

"You want me to alter a backpack?"

"I want you to cut the back off of it, hem the edges, and reattach the shoulder straps so that it's just a shell I can wear over another pack."

"Okay." She took the backpack. "I think I get what you mean. But couldn't you just carry the other pack inside this one?"

Tom shook his head. "I won't have time to stop and switch from one to the other. I need to be able to change on the run."

She unzipped the backpack and inspected it. "What is this?" She reached inside.

"Oh, those are for Jennifer." He turned to Jennifer. "As expected, the police still have your hotel room sealed off, so I bought these at one of the hotel shops."

Vegas pulled out two fancy wooden coat hangers, each holding a pair of expensive-looking white lace panties.

"Are you kidding me?" asked Jennifer. "All I asked for was two pairs of basic cotton panties. Why didn't you just buy some while you were at Walmart?"

"Sorry," he said, "but the hotel was our last stop, and this is as basic as it gets at Fontvieille Intimates. A saleswoman helped us pick them out."

Vegas held up the two pairs of panties, one thong and one bikini cut.

Tom continued, "We weren't sure what style you'd want, but the saleswoman said these are the two most popular."

"I'm cursed," said Jennifer. "I'm cursed to spend the rest of my life wearing uncomfortable underwear."

"No," said Vegas, "these are perfect."

"They are?"

Vegas turned the thong inside out. "See?" She pointed to the crotch. "These actually have a gusset lining."

Jennifer reached out and felt the material.

Vegas checked the lining on the second pair. "They should be extremely comfortable."

Jennifer finished inspecting the panties and turned to Tom. "I guess you're off the hook. If Vegas says they're okay, they must be okay."

Vegas continued examining the lacy undergarments. "These are actually really nice. If you don't end up using both of them—"

"If we don't use the extra pair," said Jennifer, "it's all yours. It's the least we can do for all your help."

Vegas smiled. "I know it's silly, but in this line of work, you can never have too much fancy lingerie."

"Okay," said Tom, "I'll let you two get back to trying on dresses. I'm going to go see how things are coming with Crocker."

"No," said Jennifer, "*I'm* going to check on Crocker, and you're going to stay and help Vegas fix that backpack like you want it. It has to leave here an hour before my dress does."

"Fine," he said. "Just find out if and when we're going to get my other bag back from the TSA. If we don't get it, all of this is a waste of time."

"I'll find out."

"And don't be gone too long," said Vegas, "because as soon as I'm done with this backpack, we have to get started on your dress. We're cutting it close as it is."

"I'll hurry back."

Jennifer dropped the red wig next to the gold dress and looked at the hodgepodge of items lying on the bed. "My small clutch definitely isn't going to hold everything I'm supposed to carry. I need to find a really big purse."

"I have something you can use," said Vegas. "It's not really a purse, but it kind of looks like one. I use it to carry all my outfits and toiletries and necessities from room to room while I'm working."

"I don't know what we'd do without you."

"Just leave me one of these pairs of panties, and we'll call it even."

"Speaking of which…" Jennifer hiked up her dress a couple of inches, reached under, and discreetly pulled off the abrasive pair of unlined panties.

Tom's eyes grew cartoonishly large.

Vegas held up the two new pairs and asked, "Which do you want?"

"Give me the bikinis."

◆ ◆ ◆

Jennifer stopped in front of the shoe wall and surveyed the lobby. She now understood why Larry had wanted extra security—the place was packed.

Neither Crocker nor Larry was visible in the sea of male faces, but she did see Scarlett, her red hair unmistakable, drinking at the bar on the far side of the room.

Jennifer squeezed into the standing-room-only crowd and picked her way toward the bar. The Prickly Pear's customers ran the gamut from impeccably dressed to borderline slovenly.

As she passed a man in a shiny purple dress shirt, something banged uncomfortably against her thigh. She looked down and saw that the man was carrying a hard-sided briefcase. Upon closer inspection, she realized that the case was actually handcuffed to his wrist.

Without a word of apology, the man clutched the briefcase tight to his chest and took a short step back.

Jennifer stepped past the nervous-looking man and pushed on for a few more feet before finding her path blocked by two extra-large T-shirts, one branded FOX MOTOCROSS and the other branded SKYDIVE SAN MARCOS. The fashion-challenged pair of broad-shouldered daredevils seemed to be competing for the attention of a petite brunette whose own wardrobe consisted of the highest heels and tiniest bikini Jennifer had ever seen.

Jennifer chuckled, more amazed than amused, as she recalled Larry's comment about those who gamble with their money and those who gamble with their lives sharing a love for prostitutes. The man in the skydiving T-shirt glanced back, then stepped aside to let her pass.

As she crossed the room, Jennifer elicited almost as many lustful stares as she had the day before on the convention center floor. By the time she reached the bar, the crowd's collective body heat had left her feeling hot and sticky. She found Scarlett chatting with a well-dressed older gentleman while a handsome young bartender poured them a round from an expensive-looking bottle of scotch.

The man said something Jennifer couldn't quite hear, and Scarlett broke into hysterical laughter. Jennifer found it hard to believe that such over-the-top cackles would fool anyone, but the man seemed genuinely pleased by Scarlett's clear appreciation for his wit.

"Sorry to interrupt," said Jennifer, "but I..." Her voice trailed off as, in one short turn of the head, Scarlett's expression changed from inviting to contemptuous.

"What?" barked the fiery redhead.

Jennifer lost her train of thought. "I... I was just wondering if you've seen Crocker in the past few minutes."

"No." Scarlett turned back toward her silver-haired admirer.

The bartender leaned across the bar. "I saw him about five minutes ago, hon. He was talking on his phone, out behind the kitchen."

"How do I get out there?" asked Jennifer.

The bartender pointed to the door at the end of the bar. "Just cut through the kitchen. Nobody will care."

Jennifer thanked him and made her way to the end of the bar. She passed through a tiny kitchen where three fry cooks—none of whom paid her any attention—busily prepared burgers and buffalo wings.

The back door was so heavy that for a brief moment she thought it might be locked. Finally, it relented and swung open. She stepped out into a small fenced-in side yard littered with garbage cans and spent beer kegs.

As her eyes adjusted to the late-day sun, she spotted her gunslinger leaning against the fence, holding the Walmart cell phone to his ear. He waved and pointed to the phone. Jennifer nodded that she understood.

"I'll make sure it's all taken care of," he said. He listened for a moment, then responded, "I understand, and I assure you that there won't be any problems." After a short pause, he said, "Okay, thanks," and hung up.

"Is everything on track?" asked Jennifer.

"As much as it can be. That was Dudka's associate Mr. Black. He and I just hammered out all the details of our upcoming meeting at McCarran International Airport. He kept talking around the issue, refusing to say anything incriminating, so the call took longer than I expected. After the third time he told me to bring a receipt for my collateral, I figured out he was telling me to bring Ashley's driver's license so that she can get past airport security."

"But we don't have her license!"

Crocker nodded. "Good thing Mr. Black doesn't actually plan to meet us at the airport."

Jennifer felt a pang of embarrassment. "Right. Sorry. Long day."

Crocker offered a sympathetic smile. "Don't feel bad—that request threw me for a second too. I'm supposed to buy two tickets to Los Angeles—one for me and one for Ashley—and meet Mr. Black and his associate at the Starbucks in concourse B. I'm to bring Ashley's license and the eight hundred thousand dollars through security."

"Nothing suspicious about that."

Crocker nodded. "He asked what I plan to tell TSA if asked about the cash. I gave your explanation about attending a cash-only foreclosure sale. That was a good idea, by the way."

"I'm just glad I had something to contribute to this bogus plan."

Crocker smiled. "After Black confirms that I have the money, his associate will exit the terminal with Ashley's license and boarding pass and return with Ashley."

"That's awfully detailed. What if they actually show up at the airport? Shouldn't we have someone there just in case?"

"I wish they were that stupid—it would make our job a whole lot easier. But these guys are smart. They'll play along with the airport plan until the last minute; then they'll zig when they're supposed to zag."

"I hope you're right."

"I'm right. We just have to hope they zig in the direction we expect. If they pick a location other than the Stratosphere, your friend is in serious trouble."

The reality of what a miscalculation might mean for Ashley hung in the air between them.

Finally, desperate to end the awkward silence, Jennifer blurted out the one question that kept eating at her: "Why are you doing this?"

Crocker furrowed his brow. "What do you mean?"

"I mean, are you just trying to live up to the marine creed of 'leave no man behind,' or is there more to it than that?"

"Marine creed? Who told you I was a marine?"

"I saw your tattoo when you got out of the shower this morning."

"Right. I forgot you saw me without a shirt on."

Jennifer felt her face flush.

"Anyway," he continued, "I wasn't a marine long enough to feel beholden to any creed. And the 'leave no man behind' mantra is used by all the armed forces."

"Then why?" she asked, her voice trembling. "You don't know Ashley, and you barely know me, so why aren't you halfway to Colorado by now?"

He placed a hand on her shoulder. "Jennifer, you underestimate how much I loved that trailer."

Jennifer half laughed and half sobbed. She wiped a tear from her eye and said, "I'm serious."

Crocker smiled compassionately. "When this is all over, I'd like nothing more than to spend a weekend analyzing my motivations with you. But if I'm going to retrieve Tom's lost luggage and get back here in time, I have to go."

Jennifer nodded. "I have to get back inside. Miss Vegas is going to alter a dress for me."

Crocker leaned forward and planted a quick kiss on her forehead before turning to leave. He walked to the gate at the end of the fenced yard, opened it, then hesitated.

He turned back. "Listen, when this is all over, you and I really are going to have a long talk, okay?"

Jennifer locked eyes with him. "You're damn right we are."

◆ ◆ ◆

For Crocker, walking into the sheriff's south area command station in Pahrump always felt like a class reunion—at least three-quarters of the deputies had studied under him at one time or another. He exchanged pleasantries with the desk sergeant and made his way back toward the sheriff's office, returning waves and acknowledging occasional shouts of "Hey, Crocker!" as he went.

The task of overseeing law enforcement in one of the nation's largest counties necessitated that the Nye County sheriff divide his time between three stations spread out over a 170-mile stretch of highway. This meant that, rather than enjoy a well-appointed office with a private receptionist, Sheriff Cargill made do with three functional but unremarkable offices, each tucked into the back corner of one of the stations.

Over the years, Crocker had spent countless hours in these offices, shooting the bull with Sheriff Cargill. But as he knocked on the door bearing the sheriff's nameplate, he worried that he was testing the boundaries of their friendship.

He listened for the sheriff's familiar call of *"Enter at your own risk."* Instead, he heard the sound of a dead bolt turning.

The door opened a couple of inches. Sheriff Cargill peered through the narrow opening, inspecting his surroundings. When he seemed satisfied, he opened the door wide and motioned Crocker inside.

"Nobody with you?" he asked.

"No." Crocker stepped into the modest office. "It's just me."

The sheriff shut the door behind him.

As Crocker took a seat across from the sheriff's desk, he again heard the faint creak of the dead bolt. "Can I infer from your sudden concern for privacy that you did as I asked?"

"You can." The sheriff walked to the other side of the desk and pulled a small black suitcase from beneath it. "I think this is what you wanted."

Crocker reached out and took the suitcase. "Did TSA give you any trouble?"

"No, I think they were afraid I was going to chew them out for placing the bag under a security hold in the first place. The supervisor I spoke to kept reminding me that in this post-9/11 world, it's better to be safe than sorry."

Crocker nodded and set the bag on the ground. "Well, I can't thank you enough for intervening. I don't know what we would have done without this."

"Don't thank me," said the sheriff, "and don't tell me what you plan on doing with it. If I knew, I might feel obligated to stop you."

Crocker gave another understanding nod. "And what about the other thing I asked you to do?"

Sheriff Cargill peered across the desk, not speaking, his eyes seeming to study Crocker. Crocker wondered if the second favor had been too much to ask.

Just as the silence threatened to become uncomfortable, the sheriff let out a loud sigh and rose to his feet. "It's over here."

He walked to the heavy metal case in the corner of the room and fumbled with his keys, eventually finding the right one.

Crocker had seen the inside of the case many times. It was where the sheriff kept his small collection of high-end firearms, including a Remington Model 700 rifle that Crocker himself had upgraded with a match-grade barrel and a custom trigger set. But when the sheriff turned back around, he wasn't holding a gun; he was holding a dingy green duffel bag wrapped in what looked like a plastic dry-cleaning bag.

Sheriff Cargill set the duffel bag on the desk. "I sure hope you're not about to do something stupid. It wouldn't look good for me to have to shoot an old friend in my office."

"Don't worry," said Crocker, studying the bag. "I'm not going to steal it."

The sheriff settled back into his chair. "I didn't figure you were, but I'd be remiss in my duties if I didn't at least warn you not to."

"Did you take the steps I suggested?"

The sheriff nodded. "I contacted Vegas Metro and requested the immediate return of the evidence; then I contacted the highway patrol and asked them to send a unit to pick it up and bring it to the station for me. No doubt every officer in the state now knows I inexplicably requested the return of nearly a million dollars in seized cash."

"Exactly," said Crocker. "Every officer, including the one who tipped off Dudka last night." He examined the plastic-covered duffel bag. "I take it I'm not allowed to open it?"

"Hell no!" said the sheriff. "It's bad enough I'm keeping it in my office and not in the evidence locker—that alone could warrant an investigation. But if I were to let you contaminate evidence in a case of this magnitude, the people who elected me would probably lock me in my own jail and throw away the key."

"I was just hoping to get an idea of how the money is bundled."

"Here." The sheriff reached into the top drawer of his desk. "These might help." He handed Crocker a manila envelope.

Crocker opened the envelope and pulled out a stack of eight-by-ten photos.

The sheriff continued, "Those are the crime-scene photos of the money. I can't let you take them, but I don't see any harm in letting you look at them."

Crocker thumbed through the pictures and noted the brown, hand-numbered envelopes stuffed with half-inch-thick stacks of hundred-dollar bills.

"Thanks," he said. "This will help."

"You know," said the sheriff, "if I knew what you were up to, I could at least position a few deputies nearby, in case you need help."

Crocker shook his head. "It's too risky." He stood and set the photos on the sheriff's desk, beside the duffel bag.

"More risky than whatever you plan to do with that?" The sheriff pointed at Tom's suitcase.

"Yes." Crocker picked up the suitcase. "Only five other people know about this, and as far as I'm concerned, they're the only ones I can trust."

"Hang on," said the sheriff. He stood and reached into his pocket. "There is one other person you can trust." He held out a business card.

Crocker set down the suitcase and took the card. It read:

WILLIAM CARGILL
SHERIFF
NYE COUNTY, NEVADA

Crocker laughed. "Sorry, Bill. I didn't mean to suggest I don't trust you."

"What?" The sheriff glanced down at the card. "Oh, no, flip it over."

Crocker turned over the card and saw that on the back the sheriff had written *SA Bruce Eastland* and a phone number.

"Special Agent Eastland is part of the FBI's organized crime division," explained the sheriff. "Apparently, he's been investigating Vladimir Dudka for years."

"You talked to this Agent Eastland?"

"I did. In fact, he's flying in on the red-eye."

"He's on his way *here*?"

"That's right. He seems to think the surveillance footage from La Condamine may be the smoking gun he's been looking for. If he can connect any of the men on that tape to Dudka, he can get a warrant to search the Winter Palace and possibly bring down the whole operation."

"That all sounds great." Crocker placed the business card in his pocket. "But none of it does me any good tonight."

"He says the FBI is willing to offer protection to both you and Ms. Williams. Are you sure you wouldn't rather just wait this out and let the feds handle it?"

"Tell him that Jennifer—Ms. Williams—and I will meet you both at the FBI's Las Vegas field office at nine o'clock tomorrow morning. If everything goes according to plan, we'll have one hell of a story to tell."

CHAPTER TWELVE

Jennifer breathed a sigh of relief as Vegas's paisley shoulder bag emerged from the X-ray scanner without so much as a sideways glance from the three security guards working the checkpoint. She mentally scolded herself for having been so nervous. A bag full of wigs and dresses wasn't likely to raise any eyebrows on the Las Vegas Strip. If the guards had searched it, the most damning thing they would have found was Vegas's assortment of condoms and lubes, which Jennifer hadn't bothered to clear out of the side pocket. The real contraband had bypassed the screening equipment an hour before, in the suitcase carried by Private Patrol Officer Matt Crocker.

Jennifer retrieved the pink and purple pack from the scanner and followed Tom toward the elevator bank. The repurposed diaper bag was a poor choice to accessorize her sophisticated little black dress; however, given the circumstances, she was satisfied that the bag, which spent most nights packed with the tools of the sex trade, was large enough to carry everything she needed and looked enough like a purse to avert suspicion.

When she caught up to Tom, he was standing in the door of an elevator packed with a half-dozen casually dressed tourists.

He turned to the uniformed elevator operator, a man of at least seventy, and said, "Here she is."

Jennifer squeezed into the car.

"So she is," said the operator. "Do you want the observation deck, the restaurant, or the lounge?"

"Level 104," replied Tom.

"Ah, the private party." The operator pressed the button. "I should have guessed as much from your sharp suit."

Jennifer smiled and winked at Tom. His navy-blue suit, though inexpensive and not quite a perfect fit, looked debonair amid the sea of T-shirts and sandals. At the office and on the conference floor, he always wore slacks and a dress shirt. Jennifer wondered if Ashley had ever seen him so dressed up.

Maybe if they both make it out of this alive...

Jennifer was vaguely aware of the elevator operator rattling off a list of facts about the Stratosphere Tower—opened in 1996 as the tallest building west of the Mississippi, almost 550 feet taller than Seattle's Space Needle, blah, blah, blah—but she was too busy sorting through a litany of unsettling what-ifs to care.

The high-speed elevator slowed. The knots in her stomach tightened.

"Level 104," announced the operator as the elevator came to a stop.

The doors opened on a central lobby area where a handful of well-dressed real estate professionals waited in line to show their invitations and be admitted into the private reception halls that ringed the lobby.

Jennifer was grateful she didn't recognize any of the guests waiting ahead of them. She was in no state of mind to chitchat about which retailers were looking to expand during the next quarter or which markets were generating the lowest cap rates.

When she and Tom reached the front of the line, one of two well-built men in dark suits held out his hand and said, "Invitation?"

"I seem to have misplaced it," she said with a polite smile, "but I'm on the list—Jennifer Williams plus guest."

The man checked the clipboard in his hand. Jennifer studied the Secret Service–style earpieces he and the other man wore and wondered if they were on the same frequency as Crocker.

After a moment, the man smiled and said, "Yes, here you are, Ms. Williams. Now if I could just see some identification."

Jennifer took her time as she pulled her wallet from the diaper bag's side pocket, where it was nestled among a handful of small items she didn't want to see tumble onto the lobby floor.

"Here you go." She handed her driver's license to the guard.

The guard inspected the license and returned it. "Thank you very much, Ms. Williams. Have a nice evening."

Jennifer smiled and nodded her thanks. She and Tom passed through the double doors and into the crowded reception area. When they were out of earshot of the guards, she stopped to place the ID and wallet back in the diaper bag.

She glanced around the room. "Do you see Crocker anywhere?" She recognized a few familiar faces in the crowd but not the face she was looking for.

"Right behind you," said Crocker.

Jennifer turned to greet him, but when she saw him, she couldn't speak. The version of Crocker standing before her was a far cry from the sleep-deprived man in the blue polo shirt and khaki shorts who'd gunned down three assailants at the Placer Gold truck stop. In sharp contrast to Tom's slightly ill-fitting suit, Crocker's was impeccably tailored, flattering both his broad shoulders and his lean physique. His hair and tie were both perfectly arranged, and his face looked freshly shaved. If not for the earpiece, he might have passed for the CEO of a brokerage firm or perhaps a wealthy developer.

"What is it?" he asked, apparently noting the surprise on her face.

"That's a nice suit," she replied.

"Good, because it's the only one I have left." He smiled. "Who knew that forgetting to pick up one's dry cleaning could come in handy?"

Jennifer returned the smile, impressed that he could make light of the loss of his trailer and so many of his belongings.

"What's the plan?" asked Tom.

"Follow me," said Crocker. "I have the perfect place for the two of you to get ready. Your stuff is waiting."

He turned and made his way toward a nearby door. Tom and Jennifer followed without a word. When they reached the door, Crocker turned and hooked his right arm under Jennifer's left.

"Tom," he said, "get on the other side."

Tom hesitated a moment, then hooked his left arm under Jennifer's right.

"Good," said Crocker. "Now, Jennifer, don't say anything, and try to look drunk."

Jennifer nodded. "I'll do my best."

Crocker pushed open the door and led Jennifer and Tom into the small service hallway. Another well-dressed security officer—this one looked a few years younger than Tom—stood beside a door labeled STAIRS.

"Hey, Crocker," said the officer. "What's going on?"

Crocker pointed to Jennifer. "Someone had a few too many."

"That didn't take long."

"It's always the corporate types, right?"

The young security officer laughed. "What are you going to do with her?"

"Well, I'm afraid if I put her in an elevator, she may puke all over it, so I was thinking I'd walk her down to the wedding chapel and let her lie down in one of the dressing rooms."

"Sounds like a plan." The security officer opened the stairwell door and held it for them.

"Thanks." Crocker led Jennifer and Tom into the stairwell.

Jennifer stumbled, playing up the role of the drunk, and let her two escorts catch her. Tom helped her to her feet and shuffled through the open door, nodding to the security officer as he passed.

The young man smiled and shut the door behind them, leaving them alone in the stairwell. Crocker and Tom simultaneously released Jennifer's arms.

"This way," said Crocker.

He led them down one flight of stairs and stopped at a door labeled CHAPEL IN THE CLOUDS. He reached into his jacket, unclipped an ID card from his inside pocket, and swiped it over the card reader beside the door.

The light on the reader changed from red to green, followed by a soft beep. Crocker opened the door, revealing another service hallway. Jennifer and Tom stepped inside.

Crocker followed and shut the door behind him. "Okay, we can talk freely. This floor is supposed to be secured, so nobody is monitoring it."

"I have a question," said Jennifer. "Why did I have to be the one who couldn't hold her liquor? Why couldn't Tom be the drunk?"

"Because," replied Crocker, "I have more faith in your acting skills than I do in Tom's."

"Good answer," said Tom.

"Indeed," said Jennifer skeptically.

Crocker grinned. "Follow me. Tom's stuff is in here."

He opened the door across from the stairwell and led them into a large room illuminated by only the lights of the city below. Windows lined the curved exterior wall, extending from the ceiling to a waist-high window ledge. Although the room overlooked nothing of note, the view from almost eight hundred feet above the city was impressive.

"Hang on," said Crocker.

He felt along the wall until he found another card reader and swiped his ID card past it. Recessed lighting in the ceiling glowed to life, bringing the small wedding chapel into full view.

The cream-colored room was wide open except for a few support columns. It was devoid of seating except for the large window ledge, which, although probably intended as a place for guests to set their drinks, looked like an excellent place to sit and admire the view. Jennifer noted the faint aroma of ammonia and guessed that the chairs had been removed so that the room could be cleaned.

"Not bad," she said. "I've always thought of Las Vegas wedding chapels as tacky, but this is cute."

"This is just one of the chapels," said Crocker. "There are two more on this floor."

Tom glanced around the empty room. "This is perfect. Are you sure we won't be disturbed?"

"Trust me, we have the place all to ourselves. Only security personnel have access to this floor, and unless my idea about bringing drunks down here catches on, there is no reason for any of the Stratosphere guards or PPOs to visit the chapels tonight."

"That's good enough for me. Where is my stuff?"

Crocker pointed to a door in the corner of the room. "I stashed it in the dressing room."

Tom walked to the door and stepped inside.

"Is that where I'm going to change?" asked Jennifer.

"Actually," said Crocker, "you get your own chapel. That way, Tom can prepare without being disturbed."

Tom emerged from the dressing room carrying a small black suitcase.

"Tom, do you need any help?" asked Jennifer.

"Nope." He set the suitcase on the floor. "This is all me."

"Here," said Crocker, "you're going to need this." He pulled the cheap Walmart cell phone from his jacket pocket and tossed it to Tom. "You're now officially on point. If, God forbid, Dudka's people try to change the venue to anywhere other than here, just keep saying no until they pick this place."

"And if that doesn't work?"

"You saved the number of the local FBI field office on your personal phone, right?"

Tom nodded.

"That's plan B."

"Not much of a plan B," said Tom.

"No," conceded Crocker, "it's not."

"So is this it?" asked Jennifer. "Will we see Tom again before the exchange?"

"Probably not," replied Crocker. "Once he assumes his role as the courier, he can't be seen with either of us."

Jennifer hesitated, not sure what she should say. Unable to find the right words, she stepped forward and embraced Tom.

"Don't worry," he said. "I'll be careful."

She held him tight. "You'd better."

Crocker placed a hand on her shoulder. She released her friend and stepped back.

Crocker extended his right hand to Tom. "I don't know if I'm supposed to say 'good luck' or 'break a leg' or what."

Tom shook Crocker's hand. "'Good luck' will do."

For a moment everyone was silent. Then Crocker wrapped an arm around Jennifer's waist and said, "I believe it's time for me to show you to your dressing room, madam."

She cast a parting smile at Tom, turned, and walked with Crocker toward the door at the far end of the chapel.

When they were halfway across the room, she stopped and turned back to Tom. "This is going to work, you know."

Tom nodded. "I know."

◆ ◆ ◆

Through the row of large windows, the city below cast just enough light for Jennifer to see that this chapel was even larger than the one in which they'd left Tom.

"Impressive," she said as Crocker shut the door behind them. "But isn't there a smaller room I can use to change?"

"The dressing room is in the far corner, but I want to show you something first."

He took her hand and led her toward the wall of windows. They moved slowly, approaching every shadow as if it concealed a hidden obstacle.

"Shouldn't we turn on the lights?" she asked.

"Not yet." He stopped at the center window. "This is better with the lights off."

Stretched out below them, the Strip glimmered in all its over-the-top glory. Lines of headlights and taillights snaked between the mammoth casinos, from Circus Circus's ancient neon clown to the emerald green of the

MGM Grand. Giant digital screens dotted the route, flashing pictures of performers and promising the highest-paying slots.

Eight hundred feet below, Sin City was alive and well, unconcerned with whether Tom Blackwell would ever have a chance to tell Ashley Thomas how he felt about her and unaffected by whatever feelings a tired gunslinger might or might not have for a down-on-her-luck real estate agent.

Jennifer turned away from the window and stared into the haze of the unlit room.

"What's wrong?" asked Crocker.

The sudden sense of powerlessness didn't translate easily into words. She thought for a moment and said, "Looking out there makes me feel small. And what we're up against is so damn big. It's a little overwhelming."

Crocker seemed on the verge of saying something but apparently thought better of it. He peered into her eyes as if he could see the wheels turning behind them.

He's worried I'm going to be a liability, she thought. *I should have kept my mouth shut.*

He glanced over his shoulder at the unlit chapel, then back at Jennifer. "Wait here a minute." He turned and disappeared into the shadows.

A moment later, Jennifer heard him fiddling with something on the other side of the room. There was a brief crackle of static followed by a familiar melody. The crooning voice of Frank Sinatra filled the room, imploring some woman—or perhaps all women—to come fly with him.

Jennifer watched Crocker reemerge from the shadows and waited for an explanation.

"I apologize if this isn't your style," he said as he removed his earpiece, "but the chapel's selection of wedding music is somewhat limited." He unhooked something from his sleeve.

"Aren't you afraid someone will hear?"

"Not particularly." He pulled a pair of wires free of his jacket. "There's nobody below us and a party going on above us." He removed a large walk-ie-talkie from beneath his jacket, wrapped the wires around it, and set it on the window ledge. "I think we're pretty safe." He removed both his holstered sidearm and his holster of ammunition and set them beside the two-way radio.

Finally free of encumbrances, he extended his left hand to Jennifer and asked, "May I have this dance?"

She hesitated, half expecting him to laugh and withdraw the hand. When he did neither, she asked, "Are you serious?"

"I'd hoped that taking a moment to enjoy the view might help us relax. But since that obviously didn't work, let's give this a try."

"Dancing?"

"Why not?"

Skeptical, she set the diaper bag on the floor and accepted his outstretched hand. He pulled her close, wrapped his free arm around her waist, and led off with his left foot.

It took her a few steps to catch on to the rhythm, but once she did, she followed with ease. Crocker was a competent dancer, and by the time Ol' Blue Eyes started into his big finish, Jennifer was actually starting to relax. As the brass band reached the peak of its final crescendo, Crocker spun her, catching her—in perfect step—just as the music came to an end.

The end of the song left the large room almost eerily silent. Jennifer released his hand and took a step back, realizing for the first time that she was the tiniest bit winded.

"I wouldn't have taken you for a dancer," she said as they walked back to their things.

"I can fake my way through a couple of steps."

"Did you take lessons?"

"Once upon a time."

"Probably trying to impress a woman, right?"

His voice grew distant. "You could say that."

Jennifer wondered what she'd said. Then she remembered Vegas's comment about Crocker's having been engaged. "Trying to impress your fiancée?"

"Yes." He stopped in front of the diaper bag and turned to face her. "Who told you?"

Jennifer hesitated, afraid she might get Vegas into trouble. Finally, she said, "I had a long talk with your secret admirer at the Prickly Pear."

"Megan. I should have guessed."

"I was talking about Vegas! How many admirers do you have there?"

Crocker chuckled. "Her real name is Megan. She's the only girl at the Pear who actually grew up around here, so the girls call her Vegas."

Jennifer found something oddly sad about this explanation. "She told you she has a crush on you?"

"No, but she's not particularly subtle about it."

"And you're not interested?"

"She's half my age."

Jennifer shrugged. "A lot of guys would consider that a point in her favor."

Crocker smiled and shook his head. "She's a sweet girl, and I'm hopeful that someday she'll wake up and realize she can do better than the Prickly Pear Ranch, but I'm definitely not interested in that type of relationship with her."

"But the two of you are close, right? I mean, you told her about your broken engagement."

Crocker's smile faded. "The engagement wasn't broken." His voice was somber but not angry. "And it's not exactly a secret—it was national news."

Oh, Christ, thought Jennifer.

Softly she asked, "What happened?"

"She was a Nye County sheriff's deputy." His voice suggested a story he'd told many times. "This was twelve years ago, when Sheriff Wilkins was still in office and Bill Cargill was just a detective for the department."

Jennifer didn't have any idea who Sheriff Wilkins was, but she figured it was enough to know he was Sheriff Cargill's predecessor.

"Anyway," continued Crocker, "I met Courtney about a year after Jeff and I opened First Shot. Back then, most of First Shot's business came from rural law enforcement agencies. Courtney came in on her own, looking for additional training to help her qualify for the county SWAT team. I agreed to work with her, and by the time she made the team, six months later, we were in love."

"She died in the line of duty?"

Crocker nodded. "We'd been together for eighteen months. The wedding was just six weeks away. The sheriff's department got a tip than an old ranch house east of town was being used to manufacture and distribute crystal meth. A warrant was issued, and the SWAT team was deployed."

"What went wrong?"

"Everything." He turned to face the window. "The ranch house was within two hundred yards of the Clark County line, which wouldn't have been a problem if the department had followed protocol and notified the Clark County Sheriff's Office of the raid. But somehow that particular step was overlooked in the planning process.

"And unbeknownst to the Nye County Sheriff's Office, the Clark County Drug Enforcement Task Force was investigating the same ranch house. Apparently, someone at Las Vegas Metro had looked at a highway map, rather than an official county plat, and concluded that the house was on their side of the county line."

"Oh no," whispered Jennifer.

"When Courtney's SWAT team broke down the door, they found two drug dealers concluding a sale to two undercover officers from the Clark County task force. But of course, Courtney and her team didn't immediately realize that two of the men were undercover officers—all four looked like drug dealers.

"At that point, both of the undercover officers should have raised their hands and announced that they were undercover police officers. But instead of raising his hands, one of the officers instinctively reached for his badge."

Jennifer felt her stomach sink.

Crocker took a deep breath. "Courtney was the second SWAT officer through the door. She heard both of the undercovers announce that they were police officers and recognized that one of them was reaching for a badge. But the third SWAT officer—the one who entered just behind her—

didn't hear them. He saw one of the men reaching for something and yelled, 'Gun!'

"Realizing that the officer behind her was about to shoot, Courtney turned and signaled him to stand down. And that's when the third drug dealer—the one none of the SWAT officers had seen, the one who'd been dozing on the couch when they burst through the door—started shooting.

"He opened fire with a piece-of-shit twenty-two revolver. He fired wildly, hitting mostly furniture and drywall. Of the six shots he fired, only one actually hit somebody."

"Courtney?"

"If she'd been facing the gunman, her body armor would have easily stopped the round. She probably wouldn't have even felt it. But because she'd turned sideways to warn her fellow officer, her left side was exposed. The round impacted just under her arm, passed between two ribs, and ripped through her aorta. She died within a matter of seconds."

Jennifer felt her eyes filling with tears. "How did you find out?"

"Bill Cargill was at the station when the call came in." A fleeting smile appeared on Crocker's face. "He jumped into a patrol car and hightailed it out to the academy, lights flashing, siren blaring. All he knew was that Courtney had been shot and was being medevaced to a trauma center here in the city. He was determined to make sure I was by her side when she went into surgery."

Tears trickled down Jennifer's face.

"Of course," continued Crocker, "there was no surgery. She was gone long before they loaded her into the chopper. In the end, Bill's determination to get me by her side simply allowed me to view her body before the coroner took her away."

Crocker walked to the window and pointed to something in the distance. "That's where I said goodbye. That hospital over there." He hesitated. "I stayed with her as long as they'd let me. When they finally made me leave, Bill was still there, waiting to drive me home."

"Was that her in the picture I saw in your trailer?" asked Jennifer. "The woman with the freckles?"

"Yeah," he said with a pained smile. "You saw that? That was my favorite picture of us."

The realization hit her. "Oh my God! You lost it!"

"It's okay. I have more pictures in Colorado."

"Another copy of that one?"

"No," he said with a sigh, "not that one. That one was taken the week before she died. She stopped by the academy to have lunch with me, and one of my students jokingly asked whether she or I was the better shot. One thing led to another, and we ended up having an impromptu competition. When it was over, another student snapped that picture. The framed copy you saw in my trailer arrived the day after Courtney was killed. The student who took it had mailed it a few days before, intending it as a wedding present."

Jennifer fought back sobs. "And now it's gone because of me."

"Hey, whoa, don't do that." He turned and place his hands on her shoulders. "You can't start blaming yourself for this mess. Trust me, that's a one-way street to someplace you don't want to go."

"Did you blame yourself for what happened to Courtney?"

"Of course—I was the one who trained her. She trusted me to teach her to stay alive, and she died. That's a lot for a guy with a broken heart to bear."

"How did you deal with it?"

"I sold my half of First Shot to my partner, Jeff; bought the trailer; and spent the next couple of years wandering around the country, just trying to make sense of things."

"Did you succeed?"

"No, I finally accepted that life doesn't make sense. That was as close as I got."

"And that was close enough?"

"I suppose. Eventually I came back to Pahrump, moved into the house Courtney and I had built, and accepted a job at the academy I'd cofounded. After that, I just took it one day at a time."

"How old was Courtney when she died?"

"Twenty-six."

Just three years older than Ashley, thought Jennifer.

Crocker reached up and wiped a tear from her cheek. "I'm sorry, I'm afraid I've failed miserably at helping you relax."

"You're sorry?" She leaned over and pulled a tissue from Vegas's diaper bag. "I'm the one who should be sorry." She wiped her eyes. "You're about to risk your life to help save my friend, and I just made you relive the most painful experience of your life."

"It's okay." He plucked the tissue from her hand. "I wanted you to know." He dabbed it under her eyes. "You know, it occurs to me that I haven't told you how amazing you look tonight."

Jennifer choked on a tear-filled laugh. "I'm wearing the same dress I've been wearing since you met me."

"That's not true. I distinctly remember you wearing a bedsheet when I woke up this afternoon."

She laughed again. "I think you must have dreamed that."

"Well, I didn't dream the way every head turned when you walked into the reception earlier. I'm clearly not the only one who thinks you're stunning."

Jennifer felt her cheeks flush. "Yes, it's amazing what a shower and a fresh coat of paint can do."

"Listen," said Crocker, "this may be a lousy time to ask, but do you think that when this is all over, you might be interested in—"

He didn't get a chance to finish the question—Jennifer's lips were pressed against his. Without hesitation, he wrapped his arms around her waist and reciprocated.

She pulled her mouth free of his just long enough to say, "I thought you'd never ask," then returned to the task at hand.

He kissed with such force that she found herself driven backward into a support column. She leaned against it as she kissed his ear.

His lips nuzzled her neck while his hand explored her body through the fabric of the little black dress. Her own fingers slid beneath his suit jacket and traced the contours of his chest.

She welcomed the feeling of being held, of being touched. His fingers found their way under the hem of her dress and caressed her thigh, inching higher, testing the water, seeking permission to proceed.

She grabbed his belt and worked the buckle. Suddenly she was airborne—both of his hands were cupped around her buttocks, and he was carrying her. She released the belt, wrapped her arms around his neck, and kissed him.

He set her on the window ledge and slid his hands under her dress. She glanced back and saw the lights of the Strip glimmering far below. She had only a moment to take in the view before she felt her comfortable new panties sliding down her thighs. She kicked off her shoes and lifted her legs to aid in the removal.

Crocker slipped the panties over her feet and stuck them in his jacket pocket.

"Look in the diaper bag," she said.

He furrowed his brow in apparent confusion.

"The bag at your feet," she added. "Check the side pocket."

◆ ◆ ◆

Out of breath and soaked in sweat, they huddled together on the window ledge for several minutes before Crocker finally climbed down and retrieved his pants from the floor. He dug through a pocket and pulled out the cell phone he'd borrowed from Vegas.

"Any messages?" asked Jennifer.

"No, but it's already five after nine. We'd better get dressed and get into position."

He helped her down from the ledge, and they set about retrieving their various items of clothing from the floor.

When they each had a small pile, Jennifer shifted all her garments to one arm and slung the diaper bag over her free shoulder. "Where is my dressing room?"

Crocker pointed to the far corner of the room. "Just feel along the wall until you find a door."

"Thanks." She wrapped her free arm around his neck and pulled his lips to hers. After several seconds, she released him, turned, and walked toward the dressing room. "To be continued, Mr. Crocker."

CHAPTER THIRTEEN

Crocker took another sip of Red Bull and tried once more to focus on the task ahead. Again, his thoughts circled back to Jennifer and their brief interlude five floors below. He set the can on the luminescent green bar and glanced around the room.

Most of the lights on level 108 had been dimmed to minimize the glare on the floor-to-ceiling windows and allow patrons an unpolluted view of the city. Compared to the high-end lounge that occupied level 107, the observation-level bar was small and simple. It had begun its life as a snack bar, selling pretzels and hot dogs to the families who came to enjoy the carnival-style rides atop the tower. Fifteen years after opening, the Stratosphere had undergone a top-to-bottom renovation that saw the bar repurposed for a trendier clientele. Now the furniture glowed, faux stars twinkled on the ceiling, and a DJ stationed near the windows spun hip-hop tunes that reverberated through the open bar and drifted down the promenade, beckoning others to join the party.

Crocker would have preferred the quieter atmosphere and older crowd one floor below, but the small, dark bar offered something the big, sophisticated lounge didn't: anonymity. He doubted that any of Dudka's goons knew what he looked like, but many of the Stratosphere's full-time security staff knew him by sight, and being recognized would further complicate an already complicated situation.

The technicians monitoring the surveillance cameras weren't a concern. They undoubtedly saw his comings and goings—though, fortunately, not in the chapels on level 103—but they could only see, not hear, and they had no way of knowing he'd deviated from his assigned tasks. For all they knew, the bar was where he was supposed to be.

The real concern was that he might bump into someone who did know where he was supposed to be, someone with a walkie-talkie who could radio down to the security office and ask whether any of the PPOs had been authorized to operate on level 108. He was tempted to remove his earpiece so as to look more like a civilian, but he knew that radio chatter between the other guards might be his first and only warning that someone knew he was off script.

He glanced over his shoulder at the growing crowd of faceless shadows mingling in front of the neon skyline. The sight triggered memories of Jennifer's writhing body silhouetted against the glimmering backdrop of the Strip.

Twenty-four hours ago, he hadn't even known she existed. Now he pondered what he'd do when she returned to her life in Texas.

He picked up the half-finished Red Bull, glanced at it, and set it down again. He had all the energy he needed. What he needed now was to get his head in the game. There was no point in worrying about his future with Jennifer when there was a possibility neither of them would survive the night.

He reached into his pocket, pulled out Vegas's phone, and checked it for the eighth time in as many minutes. He couldn't afford to miss Tom's text message, and he didn't trust himself to hear the chime over the loud music. If everything went according to plan, Dudka's people would be calling Tom at any minute to suggest a change of venue for the exchange. Everything hinged on that call, on whether Crocker had accurately predicted Dudka's next move.

The phone showed no new messages. He slid it back into his pocket and glanced around the room. He spotted the gold sequined dress and flowing red hair a full two seconds before he recognized Jennifer beneath them.

She strolled to the bar and sidled up to him. "Hey there, stranger. Looking for a date?"

"Maybe." He inspected the getup. "What'll it cost me?"

"Eight hundred thousand dollars." She slid onto the adjoining bar stool and reached for his Red Bull. "Have you heard from Tom?"

"Not a word. I'm getting restless."

She took a long sip from the can and placed it back in front of him. "How long do we wait before going to plan B?"

"We're scheduled to meet Dudka's people at the airport in ten minutes. If Tom hasn't heard from them by then, we'll call the FBI and..."

Jennifer was looking over Crocker's right shoulder.

"What is it?" He turned to see what had caught her attention.

"Don't look."

He turned back to the bar. "One of your real estate friends?"

"No."

She turned and pretended to study a drink list lying on the bar. A man in khaki slacks and a blue Hawaiian shirt passed behind them, heading toward the elevator lobby.

Crocker waited a couple of seconds, then risked a better look at the man's back. From behind, the casually dressed stranger could have been almost anybody.

"Who is it?"

Jennifer jumped to her feet. "Hang on. I want to see where he goes."

Crocker stood to join her. "Who?"

"Stay here. He's less likely to recognize me."

Crocker wanted to prod her for more information, but the man was getting away. He didn't like the idea of letting her go alone, but there was little arguing that she was virtually unrecognizable in the wig. He nodded agreement, and she trotted across the bar and down the same corridor that had just swallowed the man.

Crocker watched the mouth of the corridor for what might have been twenty seconds or two minutes—he was in no state of mind to gauge the passage of time—and then, in an effort to distract himself, made another cursory check of Vegas's phone.

To his surprise, the borrowed cell phone showed one new text message. He fumbled with the touch screen for what felt like an eternity before succeeding in opening the message. It was short and to the point:

YOU CALLED IT. MEETING NOW SET FOR 10 PM AT STRATOSPHERE. OUTDOOR OBSERVATION DECK. --TOM

As he pocketed the phone, Crocker momentarily forgot about the mystery man and imagined Mr. Black assuring Tom that meeting at the tower would be much safer than meeting at the airport. Crocker wondered how many of Dudka's goons were now monitoring police radio channels or making surreptitious phone calls to informants inside the Las Vegas Police Department, searching for any indication that authorities had been notified of the meeting. He wondered how many of Dudka's thugs were already fanning out through the tower.

His mind snapped back to the present.

Jennifer!

Now that the Stratosphere was confirmed as the site of the meeting, Jennifer's pursuit of the mystery man seemed reckless.

To hell with it. He rose to his feet. *If I'm recognized, I'll improvise.*

He'd just reached the mouth of the corridor when he saw Jennifer walking toward him. He continued down the passage, meeting her halfway.

"Well?" he asked.

She looked flustered. "I couldn't find him. He must have gotten onto one of the elevators."

"Who was it?"

"I might have been mistaken."

"Who did you think it was?"

"I could have sworn it was the highway patrolman who took my statement last night."

"Vincent Haley?"

"I don't remember his name."

Crocker took her hand. "Let's look again." He led her toward the elevator lobby.

Her tight dress and high heels left her struggling to keep up with his brisk pace. "Isn't it possible he's just—"

"This is a tourist spot. Locals don't hang out here."

"But—"

He stopped and faced her. "Tom got the call—the exchange is definitely happening here. If Haley is in the tower, it's a safe bet it has something to do with us."

Instead of giving the reply Crocker expected, Jennifer wrapped her arms all the way around him and pulled him in close. She kissed him hard on the lips. His first instinct was to push her away and scold her for her poor timing; then he felt her left hand remove his earpiece and realized she knew exactly what she was doing.

He positioned his mouth as if to nuzzle her ear and whispered, "Who do you see?"

"Haley just walked out of the men's room. It's definitely him." After a couple of seconds, she added, "Now he's walking toward the elevators." They continued the mock make-out. "He's getting on an elevator.... Just a few more...Okay."

Crocker turned his head just in time to see the elevator doors slam shut. "You're sure it was him?"

"One hundred percent. He looked right at me when he walked out of the restroom."

"He didn't recognize you?"

"No, but he was certainly close enough."

"Come on." Crocker grabbed her by the hand and led her toward the restroom.

They entered a small alcove containing three doors: one labeled STORAGE, one labeled MAINTENANCE, and one labeled MEN'S ROOM.

Crocker looked from one to the next. "Are you certain he came out of the men's room and not one of these other doors?"

"Not really."

Crocker tried the other doors first. Both were locked. He cracked the men's room door a couple of inches and peeked in at a tiny trash can and a couple of paper-towel dispensers. He opened the door and stepped inside.

The facilities were hidden behind a wall to his left. He took a couple of steps, made a U-turn around the wall, and found himself standing in the midst of a completely unremarkable and completely empty public restroom.

He checked both of the stalls and confirmed that nobody was standing on the toilet seats and that nothing was stashed in the bowls. He noticed a small storage cabinet beneath the sink but found it locked.

He backtracked around the dividing wall and checked the trash can: It contained only a couple of soiled paper towels. He peered through the small plastic windows on the paper-towel dispensers and saw nothing out of the ordinary.

I'm missing something, he thought.

He opened the bathroom door and poked his head out into the alcove, where Jennifer awaited his return. He glanced around, saw nobody, and quickly pulled her inside.

"What are you doing?" she protested. "You're going to get us in trouble."

"Relax, there's nobody here."

He led her around the bend, into the main part of the restroom.

"I guess this is the one place where we're safe from surveillance cameras," she said.

Crocker's eyes searched the room. "That's why I think Trooper Haley was up to something. He didn't come all the way up here just to use the facilities."

"Did you check the stalls?"

"Yes."

She glanced around. "What about that cabinet under the sink?"

"It's locked."

"And the changing table?"

"The what?"

She walked to the large rectangular object mounted to the wall. "Don't tell me you've never seen a baby-changing table." She flipped the latch and folded down the plastic table.

"I know what it is, but it didn't occur to me to check it." He inspected the table and pointed to what appeared to be a built-in tissue dispenser. "What's this?"

"Disposable liners. So you don't have to lay your baby on a dirty table."

The edge of one liner protruded from the plastic container. Crocker grabbed it and pulled. It slid easily from the box. He watched to see if another liner took its place at the mouth of the container but none did.

"Looks like you got the last one," she said.

"Lucky me."

He stuck a finger into the mouth of the empty dispenser. It was a tight fit, and he strained to feel around inside the plastic box. The tip of his finger grazed something that felt like leather. He pressed harder and felt a solid object shift behind the leather.

He withdrew his finger. "Any idea how to get this open?"

After a couple of seconds of experimentation, Jennifer managed to open the dispenser. Crocker reached in and pulled out a brown leather bank bag.

"What's that?" she asked.

"Evidence that our young highway patrolman is on Dudka's payroll."

"What do you think is inside?"

Crocker didn't need to open the bag—he could tell from the feel what was inside—but he unzipped it anyway, for Jennifer's benefit. Together, they surveyed the contents.

As he'd surmised, the bag contained three compact semiautomatic handguns, which he now recognized as Walther P22s, and three silencers, each of which could be threaded onto the barrel of one of the guns. The small-caliber pistols were not very powerful, but when fitted with the silencers and loaded with subsonic ammunition, a shot fired from one would be no louder than a strong sneeze.

In tonight's production of The Godfather, *the role of Clemenza will be played by Trooper Haley.*

The faintest hint of a smile formed at the corners of Crocker's mouth.

Jennifer looked at him like he'd lost his mind. "Do you find this amusing?"

"No," he replied, "but it's not surprising. A mob boss with cops on his payroll shouldn't have much difficulty slipping guns past security. Haley probably hid the bag under his shirt, flashed his badge to the guards, and bypassed the metal detectors without attracting so much as a suspicious glance."

"Well, now we have their guns, and we have a pretty good idea who's been tipping off Dudka."

Crocker zipped the bag shut. "You're half right." He placed it back inside the plastic dispenser.

Alarm washed over Jennifer's face. "What are you doing?"

He closed the dispenser. "If these guns aren't where they're supposed to be, Dudka's men will abort the exchange, and Ashley will be gone forever." He folded the changing table shut and latched it.

Jennifer looked as if she were about to say something in protest, but a chorus of men's voices interrupted.

Outside the restroom, a man with a heavy Eastern European accent asked, "Is this it?"

"*Da*," replied another, "*éto ono*."

Crocker was still processing the fact that the second man had responded in what sounded like Russian when he felt Jennifer shoving him toward one of the stalls. Since he had no plan of his own, he complied, stepping into the stall just as he heard the restroom's main door swing open with a loud thud.

"*Gde stol*," said a third man.

Jennifer followed Crocker into the stall and quickly but quietly pulled the stall door closed behind her as footsteps echoed from the other side of the dividing wall.

"*Vot*," replied one of the men.

Jennifer eased the latch into place, locking the stall door.

"Viktor," said the first man, "open the table. Dima, *prover' tualet*."

Crocker's knowledge of Russian was limited to the three or four words he'd picked up from Cold War–era spy films, but he didn't need to speak the language to know that that last word sounded a whole lot like *toilet*.

For the second time in five minutes, Jennifer surprised Crocker by kissing him. But this kiss wasn't so much romantic as abrasive. As she did this, she simultaneously untucked his dress shirt with one hand and tousled his hair with the other. Apparently satisfied with the results, she stepped back, grabbed the hem of her already ridiculously short dress, and hiked it up well above the point of decency. Crocker's brain was still playing catch-up when the stall door rattled violently.

Without missing a beat, Jennifer called out, in what sounded like a bad New Jersey accent, "Hol' ya horses, already—we're comin'."

She flipped the latch, and as the door swung open, the first thing the burly man on the other side saw was a stunning redhead pulling down the hem of her provocative gold minidress.

She looked up at the stout man in the tight black slacks and yellow dress shirt and, in the same accent, said, "It's gettin' so a gal can't even make a livin' in this town."

She reached back, grabbed Crocker by the hand, and led him out of the stall, past the confused-looking thug. Crocker saw himself in the mirror above the sink and realized what a first-class job Jennifer had done. With his hair and clothes a mess and his face smeared with lipstick, he looked like a man who'd been caught getting a little bathroom nookie.

Two men stood near the changing table. Both looked every inch the part of Eastern European gangsters. One wore a tight-fitting sharkskin suit over a half-buttoned dress shirt. The other wore all black and had his long hair pulled back in a ponytail.

The three goons watched Crocker and Jennifer walk toward the exit. As Crocker made the U-turn around the dividing wall, he gave the men a sheepish I'm-so-embarrassed look and followed Jennifer to the door.

The couple hurried into the small alcove outside the restroom and almost crashed into a squat little woman who was dragging a mop and bucket from the maintenance closet. The woman glanced up at the disheveled man and the scandalously dressed woman, shook her head in disgust, and continued on her way.

CHAPTER FOURTEEN

Jennifer closed her eyes and let the cool evening breeze wash over her, drying the beads of perspiration that still lingered ten minutes after the close encounter in the men's room. She focused on the sound of the wind and tuned out the noise of the traffic snaking along the Strip and the screams of the thrill seekers enjoying the rides on the other side of the observation deck.

She opened her eyes to find she'd squeezed the guardrail so tightly that the color had drained from her hands. She loosened her grip and felt a slight tingle as the blood returned to her fingers. She took in the view, searching for anything that might distract her from her problems. She found nothing.

Almost nine hundred feet below, men and women strolled Las Vegas Boulevard without a care more pressing than, perhaps, a losing streak at the tables. By the simple virtue of not having wandered into the Placer Gold truck stop at one o'clock that morning, they got to go on living their lives just as they always had.

To her right, Crocker leaned against the guardrail, absentmindedly seesawing a coin-operated telescope on its base.

Jennifer wasn't scared because Dudka's men had guns—she knew firsthand that Crocker could handle three armed assailants. She was scared because Dudka's men had guns inside one of the most secure buildings in Las Vegas.

Her problems were not going to end with a brief statement to the authorities and a business-class flight back to Dallas. Regardless of whether the plan to save Ashley succeeded or failed, Jennifer could not simply return to her life in Texas and assume that what had happened in Vegas would stay in Vegas.

What if, some evening six months or a year from now, she came home to find three of Dudka's henchmen waiting in her living room?

"Tell me something," she said.

Crocker stopped playing with the telescope. "Okay."

"Assuming this actually works and we get Ashley back, then what?"

"Then Tom gets her to safety, and you and I go to the feds, just like we discussed."

"And when Dudka sends his army of thugs and dirty cops after us?"

"You're worried Dudka is going to carry out a vendetta against us?"

"He dismembers incompetent employees and buries the pieces in the desert. I get the impression he's prone to holding grudges."

Crocker offered a sympathetic smile. "We made Dudka's list twenty-some-odd hours ago. Nothing we do here tonight is going to change that."

Jennifer sighed. "I just wish we didn't have to throw fuel on the fire. If we had a little more time, maybe we could come up with the money and—"

"Don't start playing that game. Take it from me, dwelling on the what-ifs gets you nowhere. We have to deal with the reality of the situation, and the reality is that we don't have any more time or money."

"Or anything else," quipped Jennifer.

"That's not true—we have friends." He pulled a business card from his jacket pocket. "And those friends are going to make sure we're safe." He handed her the card.

She examined it. "Sheriff Cargill?"

"Flip it over."

She looked at the writing on the back side. "Who is SA Bruce Eastland?"

"That's *Special Agent* Bruce Eastland. He's with the FBI's organized crime division."

"And you think he can help?"

"He's flying in from DC as we speak. First thing in the morning, you and I are meeting Special Agent Eastland and Sheriff Cargill. They're going to take care of us."

"Take care of us how? By changing our names, moving us to Idaho, and giving us jobs at the Department of Motor Vehicles?"

"Nobody said anything about witness relocation."

"How else are they going to protect us from a man like Dudka?"

"I don't know. But I do know we'll be safe. And I know that this mess will finally be out of our hands and in the hands of the professionals. For now, that's good enough for me."

Jennifer shared Crocker's desire to turn over control of the situation to a team of highly capable federal agents, but she needed to believe that doing so wouldn't mean the end of life as she knew it. She watched the handful of tourists milling about the observation deck and tried to conceive a plausible happy ending.

She was mentally sketching out the broad strokes of a scenario that involved spending a few months on a beach in South America when she saw one of the lobby doors swing open twenty feet behind Crocker. Her fantasy dissolved into stark reality as the goon in the sharkskin suit stepped out onto the observation deck, followed by the longhaired man in black.

Jennifer tucked the business card into the cleavage of her dress and, doing her best to remain calm, leaned forward and whispered in Crocker's ear, "They're here."

"The men from the restroom?"

"Yeah. Two of them, anyway."

He nuzzled her neck. "What are they doing?"

"They're splitting up. One is walking this way."

She pretended to enjoy Crocker's undivided attention as the ponytailed man in black walked past.

"They're scoping out the location," whispered Crocker when the man had passed. "Avoid eye contact—we can't afford to look interested."

Jennifer turned back toward the sea of neon lights. Crocker did the same.

He stared out at the city. "Try to act natural."

"No problem." Her voice dripped with sarcasm. "I'll just stand here mouthing 'peas and carrots' over and over until we hear from Tom."

Crocker gave her a sideways glance. "Peas and carrots?"

"That's what actors in the background of movies do so that it looks like they're having conversations."

When Crocker didn't reply, Jennifer peeked over and saw his lips moving.

They continued like that for a couple of minutes—staring out at the skyline, occasionally mouthing *peas and carrots*—until Crocker gently elbowed her in the ribs. She took a casual look around and saw the man in black headed back their way.

"Anyway," she said as if midconversation, "that's when I realized that that's just a replica and that the real Eiffel Tower is still somewhere in Europe."

Crocker laughed, and the man in black continued by without paying them any attention. A few seconds later, Crocker's jacket began to vibrate.

"Here we go." He pulled Vegas's cell phone from an inside pocket, accepted the call, and muted it without saying a word to the caller. He then forwarded the call. After a moment, his jacket began vibrating again. He reached into the same inside pocket, pulled out a second cell phone—this one borrowed from Scarlett—and offered it to Jennifer. "It's for you."

Jennifer took the vibrating phone and asked, "Should I try to warn him about the guns before I mute it?"

"No. He'd have to take the phone out of his pocket to understand you, and that might tip off anybody watching."

She accepted the call and, as Crocker had done, immediately muted it so as to avoid any suspicious sounds emanating from Tom's pants. She and Crocker held their respective phones to their ears and listened.

Tom's voice was soft and muffled. "I'm watching the two of you from the doors. Signal if you can hear me."

Jennifer waited for Crocker's nod, then ran her free hand through her hair.

"Copy that," said Tom. "We're live. You hear what I hear."

Across the way, one of the lobby doors opened, and Tom emerged onto the observation deck. His suit and dress shoes had been replaced by a long-sleeved T-shirt, a pair of cargo pants, and white sneakers. He wore the cheap canvas backpack Jennifer had seen at the Prickly Pear.

"That's your cue," whispered Crocker.

Jennifer walked casually toward the lobby doors. Neither she nor Tom acknowledged the other as they passed. She mouthed *peas and carrots* into the phone as she walked.

She passed through the same door through which Tom had just exited and sat on a bench on the small landing atop the lobby stairs. From the bench, she could watch Tom through the glass doors and keep an eye on the steps leading down to the elevators.

Tom walked to a coin-operated telescope near the guardrail and waited. He didn't have to wait long.

He'd been standing there for less than a minute when Jennifer heard a phone ring. She heard it faintly through the glass doors and loudly through Scarlett's phone.

Tom reached into his right front pocket, hesitated, then reached into his left front pocket and pulled out the cheap prepaid cell phone Crocker had given him in the chapel.

He almost pulled out the wrong phone, thought Jennifer with a shudder.

"Hello," he answered.

Jennifer couldn't hear what, if anything, was said on the other end of Tom's call, but within a matter of seconds, the man in the sharkskin suit and the man in black appeared on either side of him.

Before Tom could say anything, the man in black grabbed the cell phone from his hand and flung it over the ledge.

Tom recoiled but quickly regained his composure. "Would one of you gentlemen happen to be Mr. Black?"

"Yes," said the man in the sharkskin suit, his accent thick, "I am Mr. Black."

"Really?" asked Tom. "I would have put my money on Johnny Cash here." He cocked his thumb at the man dressed in black.

"You can call me Boris," said the man in the sharkskin suit.

Tom glanced at the other man. "I guess that makes you Natasha."

The two Russians exchanged a puzzled glance.

"You have what we want?" asked Boris.

"Do you have what *I* want?" asked Tom.

"First we see money," said Boris. "Then you get girl."

Tom reached for his pants pocket. The man in black grabbed his arm.

"Relax," said Tom, holding up his free hand in a nonthreatening gesture. "I'm just getting what you came for."

Boris nodded, and the man released Tom's hand.

Tom reached slowly into his pocket. The man in black stood ready to pounce. Tom pulled out a half-inch-thick brown envelope with a handwritten number four on it and handed it to Boris.

Boris opened the envelope and thumbed through its contents.

Jennifer had promised Larry she'd pay back the ten-thousand-dollar loan, but he hadn't seemed overly concerned about it.

When Boris was satisfied, he closed the envelope and stuffed it into his jacket pocket. "Show me the rest."

"Do I look stupid?" asked Tom.

"A little," replied Boris.

"If I hand over the money now, that'll be the last I see of it or the girl. You see the money when I see Ashley."

Boris leaned forward and whispered something in Tom's ear. He spoke too softly for Jennifer to hear. As he whispered, he opened his suit jacket so that Tom—and only Tom—could see what was concealed beneath. Jennifer didn't need to see or hear to know what Boris had revealed.

"Known for being single-mindedly ruthless and having more balls than brains," she thought, remembering Larry's warning about the Russian mob.

"Is that a gun in your pocket," asked Tom, "or are you just happy to see your money again?"

Jennifer couldn't help but smile. It was a lame joke but a clever way of letting her and Crocker know that Dudka's men were armed.

"I suggest you do not test me," replied Boris, "unless you wish to chase after your phone."

Tom snorted. "Tell you what, Ivan. If you came here to kill me, go right ahead and shoot me or toss me off the building or do whatever you've got to do. But if you came here to get your money, I suggest you show me the girl before this little powwow attracts the kind of attention you don't want."

Boris seemed uncertain. He glanced at the man in black, then back at Tom, then back at the man in black. Finally, he said something Jennifer couldn't understand. She wasn't sure whether he'd spoken Russian or was standing too far from Tom's hidden phone. The man in black responded by pulling out a cell phone of his own and placing a call.

Jennifer remembered that she too was supposed to be on a call. She let out an unconvincing laugh, glanced around the room, and saw with some relief that nobody was standing close enough to eavesdrop.

Out on the observation deck, the man in black finished his call and said something to Boris, who in turn looked at Tom and said, "We wait."

The waiting seemed to go on forever. Neither Tom nor the two thugs spoke. Jennifer grew nervous and found herself wondering if, should it come to it, Crocker could outdraw the two Russians.

After what seemed like half an hour but, according to the clock on Scarlett's phone, was actually less than ten minutes, a short, round man who made Jennifer think of Humpty Dumpty appeared at the base of the stairs, leading a young woman by the wrist.

Jennifer saw the couple for only a second or two before looking away, but what she saw in that moment both excited and troubled her. Young Ashley Thomas was alive but virtually unrecognizable. She had on no makeup, and her hair was pulled back in a tangled mess of a ponytail. She was dressed in a stained and tattered gray sweat suit and wore a pair of worn-out sneakers at least three sizes too big.

Jennifer looked down at her phone, letting strands of fake red hair obscure her face as the rotund gangster and his disheveled hostage crested the stairs and crossed to the observation deck. When the door slammed shut behind them, she jumped to her feet.

She wanted nothing more than to see Ashley and Tom's reunion first-hand, but this was her cue to exit. If things went according to plan, Ashley would be headed straight back to the elevators, and Jennifer needed to be waiting for her when she got there.

As she started down the stairs, Jennifer glanced over her shoulder and saw Crocker strolling toward the lobby doors. He would take her place atop the small landing and, should the need arise, provide cover as Ashley made her way from the observation deck to the elevators.

When Jennifer was halfway down the steps, the phone picked up Ashley's distant voice exclaiming, "Tom! What are you doing here?"

Jennifer smiled.

"Are you okay?" asked Tom.

The phone didn't pick up Ashley's response, but it did pick up Tom's audible sigh of relief. Reenergized, Jennifer cleared the last two steps in one quick stride and made her way to the elevator bank.

Out on the deck, one of the goons—Jennifer thought it was Boris but wasn't certain—said something unintelligible.

"Not until she's safe," replied Tom.

Boris—this time Jennifer was certain it was Boris—said something in protest, but Tom cut him off. "You've made enough demands. Now I'm telling you how this is going to work." Boris protested again, and again, Tom cut him off. "No, you listen, Boris. You're about to get your money, and I'm about to get my girl, and we're all going to walk away happy, so quit trying to fuck up what should be a win for everybody."

Loitering near the elevators, Jennifer wondered what Ashley thought of being referred to as Tom's girl.

"Now," he continued, "you three stooges are going to wait here with me while Ashley gets back on the elevator. When she's had time to get safely away, I'll give you the money."

There was a brief, indecipherable exchange of dialogue between the Russians; then Boris, clearly audible for the first time since Ashley's arrival, said, "Okay. She goes. You stay."

After another moment of silence, the phone picked up the sound of footsteps, followed by a loud rustling noise.

"Thank you," said Ashley, her voice so loud and clear that she had to be touching Tom as she spoke.

Jennifer dried her eyes on the back of her free hand and hoped this wouldn't be the young couple's last embrace.

"Get out of here," said Tom, his voice a bit shaky. "I'll find you when this is over."

Moments later, Ashley sprinted down the stairs, toward the elevators.

Jennifer turned toward the wall and did her best to hide behind Scarlett's cell phone and Vegas's wig. She didn't want Ashley to recognize her until they were safely inside the elevator.

Just as Ashley reached the elevator bank, a bell chimed, and the doors to the elevator on the right slid open. Jennifer peeked out from behind the cell phone and saw two people waiting inside the car. One was the elderly operator who'd complimented Tom's suit. The other was the yellow-shirted goon who'd found Crocker and Jennifer in the men's room stall.

Jennifer's heart stopped. She and the others had assumed that Dudka's goons would try to retake Ashley on the ground floor, outside the security checkpoint. The man in the yellow shirt had just tossed a monkey wrench into their plan.

While Jennifer considered her options, Ashley stepped into the car, apparently oblivious to the danger.

This left Jennifer only one option. She surreptitiously unmuted the phone, faced away from the open elevator car, and, using the same New Jersey accent she'd used in the men's room, said, "Okay, well, I'm 'bout to get on a crowded elevator, so I betta let ya go."

She hoped that Crocker had heard her and that the three gangsters standing near Tom had not. She remuted the phone and listened for any reaction from the goons. Much to her relief, she heard none.

Speaking into the muted phone, she said, "Oh really? Well, we betta just talk 'bout that later."

"Ma'am," said the elderly operator behind her, "are you going to board the elevator, or would you prefer to wait for the next one?"

"Hol' ya horses," replied Jennifer without looking back. "I'm comin'."

This contingency had been discussed in Larry's cabin but only briefly. Jennifer needed to buy Crocker as much time as possible.

"Okay," she said into the muted phone, "talk to ya soon. Love ya."

She kept her eyes down, pretending to look at something on the phone, and turned toward the elevator. It was growing increasingly difficult to hide her face, but if Ashley recognized her now, it could prove fatal.

She took a step forward and, seeing one last opportunity to buy Crocker some time, plunged her stiletto heel into the gap between the door and the elevator. She stumbled, caught herself, and knelt to free the shoe.

The elevator operator stepped forward to help her up, and she pivoted so that he stood between her and Ashley. With Ashley's view blocked, she rose to her feet and turned away from the other passengers.

She breathed a sigh of relief as the elevator doors closed in front of her. Between her rude behavior and her deliberate clumsiness, she'd bought Crocker an extra twenty to thirty seconds. And she'd done it all without letting Ashley see her face.

"Next stop," said the operator, "ground floor."

"No!" exclaimed Jennifer, realizing she'd almost made a serious mistake. "I'm getting off at level 104, the private reception."

"Not a problem," said the operator as he pressed the button. "Next stop, level 104."

The elevator began to move.

"Jennifer?" asked a soft voice in the back of the elevator. "Jennifer, is that you?"

Jennifer's blood ran cold at the sound of Ashley's voice.

How did she—

All at once, Jennifer realized her mistake. In her panic over almost forgetting to tell the operator which floor she wanted, she'd spoken to him in her everyday voice, a voice Ashley knew well.

She stiffened and watched the goon's reflection in the polished elevator doors. Had he noticed? Had he put it together? Could she play it off like she had no idea what Ashley was talking about? They just needed to survive a few more seconds until—

The thug lifted the tail of his yellow shirt and reached for something underneath.

Without thinking, Jennifer spun and charged at him. She grabbed the hand clutching the pistol and knocked it into the wall with all her strength.

The gun dropped to the floor, and the goon turned his attention to Jennifer. His two massive hands grabbed her under each arm and drove her across the elevator, slamming her into the elevator doors.

She slumped to the floor, dazed and in pain.

"What do you think you're doing?" screamed the elevator operator.

Dudka's man turned to retrieve his gun. As he bent to pick it up, Ashley lunged forward and kicked it away. It bounced off the side wall and came to rest two feet in front of Jennifer. She reached for it.

The goon grabbed Jennifer's outstretched arm and flung her to the other side of the elevator. She landed in a heap beside Ashley.

Jennifer watched from the floor as the yellow-shirted gangster bent and reached for the pistol. As he wrapped his fingers around it, the elevator doors parted in front of him.

The large man in the yellow shirt stood to find himself staring down the barrels of five handguns. Five handguns and one Taser.

While the five security guards with handguns tried to assess the situation, the security guard with the Taser apparently decided that the situation would be easier to assess when the man in the yellow shirt wasn't holding a weapon. The Taser made a horrific crackling noise, and the goon collapsed into a convulsing pile on the floor.

Jennifer's tired, bruised body begged her to lie on the floor and wait for the security guards to mop up the mess, but her brain overruled it. She sprang to her feet.

"Jennifer, what is this?" cried Ashley as the six security guards converged on the disabled Russian mobster.

"Just get out of the elevator."

"But there's no room." The young woman watched the pile of security guards struggling to get handcuffs onto the uncooperative goon.

"Just go!"

Without further protest, Ashley stepped past the befuddled elevator operator, flattened herself against the side of the open door, and slid past the writhing pile of men. Jennifer followed.

When they were safely outside the elevator car, Jennifer took a deep breath and surveyed the chaos.

"Jennifer," whimpered Ashley, "why are you dressed like a hooker?"

"I'll explain later. Just do exactly what I say. We're not out of this yet."

Ashley nodded.

"Follow me."

They crossed the lobby where Jennifer and Tom had waited in line to enter the private reception. By the sound of it, the party was still in full swing. It occurred to Jennifer that this would be a very inopportune time for her and Ashley to bump into someone they knew, but at the moment, professional embarrassment was pretty low on her list of concerns.

They ducked into the service corridor where Jennifer had done her drunk-woman routine for the guard. Thanks to the commotion at the elevators, the stairs were now unguarded, which greatly simplified this part of the plan.

Jennifer opened the door and held it for Ashley. "This way."

They hurried down the stairs, their footsteps echoing through the empty stairwell. When they reached the entrance to the Chapel in the Clouds, Jennifer stopped.

"Hang on." She dug into her cleavage and pulled out Crocker's ID card. She swiped the card over the card reader, waited for the beep and the green light, and opened the door. "Get inside."

Ashley stepped into the service hallway.

Jennifer followed and shut the door behind them. "Okay, we're safe for now, but we have to move quick." She opened the door to the chapel where she and Crocker had left Tom. "This way."

"Can't you tell me what is going on?" asked Ashley as she followed Jennifer across the chapel.

"I'll explain as much as I can while you change clothes."

"Change clothes? What is going on? How did you get away?"

Jennifer stopped at the door to the second service hallway. "What?"

"How did you get away from the Russians?"

Jennifer tried for several seconds to make sense of the question, then, realizing she was wasting valuable time, opened the door and stepped into the service hall. "I don't know what you're talking about, but we have to keep moving."

Ashley followed her across the hallway and into the large, unlit chapel where Jennifer and Crocker had made love. "The Russians told me they were letting me go because they'd finally caught you."

Jennifer stopped so abruptly that Ashley almost ran into her in the dark. "They told you what?"

"They said that you were the one they were after when they grabbed me and that they didn't need me anymore. Then they brought me here and told me that they were going to let me go but that if I called for help or made a scene, they'd kill you."

Jennifer finally understood. "They lied." She stopped beside the row of windows overlooking the Strip. "They never had me. They were just trying to make sure you cooperated."

While Ashley processed this revelation, Jennifer found the diaper bag, hoisted it onto the same window ledge that had held her during her brief romantic interlude with Crocker, and began digging through the contents.

"So you were safe all along?" asked Ashley.

"I wouldn't say I was safe, but the Russians never had me." She tossed Ashley the red spandex dress. "Put that on."

"Now?"

"Yes, right now. Do you have underwear? That dress is even shorter than this one, but I have these if you need them." She held up the extra thong Tom had purchased at the hotel boutique.

"I have underwear." The young woman hesitated. "It was the one thing I had on when they grabbed me, drugged me, and stuffed me in my suitcase."

As Ashley pulled off the dirty sweatshirt, Jennifer paused for the first time to imagine what the ordeal must have been like for her. In the dim ambient light, Jennifer searched the young woman's body for bruises or other signs of abuse. Nothing stood out.

"Are you okay?" she asked. "I mean, did they hurt you or—"

"No." Ashley leaned on the window ledge and pulled off one of the oversized sneakers. "A couple of them acted like they wanted to, but the guy in charge kept warning them not to damage the merchandise."

The phrase *damage the merchandise* made Jennifer's skin crawl. "I'm just glad you're safe."

"I'm glad *you're* safe." Ashley tossed the second sneaker to the side. "When they told me they had you, I thought for sure they were going to... I mean, after what they did to Bryan..." She stood in silence, one leg in the baggy sweatpants and one leg out of them.

"Don't think about it now," said Jennifer. "Just get dressed."

Ashley moved as if in slow motion, sliding her other leg from the sweatpants and letting them fall in a pile on the floor. She stood silent and motionless for a moment, then burst into tears.

Standing there, weeping in the glow of the Las Vegas Strip, wearing nothing but the pink cotton panties in which she'd been abducted, Ashley reminded Jennifer of a scared, lost child. Jennifer wasn't sure if it was fair to think of Ashley's tryst with Bryan as a betrayal, but even if it was, the poor girl had done her penance and then some. At that moment, any resentment Jennifer might have felt toward Ashley washed away in the young woman's tears.

Jennifer stepped forward and wrapped her arms around her friend. "You're safe now. Forget about the rest of it—you're safe."

Ashley nodded and wiped the tears from her eyes.

Jennifer stepped back and picked up the red spandex dress. "Now put this on. I promise you that Tom is going to die when he sees you in it."

A stricken look crossed Ashley's face. "Tom is still with the Russians!"

"It's okay."

"But once he gives them whatever money they're after—"

"He doesn't have the money."

"What?" shrieked Ashley.

"You're just going to have to trust me. There's a plan."

"What plan? They're going to kill him!"

"Did Tom ever tell you how he earned a living before he came to work at New Wave?"

"Yeah, he made vid—"

Ashley's answer was cut short by a chorus of muffled screams from upstairs. Then she let out her own blood-curdling scream as Tom's body fell past the large picture window to her left.

CHAPTER FIFTEEN

As a security professional, Crocker prided himself on his coolness under pressure and his ability to react and adapt. However, the unexpected sound of Jennifer's voice put those qualities to the test.

Out on the observation deck, Tom and the three goons were waiting in silence when Crocker heard the faux New Jersey accent break through on Vegas's phone.

"Okay, well, I'm 'bout to get on a crowded elevator, so I betta let ya go."

Seeing no sign that the goons had heard Jennifer's muffled voice coming from Tom's pocket, Crocker dropped onto the bench and switched his phone to the hand with the radio microphone hidden in the sleeve.

He ignored the muted phone and pressed the talk button on the covert microphone. "SSD, this is PPO Crocker." As he spoke, his free hand plucked the earpiece from beneath his jacket collar and held it to his ear.

"Security desk," responded a brisk female voice. "Go ahead, Crocker."

"Code red. Code red. Man with a gun. Tower elevator. Prepare to intercept on level one zero four. Be advised there are civilians on the elevator."

"Copy. Stand by. All SSOs and PPOs on level one zero four, proceed immediately to elevators. Prepare to intercept armed intruder. Civilians present. Use extreme caution."

"Crocker," said a deep male voice, "this is Tower Security Chief Feltoon. We need a description."

Crocker thought about the men's room. *Three guns and three goons—who's missing?*

He mashed the talk button. "Large white male. Yellow shirt."

"Copy," replied Feltoon. "Be advised the suspect is a large white male wearing a yellow shirt."

The radio was silent. Crocker glanced out at the observation deck, where Tom and his three new friends waited in awkward silence.

Crocker reminded himself to breathe. He forced himself to wait another thirty seconds, then radioed, "SSD, this is Crocker. What's the status of that intruder?"

"Stand by," came the woman's quick reply.

Crocker felt beads of sweat streaming down his forehead. He wished he could take off his suit jacket, but doing so would reveal a holstered firearm, a two-way radio, a can of pepper spray, and a set of handcuffs.

The radio hummed to life, and Feltoon said, "All security officers, be advised the intruder is in custody. The code red is canceled."

"Is everybody safe?" blurted Crocker, forgetting radio protocol.

"Affirmative," answered Feltoon. "I dropped the guy with fifty thousand volts. One of my officers got a black eye getting the cuffs on him, but aside from that, everyone is fine."

Crocker's heart was still racing. "Copy that. Crocker out."

He tucked the earpiece back into his collar. Feltoon would want to debrief him as soon as the goon was secured in the hotel's holding cell, but for now, Crocker had a rescue mission to complete. There would be time later, after getting Tom and Ashley to safety and after talking to the feds, to worry about whether this incident had effectively ended his career as a private patrol officer for Las Vegas casinos.

If all else fails, there's always the Prickly Pear.

He turned his attention back to the four-man cold war on the observation deck.

After about a minute, Boris walked over to Tom and asked, "You're satisfied?"

"We'll give her a few more minutes," replied Tom.

Boris scowled but did not reply. He wandered back to his two comrades.

A couple of minutes later, Ashley's obese escort whispered something in Boris's ear.

Boris nodded and walked back to Tom. "We wait long enough. You give us the bag."

"Just a little longer," said Tom. The self-assured cockiness was gone from his voice.

"No!" shouted Boris. He grabbed Tom by the collar. "You're stalling."

Crocker jumped to his feet and ran to the glass doors.

Out on the deck, Tom stepped forward and raised his knee on a high-speed collision course with Boris's groin.

The knee made contact with such force that Crocker reflexively flinched and covered his own crotch as he passed through the doors.

Boris released Tom, teetered backward, and fell to the ground, howling in pain as he held his crushed manhood. Tom turned to run. The goon in black lunged after him.

Tom had a good head start, but one of the coin-operated telescopes stood in his way, and the momentary loss of momentum as he sidestepped it allowed the thug to reach him and grab the loop atop the cheap canvas backpack.

Tom stumbled, and Crocker thought for sure he would fall backward into the gangster's arms. But instead of falling, Tom pointed his arms behind him like a downhill skier and let the straps slide off his shoulders. The man in black tumbled backward holding an empty shell of a backpack.

Tom kept running, a sleek red, white, and blue pack on his back. Vegas's sewing skills had paid off.

Ahead of him, the semicircular observation deck came to an abrupt end. He veered left and vaulted over the inner guardrail, landing in the narrow no man's land between it and the outer guardrail.

The man in black tossed the fake backpack to the side and climbed to his feet. The other two thugs joined him. They walked slowly toward Tom, who, standing between two rows of iron bars, looked like a caged animal.

Tom glanced back at the approaching gangsters, then scurried up the outer guardrail.

Crocker noticed that the handful of tourists milling about the observation deck had stopped to watch the scene unfold.

Tom slid down onto the ledge overlooking the nine-hundred-foot drop.

"*Durak,*" muttered Boris. The other two goons laughed.

The three gangsters lined up along the inner fence. Tom clung to the bars of the outer fence and stared back at their grinning faces. There was no place left to run.

Crocker, along with a handful of tourists, moved in for a closer look.

Boris's grin faded.

You're catching on, aren't you? thought Crocker with a smile of his own. Tom's plan to hang around after the conference and try to win a little money at the skydiving tournament might have crashed and burned, but his plan to pull one over on Dudka's goons was right on track. He turned toward the ledge, took two quick steps, and leapt into the black abyss.

The tourists' cries of surprise and horror drowned out Boris's tirade of what Crocker assumed could only be Russian profanity.

As the shrieks and hollers faded, there was a sound like a clap of thunder. Tom's parachute had opened.

CHAPTER SIXTEEN

Every head on level 107 turned as the sultry duo entered the lounge. Jennifer ignored the men's leering stares and the women's contemptuous glares and glanced back at the raven-haired beauty in the painted-on red dress, who bore only the slightest resemblance to New Wave Commercial's blond-haired wunderkind.

Ashley offered a weak but reassuring smile, and Jennifer noted with some relief that the young woman's makeup remained free of streaks. Seeing Tom fall past the chapel window had unleashed a torrent of emotion in the recently freed hostage, and despite Jennifer's repeated assurance that Tom's fall was part of the plan, it had taken several minutes to get the floodgates to close.

The swanky lounge was a circular loft centered above the tower's signature attraction, a rotating five-star restaurant. Jennifer paused near the bar and surveyed the room. Somewhere on the other side of the lounge, a live band played soft jazz.

Her gaze fell on one of the tables near the loft's outer rim, and for a fleeting moment she saw Bryan waiting there for her. It was the table they'd shared a year before, when he was still alive and still married and still the forbidden object of her desires.

There he'd confided that his marriage was ending, and she'd sat across from him, thinking, *Maybe next year things will be different.*

She blinked away the ghosts and surveyed the bar once more. The table she'd once shared with Bryan was empty, but two tables to the left, a waving arm beckoned. She returned Vegas's wave and led Ashley to the table.

Vegas bounded from her chair, almost bouncing out of her tiny leopard-print dress, and greeted Jennifer with a bear hug. "You made it!"

Jennifer couldn't help but smile at the young woman's exuberance.

Vegas released her embrace. "Any word from Matt?"

"Not yet." Jennifer set the diaper bag on the table. "But he still has a few minutes."

"I wish you could have been here when Tom jumped. Everybody screamed, and then this one lady down in the restaurant started hollering for someone to call 911, and then some guy up here in the bar yelled back, 'You'd better tell them to bring a snow shovel and some Hefty bags.'"

Jennifer winced and looked at Ashley, expecting tears. Much to Jennifer's relief, the floodgates held.

"Come to think of it," continued Vegas, "I suppose that's kind of morbid, considering most of these people really thought he'd died. But I couldn't stop laughing."

"Ashley," said Jennifer, "I want you to meet Vegas. She helped us put this together."

Before Ashley could reply, Vegas stepped forward and wrapped her arms around her. "I'm really glad you're safe."

"Thanks," said Ashley, casting a bemused glance at Jennifer. "I appreciate your help."

Vegas let her go. "Forget it. Scarlett and I were happy to help."

"Where is Scarlett?" asked Jennifer.

"She went to offload a few of these mango martinis." Vegas nodded toward the empty glasses on the table. "Of course, knowing her, she probably got sidetracked soliciting some—"

"I wasn't soliciting anything," protested Scarlett from behind them. "I was waiting in line to use the little girls' room."

Jennifer turned to find the less amiable half of the Prickly Pear pair wearing a slinky white dress that blended seamlessly with her fair skin and made her dark red hair seem all the more brilliant.

"Ashley," said Jennifer, "this is Scarlett, another member of our ragtag band."

Ashley extended a shaky hand. "It's nice to meet you."

"Hi," replied Scarlett, ignoring the hand. "Jenny, you're paying our tab, right? Because we've been here for like two hours, and these drinks aren't cheap."

Before Jennifer could reply, a loud, sensual moan called out from the diaper bag.

"Good," said Scarlett, "you didn't lose my phone. Can I have it back now?"

"Hang on." Jennifer reached for the bag as it moaned again. "That might be Crocker."

She pulled Scarlett's phone from the bag and answered, "Hello?"

"It's me," replied Crocker. "Larry just picked me up."

"Is Tom with you?"

"Yeah, he's lying down in the backseat. He had a pretty rough landing, but Larry got him into the car, and they got away before the cops arrived. He'll be okay."

"Is it safe for us to leave?"

"As safe as it's going to get. Hotel security nabbed the three goons from the tower when they got off the elevator, but you can bet Dudka has people watching the exits."

"Don't worry," replied Jennifer, eyeing Ashley's disguise, "we'll walk right past them."

♦ ♦ ♦

It was impossible not to notice the four provocatively dressed beauties crossing the casino floor. They navigated the throngs of gamers and strutted past a half-dozen surly-looking men loitering near the main entrance.

The four women attracted a lot of attention but no apparent suspicion as they made their way out of the casino and into the waiting limousine.

Jennifer held her breath and watched the rear window as the car pulled out of the drive and onto the narrow side street. When it made the right turn onto Las Vegas Boulevard, she exhaled and slumped into her seat.

Across from her, Vegas squealed with delight. "We did it!"

Jennifer still couldn't believe it. "I guess we did."

Beside her, Ashley's facial expression relaxed into something that was almost a smile.

Only Scarlett, who sat alone near the front of the passenger compartment, engrossed in her recently reacquired cell phone, seemed unmoved by the success of the rescue mission.

"I think this calls for a celebration," said Vegas, reaching for the mini-fridge. She opened it and pulled out a half-size bottle of champagne. "I'm sure Larry won't mind if we add this to the tab." She giggled and peeled the foil from the cork.

"Fuck!" exclaimed Scarlett.

The other women froze.

After a tense silence, Jennifer found the courage to ask, "What's wrong?"

The fiery redhead dropped the phone onto her lap. "The bastard canceled on me."

"What?"

"I sent a text to my eleven o'clock, to let him know I'd be a little late, and he replied that he can't make it tonight. That son of a bitch had me booked for the whole night."

Jennifer covered her mouth to keep from laughing.

"You think this is funny?" snapped Scarlett.

"Not really." Jennifer contained herself and wiped her eyes. "But the way you yelled, I thought we were about to be gunned down by a Russian death squad or something."

Vegas struggled to suppress her own giggles as she offered her angry coworker a reassuring smile. "She didn't mean anything by it. You just caught us off guard."

"Whole night shot to hell," muttered Scarlett.

"It's still early. When we get back, why don't you join the lineup with me?"

Scarlett looked mortified. "Are you kidding? The lineup?"

"It was just a suggestion."

"Excuse me," interjected Ashley. "What exactly do the two of you do for a living?"

There was a brief pause while everyone processed the question, then both Jennifer and Vegas erupted in laughter.

"Hang on," said Vegas, still laughing as she twisted the cork on the champagne bottle. "Let me get you a drink first."

For the next hour and fifteen minutes, Vegas, who became more loquacious with each glass of champagne, carried the conversation with anecdotes of life at the Prickly Pear.

For her part, Jennifer nursed a flute of bubbly and interrupted only occasionally to ask Ashley if she was okay.

Aside from declining champagne in favor of bottled water and repeatedly assuring Jennifer that she was fine, Ashley spoke only once: During Vegas's story about a customer with an odd shower fetish, she commented that she currently might consider such a perverted request if it meant getting to take a hot shower.

Scarlett, who'd apparently heard Vegas's stories before, ignored the other passengers and entertained herself by sending and receiving text messages.

When the limousine turned left at a sign proclaiming WORLD-FAMOUS PRICKLY PEAR RANCH – 2.5 MILES, Vegas brought her latest anecdote to an abrupt halt. Jennifer sat up straight and placed her half-full glass of champagne in a cup holder.

"What's going on?" asked Ashley.

"We're almost there," replied Jennifer. "We're practically in Dudka's backyard, so we need to get you and Tom loaded up and on your way as quickly as possible."

"On our way where?"

"Tom will explain everything. For now, you just need to trust us."

The four women rode in silence until the Prickly Pear's well-lit sign—a neon depiction of a bikini-clad woman straddling a cactus as if it were a bucking bronc—came into full view.

"Is that it?" asked Ashley.

"That's the Pear," answered Vegas with a note of pride.

Ashley stared out the window as the limousine sped toward the brothel. "Shouldn't we be slowing?"

"Nope," replied Jennifer.

The driver gave the horn two quick honks as the car flew past the entrance. Jennifer held her face to the window and watched a pair of headlights pull out of the driveway and fall in behind the limo.

"They're behind us," she said.

"Who is?" gasped Ashley.

"Tom and the others."

"Relax," said Vegas in her usual carefree tone. "It's all part of the plan."

Without warning, the limousine decelerated rapidly, then shook violently as the pavement gave way to a dirt road. The four passengers bounced in their seats.

Ashley braced her hands against the ceiling. "Is this part of the plan?"

"Yep," replied Jennifer.

"How far do we have to go? I'm not sure how much of this I can take."

"Just a couple of miles," said Vegas, who seemed to be enjoying all the excitement. "Watch the side of the road for a white fence post standing out there all by its lonesome. That's roughly the halfway point."

Ashley peered out the window. "It's awfully dark."

Vegas laughed. "That's 'cause we're in the desert."

I wish I were having as much fun as she is.

Jennifer watched the headlights cutting through the dust behind them and tried to ignore her creeping sense of nausea.

"We just passed it," said Ashley. "We just passed the white post."

"Welcome to California," said Vegas.

"What?"

"We just crossed the state line. We're in Cali now."

"Where are we going?"

"You should be able to see it just over this hill."

Jennifer turned and stared into the blackness ahead. As the limo crested the hill, a line of lights resembling a small city came into view.

Thank God, she thought, still fighting back the onset of motion sickness.

She watched the lights grow larger and brighter as the car bounced down the dirt road. Behind the limo, the other vehicle kept pace. When they were just a few hundred yards from the source of the lights, the bouncing stopped.

"Are we back on the pavement?" asked Ashley.

Vegas shook her head. "Dry lake bed. It's super flat, so people come out here to, like, race cars and stuff."

Now that the ride was smoother, Jennifer could make out the source of the lights. Silhouetted against the sky was a makeshift city of tents and motor homes—hundreds if not thousands of them.

The limo slowed to a crawl as it approached the encampment. The other set of headlights followed close behind.

"Who are all these people?" asked Ashley.

"According to your boyfriend, they're three thousand of his closest friends," replied Vegas.

"Boyfriend? You mean Tom? Tom's not my boyfriend."

"Well, he should be. He jumped off a building for you."

Jennifer grinned. Ashley turned red and looked away.

The limo traveled down a de facto Main Street that lay between the rows of tents and travel trailers. The driver navigated the narrow path, stopping or veering occasionally to avoid a pedestrian or an oncoming golf cart. The hodgepodge of residents stared at the limousine with curiosity and amusement. A shirtless man and a bikini-clad woman, both with shoulder-length dreadlocks, approached and tried to peer through the tinted windows. Three young men with crew cuts and crisp, clean United States Air Force T-shirts fell in behind the second vehicle and trotted along, apparently determined to catch a glimpse of the mysterious VIPs. Others did the same, and by the time the cars passed out of the encampment, a small entourage followed.

The two vehicles parked twenty yards past the tent city, beside a white trailer marked GROUND CONTROL.

"This is it," said Jennifer, staring out the window at the small crowd lingering near the edge of the encampment.

"What now?" asked Ashley.

As if in reply, Vegas grabbed her shoes from under the seat, opened the door, and climbed out.

Jennifer gestured toward the open door. "Now we get you the hell out of Dodge."

Ashley hesitated only a second before grabbing her own shoes and climbing out of the car. Jennifer scooped up the diaper bag, which now contained her stiletto heels, and followed.

The night air was at least ten degrees cooler than it had been in the city. Jennifer crossed her arms and wondered for a moment if perhaps she should have hung on to the filthy sweat suit Ashley had worn to the Stratosphere. At least the packed earth under her bare feet still radiated some of the day's warmth.

As Scarlett stepped out of the car, a man somewhere in the crowd of spectators yelled, "Oh, it's just hookers."

Amid a chorus of laughter and catcalls, the spectators began to disperse.

Jennifer turned her attention to the vehicle that had tailed them, an ancient green Land Rover.

The front passenger-side door opened, and Crocker stepped down. He walked to the limousine and knocked on the driver's window, which promptly opened. He handed something to the uniformed driver, uttered a few inaudible words, then walked back to the quartet of women.

He waited while the limousine made a wide circle in the open patch of desert and disappeared back down the makeshift Main Street.

When the noise had passed, he extended a hand to Ashley and said, "Ms. Thomas, I'm Matt Crocker. It's a pleasure to finally make your acquaintance."

Ashley accepted the hand and said, "The pleasure is all mine, Mr. Crocker. I don't know how I'll ever thank you for everything you've done."

"That's not necessary. But if you want to thank someone, thank Tom— he did the dangerous part."

"Where is he?" She glanced at the Land Rover. "Can I go talk to him?"

Crocker glanced back at the car. "It's probably better if you wait."

"Is he hurt bad?" asked Jennifer.

"He's hurt?" shrieked Ashley, the words trailing off as she sprinted toward the Land Rover.

Jennifer followed as quickly as her bare feet would carry her. Ashley reached the car first and threw open the back door.

Tom lay in the backseat with his legs propped over the seat in front of him. Larry was turned around in the front seat, using a pocketknife to cut off Tom's cargo pants. The right pant leg was ripped and spotted with blood.

"Hey!" exclaimed Tom as Jennifer skidded to a stop beside Ashley. "Can't a guy have a minute to change clothes?"

Crocker, who'd made no effort to run, joined Ashley and Jennifer at the open door. "As I was saying, it would probably be better if you wait until he removes his gear and gets dressed."

Ashley's eyes locked onto Tom's bloody pants. "Are you hurt?"

"I just skinned up my leg," he replied. "It's no big deal except that it's making it even harder to get out of this ridiculous getup."

Jennifer inspected the *getup*, as Tom had called it. The waist of his cargo pants hung at midthigh, revealing a pair of gray boxer shorts cinched tightly to his crotch by the nylon harness. Without the cover of the cheap canvas backpack, the rig's straps and handles were visible protruding through strategically placed slits in his oversized T-shirt.

"What happened?" asked Ashley, her voice calmer.

"When I landed, a gust of wind picked me up and dragged me halfway across the parking lot of the Blue Parrot. It would have pulled me out into Las Vegas Boulevard if I hadn't grabbed a car bumper and held on for dear life. Larry ran over and cut away the parachute with his knife."

"Why did Larry have to do it?" asked Jennifer. "I thought the plan was for you to cut it away yourself as soon as you landed."

"It was," said Tom, "but when I was repacking my main chute in the chapel, I started worrying that it might not open in time. I mean, it's a great canopy, but it's designed to open comfortably, not quickly."

"So what did you do?"

"I used my reserve chute instead. It's designed to open quick as shit, comfort be damned."

"But why couldn't you cut it away yourself?"

"Because a reserve chute doesn't have a cutaway handle." He pointed to a red, pillow-shaped handle protruding from a vertical slit on the right side of his T-shirt. "Which means that the only way to cut one away is to saw it off with a knife." He touched a jagged nub of nylon webbing protruding from the left shoulder of the harness and fondled it mournfully. "I almost had this damned thing paid off."

A loud ripping noise filled the Land Rover as Larry tore away the tattered cargo pants. He tossed the ruined garment in Tom's lap. "There you go, kid. Now get out of my car before you get blood on the seats."

Tom snorted and made his way to the open door. "Like anything could hurt this tank." He stepped out onto the lake bed. "I still say we should have taken your other car."

Larry rolled his eyes. "Yeah, there's nothing less conspicuous than three grown men crammed into the front seat of a yellow Corvette."

Tom took several seconds to examine his bloody leg and what remained of his getup. Finally, he grabbed the front of his T-shirt and tugged at it. The sliced and diced garment tore free.

"Ooh, take it off," cheered Vegas.

Ashley cast a sideways glance at the young woman.

Tom tossed both the ripped shirt and the ruined pants into the backseat of the car.

"Dammit," yelled Larry from the front seat, "don't throw your trash in here."

Crocker laughed. "Don't worry, Larry. I'll get it when we get back to the Pear."

Tom undid the harness straps and tossed what was left of his skydiving rig on top of the ruined clothes.

"Is that trash too?" asked Larry.

"Hell no." Tom looked a bit comical standing in the glow of the Land Rover's dome light, wearing nothing but gray boxer shorts and white sneakers. "The harness and main chute are fine. It just needs new reserve risers and a new reserve chute." He turned to Crocker. "Somewhere around here is a parachute rigger named Chuck. I'm going to get word to him that he needs to stop by the Pear and pick up my rig. Hopefully, he can repair the damage."

Crocker nodded. "I'll tell Dottie to—"

"I'll make sure he gets it," interrupted Vegas.

Ashley stared at Vegas for a moment before turning her attention back to Tom. "So you go to all the trouble of saving me, then you don't even tell me hello?"

Tom stared at his feet. "Sorry." He looked up. "I guess I'm still kind of focused on the mission." He glanced around for support but seemed to find none. "How are you?"

Ashley gave an exasperated snort and marched over to the awkward young man in the boxer shorts and tennis shoes. "That's not how you greet the woman you just saved." She placed her hands on his shoulders. "This is how you greet the woman you just saved."

With that, she leapt into his arms, wrapped her legs around his waist, and assaulted him with a kiss that sent him stumbling backward against the Land Rover. He steadied himself against the side of the car and, with his balance restored, set about keeping up his end of the kiss.

Jennifer didn't want to stare, but it was hard not to. The kiss went on and on with no sign of stopping.

Behind her, Vegas whispered, "See, she just needed a little nudge."

Jennifer turned and whispered, "Were you deliberately trying to make her jealous?"

Vegas smiled and shrugged.

Jennifer chuckled. "Crocker was right—you're a lot smarter than you let on."

Vegas opened her mouth to speak, but her voice drowned beneath a cacophony of noise as, somewhere nearby, a pair of large engines fired to life. The ruckus caught the attention of everyone, including the two lovebirds, and brought the kiss to a reluctant end.

Tom lowered Ashley to the ground. Together they followed the rest of the group around the Land Rover, in the direction of the roaring engines. For a moment, the source of the sound wasn't clear. Then the craft's exterior lights came on, and the small airplane lit up like a Christmas tree, fifty yards down the dirt landing strip.

"What's that?" asked Ashley.

"Our ride," replied Tom.

CHAPTER SEVENTEEN

As one of the few First Shot instructors with no wife or kids, Crocker often volunteered to perform what the other instructors disdainfully referred to as *Sunday chauffeur service*. On a Sunday before a busy week, he might make as many as three trips out to the private airstrip on the north side of Pahrump, to pick up students who'd arrived by private plane.

Though he'd never flown in anything smaller than a commercial airliner, Crocker had witnessed the arrival of everything from two-seat prop planes to lavish private jets. He knew little about aviation and cared even less, but thanks to six Arizona Department of Public Safety officials who'd flown in three weeks earlier, he knew that the low-wing, twin-propeller aircraft cutting across the dry lake bed was called a King Air. The six senior DPS officers had spent the fifty-five-minute drive between the airport and the academy bragging about their own King Air and lamenting the fact that more often than not, budget cuts kept it grounded unless the governor needed to be somewhere in a hurry.

Of course, unlike the plane now taxiing down the dirt strip, the King Air from the great state of Arizona didn't have a stylized Texas flag and the words LONE STAR SKYDIVING painted on its tail.

Crocker and his cohorts watched the approaching plane as if it were the first flying machine they'd ever seen. Even Larry abandoned the comfort of his car and joined them at the edge of the temporary runway to watch the long-nosed bird taxi down the dirt strip. Only Tom, who stood at the rear door of the Land Rover, frantically pulling clothes from a suitcase, and Ashley, who sat on the car's bumper, watching him, were not transfixed by the plane.

As the aircraft rolled to a stop in front of the small band of onlookers, Larry placed a hand on Crocker's shoulder and shouted over the noise of the engines, "You gotta hand it to the kid—he knows how to make an exit."

"Yes, he does," shouted Jennifer, her eyes fixed on the plane.

The engines whined, and the propellers slowed to a stop. As the plane grew silent, Crocker and Larry glanced back at Tom, who, still dressed in his boxers and sneakers, was hopping on one foot and trying to slide the other into a pair of Bermuda shorts.

"I'm not saying I'd want him dating my daughter," added Larry, no longer shouting, "but the boy is okay."

"If you had a daughter," replied Crocker, "guys like Tom would be the least of your worries."

Larry laughed and slapped Crocker on the back. "You got that right."

Scarlett turned from watching the plane and wrapped her fingers around Larry's right arm. "Can we go now? Vegas and I are freezing."

"I'm okay," said Vegas, still watching the plane.

"Well, you're a freak," said Scarlett. "But I didn't grow up in the desert, and I can't handle these thirty-degree temperature swings. I need to either get inside or put on some warmer clothes."

"You don't want to wait to see Tom and Ashley take off?" asked Larry.

"I've seen planes take off before."

Larry frowned.

"Please, Lare-Bear," she intoned in a childlike voice. "It's been a long day, and I just want to go back to your place and take a hot shower."

He turned to Vegas. "What do you want to do?"

"If Scarlett is cold, we can go. Besides, I need to get a spot in the lineup if I'm gonna make any money tonight."

Larry glanced back at the plane. "To hell with it." He turned to Crocker. "Just give me a call when you're done here, and I'll run down and pick you up."

Crocker smiled. "Whatever you say, Lare-Bear."

"Careful with that, or you'll be walking back. You still have Vegas's phone, don't you?"

"He'd better," interjected Vegas.

"I do," replied Crocker.

"Good," she said, "I need that back at some point. And my wigs. And my dresses. And my bag. And—"

"We get the point," said Larry.

"Sorry. I just want to make sure I get my stuff back."

"Don't worry," said Jennifer. "As soon as I get to the Pear, I'll round up your things and bring them to you."

Vegas grinned. "Thanks."

Larry turned to Jennifer. "And after that, we'll celebrate with those drinks I promised you. I make a margarita that'll knock the sequins off that dress."

Before Jennifer could respond, Tom—now dressed in the Bermuda shorts and a black T-shirt branded DALLAS STORM on the front and CHAMPION 4-WAY SKYDIVING TEAM on the back—shuffled by, dragging his suitcase with one hand and Ashley with the other.

"I don't know what you're all standing around for," he called. "Let's get this show on the road."

"Hey!" yelled Vegas. She ran to catch up to them. "I know you're on the run and all, but you could at least say bye." She wrapped her arms around him.

He released the suitcase and returned the hug.

"Watch your back," she said. "When Dudka finds out what happened, he'll be out for blood."

"I know. We'll be careful."

"And you," she said to Ashley, "you take good care of him. Not every girl gets a knight in shining armor, you know."

Ashley nodded.

Vegas turned and chased after Larry and Scarlett, who were already climbing into the Land Rover.

"All right," called Larry from behind the steering wheel, "you kids get out of here while you still can. The next time you're out this way, we'll have a proper celebration."

"I'll take you up on that," called Tom as Vegas climbed into the backseat.

The SUV growled to life, made a slow U-turn on the landing strip, and disappeared into the tent city. As the taillights faded from view, a loud rapping drew Crocker's attention back to the plane, where Tom stood behind the left wing, pounding on the cabin door.

To Crocker's surprise, the door was made of what looked like thin Plexiglas. The King Air from Arizona had featured a sturdy metal door equipped with built-in stairs that folded down for boarding. He wondered if the skydivers needed a door they could see out of or if this plastic replacement was some sort of quick fix, akin to taping garbage bags over a broken car window.

A man appeared on the other side of the door and tugged at a handle near the floor. The door slid up into the fuselage, and Crocker realized why the heavier door had been replaced: The skydivers needed one they could open in flight.

The pilot crouched and placed his palms on the lower edge of the door frame, which was a good three to four feet above the ground. He dangled his legs from the plane and lowered himself onto the runway. When his feet were firmly planted, he surveyed the welcoming party.

Though he wasn't very tall, the man had a powerful build. His chest bulged under his tight green T-shirt, and his thick arms spoke of a life of vigorous activity. His well-lined face was clean shaven, and he wore his gray hair cropped short.

Ex-military, thought Crocker.

When he'd finished his inspection, the man turned to Tom and bellowed, "Hollywood, what the hell have you gotten yourself into?"

Jennifer glanced at Crocker. Crocker shrugged.

"It'll be easier if I wait and fill you in once we're airborne," said Tom.

"Fair enough," said the man. He turned to Ashley. "You must be the source of the problem."

Ashley flinched. "Why do you say that?"

"Because guys are always getting themselves into trouble over pretty women." He extended his right hand. "Brent Brewer, drop zone owner and pilot, at your service."

She shook his hand. "Ashley Thomas, source of the problem, at yours."

He laughed. "Hollywood, you better hang on to this one."

Crocker approached and extended his own hand. "Brent, I'm Matt Crocker. I want to thank you for helping us out."

Brent gripped the hand and said, "Glad to meet you, Matt." He paused mid-handshake, studied Crocker for a moment, and asked, "Army?"

"Umm ... marines, actually."

"Well," said Brent, releasing Crocker's hand, "just don't call me a squid, and we'll get along all right."

Jennifer joined them.

The old man's eyes lit up. "You must be the other source of the problem."

Jennifer offered her hand. "Jennifer Williams. Pleased to meet you."

Brent accepted the handshake. "Will you and Matt be joining us for the trip?"

"I'm afraid not. We still have some cleaning up to do here."

"I never cared much for that part. Preferred to drop my ordnance, return to the boat, and leave the cleaning up to the marines." He winked at Jennifer.

She chuckled.

"Do you need fuel," asked Crocker, "or are you ready to take off?"

"All I need are my two passengers."

"Then perhaps we should get them in the air before we push our luck any further."

"It's that serious, is it?"

"It is."

Brent nodded and turned to Ashley. "Ms. Thomas, I have a stepladder in the plane, but if you're comfortable letting an old man give you a boost, we can skip the ladder and get you in the air that much quicker."

Ashley grinned. "A boost will be just fine, Mr. Brewer."

"That's Commander Brewer." Brent made a stirrup with his fingers. "Lieutenant commander. Retired, of course."

Ashley wrapped her left arm, still holding the stiletto heels, around Brent's neck and stepped into the stirrup with her right foot. "I'm really not dressed for this."

"Don't worry," said Brent, averting his eyes as he hoisted her up into the plane, "I promise not to look up your dress."

"Your dress!" exclaimed Jennifer as Ashley's rear settled inside the doorway.

"What?" Ashley pulled her dangling legs into the plane.

"I almost forgot—I need your dress. And your shoes. And the wig."

"What does that leave me? I'm not flying all the way to Timbuktu in just my underwear."

"No," said Jennifer, digging through the diaper bag, "I have these." She pulled out a small bundle of clothes and a pair of flip-flops and held them up for Ashley. "Donations from Vegas."

Ashley accepted the bundle and examined the clothes—a white tank top and a pair of pink terry-cloth shorts that in some circles might have passed for underwear. "This is all I have to wear?"

"You can buy some more clothes once you get there."

"Just so you know," said Brent, "the temperature when we land should be somewhere in the mid-forties."

"Really?" asked Jennifer.

"The mid-forties?" exclaimed Ashley. "I'll freeze!"

"Relax," said Tom. "I have something that will keep you warm."

He dropped to the ground and dug into his suitcase.

"You have something I can wear?" she asked.

"Here." He held up a red, white, and blue jumpsuit. "If this can keep me warm in the air, it should keep you warm on the ground, at least until we find you something else to wear."

She took the jumpsuit and stared at it skeptically.

"And here." He reached back into the suitcase. "Wear these under the sandals." He pulled out a balled-up pair of white tube socks.

Ashley took the socks. "The fashion statement is complete."

"It's a getaway, not a fashion show," said Crocker, worried that they were wasting time. "Get back in the plane and change. Make it quick. The rest of us will wait out here until you're done."

"All right." She held out Vegas's stiletto heels to Brent. "Could you hand these to Jennifer?"

He took the shoes. "I'm at your service."

Ashley disappeared into the plane, carrying the jumpsuit and socks. A second later, she reappeared in the doorway. "Jennifer, could you help me?"

"You need help?" asked Jennifer.

"Just come." Ashley disappeared back into the plane.

Jennifer glanced first at Matt, then at Brent, as if asking permission.

Brent responded by setting Ashley's shoes on the ground and making another stirrup with his fingers. Jennifer set the diaper bag on the ground and placed a bare foot in Brent's hands. He hoisted her with ease, allowing her to drop seat-first inside the door. She used both hands to hold down the hem of the gold dress as she rose to her feet.

"There are no seats in here!" she exclaimed.

Brent offered a patient smile and explained, "Seats just get in the way when you're wearing thirty pounds of gear."

Jennifer nodded as if she understood and disappeared into the plane, leaving the men to wait alone.

After a brief silence, Crocker turned to Brent and asked, "What do you think the flight time will be?"

Brent stroked his chin. "Wheels up to wheels down, about an hour and a half, give or take."

Crocker performed a couple of quick calculations in his head and turned to Tom. "Accounting for the time difference, that puts you into Cortez around three a.m. The rental car should be parked outside the FBO. My friend said she'll leave the keys under the bumper."

"Do you know what type of car?" asked Tom.

"No, but it's going to be parked in a spot reserved for the U.S. Forest Service, so it should be easy to find."

"Sounds foolproof."

"If you follow the directions I gave you, you'll pass a Walmart and a Denny's about five miles from the airport. Stop at the Denny's and get yourselves some breakfast. Then run into the Walmart and grab some clothes and toiletries for Ashley. Get some groceries, too—I haven't been home in nine months, so there won't be a thing to eat in the house."

"Can't we come back for some of that stuff later? We're going to be worn out by the time we get there."

"It's better if you do it now. The sun won't be up until almost six, so you want to kill time until at least five, before starting out of town. Any earlier than that, and you'll be driving the trail in the dark. That's a dangerous prospect for someone who doesn't know the road."

"If you say so."

"I'm not kidding. If it's still dark when you turn off the pavement, you park and wait until the sun comes up. That mountain trail is treacherous enough in the daylight."

"All right, point taken."

"Once you get to my place, just lay low. Don't go into town, and don't let anyone—and I mean *anyone*—know where you are. If you need to get hold of Jennifer or me, you can reach us through Sheriff Bill Cargill at the Nye County Sheriff's Office. There's no cell service at the house, but if you continue up the trail for another hundred yards or so, you'll reach a high spot where you can get a signal."

"Sounds like the setting for a horror film," said Tom.

Brent snorted. "Sounds like paradise."

"Do you know how to light a hot water heater?" asked Crocker.

"Yeah," said Tom, "I—"

Jennifer appeared in the door, carrying the red spandex dress and the black wig. Ashley stood beside her, hair a mess, looking a bit like a disheveled comic-book hero in the red, white, and blue jumpsuit.

Both women's makeup was streaked with tears.

Crocker locked eyes with Jennifer. "Is everything okay?"

"Can I have a hand down?" she asked, her voice barely rising above a whisper.

Brent moved toward the door, but Crocker stepped in front of him and offered his own hand. Jennifer accepted and climbed down without a word.

Tom looked at Ashley. "Are you all right?"

She turned and disappeared into the plane.

Brent, who looked thoroughly perplexed, glanced at Crocker and held open his arms as if to ask, *Now what?*

"I think you better just go," said Crocker. "The important thing right now is to get Tom and Ashley away from here."

Brent nodded and motioned Tom toward the door. "Let's go, Hollywood. You don't get a boost."

Tom hoisted himself into the plane.

From the doorway, he looked back at Crocker and Jennifer and said, "I...I guess we'll see y'all real soon."

Without waiting for a response, he turned and disappeared into the cabin.

Crocker wrapped an arm around Jennifer, who seemed not to notice.

"It sounds like they're playing me off," said Brent. "Ms. Williams, Mr. Crocker, it was a pleasure to make your acquaintances, and I wish you the best of luck in cleaning up whatever mess Hollywood and his girl left behind." He pulled himself up into the plane, turned, and added, "You might want to stand clear so we can take off."

With that, he closed the Plexiglas door and disappeared.

CHAPTER EIGHTEEN

A gentle squeeze to her hand brought Jennifer back to the present. She glanced to her right and saw Crocker standing beside her. She looked for the plane and saw its lights fading into the night sky. She vaguely remembered watching it make a hairpin turn and accelerate down the dirt strip. Now it was at least a mile away.

"Did you hear me?" asked Crocker.

She shook her head.

"I asked if you're cold."

"I don't know. I guess. A little." As the words passed her lips, she realized she was actually quite cold. The empty runway, lit only by the moon and the faint glow of lights from the tent city, offered no warmth and no protection from the desert wind.

Crocker released her hand and took off his suit jacket. "Here"—he draped the jacket over her shoulders—"this should help."

"Thanks."

Somewhere in the distance, a live band played a cover of a Rolling Stones tune. The music carried over the dry lake bed and mingled with the voices of revelers gathered in small pockets throughout the tent city. Jennifer listened to the chorus of sounds, peripherally aware of Crocker's fixed gaze.

"Are you going to tell me what happened between you and Ashley?" he asked.

"You should call Larry to come get us. We may not be safe out here."

After a long silence, Crocker said, "The phone is in the right inside pock- et of my jacket."

She stared at him for a couple of seconds before realizing he meant the jacket she was wearing. She opened it and reached into an empty pocket.

"The *right* pocket," he reiterated.

She reached into the other side, pulled out the phone, and handed it to him. Across the lake bed, the Rolling Stones tune came to an end, and the band, apparently beholden to no particular period or genre, launched into a Garth Brooks number.

"We seem to have a minor hiccup," said Crocker.

"Hiccup?"

"The phone is dead."

Jennifer processed his words slowly.

"It's an old phone," he added. "Using it to listen in on Tom's conversa- tion must have drained the battery."

"Does that mean we're stuck here?"

"Nah, we just need to find someone who'll let us use their phone."

She glanced at the rows of tents and RVs. "Fine. Let's go." She turned and walked toward the temporary Main Street.

"Hang on," said Crocker.

She stopped and looked back. "What?"

"I hate to be a... What's the nonracist equivalent of 'Indian giver'? Anyway, I hate to be one, but I'm going to need my jacket back."

"Why?"

Crocker held open his arms and waited.

After a long moment, she finally got his point. The pistol and other secu- rity items clipped to his belt didn't exactly invite hospitality.

She slipped off the jacket, tossed it to him, and resumed her walk toward the tent city. Her bare feet moved briskly over the smooth ground. She heard Crocker's hurried footsteps behind her.

He fell into step on her right. "I wish you'd talk to me."

She glanced at him but didn't speak. He carried the diaper bag, which she'd forgotten. They passed silently between rows of unlit tents and motor homes.

"Even if you don't want to tell me what's bothering you," he continued, "I wish you'd say something. You're kind of scaring me."

Jennifer searched for something to say, anything to get him off her back. Finally, she looked at him and asked, "What's a squid?"

"What?"

"Brent told you not to call him a squid."

"Oh," said Crocker, sounding a bit relieved that she had a logical reason for asking about cephalopods. "It's a derogatory term for someone in the navy."

"Used by the marines?"

"Primarily. The old joke is that marines call sailors squids because a squid is a lower form of marine life."

"Funny."

"I suppose."

"Why do you get embarrassed whenever someone asks about your military service?"

"What? No, I don't."

"Yes, you do. I thought maybe I imagined it the first time, when I asked about your tattoo, but you did it again when Brent asked if you were in the army. You answered like you were ashamed."

"I'm not ashamed. I just…I don't feel right claiming military service."

"Why? Weren't you in the military?"

"I was. For almost six months."

Jennifer waited for an explanation.

"When I graduated college, I found that nobody was hiring philosophy majors, so I joined the marines."

"Philosophy?"

"Yes." He hesitated as if expecting a follow-up question. "Anyway, I was well on my way to becoming a military policeman when I collapsed during a run and had to be hospitalized. The doctors diagnosed me with adult-onset asthma and sent me home."

"They kicked you out?"

"*Medical discharge.* The Cold War was over, Congress was hacking away at the DoD budget, and America had no use for a marine who might collapse on the battlefield."

"Do you still have asthma?"

"My chest sometimes tightens up when I work out. I keep an inhaler in my gym bag. It's no big deal."

"What did you do after you were discharged?"

"I came home and tried to get a job on a civilian police force. But every department I applied to took one look at my military record and disqualified me on medical grounds."

"So you got into instructing?"

"First, I spent a couple of years driving armored trucks in San Diego. Then I took a job at a private security firm in Salt Lake City. That's where I met Jeff Flitcraft. Jeff was a former member of the air force pistol team, and he shared my disdain for the antiquated training methods utilized by the military, most police forces, and, of course, the firm we worked for. We started developing our own training methods, and two years later we moved to Pahrump to start First Shot."

"I understand wanting to start your own business," she said, "but how the hell did your Realtor sell you on"—she waved an arm at the desert—"*this*?"

"It was a logistical decision. We wanted to be within sixty miles of an international airport, we saw the advantage of locating near a thriving tourism hub, and after putting up with the teetotalers in Utah, we both really liked the idea of living an hour west of Sin City."

Jennifer pictured Crocker in his late twenties, unleashed on the Las Vegas Strip after two years spent sipping near-beer within sight of the Mormon Tabernacle. It was almost enough to make her smile.

"There," said Crocker, pointing to a group of people huddled around a campfire beside a travel trailer. "One of them will have a phone."

The travel trailer looked to be at least two decades newer than the one Crocker had referred to as his winter home. A middle-aged man wearing baggy purple pants stood near the door, talking to a middle-aged woman in a maroon jumpsuit. On the ground, a young man and a young woman cuddled beside the fire, sipping bottles of imported beer. Both wore orange T-shirts emblazoned with GRAVITY RATS.

Crocker and Jennifer stopped in front of the campfire.

"You lost?" asked the female Gravity Rat.

"Not so much lost as stranded," replied Crocker with a friendly smile. "We need to call for a ride, but our phone is dead."

The lady in maroon turned and disappeared into the trailer.

"Did you come out to watch the jumping?" asked the male Gravity Rat.

"Actually," answered Jennifer, "we were visiting a friend."

"A skydiver?"

Jennifer nodded. "His name is Tom Blackwell."

No spark of recognition.

"If I'm not mistaken," said Crocker, "the other skydivers call him Hollywood."

"You're friends of Hollywood Tom?" asked the girl.

Before Crocker or Jennifer could reply, the trailer door opened, and the woman in maroon reappeared carrying a cell phone.

"They're friends of Hollywood Tom," said the man in the purple pants.

The maroon lady nodded and held out the phone to Crocker. "Are you trying to catch a ride back to Vegas?"

Crocker shook his head and accepted the phone. "Just back to the pavement."

The man in purple grinned. "Don't tell me you're trying to get this pretty lady back to one of those brothels before they charge you for an extra hour."

Jennifer took a deep breath and reminded herself that she was, in fact, wearing a wig and dress borrowed from a prostitute.

The maroon lady shot the man a dirty look, and his grin faded.

"Sorry," he said. "Only joking."

"Don't mind him," said the woman. "He was born without a filter between his brain and his mouth."

"The truth is," said Crocker, "I'm the one who works at a brothel, not her. I'm a security contractor for the Prickly Pear Ranch."

"If that's as far as you're going," said the man, "I can give you a ride."

The woman shot him another dirty look.

"Just to drop them off," he added.

"Would you mind?" asked Jennifer. "I hate to be a bother, but we're cold and tired, and it would sure be a big help."

"It's no problem," replied the woman. "We'll *both* take you."

The man frowned at the woman. "I said I wasn't going to stay."

"Just make room in the truck," she said.

The man grumbled and walked behind the trailer, disappearing into the shadows.

Crocker handed the unused phone back to the woman.

"Have a seat by the fire," she said. "It'll just take a minute to clear out the back of the truck."

The back? thought Jennifer as the woman followed the man behind the trailer.

Crocker dropped to the ground, showing little concern for his suit, and sat cross-legged in front of the fire. Jennifer moved slowly, more out of concern for the dress's short hemline than for the dress itself.

The young woman in the orange Gravity Rats T-shirt smiled at her. "I like your outfit."

"Thanks," said Jennifer. "I borrowed it from a friend."

"It's very sparkly."

"And very short." Jennifer kept her knees together and sat on her heels.

"Would either of you like a roasted marshmallow?" asked the young woman. "We made s'mores earlier. We're out of chocolate bars, but I think we still have a bag of marshmallows left."

Crocker smiled politely. "I'm fine, but thank you."

Jennifer was tempted—she hadn't eaten in hours—but worried that molten sugar wouldn't sit well on an empty stomach. "No, thank you."

The warmth of the fire was a welcome reprieve from the cool desert night. She inched forward on the hard ground and warmed her hands over the flames. "I can't remember the last time I sat in front of a campfire."

"That's a shame," said Crocker. "I build them all the time at my place in Colorado." He hesitated before adding, "Maybe you should come visit me sometime this summer."

Jennifer kept her eyes fixed on the fire.

"It's a beautiful place," he continued. "You've never seen so many stars."

Jennifer glanced around, looking at anything and everything but Crocker. Behind the trailer, a diesel engine roared to life.

"That must be our ride," she said, a bit too eager to change the topic.

Light flooded the small dirt street beside them as the old pickup turned out from behind the trailer and stopped a few feet away.

The woman in maroon leaned out the passenger-side window and hollered, "Hop in the back. We'll run you up to the pavement."

Crocker jumped to his feet and held out a hand for Jennifer.

She accepted the hand and glanced back at the young couple as she stood. "It was nice to meet you."

"You too," said the young woman.

Jennifer wanted to ask their names so that she could tell Tom, but she felt Crocker dragging her toward the truck. She waved and the young woman waved back.

Crocker lowered the tailgate and helped her into the bed of the pickup. When they were each seated on opposite wheel wells, he knocked on the rear window and gave the driver a thumbs-up.

The truck started forward. Jennifer crossed her arms and ducked down behind the cab to cut the wind chill.

"Here," said Crocker, removing his jacket. "I think I can take this off now."

Jennifer accepted the jacket and draped it over her shoulders. For the next couple of minutes, neither of them said a word. When they reached the edge of the tent city, the truck picked up speed.

She trembled under the jacket. "I miss the fire."

"There's one waiting for you in Colorado if you're interested. The offer is still on the table."

She looked away.

Crocker sighed. "I don't get it. Three hours ago, you and I... Now you won't even look at me. What did Ashley say that—"

"She said she was sorry!"

"What?"

"She said she was sorry for sleeping with Bryan."

"Your boss? I'm not sure I—"

"He came to our room looking for *me*. Do you understand now? He was looking for *me*! But I wasn't there. And he was drunk and lonely, and she was drunk and lonely, and..."

Crocker was silent.

Jennifer took a deep breath. "And the guy I was supposed to live happily ever after with ended up sleeping with my twenty-three-year-old protégée instead."

Crocker seemed dumbfounded.

Jennifer wiped her eyes. "He was supposed to be with me, but he slept with her, and now he's dead. And I don't know if I'm supposed to be mad at him for sleeping with her or at her for sleeping with him or at myself for overreacting and running off in the middle of the night and getting him killed."

Crocker opened his mouth, hesitated, then closed it.

"I would have been fine," she continued, "just thinking I'd imagined the connection with him. Just believing she'd slept with him without knowing how I felt about him. Just assuming it was never meant to be. But now I'm left thinking that it *was* meant to be and that he or she or I or all three of us screwed it up."

Crocker opened his mouth again. Then he closed it again.

"And on top of all that," she said, "I'm left trying to figure out how I feel about you. You're so goddamned persistent, and I can't tell if I have real feelings for you or if what I'm feeling is just my mind's way of blocking out all the fear and pain I should be feeling."

The rough dirt road gave way to smooth asphalt. Jennifer glanced up, wiping tears from her eyes, and saw the giant neon woman straddling the giant neon cactus, ahead on their right.

A moment later, the truck pulled into the Prickly Pear parking lot and stopped.

The woman in maroon leaned out the passenger-side window and yelled, "All ashore who's going ashore."

Jennifer felt as though she were viewing the world through the wrong end of a telescope. From a distance, she watched Crocker crawl out of the pickup, open the tailgate, and offer his hand. With great effort, she willed herself to accept the hand and climb out of the truck.

When the tailgate was shut, the woman in maroon yelled, "You two have a good night. Tell Hollywood we said hi."

Tell Hollywood who *said hi?* thought Jennifer as the truck pulled away.

"Jennifer," called Crocker.

Some part of her mind registered that this was at least the second time he'd called her name.

"Uh-huh?" she replied.

"Why don't I drop you at the Champagne Suite before I head over to Larry's cabin? I'll tell him and Scarlett you weren't feeling well and went to bed."

Bed sounded good. Very good.

But a drink sounded better.

"No," she said, "I'll make an appearance. C'mon."

She took off across the parking lot, ignoring the rocky asphalt digging into her feet. She heard Crocker's footsteps behind her as she marched around the outside of the main building and made her way past the other cabins.

She made no effort to walk fast, but by the time she reached Larry's front door, Crocker lagged at least ten yards behind. She gave three hard knocks and waited.

Crocker caught up to her just as the door opened. Scarlett stood in the entry hall, wearing the same silk kimono and Japanese slippers she'd worn at the brainstorming session earlier that day. She nodded to her guests, turned, and retreated into the cabin.

"After you," said Crocker.

Jennifer followed Scarlett into the living room, where Larry waited in his armchair. Across from him, on the couch where Jennifer and Crocker had sat a few hours before, rested a distinguished-looking gentleman of perhaps sixty-five.

I do not have the energy to make small talk with one of Larry's high rollers, thought Jennifer.

Crocker's fingers dug into her shoulder, bringing her to an abrupt halt.

The well-dressed gentleman smiled under his thick gray beard and rose to his feet. "Ms. Williams, Mr. Crocker," he said, his Eastern European accent faint but unmistakable, *"Ochen' priyatno."*

Jennifer's blood ran cold as she felt Crocker pull her close. When she found her voice, it was a harsh whisper. "Is that one of Vladimir Dudka's men?"

"No," replied Crocker. "That *is* Vladimir Dudka."

CHAPTER NINETEEN

Crocker glimpsed the muzzle of a gun to his left and froze in place, listening for either a command or a gunshot.

Over his right shoulder, a man with a thick Eastern European accent said, "Leave it in the holster."

Crocker looked down and saw his own fingers wrapped around the grip of his sidearm. He had no memory of reaching for it—a lifetime of training had almost gotten him killed. Moving in slow motion, he let go of the pistol and raised his hands.

He looked to his left and saw a muscular, clean-shaven man of about fifty holding a small Makarov handgun. The man stood several feet away, suggesting at least some formal training. A street thug would have pressed the gun in close, for dramatic effect.

Crocker glanced over his right shoulder and saw that the man with the accent was at least twenty years younger. The younger man wasn't holding a gun, but Crocker had little doubt there was one concealed somewhere beneath the man's button-down shirt.

Maintaining the pleasant tone of his greeting, Dudka said, "Mr. Crocker, if you'd be so good as to let Sasha disarm you, my dear friend Ilya won't have to shoot you in the face."

Crocker gave a slow nod.

The younger man stepped forward and unholstered Crocker's gun. When he had the pistol in hand, he pulled the diaper bag from Crocker's shoulder and took a step back. He dropped the bag on the floor and unloaded the gun with surprising speed. When he was done, he shoved the empty weapon into the waistband of his pants and returned to Crocker's side.

He plucked the radio and other items from Crocker's belt and pockets and tossed them one at a time onto the floor beside the diaper bag. When the belt was empty, he wrapped his hands around Crocker's left ankle and frisked up one leg and down the other. He then stood and frisked Crocker's waistband and shirt.

Apparently satisfied that he'd relieved Crocker of anything that might pose a threat, Sasha turned and placed his hands on Jennifer's shoulders. She flinched but maintained her composure. He removed the suit jacket and checked the pockets. He found Vegas's phone, inspected it, and stuffed it into his hip pocket. When he'd finished searching the jacket, he tossed it onto the pile of security tools lying next to the diaper bag. After a quick visual inspection of Jennifer's outfit, he knelt, wrapped his fingers around one of her bare thighs, and slid his hands up under the hem of her gold sequined dress.

Jennifer cringed, and Crocker opened his mouth to protest, but Dudka spoke first.

"Sasha, this is not a recreational activity. If there were a gun under that dress, I'd be able to see it from here."

Sasha released Jennifer's thigh and, in his heavy accent, said, "Sorry, boss." He rose to his feet. "They're clean."

"Wonderful," said Dudka with a smile. "Now we can all be friends."

Crocker lowered his hands and immediately felt Jennifer's fingers dig into his forearm. She stared at him with eyes that pleaded for answers he didn't have.

Dudka waved them forward. "Let's have a seat, shall we?"

Crocker led Jennifer, who moved as though her joints had rusted over, into the sitting area.

Dudka returned to his seat on the couch and motioned for the two of them to sit on the fireplace hearth between him and Larry. As they sat, Crocker cast a near-fatal glance at Larry.

Larry recoiled. "Don't look at me, pal." He cocked his head toward the kitchen door, where Scarlett stood sipping a bottle of Miller Light. "She blindsided both of us."

Jennifer's eyes locked onto the redhead. "You?"

"What?" asked Scarlett. "You don't think the dumb hooker can come up with a plan of her own?" She walked to the couch and sat beside Dudka.

Dudka laughed. "You know what they say about a woman scorned."

Jennifer's gaze remained fixed on Scarlett. "This is who you were texting in the limo, isn't it?" She nodded toward Dudka. "The client who canceled?"

Dudka laughed again. "That would be young Sasha here. Apparently, he and Ms. Scarlett have a monthly arrangement." He glanced at Scarlett. "A poor investment if you ask me, but such is the nature of youth."

Scarlett scowled.

"Mr. Dudka," interjected Larry, "you may not be aware of this, but I have friends in Chicago who—"

Dudka erupted in laughter. "I know all about your friends, Mr. Chappell. I'm not afraid of Cosa Nostra."

Larry's eyes widened.

Dudka continued, "I dealt with the Italians twenty years ago when they swooped into Russia hoping to pick at the carcass of the Soviet Union. We sent those potbellied bankers crawling back to their seaside villas with their tails between their legs."

Scarlett giggled. "So much for being connected, huh, Lare-Bear?"

Such intense anger flashed in Larry's eyes that Crocker felt certain his friend was about to reach out and strike the young woman. Then, just as quickly, the anger faded, and Crocker saw the pained eyes of a lover betrayed.

Dudka went on: "I'm not intimidated by men who've spent their lives gorging on wine and pasta. If you want to impress me, make some friends who've known hunger."

Jennifer's voice shook. "So you're going to...what? Take your revenge on us? Bury us in the desert? We're not the ones who lost your money at the blackjack tables. We're not the ones—"

"Ms. Williams," interrupted Dudka, his voice calm, "I'm much less concerned with assigning blame than with retrieving my eight hundred thousand dollars."

"Take it up with the Nye County Sheriff's Office," said Crocker. "I don't know what Scarlett told you, but we don't have your money. We never did."

"She told me as much. She also told me you have a plan to replace it."

"What?" Crocker looked to Scarlett for an explanation.

She smiled. "Five hundred players checking in over the course of five hours, a tournament room located nowhere near the vault, and a million dollars sitting in a glass safe in the center of the gaming floor."

♦ ♦ ♦

Scarlett's recital of Crocker's words hung in the air.

Jennifer's mind scrambled to arrange the pieces of the puzzle. "You're talking about the poker tournament—La Tournament or whatever it's called?"

"Le Tournoi," said Crocker. "Scarlett, what the hell have you gotten us into?"

"She's offered you—all of us—a way out of this mess," said Dudka.

"You can't seriously expect me to rob a Las Vegas casino. You may be greedy and corrupt, but you're not stupid."

"It's neither greed nor stupidity, Mr. Crocker. It's necessity. I'm a businessman, and as such, I have overhead to cover and, more significantly, partners to compensate. A loss of this magnitude is simply unacceptable."

"If you're a businessman," said Jennifer, "write it off."

Dudka snorted. "Thanks to our local economy, I'm drowning in write-offs—two failed restaurants, an abandoned real estate development, and a winery that consistently operates at a loss. But the IRS doesn't offer a deduction for money seized in a botched robbery." He hesitated. "And my partners don't accept excuses in lieu of cash."

Jennifer knew plenty of people who'd lost their shirts on botched real estate developments, but she was astonished that someone could so effortlessly traverse the line separating legitimate business ventures and criminal endeavors.

Beside her, Crocker shifted uncomfortably on the stone hearth. "How exactly do you expect me to steal eight hundred thousand dollars from Le Tournoi?"

Dudka grinned. "Any way you can."

"And if I refuse? Do I end up a headless, limbless corpse like your three couriers who got arrested in California?"

Dudka's grin faded; his eyes narrowed. "If you refuse, Sasha and Ilya will disperse your remains across twenty thousand square miles of desert, and I'll recoup some small fraction of my loss by selling Ms. Williams to one of my clients overseas."

Jennifer emitted a shallow gasp.

Dudka turned and looked her over. "Don't take this personally, dear, but your young blond friend would have fetched a much better price. You're pretty enough, but you have some—what's the term?—*city miles* on you."

Jennifer winced, both at the threat of being sold as a sex slave and the suggestion that she was too old to fetch a good price. She opened her mouth to tell him to go fuck himself, but a hiss of static from the intercom box near the door preempted her.

Sasha pivoted toward the source of the noise and placed one hand atop a small bulge at the back of his shirt.

"Hey, guys," crackled Vegas's girlish voice over the intercom. "Anybody there?"

Dudka looked at Scarlett. "Take care of it."

She walked to the intercom and pressed the talk button. "What do you want, Vegas?"

The box hissed again. "Are Matt and Jennifer back yet? I want to stop by and pick up my phone and wigs and things before I join the lineup."

"Sorry, they're not back yet."

"Can I come wait for them with you guys? I really need my stuff."

"Tell her you'll bring it to her," said Dudka.

Scarlett pressed the button. "Larry and I are kind of...umm...busy right now, but as soon as Matt and Jennifer get back, I'll grab your stuff and run it down to you. Okay?"

"Busy, huh?" Vegas giggled. "Okay, I guess that'll work. Just don't take too long. None of my regulars can reach me if I don't have my phone."

Scarlett returned to the couch and reclaimed her seat beside Dudka.

"Should this concern me?" he asked.

"Nah. Vegas just wants that phone Sasha found, plus the wigs and dresses she loaned Jennifer."

"Fine. Take them to her."

"Now?"

"Yes, before she gets impatient and comes looking for them."

Scarlett sighed and stood again. "Sasha, hand me that ugly-ass bag you took."

He picked up the diaper bag and tossed it to her.

"Hey!" She reacted just in time to catch it. "I said *hand* it to me."

He shrugged.

Scarlett turned to Jennifer. "I need those too."

"Need what?" asked Jennifer.

"The wig and dress. Take 'em off."

Jennifer recoiled. "Fuck you. I'm not taking off my dress."

Scarlett looked back at Sasha. "Get the dress."

He took a step toward Jennifer, who felt the same panic she'd felt at the Placer Gold truck stop.

"No!" she screamed.

Crocker jumped to his feet and stepped between Sasha and Jennifer. Ilya raised the Makarov and pointed it at him.

Crocker looked at Dudka and said, "If you want my cooperation, you'll let her change in the bathroom."

Nobody moved or spoke. Ilya kept his gun trained on Crocker's head. Dudka seemed lost in thought.

Finally, the Russian mob boss looked at Jennifer and asked, "You have something else to wear?"

Jennifer nodded and pointed to the diaper bag. "In there."

Dudka turned to Sasha. "Check the bag. Make sure she doesn't have a phone or a weapon."

Sasha retrieved the bag from Scarlett and began sifting through the compartments.

Dudka continued, "Ms. Williams, I will give you exactly three minutes in the toilet. You will leave the door cracked. If you take longer than that, I'll send in Sasha to deal with you as he sees fit."

Jennifer nodded, her heart still pounding from the threat of having her clothes ripped off.

Dudka turned to Scarlett and added, "You get dressed too. I intend to move this party someplace I can control."

Scarlett offered a coquettish smile. "Whatever you say." She untied the kimono and let it slide from her shoulders and drop to her feet. Completely naked, she kicked the silk garment to the side and whispered, "Be right back."

Crocker's and Sasha's eyes followed the nubile young woman as she jiggled her way across the living room and into what Jennifer assumed must have been the master bedroom.

Dudka's gaze remained fixed on his two hostages. "Sasha, does that satchel contain anything that should concern me?"

"*Nyet*," replied Sasha as he palmed a handful of condoms into the front pocket of his jeans. "Clothes. Makeup. A wig. Rubbers."

Dudka nodded and turned to Larry. "Where is the toilet?"

Larry pointed to a door near the entryway. "There."

Dudka turned back to Sasha. "Give her the bag, and check the toilet."

Sasha tossed the bag at Jennifer's feet and marched off toward the bathroom.

Dudka glanced back at Jennifer and nodded toward the bag. She leaned forward and grabbed it.

The sound of drawers and cabinets being yanked open and slammed shut echoed from the bathroom. A moment later, Sasha emerged carrying a pair of styling shears and a nail file.

"Clean," he said.

Dudka checked an expensive-looking wristwatch. "Ms. Williams, your time starts...now."

For a brief moment, Jennifer thought he was joking. When she realized he wasn't, she jumped to her feet and ran toward the bathroom.

Dudka added, "Please be so kind as to leave the door cracked a few inches. If Sasha hears anything out of the ordinary, he has my permission to conduct as thorough an investigation as he sees fit."

Once inside the bathroom, it took all Jennifer's willpower not to slam the door and lock it behind her. Her every instinct told her to put as many barriers as she could between herself and Vladimir Dudka's goons.

She summoned her self-control and left a half-inch crack between the door and the jamb. Almost immediately the door pressed back against her hand, opening an extra three inches.

"Like this," said Sasha as he pushed from the other side.

"Okay, okay!" pleaded Jennifer, not wanting him to open the door any farther.

Ever cognizant of the ticking clock, she dropped the diaper bag on the counter and dug through it. For the moment, she was less interested in finding her clothes than in finding anything Sasha might have overlooked, anything that might help her and Crocker.

She pulled out useless item after useless item—her uncomfortable stiletto heels, the clothes and wig Ashley had worn, her overpriced little black dress, the extra pair of panties Tom had bought, Vegas's makeup kit, a pack of tissues—nothing that was going to save the day. She checked the side pocket and found that Sasha had cleaned out the stash of condoms, leaving only a bottle of K-Y Liquid and a couple of Viagra tablets.

Panic began to set in. If she and Crocker couldn't find some way to escape before Dudka's men dragged them off to God knew where, they might never be heard from again.

"Two minutes," called Dudka from the living room.

Does he mean that I have two minutes or that I've used two minutes? wondered Jennifer, her panic level rising.

With no time to waste, she pulled the bright red wig from her head, stripping bobby pins from her hair. She dropped the wig onto the counter and, stretching her right arm to its limit, yanked down the zipper on the gold sequined dress. She reached for the hem of the dress and, finding it even higher than she remembered, pulled the whole thing up over her head.

As she dropped the dress onto the counter, she saw a small white card flutter to the ground. She knelt and picked it up.

It was Sheriff Cargill's business card, the one Crocker had given her atop the Stratosphere. She flipped it over and saw the handwritten phone number for FBI special agent Bruce Eastland.

If only I had a phone.

That thought gave way to another. Jennifer dropped the card onto the counter and dug through the pile of items she'd removed from the diaper bag.

♦ ♦ ♦

Sasha eyed the bathroom door as if ready to pounce. Crocker prayed Jennifer wouldn't try anything desperate.

To his left, Ilya stood with his pistol pointed low, at the ready. Crocker studied the gun out of the corner of his eye and noticed that the muzzle end was thicker and rounder than that of a standard Makarov. He'd heard that select units of the Soviet special forces were issued Makarovs equipped with integrated silencers, but those guns were ghosts, something one expected to find displayed in a museum, not carried by a mob enforcer.

It occurred to him that he hadn't heard Ilya speak. It was possible the man didn't speak English. Knowing for sure could prove to be of vital strategic importance.

He caught Ilya's eye and asked, "You were Spetsnaz, weren't you?"

Ilya watched Crocker in silence. Finally, he smiled and, in a posh English accent, replied, "No, Mr. Crocker, my talents lie elsewhere."

Both Ilya and Dudka burst into laughter as Crocker stared in disbelief.

The bedroom door swung open, and Scarlett emerged wearing a pink jogging suit. She glanced around and asked, "Is the bitch done changing?"

Larry pivoted in his chair and replied, "Darling, there is only one bitch in this house, and right now she's wearing the velour tracksuit I bought her."

Scarlett smiled and walked to the couch.

Dudka looked at his watch and said, "Time is up. Get her out here."

Sasha gave the bathroom door a shove. It swung open just as Jennifer pulled the little black dress down over her hips.

Sasha filled the doorway, blocking her exit. The two of them stood almost nose to nose.

Jennifer turned to her left and raised her right arm. "Zip me."

The young man glanced around as if suspecting a trap. When he'd apparently concluded that the dress wasn't wired to explode, he reached forward, grabbed the zipper, and jerked it violently upward.

"Thanks." She bent down to put on her high heels.

Sasha grabbed the packed diaper bag from the counter.

"Search every pocket of that thing," said Dudka. "Make sure she didn't slip a note into it. Then give it and the phone to Ms. Scarlett to deliver to her friend."

"*Khorosho.*" Sasha knelt to inspect the bag.

"Once the bag is delivered, you and Ms. Scarlett follow in Mr. Chappell's car. His absence will seem less suspicious if his car is gone." Dudka pointed to Crocker's pile of security items lying on the floor. "Don't forget all of that."

"*Khorosho.*"

Crocker tried to remember if his alma mater had offered Russian as a foreign language. At the moment, his four semesters of Latin were not coming in handy.

Dudka scanned the room and said, "Ilyusha, would you be so good as to ask Jesse to pull the van up front? It's time to go."

CHAPTER TWENTY

The back of the cargo van smelled like a gym locker room. There were no windows and no seats, just worn carpet stained with God knew what. Jennifer thought she detected a hint of urine beneath the overpowering stench of sweat.

Squeezed between Crocker and Larry, she felt almost claustrophobic. The three prisoners rode with their backs against the front bulkhead, facing rearward. Across from them, Ilya leaned against the rear cargo door, his eyes alert, his gun at the ready.

Jennifer wasn't sure how long they'd been on the road—at least thirty minutes. She glanced once again at Crocker, hoping for a bit of reassurance, but his eyes were still shut.

As soon as they'd turned out of the Prickly Pear parking lot, Crocker had closed his eyes and disappeared into his own world. His occasional head tilts—slow and deliberate—were the only indication he wasn't asleep.

After a couple of failed attempts to coax information from Ilya, Larry had settled for staring at the floor. For the past twenty-some-odd minutes, they'd ridden in silence.

The van slowed, made a sharp turn to the right, and eased to a stop. Jennifer heard a series of hums and creaks that she recognized as the sound of a garage door closing.

Crocker opened his eyes. "Is this it?"

Ilya smiled and, in his incongruous English accent, replied, "Home sweet home."

The sound of the garage door ceased, and Ilya turned toward the rear of the van just as the cargo door swung open. Outside, Dudka waited beside a toadlike little man who held the largest handgun Jennifer had ever seen.

Dudka surveyed the prisoners and said, "Jesse, help Ilya escort the men to the basement. Make sure they're secure; then come help my team load the van."

In a raspy voice, clearly American, the rotund man replied, "Whatever you say, boss."

"Ilyusha, stay with the men until Sasha returns; then come find me. I'll be in the bedroom with Ms. Williams."

Jennifer glanced at Crocker, her eyes screaming, *THE BEDROOM?*

Crocker didn't respond, and Jennifer prayed he hadn't taken leave of his senses.

Dudka extended a hand into the van. "Shall we?"

She glanced at Larry. His eyes conveyed at least some hint of sympathy. Reluctantly, she crawled forward, accepted Dudka's outstretched hand, and let him help her out of the van.

To her surprise, she found herself standing in a standard two-car garage containing two identical white vans. She'd expected something a bit more elaborate, perhaps a row of expensive sports cars or a wall of torture implements.

Dudka positioned himself behind her and pointed to a door in the corner of the garage. "This way."

She walked to the door and glanced back at Dudka.

"You can open it," he said. "The bedroom is to your left, at the end of the hall."

She turned the knob and gave a slow push. The door opened, and she stepped into what looked like a standard suburban home. To her right was a living room that might have been lifted from one of the hundreds of ranch-style homes she'd shown during her brief stint as a residential Realtor. To her left was a short hallway with two open doors on the right and a closed one at the far end.

She turned down the hallway and moved slowly toward the far door. She could hear Dudka's footsteps a couple of paces behind her.

She approached the first open door and recognized the foul stench of a well-used bathroom. A quick glance as she passed confirmed that it had not been cleaned in a very long time.

As she approached the second door, the smell of the bathroom gave way to a caustic industrial smell. Glancing inside, she saw a four-poster bed, atop which rested a pile of guns. Two large men in sleeveless shirts sat on the once-white bedspread, which was now ragged with holes and stained with splotches of dark gray, cleaning a pair of military-style rifles.

Jennifer recalled once seeing a news report about a police raid on a Dallas home that had been found to contain a meth lab. The neighbors interviewed for the story had expressed shock and outrage that their quiet middle-class subdivision could play host to a drug lab. She wondered what the residents of this neighborhood would think if they knew they were living next to a safe house for the Russian mob.

She reached the closed door at the end of the hallway, placed a hand on the knob, and hesitated. From somewhere far behind her, she heard the toadlike little American barking orders at Crocker and Larry as he led them to the basement.

She shuddered to think what might be in the basement. Still, she wished she were going with them.

A hand settled onto her right shoulder. She almost screamed.

"It's unlocked," said Dudka.

She turned the knob, and the door opened to a tastefully adorned but horribly unkempt master bedroom. Everything in this house needed a good scrubbing.

As she took a step forward, she glanced over her shoulder at Dudka.

"On the bed, please," he said.

In the center of the room, a king-size bed with a wrought iron frame was topped by a tangle of soiled sheets.

Soiled with what? she thought as she approached the foul mess.

She saw a small love seat across from the bed and pointed to it. "Couldn't I just sit on—"

"The bed," he repeated.

She walked to the bed, placed a steadying hand on the ornate iron footboard, and turned toward Dudka as she sat.

He pointed to the center of the bed and said, "Lie down."

She thought briefly about lunging forward and running at him with all her strength. If he was slow to react, she might knock him to the ground and make it into the hallway. But would she make it past the two goons cleaning machine guns? Who else might she encounter before she found an open door?

She thought about screaming. She might attract the attention of a neighbor, but how long would Dudka let her scream before striking her or... worse?

Her arms shaking, she pushed herself back onto the bed. As she slid across the sheets, which she now saw were stained with blood and any number of unidentified bodily fluids, her eyes came to rest on the footboard. She froze.

Dangling from the ornate metalwork were two pairs of handcuffs, spaced roughly three feet apart.

She tried to think of something to say—a plea she could make, a deal she could offer, anything that might persuade her captor to change course.

As the wheels turned inside her head, she watched Dudka walk to the edge of the bed.

You can't let him cuff you, she told herself.

His left hand reached out and grabbed her right leg.

If you let him chain you to the bed, you'll be out of options. You'll have no chance of escape.

His right hand found the nearest handcuff.

Whatever you're going to do, you have to do it n—

The cuff sounded like a gunshot as it snapped shut around her ankle.

She stared at the second cuff, three feet to the left, and realized there was no longer any point in resisting. No matter how hard she fought, she'd never break free of that first handcuff. She glanced over her shoulder and, as she expected, saw a pair of handcuffs hanging from each corner of the headboard.

Conceding defeat, she placed her left foot in front of the second cuff and said, "Please don't fasten this one quite so tight."

Dudka chuckled.

Of course, she thought. *Making the cuffs too tight is part of the fun.*

With a smile, he said, "I appreciate your cooperation, Ms. Williams, but I really don't think there is any need for the other cuffs." He pointed to her shackled ankle. "This should keep you from going anywhere."

◆ ◆ ◆

Crocker leaned against the narrow support column and waited patiently as the squat little American with the sandpaper voice cuffed his hands behind him. A few feet to his left, Larry stood against an identical column, his hands already cuffed behind him.

We look like we're awaiting a firing squad, thought Crocker.

Of course, there was no firing squad before him, just a middle-aged gangster resting at the foot of the stairs. Even lounging against the basement steps, Ilya looked as alert as ever. He wore the same thousand-yard stare Crocker had seen a dozen or so times over the years. Something in those eyes suggested Ilya might have actually been part of a firing squad or two.

Crocker felt a chill along his spine and reassured himself that Dudka's goons wouldn't touch him until he'd stolen—or at least tried to steal—the money from the tournament.

And Jennifer? Will they extend her the same courtesy?

He did his best to push the thought from his mind. Focusing on the what-ifs wasn't going to get him out of this basement, and it wasn't going to help Jennifer or Larry. He needed a plan.

Behind him, the fat American finished with the handcuffs. Crocker caught a strong whiff of cigarettes and body odor as the unpleasant little man, now breathing heavily, passed by and disappeared up the stairs. A few seconds later, the door at the top of the stairs slammed shut.

Crocker glanced over his shoulder at Larry, then back at Ilya. Nobody spoke. The basement was eerily quiet. He slid down the support column and lowered himself into a sitting position. A moment later, he heard Larry do the same.

The concrete floor and cinder-block walls, coupled with the dim lighting, created a dungeonlike atmosphere. It occurred to Crocker that the basement might be soundproof. Another chill ran down his spine.

Stop psyching yourself out, and concentrate on what you know, he thought. *What do I know?*

He knew that basements were not and had never been a common feature in Southern Nevada homes. He'd seen only three or four in all his years in the area.

He knew that, despite the half-hour drive from the Prickly Pear, they'd traveled no more than fifteen or twenty miles in the van. His intense focus on the number and direction of turns had failed him somewhere along the route—according to his mental map, they should have been in the middle of the desert, nowhere near the type of tract home in which he now found himself—but he distinctly remembered one stretch in which they'd made three lefts, four rights, and three lefts, in that order. The driver had gone to a lot of trouble to disguise a couple of right turns.

They hadn't traveled very far, and they hadn't started up any mountain passes—the incline would have been unmistakable. That meant they were in one of the few basements in the Pahrump Valley. If he could pass a message to one of the other security guards at the tournament, this information would give the authorities a starting point for a search. He thought it might be possible for the FBI to search all the Pahrump basements in a matter of hours.

The plan had only one flaw.

Once I hand over the stolen money, we'll be dead in a matter of minutes.

♦ ♦ ♦

The lock on the bedroom door made two loud clicking noises. Jennifer had just enough time to stop fiddling with her shackled foot and lie back before the door swung open. Dudka entered carrying a small tray of food.

"It seems," he said, "that my men haven't been to the market in quite some time, but I found a few items that look as though they're probably safe to eat." He set the tray, which was loaded with crackers, cubes of cheese, slices of some sort of dry salami, and two small Dixie cups of what appeared to be tap water, on the corner of the bed. "I'm sure this no more lives up to your standards than it does mine, but perhaps we can make do for now."

His mock congeniality made the hair stand up on the back of Jennifer's neck. She wanted to tell the patronizing son of a bitch to go fuck himself, but instead, she forced herself to mutter a soft, "Thank you."

He set about piling a cracker with meat and cheese. "What kind of host would I be if I didn't feed you?"

It occurred to Jennifer that she hadn't had a real meal in well over twenty-four hours. Aside from a few bites of the sandwich Vegas had brought her, she hadn't eaten anything since leaving the fancy steak house where she and the rest of the New Wave staff had gorged themselves at the company's expense. She recalled Bryan's toast—congratulating everyone on a productive first day—and the way he'd winked at her as everyone clinked glasses. Now she was sitting across from the man who'd had him killed.

"Aren't you hungry?" asked Dudka.

Jennifer realized he was holding out a cracker loaded with salami and cubes of cheese. She reached forward and took it. "Thank you."

"I really do apologize for the meager spread," he said as she took a bite of the cracker. "My men are not particularly domestic, as you can probably tell from the state of this room."

Jennifer looked around as she chewed. Her gaze fell on the stained sheets, and she gagged, almost choking on the bite of cracker. She grabbed one of the Dixie cups and drained half the liquid in one swallow. The drink succeeded in washing down the bite of cracker but burned her throat in a way she hadn't expected. She coughed up a mouthful of what smelled like nail polish remover.

Dudka patted her on the back like a concerned friend. "My dear, I'm so sorry. I should have warned you it's vodka—some of Russia's best, though I fear the quality may have been lost on you."

She waved him off and, as she got the coughing under control, said, "It's fine. I just wasn't expecting it."

Dudka stood. "Let me see if I can find you some water."

Jennifer nodded, still trying to catch her breath. "I'd appreciate that."

He exited through the door. She heard him lock it behind him.

She glanced at the cup in her hand. She was in a bad place with bad people, and she needed something to steady her nerves. She swallowed the rest of the ice-cold vodka and set the empty paper cup on the tray.

Feeling less shaky, she returned her attention to the handcuff shackled to her right leg. It looked like the real deal, not some novelty item from a sex shop. It wasn't something she could pick with a hairpin.

She looked at the unused handcuff a few feet to the left and at the two hanging from the corners of the headboard. She imagined that with all four cuffs in use, her limbs would be pulled taut, holding her spread-eagled on her back. She looked once again at the stains on the sheets and mustered all her willpower to swallow the scream welling inside her.

Somewhere deep in the Nevada desert, she'd stumbled into the seventh level of hell.

She heard the turning of the dead bolt and tried to regain her composure as the door opened.

Dudka entered carrying a soda can. "My men seem to be out of bottled water. Would you settle for a Coca-Cola?"

She debated asking for tap water but decided not to press her luck. "Sure. That'll be fine."

Dudka handed her the Coke and took a seat on the corner of the bed.

Jennifer sipped the soda. When she'd washed the taste of vodka from her mouth, she lowered the can. "I take it you don't spend much time here?"

"Not when I can help it." He chuckled. "My men are lousy housekeepers, and the fringe benefits aren't to my liking."

Without pausing to consider her words or the possible repercussions, Jennifer replied, "Really? Who doesn't enjoy a little rape every now and then?"

Dudka stared deep into her eyes. "You judge something you couldn't possibly understand. You've lived your whole life in one tiny, affluent corner of the globe, yet you presume to know how the world works."

"I know how sex trafficking works. I know how this bed is meant to work. When you and your men are too broke or too lazy to pay for sex—because God knows no woman would give it to you for free—you drag in some poor girl from the Second or Third World and prove what big men you are by chaining her to this bed and—"

"Ms. Williams," Dudka interrupted, "I won't pretend that my employees are gentlemen, but the demands of their work require that I allow them a bit of latitude. Like a wine distributor who overlooks the occasional opened case, I turn a blind eye when, from time to time, my men wish to sample the merchandise."

The callousness of his words left Jennifer speechless.

"But," he continued, "don't confuse me with my men. I was a dedicated soldier until the West corrupted the Soviet way of life, and I fought for the new Russia until I was betrayed by ambitious comrades whom I mistook for friends. Now I am a simple rancher. I buy livestock from poor countries and sell it to rich countries."

Jennifer's eyes widened.

Dudka said, "You come from Texas. You must have seen cattle grazing."

Still processing the fact that Dudka knew where she was from, Jennifer gave a slow nod.

Dudka continued, "Those cattle have more promising futures than do the women we find in the squalor of places you couldn't point to on a map—countries that have been forgotten by the United Nations, regions the Red Cross planes won't even fly over. So we offer those women something better. And they come *willingly*."

Jennifer shook her shackled foot, rattling the handcuff. "You call this 'willing'?"

"Sometimes they have buyer's remorse. Sometimes they have to be taught how the game is played. But there is no turning back. They entered a binding agreement the moment they stepped into a truck or a train car with one of our recruiters. My investors incur considerable expense bringing the women to this country, and the men who serve me here have no tolerance for a whore who waits until her feet touch the land of the free to suddenly have second thoughts about holding up her end of the bargain."

Jennifer shuddered at the realization that Dudka believed what he was saying. "And what about Ashley? What about the twenty-three-year-old American girl you kidnapped? She wasn't from some Third World slum. She didn't come willingly. How does your warped mind justify that?"

"The same way I'll justify what I do to you if Mr. Crocker doesn't come through for us." Dudka's tone lacked even a hint of emotion. "In the end, this business, like any other, is all about the bottom line."

◆ ◆ ◆

Crocker sat with his eyes closed, retracing the van's path in his mind, trying to figure out where his calculations had gone wrong. The creak of a door and the sound of footsteps interrupted his train of thought.

He opened his eyes just as Sasha and Scarlett reached the bottom of the stairs. Ilya rose to his feet and let them pass. Against the gloom of the empty basement, Scarlett's pink jogging suit and red hair stood out like a pair of road flares.

"Hiya, guys," she said with a grin. "Miss me?"

Neither Crocker nor Larry responded.

Ilya whispered something into Sasha's ear, then disappeared up the stairs.

Sasha stepped forward and inspected the two prisoners. "It seems," he said in his thick Russian accent, "that Scarlett and I are to be your babysitters for the time being. I trust we will all get along." He leaned down so that his face was only a couple of feet from Crocker's. "No heroics from you, mister hero. Okay? Not unless you want me to pay a visit to your girlfriend upstairs. Understand?"

Crocker nodded.

"Good." Sasha walked to the staircase and took Ilya's vacated seat on the first step. "We will be like happy family."

Despite himself, Crocker replied, "And all happy families are alike—right, Sasha?"

Sasha and Scarlett stared blankly.

Larry snorted—almost a laugh but not quite. "Wrong crowd, Crocker."

Scarlett took a step closer to the two hostages. "What is that supposed to mean?"

"It means," replied Larry, "that if Crocker's joke had been any farther over your head, they would have seen it upstairs."

Her face grew angry. "What joke?"

Crocker hoped that Larry would just let it go. *Save the jilted-lover routine until you're not handcuffed to a column.*

Larry laughed out loud. "You wouldn't get it even if I explained it. It's a reference to a book that doesn't have any pictures."

Crocker saw the fire in her eyes and wished Larry would shut up. He thought Larry was about to catch a slap across the face, but instead, Scarlett turned and walked to Sasha. She leaned down and whispered in the Russian's ear.

Sasha laughed and nodded.

As the young gangster rose to his feet, Scarlett turned and smiled at the two hostages. "You two don't mind if Sasha and I kill a little time while we wait for Ilya, do you?"

Crocker saw where this was going. What Scarlett had in mind was intended to sting Larry worse than a slap across the face. In one swift motion, she dropped her pink sweatpants to the ground and stepped out of them. Crocker was certain no one in the room was surprised to see she wasn't wearing underwear.

She turned and leaned forward against the stair railing, her bare ass glistening in the dim basement light. As the Russian fumbled with his belt, the pretty redhead smiled back over her shoulder and winked at Larry.

♦ ♦ ♦

Jennifer choked down another bite. Old salami and cheese sandwiched between stale crackers wasn't one of her favorite meals, but she was feeling light-headed and hoped the food might help.

A loud knock at the door made her jump and almost knock over the tray.

Beside her, Dudka turned his gaze to the door. "What is it?"

The door opened, and Ilya waved to him from the hallway.

Dudka turned back to Jennifer. "Excuse me. This will only take a moment."

He stood and followed Ilya into the hallway, locking the door behind him as he went. Jennifer noticed for the first time that the doorknob was reversed—it locked from the outside and required a key from the inside. In the scheme of things, it made perfect sense.

She dropped the half-eaten cracker sandwich onto the tray and turned her attention once again to her shackled ankle. The handcuff itself was a lost cause—she couldn't pick it, and she certainly couldn't break it—so she focused on the footboard. Might there be some way to disassemble or break the intricate ironwork and slip the other end of the handcuff free?

She saw that the footboard was a solid mass of welded wrought iron. Her leg would break before the footboard would.

From somewhere inside the house, a faint but shrill noise made the hairs on her arms stand on end. It was a woman's scream.

What kind of monsters—

She heard it again. But this time... This time it sounded almost like...

She heard it once more and realized that it did, in fact, sound like screams of pleasure.

She heard the doorknob and rolled back toward the tray of food. She was reassembling her half-eaten cracker sandwich when Dudka reentered the room.

"My apologies," he said, "but my dear friend Ilya was just updating me on the preparations for tomorrow's activities. I wasn't aware of the lateness of the hour. I'm afraid I'll have to leave soon, which is truly a shame because I had hoped to get to know you a little better. I make very few new friends in my line of work."

"So stick around," said Jennifer, worried that whoever replaced him as her guard might not be quite so...polite.

Dudka smiled. "I wish I could, but I'm afraid I must oversee the final stages of this operation myself. My underlings have made too many mistakes already, and I simply can't afford any more."

Jennifer wasn't sure what he meant, but she nodded anyway.

Dudka sat on the corner of the bed and placed a hand on her leg, an almost paternal gesture lacking any hint of sexuality. "We have a few more minutes before I have to go," he said. "Tell me a little bit about yourself. Who is Jennifer Marie Williams?"

♦ ♦ ♦

When she was done wiping down her nether regions, Scarlett balled up the old towel and tossed it back into the pile of laundry where Sasha had found it.

He sat on the bottom step, buckling his belt.

The show had been a bit too theatrical for Crocker's taste—too much screaming and moaning. Scarlett was a skilled actress, but her act was geared toward lonely men who wanted to believe.

To Crocker's left, Larry had made no apparent effort to either watch the spectacle or avert his eyes. He'd paid it no more attention than one might pay an obnoxious TV commercial.

Scarlett pulled up her sweatpants and smiled at her hulking former lover. "How did you enjoy the show, Lare-Bear?"

Larry shrugged. "I've seen it before."

"Not from that angle, you haven't."

He chuckled. "I'm sorry to burst your bubble, sweet cheeks, but guys who date whores don't get jealous when the whores fuck other guys. It comes with the territory."

Scarlett glared at him.

He continued, "I've been in the business for a lot of years, and I've dated a lot of working girls. Do you really think you're the first one I've seen with another man's cock in her?"

Scarlett looked ready to tear out Larry's throat.

Something in her eyes set off an alarm inside Crocker's head. Without thinking, he called out, "Scarlett!"

Her furious eyes homed in on him. He'd spoken reflexively, with no plan, hoping to turn her attention away from Larry. Now he worried that if he didn't think of something to say, he might become the target of her rage.

"Tell me something," he said. "What are you getting out of this? What is Dudka paying you?"

She stared at him for a moment. Then the corners of her lips turned upward, transforming her sneer into a shallow smile. "Just a small finder's fee." Her smile widened. "One point two million dollars."

This time it was Sasha who chuckled.

"What?" she snapped.

Sasha simply shook his head and laughed again.

"One point two million?" asked Crocker. "You think Dudka is going to pay you one point two million dollars for helping him retrieve eight hundred thousand?"

Scarlett scowled. "No, dipshit, he's going to pay me one point two million dollars for helping him steal six million."

It took Crocker a moment to process this. Then it was his turn to laugh. "You think I'm going to steal six million dollars from a poker tournament?"

Scarlett clenched her jaw. "Five hundred players at ten thousand apiece and a million in the glass vault—that's six million dollars. Twenty percent of six million is one point two million."

Crocker could no longer control his laughter. He was in his current predicament because Scarlett the harlot was good at basic math but bad at basic logic. Both Larry and Sasha had also succumbed to full-blown fits of laughter.

Scarlett's eyes darted from man to man. "What?" she screamed. "What is so damned funny?"

Crocker brought his own laughter under control, and the other two, apparently wanting to hear his explanation, followed suit.

"The thing is," he said, "fewer than half of the contestants pay by cash. And the glass vault in the center of the gaming floor is impenetrable. The sides are eight-inch-thick bulletproof glass, and it's surrounded by six heavily armed guards, with two more on standby in the cash cage. And that doesn't count the usual security officers stationed in the room and throughout the rest of the casino. It's more heavily guarded than a presidential motorcade."

"What does that mean? You mean you're only going to get..." She paused and squinted her eyes. "Two and a half million?"

Crocker shook his head. "A million dollars at the absolute most."

Sasha tried to contain his laughter. Larry did not.

Crocker continued, "At random intervals during registration, one of the vault managers brings us a fresh cash cart. Then we escort him as he takes the partially filled cart back to the vault. Once the money is in the vault, it's gone forever. The U.S. Army couldn't penetrate a casino vault."

He could see the wheels turning behind Scarlett's eyes as she did the math.

A stricken look crossed her face. "So you're saying that the most I'll get is two hundred thousand?"

"If you're lucky."

She shot Sasha a look. "You knew about this?"

Sasha recoiled a bit. "I know casinos. I know they don't leave six million dollars for bored security guard to steal."

"But I said—"

"You say that man who cost us money has plan to steal it back. We promise you finder's fee. You never say six million dollars; we never say one point two million dollars. You make assumptions."

She glared at him.

He leaned forward and added, "Two hundred thousand is good money. If you don't want it, give it to me."

Scarlett shot him a look. "I make more than that in a year at the Pear."

Larry laughed again. "Not anymore, you don't."

Scarlett slowly pivoted toward him.

He continued, "If it makes you feel any better, think of it as your severance pay."

Scarlett's gaze came to rest on her former boss-cum-lover. The look in her eyes scared Crocker.

Larry didn't see it. He was balled up in laughter at his own joke. Sasha was laughing too.

Crocker didn't think either of them would be laughing if they could see Scarlett's eyes.

Still looking down, Larry said, "Maybe you should charge your friend there for that freebie you just gave him." He fought back laughter as he spoke. "In fact, maybe you should ask him if he's ready to go again. It sounds like you're going to need the money."

Scarlett's hands balled into fists.

"But could you do me a favor?" asked Larry as he raised his gaze. "Could you face another direction? I'm not sure I can stand another three minutes watching his hairy balls bounce off your cottage cheese ass." His last word trailed off as he saw the look in Scarlett's eyes.

She took a long step toward him and swung her right foot forward like a field-goal kicker. He tried to move his head to the side, but it was too late. Her instep connected with the underside of his jaw and sent a spray of blood across the room as his head jerked violently backward.

He slumped to his right, not unconscious but not fully conscious. Crocker looked to Sasha, hoping the Russian would intervene, but Sasha just sat there in wide-eyed surprise.

Before anyone could say anything, Scarlett took another step forward, raised the opposite foot, and brought it straight down on Larry's face. His nose snapped to the right and gushed blood. As if spurred on by the sight of blood, she let loose a flurry of kicks and stomps, beating him mercilessly about the head and chest.

Crocker looked pleadingly at Sasha and yelled, "Do something!"

The young Russian, perhaps fearing retribution if he lost a hostage, jumped to his feet and lunged at Scarlett. He grabbed her by the shoulders, pinned her arms behind her, and dragged her—legs still flailing—away from the bloody mess that had been Larry Chappell.

Crocker looked at Larry's limp body and noted with some relief that his old friend was still breathing. Barely.

◆ ◆ ◆

Under normal circumstances, small talk came easily to Jennifer. But these circumstances were far from normal. She wasn't sure if Dudka was genuinely interested in her life or simply killing time.

Perhaps he's deciding how to market me to potential buyers, she thought as he rattled off one mundane getting-to-know-you question after another.

She felt as though she were on the world's most uncomfortable speed date. The man who'd ordered the death of her boss and tried to sell her friend into sex slavery and who somehow knew her middle name now wanted to know about her interests and aspirations.

"Is that too personal?" he asked.

Jennifer realized she'd missed his last question. "I'm sorry, what?"

"I asked how it is that a beautiful woman like you is still single at your age."

Beautiful? she thought. *You mean despite all those "city miles"?*

She shrugged. "Unlucky at love, I guess."

Dudka offered a sympathetic smile. "Always a bridesmaid, never a bride?"

His overly friendly tone made her cringe. She swallowed and said, "Something like that."

"All those years without a marriage proposal, watching your friends start families, that must be difficult."

For a brief moment, she contemplated trying to kick him in the head with her free foot. Such an action would certainly invite harsh retribution, but that almost seemed preferable to continuing the current conversation.

Dudka waited patiently for an answer.

Finally, she said, "I was married once. Briefly."

"Really?" He uncrossed his legs and leaned in closer. "Why didn't it last? Was he a philanderer? Abusive?"

"No." The urge to kick him grew stronger. "It was nothing like that."

"Then what?"

Jennifer sighed. "I was about to turn thirty. I was feeling a little desperate. I said yes when I should have said no."

He nodded as if this made perfect sense. "In my line of work, I run across a lot of women who say yes when they should say no."

Jennifer wasn't sure if that was supposed to be a joke. She didn't respond.

"Was it a painful divorce?" Dudka asked.

Jennifer shrugged. "He was in love. He didn't take it very well when I told him I wasn't."

"He made it difficult for you?"

"You could say that."

"How?"

"He made sure the people in our lives, even my own family, understood that I was the one who'd given up on the marriage. Most of our friends sided with him. Some haven't spoken to me since."

"How long ago?"

Jennifer thought for a moment. "Nine years, almost to the day."

"To the day?"

She nodded. "He made sure the hearing fell during my annual real estate conference in Las Vegas. I had to choose between letting the judge rule in my absence or taking a forty percent pay cut for the year."

"Which did you choose?"

"On the advice of my lawyer, I attended the hearing. In fourteen years as a commercial Realtor, that's the only conference I've missed, until now."

Dudka chuckled. "Your current predicament must make you nostalgic for divorce court."

"I suppose. Maybe."

She was vaguely aware that Dudka was attempting to say something profound about love, but she'd tuned him out. She was thinking about Crocker and the way she'd treated him on their walk back from the airfield. Perhaps there was a reason she was still single.

A loud knock on the bedroom door cut her self-loathing short.

Dudka turned toward the door. "Yes?"

From the other side, Ilya said, "It's time."

"Thank you, love." Dudka rose to his feet and offered Jennifer a polite smile. "It has been a pleasure getting to know you, and if we do not meet again, I want to thank you for being such good company."

Jennifer didn't reply.

He walked to the door and glanced back before stepping outside. "If I might offer a word of advice—your chaperone for the remainder of the day will be young Jesse, whom you met ever so briefly when we arrived. He's a good soldier, but his manners, particularly with the ladies, are sometimes lacking. You might want to be a bit more discreet in how you lounge about in that short dress of yours."

Without waiting for a response, he stepped out of the room and locked the door behind him.

CHAPTER TWENTY-ONE

Between Ilya's constant lane changes and the foul odor in the back of the van, the only thing keeping Crocker from throwing up was the fact that he had nothing in his stomach. He'd managed perhaps two hours of sleep chained to the support column. A few minutes after Sasha had dragged Scarlett from the basement, Ilya had returned to assess the damage. He'd walked to the bottom of the stairs, taken one look at Larry, and left, turning out the lights as he went.

Crocker didn't remember dozing off, but he'd awoken to a dull pain in his shoulders and a sour taste in his mouth. He'd sat in the dark for perhaps an hour more, listening to the gurgling sound of Larry's breathing. Finally, Ilya and the fat little American had returned with a meager hodgepodge of toiletries and waited as he did his best to make himself presentable.

The collection of hygiene products had consisted of a pink disposable razor, an almost-empty tube of toothpaste, and a stick of women's deodorant. Without the luxury of a toothbrush, soap, or even water, Crocker had improvised, brushing his teeth with his finger and slathering on the deodorant as a weak substitute for a shower. He'd had difficulty getting the well-used Bic Lady Shaver to do its job, but the fat American had solved the problem by tracking down a bottle of sex lube and instructing him to use it like shaving cream. In the end, the sex lube had served as not only shaving cream but hair gel.

Crocker rode alone in the back of the windowless cargo van. He was pretty sure Ilya was alone in the cab. It seemed that the rest of Dudka's men were otherwise engaged. Aside from Ilya and the fat American, the only person he'd seen during the walk to the garage—including a brief stop at a disgusting bathroom where he'd been allowed to use a toilet that wouldn't flush—was Scarlett, who was sleeping on a couch near the entrance to the basement.

He'd paused beside her and thought, *One swift kick to the throat would save them the trouble of cheating her out of her finder's fee.*

Ilya made another sudden lane change, and Crocker tumbled to his left. He righted himself and noted that he was now sliding toward the front of the van rather than the back. They were on the downhill side of the pass.

Halfway there. If I'm going to think of a way out of this, I'd better do it fast.

He surveyed his surroundings once more. He'd already confirmed that there was no way to open the cargo door from the inside, and he'd failed to locate any exposed wiring. Of course, neither the door nor the wiring was a truly viable option. The standard tips for somebody trapped in the trunk of a car—tips he'd taught in hundreds of self-defense courses—didn't apply here. The problem wasn't that the back of a cargo van was so different from a car trunk; the problem was that escaping, disabling the vehicle, or attracting the attention of a passing police cruiser would condemn Jennifer to death. He had nothing more than a vague description of the inside of the house where she was being held. He knew that it had a basement and that it was somewhere in the Pahrump Valley—not nearly enough information to help the police find her before Dudka's men turned her into cactus fertilizer.

If they haven't already.

He was developing a case of the shakes.

Get a grip, he thought. *Of course she's still alive. Killing her would be a waste of valuable merchandise.*

◆ ◆ ◆

The master bathroom wasn't quite as disgusting as the guest bathroom Jennifer had passed in the hallway, but it was bad enough to make her long for some of the seedier service station restrooms she'd encountered. She closed the toilet lid and, moving slowly so as to avoid the telltale clink of porcelain on porcelain, lifted the lid off the tank. She set the heavy lid on the floor, beside the bucket of water provided by the fat man with the gravelly voice.

She now understood why Dudka had brought her a soda instead of tap water: The house didn't have running water. Dudka and his men seemed to be using a foreclosed home as a temporary base of operation.

The fat man's instructions for flushing the toilet had been simple: *"Hold the bucket a couple of feet above the bowl and pour. The toilet will flush on its own."* However, if she did that, the fat man would hear and come drag her back to the bed. She needed a few seconds alone with the empty bucket.

She lifted the bucket, which was heavier than she'd expected, and poured the water into the empty tank. She poured it slowly to ensure the fat man would mistake the sound for a bodily function. When the bucket was empty, she walked to the shower, eased open the large glass door, and stepped inside.

The shower was an expensive custom job: Mexican tile, stainless steel knobs, and dual showerheads. She flipped the bucket upside down and set it on the tile floor, just beneath a high sliver of a window that let in natural light. She stepped onto the bucket, keeping her feet near the edges so as not to collapse the thin plastic bottom, and strained up onto her tiptoes.

The window was about three feet wide and about six inches tall—small enough that her captors weren't worried about her escaping through it but large enough that she was able to see out. Standing on her toes, she had a narrow view of the backyard.

What must have once been a well-landscaped oasis was now a graveyard of dead vegetation. A stone path separated the skeletons of several long-forgotten shrubs from a large patch of brown grass. A high wooden fence bordered the yard on all three sides. Behind the back and right fences, yellowed pine trees rose thirty feet into the air, blocking the view of any neighboring houses. There were no pine trees to the left of the yard, just a children's swing set peeking over the fence.

Jennifer felt a surge of excitement and had to grip the window ledge to keep from falling off the bucket.

Next door was a normal suburban family. Next door was safety.

◆ ◆ ◆

Crocker heard the crunch of gravel as the van slowed to a stop. A moment later, the back door cracked open, and Ilya tossed a paper grocery sack into the cargo hold.

"Almost showtime," said the mobster in his proper English accent. "Get ready."

The door slammed shut, and seconds later the van was back on the road. Crocker pulled the bag to him and looked inside. Stuffed on top was his suit jacket.

He shook out the jacket, looked at the wrinkles, and thought, *I am never going to work in this town again.*

Beneath the jacket were the security items Sasha had taken from him the night before, with the exception of his radio, his OC spray, and his gun. The radio wasn't a problem—each casino issued its own radios, so he'd get a new one at check-in. He could simply claim to have forgotten his OC spray and borrow a can from the security office, but he hadn't the foggiest idea how he was going to explain showing up without a gun.

Maybe I can tell them I've taken a vow of nonviolence.

He inspected the items one by one and attached them to his belt. He was maneuvering the handcuffs into their too-small leather holster when the van decelerated and pulled off the main road again. It made a couple of quick turns and backed to a stop. Crocker heard the cab door creak. Then the back door swung open.

He moved to climb out.

Ilya raised a hand to stop him. "It's better if we do this in here." He climbed into the cargo hold, leaving the door cracked behind him, and knelt beside Crocker. "We're at the Desert Springs Motel across the street from La Condamine. You'll walk from here. Once you have secured the money, you will exit the building through the south service entrance. I'll be waiting in the employee parking lot. You will load the cash into the van and shut yourself in. Do I make myself clear?"

"Yeah, I got it—you don't want to be seen by the hotel security cameras."

"I hope you understand what is at stake here, Mr. Crocker. I won't pretend we have the ability to monitor your every move inside the casino, but we have enough well-placed informants that you'd be wise to stick to the plan. If a call goes out to 911, I can assure you that Ms. Williams will be dispatched before the first police units are."

"I got it."

"And I know how to spot a tail. If I see any cars following us or notice any helicopters loitering above us, I'll drive you out to Death Valley and put a bullet in your brain. Then Vlad will throw dear Ms. Williams to the wolves."

Crocker said nothing.

Ilya reached under his shirt. "I believe you'll need this." He produced Crocker's compact nine-millimeter Glock and held it out, butt-first.

Crocker hesitated, wondering if it was some sort of trick.

"Go ahead."

Crocker took the gun and rested it on his open palm, feeling the weight. "It actually feels like it's loaded."

"Of course it's loaded. You couldn't very well pass weapon inspection with an unloaded gun. Just make sure nobody disassembles it, or they may notice that the striker tip has been filed off your firing pin."

Crocker slipped the gun, which was now strictly for show, into its holster.

Ilya chuckled. "Deactivating your gun was relatively simple compared to this." He reached into his front pocket and pulled out Crocker's OC spray. "One of our men had the bright idea to drain the contents by poking a hole in the bottom. He spent the next hour rubbing sour cream in his eyes."

Under other circumstances, the thought of some goon emptying a can of military-grade pepper spray into his own face would have made Crocker laugh, but he was too unsettled by the thoroughness of Dudka's men. He slipped the empty spray canister into its holster.

Ilya glanced at his watch. "It is almost five thirty. Registration opens at six. You have until eight. Do you have any questions?"

Crocker had plenty of questions but none that Ilya could answer.

◆ ◆ ◆

Salvation was perhaps thirty feet away, on the other side of that high picket fence beyond the walls of Dudka's run-down ranch-style safe house. But it might as well have been back in Texas for all the good it would do Jennifer. Until her bathroom break, she'd considered herself lucky that Jesse, the foul-smelling American with the toadlike features, hadn't spent much time in her room. Now she needed him close if she was to have any chance of getting free of the leg iron.

Here goes nothing.

She grabbed her shackled leg and, doing her best to sound urgent, yelled, "Jesse! Jesse! Jess—"

The door swung open, and Jesse rushed in, the monster handgun in his right hand and a *Hustler* magazine in his left. He raised the pistol and scanned the room in a panic.

"What? What is it?" he growled.

"It's my leg," she said. "It's cramping. I need to walk it off."

He lowered the gun. "Forget it."

"Please. I'm in pain."

He offered a wide, shallow grin that made him look even more like a toad. "I'll rub it if you want."

Jennifer cringed. She massaged her calf and said, "Thanks, but I—"

"What the fuck is all the yelling about?" asked Scarlett from the doorway.

Jesse glanced back over his shoulder. "Your friend has a leg cramp. I was just going to rub it for her."

"No," said Jennifer, "I'm fi—"

"Or...," continued Jesse, clearly on the trail of a good idea.

"Or what?" asked Scarlett.

Jesse stared at her a moment longer. "Or *you* could rub it for her."

"Why would I—"

"No!" exclaimed Jennifer. "Really. It's fine."

Scarlett's scowl slowly bloomed into a smile.

Ah, hell.

Scarlett approached the bed. "Are you in pain?" Her voice was a disturbing parody of a little girl's. "Do you need Nurse Scarlett to make you feel better?"

Jesse's grin widened.

This is not good.

Scarlett sat on the corner of the bed and pointed to the shackled ankle. "Is it this leg?"

Jennifer didn't reply.

"Yeah," said Jesse, perching himself on the arm of the love seat directly across from them, "that's the one."

"Hmmm," said Scarlett. "I don't have any massage oil, but maybe..." She looked at her open palms for a moment, then slowly licked each one from bottom to top.

Jesse leaned forward intently.

Scarlett began rubbing her two moistened palms together, like a masseuse preparing for a client.

Jennifer strained against the handcuff.

"Relax, Jen-Jen." Scarlett grinned. "I'm a professional." She wrapped her hands around Jennifer's calf and began rubbing.

Jennifer's face contorted into a disgusted grimace.

Scarlett's hands massaged upward, past Jennifer's knee.

Jesse stood up for a better look.

Scarlett's hands continued up over Jennifer's thigh and under the hem of the little black dress.

It occurred to Jennifer that Scarlett was the fourth person in two days to slip a hand under her dress and the third to do so unbidden.

The traitorous redhead never saw the kick coming. Jennifer's free leg caught her in the side of the head and sent her tumbling off the bed.

Scarlett staggered to her feet. "You stupid bitch!"

She lunged at Jennifer, but Jesse intercepted and wrapped a beefy arm around her waist. "All right, show's over. Outside." He dragged her to the doorway, shoved her into the hall, and shut the door.

From outside, she kicked the door a couple of times and shouted, "You're going to pay for that, you bitch!"

Jesse smacked the door with the palm of his hand and shouted, "That's enough!"

Scarlett kicked the door once more. "Fuck both of you." She stormed off, her footsteps fading into the distance.

Jesse placed his ear to the door. When he seemed satisfied that Scarlett was actually gone, he stepped outside and pulled the door shut behind him.

Jennifer shivered as her body processed the overload of adrenaline.

So much for that brillian—

The door opened and Jesse stepped back into the room. He pulled a key from his pocket and locked the dead bolt.

Is this good or bad? thought Jennifer.

He walked to the foot of the bed and stared at her.

Bad.

He grabbed her free ankle and stretched it to the far corner of the bed.

"Hey!" she screamed.

He grabbed the nearby cuff and snapped it around the ankle.

She grabbed the hem of her dress and held it down between her legs, which were now stretched in a wide V.

"What do you think you're doing?" she asked, trying to keep her voice calm.

Without answering, he reached into his pocket and pulled out another key. He grabbed the ankle that had been chained to the bed for the past several hours and used the key to release the handcuff. He slipped the key back into his pocket and reached down to retrieve his dropped magazine.

Jennifer rubbed the freed ankle. "Thank you."

"Fuck you, bitch." He stood, clutching his magazine. "If it were up to me, I'd have let that redheaded cunt tear your throat out. But I'm under strict orders—nobody touches you until your boyfriend gets back with the cash."

He dropped onto the love seat and began thumbing through the wrinkled copy of *Hustler*.

Well, thought Jennifer, *at least now he's close.*

♦ ♦ ♦

Crocker stood at the back of the small cluster of private patrol officers, trying not to catch the eye of the woman with the clipboard. His face felt flushed, and despite the powerful air-conditioning inside the tournament room, he was sweating. He suspected that to an objective observer, he looked every bit the part of a would-be thief.

His eleven teammates, all male, ranged in age from mid-twenties to late sixties. He knew most from past jobs. Two were new. Both of the rookies looked to be in their late twenties or early thirties and carried themselves with a confidence that screamed *ex-military*.

Just what I need, he thought, *a couple of soldiers of fortune looking to prove themselves.*

The woman with the clipboard glanced up at the men, then back at the clipboard. Crocker wiped his brow on his jacket sleeve. Aside from an occasional murmur, the room was quiet.

He surveyed his teammates and tried to assess which might trade starting positions with him if he didn't get a lucky draw. Trading positions was technically forbidden—there was a reason the assignments were random—but it was done from time to time. Unless another patrol officer complained, casino personnel were unlikely to notice.

The woman raised her eyes to the men and gave a practiced smile. "Can everybody hear me okay?"

The crowd murmured in the affirmative.

"Wonderful," she replied. "Well, for those of you who don't know me, I'm Alicia MacAdams, director of operations here at La Condamine. Mr.

Hernandez, our chief of security, is attending to other matters, so I'm going to give you your starting positions. I'll read these off alphabetically, so please pay attention."

Crocker's heart felt like it was trying to escape through his rib cage.

No whammies. No whammies.

The woman continued, "Arredondo, you're at the safe. Bucci, you're on the floor. Cox, you're in the cash cage. Crocker, you're at the safe."

Mother fu—

"Wait a minute," she said. "Sorry, I read from the wrong line. Cox, you're on the floor with Bucci. Crocker, you're in the cash cage. Guzman, you're at the safe...."

She kept reading but Crocker didn't hear. He'd just had his first stroke of good luck in two days.

♦ ♦ ♦

Jennifer hadn't actually needed to pee again when she made the request—she'd simply wanted to be free of the handcuff and out of Jesse's sight—but his refusal to let her go had flipped some sort of mental switch, and now all she could think about was how badly she needed to pee.

She wondered briefly if wetting herself might earn her a trip to the bathroom, but that plan had two major flaws: If Jesse still refused to let her go, she'd have to sit in a puddle of her own urine, and unless Jesse was into that sort of thing, wetting herself would almost certainly rule out plan B.

She didn't like thinking about plan B. It was a last resort. She much preferred plan A, in which she knocked the fat son of a bitch unconscious with the heavy ceramic lid to the toilet tank.

"Jesse," she pleaded, trying to sound sweet and pitiful, "I really do need to use the toilet."

"Tough shit," replied the fat man. "You went an hour ago. I'll take you again in another hour or so."

"This isn't going to wait another hour or so."

"Not my problem."

She thought for a moment. "If you have to explain to your bosses why their mattress is soaked with urine, will that be your problem?"

Jesse sighed. He set down the magazine and rose slowly to his feet.

That did the trick.

He walked to the edge of the bed, grabbed her ankle, and fished the key from his pocket.

"Thank you," she said, still trying to sound sweet. "Really, I mean it."

Jesse snorted and inserted the key into the cuff. With a quick twist of his wrist, the cuff sprang open. "Let's get this over with."

Jennifer jumped up and shuffled toward the bathroom door, resisting the urge to run. Jesse followed.

She stepped into the foul-smelling master bathroom and swung the door closed behind her. It stopped an inch short of the latch and swung open again.

Jesse stood in the doorway. "If you need to go so badly, you can go with the door open."

Fuck.

◆ ◆ ◆

Crocker's lucky streak had lasted all of about ten seconds. His relief at being one of three patrol officers assigned to start the day in the cash cage—the only position where he could conceivably steal a large sum of money—was soon overshadowed by the realization that he would share the assignment with the two new guys, Hall and McMahon.

He knew he could count on longtime colleagues to give him the benefit of the doubt if he broke protocol or acted suspicious, but he couldn't expect such courtesies from strangers, particularly two gung-ho rookies champing at the bit for a little excitement. He'd drawn a good hand, but the house had matched it.

For the moment, the mood in the cage, which handled all entry fees paid with cash or cashier's check, was light. Only about a dozen early birds had been waiting outside the cage when it opened at six, and only two of them had paid cash. Money had continued to trickle in for the past hour, but by Crocker's count there was still less than a hundred and fifty thousand dollars in the cash cart. Things would almost certainly start to pick up soon, but for now a WINDOW CLOSED sign blocked one of the two cashier windows. The two cashiers—a plump, middle-aged woman and a stick-thin man at least twenty years past middle age—alternated between working the open window and chatting with the private patrol officers.

"You gotta understand," continued the male cashier from his swivel chair in front of the closed window, "that those flyboys from Nellis tended to look down their noses at any fellow not in uniform. So one Saturday night, a couple of them sit down at my table over at Caesars, each with a showgirl on his arm, and start giving me the third degree about why ain't I serving my country like a good American."

Patrol Officers Hall and McMahon seemed genuinely enthralled by the story.

"Now, mind you," added the cashier, "these two greenhorns hadn't seen no action beyond a jet trainer, and I'd done two tours in the bush. But I didn't say nothing right then. I just dealt the cards and kept smiling like I was supposed to. After a couple of hours, both of them are drunker 'n' snot, and one of them is losing pretty bad, and he starts getting loud."

The female cashier took an envelope of cash from a woman at the window and placed the bills in the counting machine. Crocker added it to his mental tally, which was still nowhere near eight hundred thousand.

The male cashier continued, "This guy accuses me of cheating him and threatens to take me outside and whoop my ass. It's all I can do to keep from laughing, because this kid is too drunk to walk, much less fight. But I see a couple of our security guys walking toward my table and—" He paused. "You gotta understand that back then the security guys on the floor were real security guards, guns and everything, not bellhops with pepper spray like we have now. Before the corporations took over and tried to rebrand Las Vegas as a family destination, we never had to call in freelancers to handle our business. No offense."

"None taken," said McMahon, the larger of the two new guys.

"The Strip was a different place in those days, you know? People still dressed up before coming downstairs."

"Dressed up?" asked Hall, the shorter, boxier rookie. "You mean beyond matching their socks to their sandals?"

"Ha!" snorted the old man. "Back when the boys from Kansas City and Chicago ran things, one of our armed guards would toss you out on your ass if you walked onto the gaming floor dressed like that. When the mob left town in 'eighty-four, they took all the guns and suits with them."

The two new guys laughed. Crocker gave a polite smile. He'd heard the same line from at least a dozen old-timers over the years.

A loud buzzer cut through the cash cage, bringing everyone to attention.

The male cashier spun his chair back toward the closed window and acted busy.

"What's that?" asked McMahon.

"Door buzzer," said Crocker. "Probably the vault manager." He checked the video monitor above the door and saw a high-angle black-and-white image of a broad-shouldered man of perhaps thirty-five wearing a La Condamine blazer and pushing a cash cart.

McMahon moved toward the door. "I got it."

"Hang on," said Crocker. "I don't recognize him. Tell him to come around to the window and show his ID."

The old cashier glanced at the monitor. "It's okay. He's on loan from one of our sister properties, filling in for either Ted or Todd. I forget which one it is, but one of them is gone for a funeral or something."

Fuck, thought Crocker, *now I'm dealing with* three *new guys*.

McMahon stood with his hand on the door handle, awaiting an answer.

"Okay," said Crocker, "let him in."

McMahon opened the door, and new guy number three pushed the fresh cart into the cage.

"Morning," said the vault manager. "Is my baby ready to be put to bed?"

"Just about," replied the old cashier. "It's a light load."

"It's early." The vault manager positioned the empty cart beside the one the cashiers had been filling. "Things will pick up."

The old cashier walked to the small metal desk in the back corner of the room. On the wall above the desk hung a ring of keys on a lanyard. He grabbed the keys and walked back to the partially filled cart. The retractable leash unreeled behind him like a fishing line.

Crocker watched as the old man flipped through the keys, found the one that matched the number on the side of the cart, and locked the small steel door.

"McMahon," said Crocker, "it's time to pop your cherry. You'll escort this first deposit."

♦ ♦ ♦

Jennifer's dignity was long gone, but her modesty remained intact. After confirming that her little black dress would not keep her covered while she peed, she'd thrown a towel over her lap, to the obvious disappointment of her chaperone. Now back on the bed, with her foot chained to the footboard, she searched for the courage to implement plan B.

Some small part of her still hoped that help was on its way, that a search-and-rescue team led by Sheriff Cargill would burst through the door and put a bullet between Jesse's eyes. But she knew she couldn't count on that. Even if somebody knew to look for her, how would they ever locate this hellhole? She had to save herself.

She watched Jesse and wondered how long it had been since he'd slept. Based strictly on her sense of smell, she guessed that his day had started at least twenty-four hours ago. That wasn't much to go on, but it offered a kernel of hope. If he was even more sleep deprived than she was, that might give her an advantage. She watched for any signs of fatigue.

Sitting on the love seat, thumbing through his tattered copy of *Hustler*, he looked all too alert.

Just do it, she thought. *If you don't, you're as good as dead.*

She watched her toadlike captor and considered for a moment that a quick death might be preferable to seeing this plan backfire. Then she remembered that hers wasn't the only life on the line. Wherever they were, Crocker and Larry were running out of time just as quickly as she was.

Fuck it.

She stretched back and laid her head on a filthy decorative pillow.

"It's too hot in here," she said. "Can you turn down the air-conditioning?"

Jesse glanced up from his magazine. "There ain't no air-conditioning."

"No air-conditioning?" she asked, feigning dismay.

"Nope. Gets hot as hell here during the day."

She uttered a pouty humph and began fanning herself with the hem of her dress.

Jesse stared across the top of his magazine. The girls of *Hustler* were apparently forgotten. He had a front-row view of a pair of real legs disappearing into a pair of bikini-cut lace panties.

♦ ♦ ♦

Like every other cash cage at La Condamine, this one featured a large digital clock mounted above the cashiers' windows, visible only from the inside. Gamers were encouraged to lose track of time; employees were not. The clock read 7:47. Crocker stared at the numbers and fantasized about being on a big Boeing jet, headed someplace far, far away.

He watched as 7:47 turned into 7:48 and discovered that, without intending to, he'd brought his right hand up to the bulge in his jacket, as if some part of his brain perceived the clock itself as the threat. He patted the bulge and reminded himself that without a functioning firing pin, his gun was no threat to the clock or anything else.

He glanced at the video monitor above the door and saw only a patch of empty carpet.

Come on, already.

Ilya's eight o'clock deadline was just twelve minutes away, and the vault manager still hadn't returned for the second deposit. The random pickups could occur as close together as half an hour or as far apart as ninety minutes.

Luck, be a lady, you bitch.

At the windows, both cashiers logged envelopes of cash as fast as they could. The fresh cart left by the vault manager now held almost nine hundred thousand dollars. By eight o'clock, it would hold close to a million. Unfortunately, Crocker couldn't wait that long.

He sat on the metal desk, twirling the ring of cart keys on the attached lanyard, like a Victorian gentleman twirling a pocket watch.

The attached key ring was one of the oldest and most effective security measures in the casino business. The ring held one key for each cash cart used in that cage. The vault contained a complete set of keys for all the carts used in the casino. There was no master key, and because the key rings couldn't be removed from the cage or the vault, there was no way to open a cart en route without picking, drilling, or blowing the lock.

A more modern safeguard ensured that a would-be thief couldn't simply walk out the front door with a cart full of cash: Buried inside each cart was a radio-frequency identification tag that triggered an alarm and initiated a lockdown if the cart got too close to an exit.

Crocker watched the female cashier take a stack of cash from the currency counter and wrap a paper band around the bills. The bundle went into a drawer in the cash cart, alongside a dozen or so identical bundles.

So close yet so far.

He'd considered a dozen ways of trying to steal the money while still in the cage, but he could not conceive of a single scenario in which he made it out of the casino with the money. He had no plan B. His only chance was—

The buzzer sounded.

His eyes found the monitor.

Thank God!

There on the black-and-white video monitor was the vault manager waiting with a new cart.

"McMahon," snapped Crocker, "get the door. Hall, help wheel in that cart."

The vault manager wouldn't actually need help, but Crocker needed both McMahon and Hall facing the door. As they turned away, he reached down by his thigh and slid the cart key into the narrow gap separating the desk's top drawer from the one beneath it.

McMahon grabbed the door handle and rotated it to the right. As the heavy bolt dropped, Crocker pulled up on the ring, snapping off the key at its base.

The female cashier was just putting her last bundle of cash into the cart.

Crocker pulled the freed key from between the drawers and stood. "Here, let me get that for you." He carried the key to the cart, the lanyard unreeling behind him.

"Oh, I don't mind." She held out her hand for the keys. "I can get it."

Crocker knelt beside the cart. "I insist. My mother would slap me upside the head if she saw me letting a lady get her own door. Even the door on a cash cart."

The woman seemed both flattered and confused. "Well, thank you."

Crocker shut the small steel door and, holding the freed key so that it appeared to still be attached to the ring, locked the cart.

"Do you want me to take this deposit?" asked Hall.

"No," replied Crocker, "I think I'd better handle this one." He stood and walked the key ring back to the security desk, moving slowly enough to let the lanyard retract.

"What's the total?" asked the vault manager.

Crocker palmed the freed key as he hung the rest above the security desk.

"Nine forty," replied the female cashier.

Crocker turned back to the group, slipping the key into his jacket pocket as he did.

"So close," said the vault manager.

Crocker froze.

The vault manager gave the female cashier a good-natured grin. "A few more minutes, and you'd have had a million dollars in there."

"Maybe next time," she said.

The vault manager looked at Crocker. "Shall we?"

Crocker checked the clock. He had ten minutes.

◆ ◆ ◆

La Condamine certainly wasn't the oldest casino on the Strip, but it was old enough to predate the poker craze of the early twenty-first century. Shortly after ESPN had bestowed professional-sport status on Texas Hold'em, the managers at La Condamine had ordered the smallest of the resort's three conference halls converted into a tournament room.

Only one shortcoming marred the otherwise seamless conversion: Because the new tournament room resided on the opposite side of the resort from the main gaming floor, tournament deposits en route to the vault had to travel via publicly accessible corridors.

Crocker trailed the vault manager, who had the undesirable task of pushing the heavy cart against the flow of people migrating toward the tournament room, and went through the motions of scanning for security threats.

They continued upstream for a little more than two hundred yards before emerging from the conference-center access corridor into the expansive hotel lobby.

The vault manager stopped and wiped his brow. "That was a goddamned workout."

"We should keep moving," said Crocker. "It's not safe to stop."

The vault manager nodded. "Just give me a second to catch my breath. I'm Bruce, by the way." He extended his right hand.

Crocker accepted the handshake. "I'm…Matt." He wasn't sure what he hoped to accomplish by introducing himself as Matt instead of Crocker, but intuition told him to distance himself from the man he was about to rob.

"Nice to meet you, Matt. Shall we get going?"

Without waiting for a reply, Matt's new friend Bruce resumed pushing the cart across the lobby.

Crocker followed, looking left and right, feigning a typical security scan. His eyes kept coming back to the restroom sign at the far end of the lobby.

Giving the best performance he could muster under the circumstances, he said, "Speed it up a little, Bruce. There are a couple of guys on our six acting suspicious."

Bruce turned to look back.

"Don't look!" snapped Crocker. "Just walk." He raised his sleeve mic to his face and, without actually depressing the talk button, said, "Security, this is PPO seven escorting Tango Romeo full. I may have a tail. Main lobby." He waited a second and added, "I see two.... No, make that three."

Bruce's legs were pumping. Crocker was pretty sure he'd never seen a fully loaded cash cart move so fast. The restroom sign was just a few yards ahead, on the left.

"Negative," said Crocker into the dead mic. "The nearest secure was a hundred feet back, and we can't turn around. I don't think we can make the next one." He tapped Bruce on the shoulder and pointed to the restroom sign. "Turn in there." Into the dead mic, he said, "We're going to secure ourselves inside restroom L3. Send SRT."

Bruce turned toward the men's room. Crocker slapped him on the shoulder and pointed to the third door, the one with a pictogram of a family on it. "That one."

The cart barely fit through the restroom door, which Crocker was relieved to find unlocked. As soon as they were both inside, Crocker locked the door behind them and concluded his Oscar-worthy performance by lifting the mic and saying, "We're secure inside. We'll wait for SRT."

In truth, the SRT was precisely what Crocker wanted to avoid. What the old cashier had said about most casinos no longer stationing armed guards on the floor was true, but every casino on the Strip employed an armed special response team, or SRT. In high-end casinos like La Condamine, the SRT was made up of highly paid ex-SWAT officers who spent their days playing cards in a hidden room, on standby in case of a shooting spree or a child abduction or some other event that necessitated an immediate armed response.

Crocker surveyed the restroom. Along with the hotel's guest rooms, the restrooms were among the few areas at La Condamine not covered by multiple surveillance cameras. He held a finger to his earpiece and listened for the hiss of static that would precede an incoming transmission asking why he and the vault manager had just escorted a million dollars into the restroom. He'd worked out a fairly plausible excuse about needing a secure spot to fix a jammed wheel on the cash cart, but there was no hiss and no question.

Finally some luck, he thought.

With more than a thousand cameras to monitor, it was possible the forty video techs were all watching something else. The deposit from the tournament room might not be the most interesting thing happening at La Condamine at that moment.

That's about to change.

He turned to Bruce. "Push the cart into the corner by the baby-changing table. I'll guard the door."

Bruce hesitated. "Yeah. Sure." He muscled the cart toward the corner.

Crocker turned toward the door and drew his gun. He pointed the gun at the door and listened to the clattering of the cart's wheels on the tile floor.

The clattering stopped.

"Like this?" asked Bruce.

Crocker took a deep breath, spun, and pointed the gun at Bruce. "Don't m—"

Bruce had a Glock 23 trained on Crocker's head.

Since when do vault managers carry guns?

The shadow of a smile formed at the corners of Bruce's mouth. "Take it easy, Mr. Crocker. Mine is bigger, and it has all its parts."

CHAPTER TWENTY-TWO

The barrel of a Glock 23 is one millimeter wider than the barrel of a Glock 19. Crocker's own Glock 23 was in the evidence locker at the Nye County sheriff's station, and his Glock 19 had been reduced to an expensive paperweight, but his expertise with both told him he was staring down the barrel of a Glock 23. The eyes of the man holding it told him it wasn't an idle threat.

Crocker lowered his inoperable nine-millimeter. "Who are you?"

The man kept the .40-caliber raised. "Set your gun on the ground, place your hands on your head, and take a step back."

"If you're so sure my gun is deactivated, why—"

"Because I hear you're a resourceful guy. Now do it."

Crocker set the gun on the tile floor and took a step back.

"Hands," said the man.

Crocker placed his hands on his head and interlaced his fingers.

The man relaxed his posture, removed his left hand from the pistol, and pulled a black ID wallet from inside his La Condamine blazer. "Catch."

Crocker barely had time to reach for the wallet as it soared toward him. He trapped it between his hands and pulled it in for inspection. There were no markings on the outside. He flipped it open.

Inside were a gold badge and two ID cards:

BRUCE EASTLAND

SPECIAL AGENT
FEDERAL BUREAU OF INVESTIGATION

Crocker stared at the credentials and searched his memory for the missing piece of the puzzle.

"Mr. Crocker."

He looked up.

Special Agent Eastland continued, "Acknowledge that you understand I'm on your side."

Crocker nodded.

"Okay." Eastland slipped his gun into a holster concealed beneath his jacket and pulled a white business card from one of the jacket pockets. "What kind of time frame are we looking at? When and where are you supposed to deliver the money?"

"I have maybe five minutes to get the cash to the employee parking lot. How did you...I mean, who—"

"Trade me." Eastland held out the card.

Crocker exchanged the FBI credentials for the card. It was one of Sheriff Cargill's business cards. "How did he—"

"Other side."

Crocker looked at the back of the card and smiled. It was the card he'd handed Jennifer on the observation deck of the Stratosphere. Above where the sheriff had written *SA Bruce Eastland* was a line of smeared text scrawled in what looked like eyeliner:

Dudka has us

Below Eastland's phone number, the message continued:

Forcing Matt to rob tourn

Crocker looked up at the FBI agent. "Where did you get this?"

"A young woman by the name of Megan Burnett."

"Vegas? How?"

"As she tells it, she put on a pair of underwear and felt something that didn't belong. Someone had tucked that into the lining of the crotch."

◆ ◆ ◆

Jesse threw the *Hustler* magazine hard enough to sting Jennifer's cheek.

"What the hell?" she screamed. She grabbed the magazine and tossed it back.

He batted it away. "Knock it off already!"

"Knock what off?"

The fat American stood and pointed a sausage link of a finger at her. "You know exactly what. Cross your fucking legs, and quit flapping your fucking dress. I don't want to look at your underwear, and I'm not going to let you get me into trouble."

"I'm just trying to stay cool," she said in her best pouty voice.

"Well, find some other way to do it because if you lift your dress one more time, I'm going to chain your fucking hands to the headboard. Understand?"

"Fine." She crossed her arms and pursed her lips like a petulant child.

Jesse scooped up his magazine and dropped his heavy frame back onto the love seat. He flipped through the tattered copy of *Hustler* but kept his gaze fixed a couple of inches above the pages, on the bed.

Jennifer arched her hips ever so slightly and slipped her hands behind her backside. They slid up under her dress, then back down. They emerged from beneath the hem, dragging her silk bikini-cut panties over her thighs and past her knees.

"Oh, what the fuck?" Jesse jumped to his feet.

"What?" She used her free foot to slide the underwear past the shackled ankle and dropped them so that they hung from the handcuff chain. "You said to find some other way to stay cool, so I did."

Jesse opened his mouth to say something, but Jennifer cut him off. "I'm not sure you understand how steamed up us ladies get down there. You don't want me all hot and sweaty, do you?"

Jesse crumpled the magazine between his hands and dropped onto the love seat, veins bulging from his shiny red face.

♦ ♦ ♦

Special Agent Eastland finished dumping the contents of the trash can onto the restroom floor and righted the can beside the cash cart.

Crocker checked the can and saw some sort of pink liquid, possibly a discarded soft drink, congealed in the bottom of the trash bag. "Let's hope Dudka doesn't mind his money a little sticky."

"He won't have it long enough to notice." Eastland produced the other copy of the cart key—the one that wasn't supposed to leave the vault—and unlocked the cash cart.

"What if they spot the tracking device?"

"Not likely." Eastland reached into his jacket, which seemed to hold no end of surprises, and pulled out a stack of hundred-dollar bills bundled in a paper La Condamine band like the rest. He tossed the bundle to Crocker and knelt beside the cart.

Crocker examined the bundle. "This is it?"

"Same thing we use to catch bank robbers." Eastland began transferring the real bundles of cash from the cart to the trash can. "The center of that stack is hollowed out, and a transmitter is hidden inside. It's not as flexible as a real stack of bills, but other than that, it's a perfect decoy."

"I hope you're right." Crocker tossed the fake bundle into the trash bag with the real ones. "But I wouldn't put it past this guy to thumb through each stack on the drive back."

"Thumbing is fine as long as he doesn't remove the band or try to fold the bundle in half. Who do they have escorting you?"

"British guy. Goes by Ilya."

Eastland stopped transferring the money and turned toward Crocker. "Ilya Boystov?"

"I don't know. We weren't formally introduced."

Eastland shook his head and resumed transferring the money. "Boystov isn't British. He has that accent because the KGB trained him to blend into English society. The Soviets trained a lot of spies like him. Some had English accents; some had Boston accents; some sounded like they grew up on a Louisiana bayou. The KGB turned out some damned fine operatives, and Vladimir Dudka trained the best of them."

"Trained them?"

Eastland dropped four more cash bundles into the trash can. "Dudka was a senior instructor at the Andropov Institute, the KGB's top intelligence school. That's where he and Boystov met and became romantically involved."

"They're a couple?"

"Straight out of a Shakespearean tragedy." Eastland dropped a handful of cash into the trash can. "By the time the Soviet Union fell, Dudka and Boystov's relationship was an open secret among the higher-ups in the Russian intelligence community. The other intelligence officers probably would have gone on guarding that secret if Dudka hadn't stirred up trouble between the president and the parliament."

"Wait, didn't Yeltsin send in the military to dissolve the Russian parliament?"

"Yeah, and he never would have gotten away with it if Dudka hadn't been forced into exile months before." Eastland grabbed the last four bundles from the cash cart. "At the time, Dudka's relationship with Boystov was still a crime under Russian law. Yeltsin's allies in the intelligence community used that fact to push Dudka out of the picture." He dropped the remaining cash into the trash can and stood.

Crocker had a dozen questions, but they would have to wait.

Eastland bent and picked up the disabled Glock 19. He studied it, then pulled his own Glock 23 from its holster. He held the two guns side by side. "Do you think they'd notice if we traded?"

"Unfortunately," said Crocker, "I do."

Eastland handed over the nine-millimeter. "Blunted firing pin?"

"Yeah." Crocker holstered the weapon.

"Want mine?"

"Your firing pin?"

"We could change them out in a couple of minutes."

Crocker shook his head. "We don't have a couple of minutes. Besides, Ilya will take the gun first chance he gets. If he realizes I changed out the firing pin, he's going to get real curious about where I got the replacement."

Eastland reholstered his .40-caliber. "I guess you're just going to have to trust the Bureau to do its job."

Crocker pulled the half-full trash bag from the can. "Just make sure your people keep their distance. You might want to let them know they're tailing a fucking KGB agent."

◆ ◆ ◆

Jesse glanced up from his reading material, stared for a moment, then ripped the magazine in two, tossing the halves in opposite directions as he leapt to his feet.

"Enough!" he screamed.

"What?" Jennifer continued rubbing her inner thighs through the thin material of her dress.

Jesse took a step toward her. "Stop touching yourself!"

"You mean this?" She exaggerated the rubbing motion. "I'm just wiping away the moisture."

"I swear to God I'm going to ..."

"Going to what? Keep whining like a little bitch?"

"I'm going to teach you what happens to teases around here, you fucking—"

Jennifer laughed. "Teach me with what? Even if you could find your tiny cock under that giant gut, you and I both know Dudka has your balls in his pocket."

In a clumsy flurry of hands, the fat American undid his belt and dropped both his pants and boxers to the floor.

Jennifer swallowed hard.

Moment of truth. Play it through.

Jesse shuffled toward the bed, his pants still around his ankles.

Jennifer laughed again. "At least take off your pants, you fat fuck. You look like a little boy trying to make it to the potty."

Jesse kicked off his shoes and stepped out of his pants and underwear. He climbed onto the foot of the bed and crawled toward her, wearing nothing but a shirt.

"Is it down there?" She tried to keep her voice from shaking. "I can't see it from here, but maybe if you get a hand mirror and some binoculars, I can talk you in."

She was only half joking—she knew there must be a penis somewhere between his legs, but it was obscured by rolls of fat and the tail of his tent-size shirt.

"Don't worry," he replied as he positioned himself over her, "you're going to know exactly where it is in about five seconds." His left hand held on to the headboard, supporting his weight. His right hand searched for the hem of her dress.

The smell of his unwashed body was almost too much. Jennifer caught her breath and said, "Just to be on the safe side, tell me when it's in so that I know to start moaning."

He looked down, trying to locate the target under his massive belly. "Don't worry, bitch. You'll—"

The snap of the handcuff sounded like a clap of thunder. Jesse looked at the headboard. His face barely had time to register that his left hand was cuffed to the wrought iron bed frame before Jennifer's right hook connected with his nose, sending a spray of blood across the sheets. His meaty jowls were still quivering when her right knee found his testicles, which were still located between his legs after all. He rolled to the side, and Jennifer found herself no longer trapped beneath him. She scrambled toward the foot of the bed and dove over the edge.

She landed on the floor, her shackled leg dangling from the footboard. The bed shook violently as Jesse lunged for her. With his hand cuffed to the headboard, his reach came up a good foot short of the footboard. He kicked but only succeeded in striking the end of her shackle.

Jennifer found his pants lying next to her and searched the pockets and waistband.

Where is it?

She found herself in the grips of panic, thinking that perhaps his giant handgun was hidden somewhere beneath his shirt. Then she remembered his brief departure after Scarlett's dramatic exit. Apparently, he was smart enough not to keep a gun within reach of a prisoner.

She found the key ring and searched it for anything that might be a handcuff key.

"Help!" screamed the pantsless goon. "I need some help in here!"

Jennifer found a key that looked like a small antique door key. It fit into the hole on the handcuff. She turned it, and the cuff sprang open. Her foot fell free.

She pulled the keys from the open cuff, jumped to her feet, and ran toward the door. Halfway there, she felt something trailing from her left foot and stopped. She looked down and found her underwear wrapped around her ankle.

She contemplated leaving them behind but decided she was vulnerable enough without going commando. She stepped through the free leg hole and pulled them up as she resumed her run.

"Somebody come shoot this bitch!" screamed Jesse.

Jennifer tried the bedroom door. As expected, it was locked.

Jesse tugged at the handcuff, rattling the bed frame. "She's trying to escape!"

The key ring held three house keys. Jennifer tried the first one. It didn't fit.

"Hurry!" shouted Jesse, his voice shrill from the strain.

She tried the second key. It fit but did not turn. She tried the third one. Nothing.

No! It has to be one of these!

She jiggled the third key, but it still didn't budge. She heard footsteps in the hallway.

"Just shoot through the damned door!" screamed Jesse.

Jennifer tried the second key again. This time, she jiggled it as she had the third. The lock turned.

The footsteps stopped on the other side of the door.

She hesitated with her hand on the knob.

Stay or go?

If she opened the door, she might step into a hail of bullets. If she stayed, she would face the fat goon's wrath.

She opened the door and bolted, head down, arms up.

When she saw the deer-in-the-headlights expression on Scarlett's face, she knew she'd made the right call.

The young redhead was alone and unarmed. She tried to get her hands up but didn't react quickly enough. Jennifer dipped a shoulder and caught her square in the chest. Scarlett tumbled backward, landing hard on the expensive Mexican tile.

Jennifer continued into the living room and spied daylight to her left. She surveyed the room, saw nobody else, and turned toward the source of the light, a large sliding glass door on the other side of the room.

She skidded to a stop in front of the door, grabbed the handle, and pulled with all her strength. It didn't budge. She flipped the small lever on the door handle and tried again. It still didn't budge. Then she saw the metal rod bolted into the door track. There was no way to make the door slide.

She looked back across the living room and saw the front door. It was blocked from the inside by the type of steel security gate used on the outside of doors in bad neighborhoods.

She glanced down at the ring of keys still clutched in her right hand. One of those keys might open the security gate, but she was running out of time.

She turned back toward the inoperable sliding glass door and saw the plastic houseplant sitting a couple of feet to the right, in a heavy ceramic pot.

The discarded key ring clattered across the tile floor. Jennifer grabbed the pot, took a step back, and tossed it, plant and all, through the glass door. The door exploded, sending shards of glass crashing onto the patio.

She took a running start and hurdled the debris field. Her bare feet cleared the shards by little more than an inch. As she emerged into the sunlight, she heard Scarlett shouting something from inside the house but didn't stop to listen. The desert heat had never felt so good.

When her feet hit the dead grass, she veered left toward the swing set that peeked over the high privacy fence.

"Help!" she screamed. "Nine-one-one! Fire!"

She reached the fence and glanced back long enough to confirm that nobody was behind her.

She climbed the fence rails like ladder rungs. At the top, she crouched on the flat, narrow ridge and inspected her prospective landing area. A hedge of cacti and yuccas lined the base of the fence. Dropping straight down didn't look like the best option.

The nearest leg of the A-frame swing set was maybe four feet from the fence line. She glanced back over her shoulder again. The yard behind her was still empty.

She spread her feet wide and stood uneasily, balancing atop the fence. When she thought she had sufficient height, she leaned forward toward the swing set.

Her left foot slipped. A splinter of wood dug into the heel. She resisted the urge to lift the foot, but her balance was already lost.

Using what little grip her right foot still had on the narrow fence top, she pistoned her leg as hard as she could, launching herself toward the swing set.

She grabbed the leg of the swing set just as both of her feet came free of the fence and dropped below her. Her grip held for only a fraction of a second, but it was long enough to swing her clear of the cactus hedge and break her fall onto the hard-packed earth.

Dazed, she sat up and screamed, "Help! Somebody call 911! Fire!"

She couldn't remember where she'd heard that a bystander is more likely to respond to a cry of *"Fire!"* than to any other plea for help, but she needed whatever advantage she could get.

She surveyed her surroundings and saw with great dismay that the yard she'd fallen into looked no better than the one she'd just left.

God, please don't let this be another abandoned house.

She grabbed the leg of the swing set and pulled herself to her feet. Her body had sustained a few bruises, but she had no difficulty walking. The walk turned into a run.

When she reached the porch, she slowed and looked at the patio table. A half-full mug of coffee and an ashtray of cigarette butts rested beside a folded newspaper.

She felt a sudden surge of adrenaline. She took two quick steps and began pounding on one of the ornate French doors.

"Help! Open up!" she screamed. "Please! I need help!"

The last pound of her fist found only air as the door opened in front of it.

Behind the door stood a pale-skinned man wearing a pair of boxers. His hair was a tousled mess.

"Please," she said, "I need to call—" She hesitated. This man was familiar to her. She continued, "I need to call the police. I—"

The police.

His hair was a fright, and he was definitely out of uniform, but he had the same stupid grin he'd had outside the Placer Gold truck stop.

When his left hand emerged from behind the door, she wasn't surprised to find it holding a gun. She'd last seen him just after he planted three guns inside a baby-changing table in a men's room.

CHAPTER TWENTY-THREE

Jennifer's pulse throbbed uncomfortably in her temples. She opened her eyes but saw only a dark blur. She wanted to sit up, but her hands and feet refused to cooperate. Her mind juggled disjointed fragments but couldn't process anything beyond the sound of heavy breathing.

Who the hell is panting in my ear?

She listened.

Fuck, it's me.

The dark blur became a light blur. Objects began to take shape. The room in front of her was tilted ninety degrees to the right. A pair of skylights to the right cast a hazy glow over a dozen or so big blue barrels on the floor to the left. She tried again to sit up but found that her hands and feet were bound.

She closed her eyes and tried to concentrate. The tile floor felt cool under her cheek. How much time had passed? Had she lost consciousness? Was it possible to lose consciousness from a blow to the stomach?

She remembered fixating on the gun and being surprised by the punch. She remembered gasping for air and collapsing to her knees as her field of vision narrowed. Beyond that, she recalled only fragments: the sensation of being dragged, a man's voice mumbling about *"inept commie fucks."*

With each breath, the throbbing in her head subsided, and she became increasingly aware of an acrid stench like cat urine in a gym locker room.

She opened her eyes again but saw only the floor tiles beneath her and the unfurnished den full of fifty-five-gallon drums in front of her.

She wiggled her extremities, checking for injuries. Her hands tingled from lack of circulation. Trooper Haley had made the cuffs too tight. She strained her neck and glanced back over her right shoulder. The zip ties around her ankles weren't as bad, but the plastic edges dug into her skin whenever she wiggled her feet.

"Move it," said Haley somewhere behind her.

She lifted her shoulders and rotated her head to the left as two pairs of legs shuffled past. Trooper Haley, still shirtless, had put on a pair of khaki pants and tucked his gun into the back waistband. The woman with him wore no pants at all, just a baggy gray sweatshirt that barely covered her hips. Watching the woman from behind, Jennifer could make out little more than unkempt hair and bruised legs.

The duo continued twenty feet down a narrow hallway before stopping in front of a door to the right. The woman stood motionless, facing the far end of the hall as Haley unlatched three keyless dead bolts and pushed open the door.

He grabbed the woman by her shoulders and pointed her toward the open door. "Let's go."

She cast a lazy glance back at Jennifer, revealing the soft features of a teenage girl and the glassy eyes of a doll. She was in shock or on drugs or both.

Haley gave the girl a shove. She stumbled into the room.

Jennifer recalled Dudka's ranching analogy: *"I buy livestock from poor countries and sell it to rich countries."*

Her stomach churned.

Haley shut the bedroom door and fumbled with the first dead bolt.

Three loud knocks echoed from somewhere behind Jennifer.

"Hang on," shouted Haley as he worked the second lock. When he'd finished with the dead bolts, he hustled toward Jennifer and disappeared behind her.

Three more knocks, louder and quicker than the previous three, shook the walls.

"Coming!" he shouted.

Jennifer rolled to her right to get a better view. Behind her was a small foyer that terminated in a wooden door covered by a familiar-looking security gate. Haley fished through his pockets and pulled out a key ring. He searched through the keys, found one, and tried it. It didn't work. He searched again.

Three more knocks.

"Goddammit," he yelled, "I'm fucking with your stupid gate! Just give me a minute!" He got the gate open and began searching for the key to open the wooden door. "So help me," he muttered, "if that son of a bitch knocks again—"

The door swung inward on Haley. He jumped out of the way.

Jesse stood on the other side, his own key ring in hand.

Jennifer's mental fog lifted.

Fuck.

The fat American had taken the time to put on his pants but not to buckle them. Like Haley, he was barefoot. He took a step into the house and bellowed, "Where is that fucking cun—"

His gaze locked onto Jennifer at the end of the foyer. His eyes lacked any hint of humanity. He lunged forward with surprising speed. In a flash, he was over her, lifting her by her hair.

The shrillness of Jennifer's scream surprised even her. She tried to get her feet under her, anything to take her weight off her hair.

His hands found their way to her throat and continued to lift as if he wanted to detach her head from her neck. She pressed up on her toes, trying to relieve the pressure on her throat. Her vision grew red.

Somewhere behind that crimson curtain, Trooper Haley said, "If she dies, that's on you. I'm just here to babysit. You can explain to Ilya what happened to…"

Jennifer collapsed onto the ground, choking for air. When she opened her eyes, Jesse had his hands on his knees, panting like a man who'd just run a marathon.

Nearby, a woman laughed.

The red devil. A chill ran down Jennifer's spine.

Scarlett stood in the open doorway. "Are we moving the party over here?" She crossed the foyer.

Haley watched her approach. "For you, sweetheart, we'll move the party anywhere you like."

"Forget it," said Jesse. "She's nothing but trouble."

Scarlett glared at him. "I uncuffed you, didn't I?"

Haley gave a snorting laugh and glanced back at Jennifer. "No wonder you want to kill this bitch."

Jesse's face flushed.

Scarlett stopped in front of Jennifer. "Kill her? Not yet. We might need her." She turned back to Jesse. "That's the problem with you men. No subtlety. No nuance." She looked down at the fat goon's unfastened pants and said, "Let me show you how this is done."

Jesse recoiled as she reached for his crotch.

"Relax." She gripped the buckle of his leather belt and pulled it free of his pants. "Watch and learn." She dangled the belt from one manicured finger and turned toward Jennifer.

Jennifer saw the light from the door reflected on the belt's engraved silver tip and shot a desperate look at Trooper Haley. "Your friends will be back with Crocker soon, and I don't think—"

"Uh-huh," said Scarlett. She pressed her left foot between Jennifer's shoulder blades, pinning Jennifer's chest to the ground.

Jennifer struggled to roll to one side or the other but couldn't break free.

Scarlett danced the silver tip along Jennifer's back. "Before my mom would whip me, she'd say, 'This is going to hurt me more than it hurts you.'"

"Please don't," begged Jennifer.

"Of course," continued Scarlett, "the bitch always said it with a smile."

The belt hummed through the air. Jennifer's brain processed the loud snap a millisecond before the pain in her backside shut out all other senses.

Her scream prompted both Jesse and Trooper Haley to take a step back.

"See," said Scarlett. "This is much more fun than killing her."

Two more sharp hums and two more loud snaps followed in quick succession. Jennifer's screams turned into gasping sobs. Tears streamed from her eyes.

"If you kill her," continued Scarlett, "the fun is over in a minute." She struck again.

Jennifer pressed her face into the floor and screamed through gritted teeth.

When the scream had faded, Scarlett added, "But this can go on for hours." She gave three more quick lashes. The last two landed inches below the hem of Jennifer's dress, welting bare skin.

The world around Jennifer seemed momentarily far away, then once again close. She struggled to catch short breaths between sobs.

"Okay, okay," said Jesse. "My turn."

"Hold your horses," said Scarlett.

The next three lashes struck at the back of Jennifer's knees. Her mind threatened retreat, but she clung to consciousness. She focused on keeping her face to the ground, in case Scarlett aimed the next blow at her head.

Scarlett lifted her foot from Jennifer's back. "Okay, big guy. Your turn."

Jennifer turned her head and, through tear-clouded eyes, saw Scarlett hand the belt to Jesse. The fat goon's foot crushed down on her back with such force that her lungs struggled to fuel her sobs.

"Stop!" she gasped.

Jesse chuckled. "That's right, bitch. Beg me."

She tried to face away from him, but his weight pinned her head in place.

He's not going to stop until he kills me.

He ground his toe into her back and glanced over at Scarlett. "All right, Fire Crotch, give me a countdown."

"Like 'three, two, one' or 'ready, set, go'?"

"I don't—" He hesitated. "Shit."

"Is that them?" asked Haley.

"Yeah," replied Jesse. "That's them." He took his foot off Jennifer's back.

Outside, a car horn let out two quick beeps. The rumble of the engine was faint but audible.

Jennifer choked back a sob. *Saved by the—*

The lash struck her with such force that she didn't even scream. Instead, she felt the breath escaping her body and consciousness slipping away.

When the world came back into focus, she was slung over Jesse's shoulder, being carried out into the morning sun. The pain from her backside brought to mind the hot glow of a branding iron. She felt a warm trickle on her leg and realized that the fat man had drawn blood.

She looked around but wasn't sure whether she was conscious or dreaming. Two well-constructed renditions of the classic ranch-style home—complete with wide driveways, big yards, and brick mailboxes—sat side by side, all alone, surrounded by desert as far as the eye could see. The paved street in front of the two houses stretched into infinite nothing in both directions. No other structure of any type was visible. Jennifer had the surreal sensation of being inside a desert mirage.

Your next stop, the Twilight Zone.

The white cargo van she'd ridden in the night before was parked in the driveway on the right, next to Larry's yellow Corvette. Jesse cut across the yard toward the van, leaving Jennifer facing the wrong direction. Only by arching her back and straining her neck was she able to glimpse the van and her captors.

Scarlett and Trooper Haley were already at the driver-side window, talking to Ilya, when Jesse got there with Jennifer.

Ilya was saying, "That doesn't explain what happened to your clothes."

Haley rubbed the back of his neck. "The thing is, she showed up just as I was getting ready to try out one of the new girls."

"I told you to *watch* them."

"Yeah, and I was watching 'em. None of *my* prisoners got loose. Remember, I'm doing you a favor—I get paid to provide information, not plant guns and guard kidnapped women."

"If you're not happy with the compensation..."

"No, the money is fine, but don't give me shit about—"

Ilya held up a hand to silence Haley. "We'll discuss this later. Go to the garage next door, and fetch three empty drums."

"Send Jesse. The fumes in there make my eyes burn."

"Jesse is carrying Ms. Williams, so you fetch the barrels. You'll have to carry them one at a time. If there are only two empties, we can make do, but we're going to need at least two."

"On second thought," said Haley, "when this shit is over, we're going to renegotiate my fee."

Jennifer quit straining to look over her shoulder and watched Trooper Haley jog barefoot and shirtless toward the house they'd just left. Behind her, a car door opened. She heard feet on the driveway.

"Jesse," said Ilya, "take Ms. Williams to the basement, and wait there while I bring Mr. Crocker."

"Right, boss."

The fat goon lumbered toward the house, giving Jennifer her first unobstructed view of the van. She watched Ilya pull a partially filled garbage bag from the cab.

Jesse stopped at the front door and adjusted his burden.

Ilya stared at Scarlett for several seconds, as if considering his next move, then held out the bag. "Take this to the master bedroom, and wait there with it. I know exactly how much is inside, so do my men a favor and don't..." Jennifer lost the conversation as Jesse carried her into the house.

◆ ◆ ◆

Crocker picked his way down the basement stairs, testing his footing before transferring his weight, fully aware that with his hands cuffed behind his back, a misstep could be fatal.

Ilya nudged him from behind. "Move it."

Maybe a misstep is what he's hoping for.

The stale air reminded him of a cave he'd toured as a child. The smell paired with the dim lighting to create the sensation of descending into a tomb or catacomb, something more foreboding than the basement of a suburban home.

But this isn't a suburban home, not really.

While being escorted from the van to the house, he'd taken one look at his surroundings and realized where he was. An hour before, that information might have saved his life. Now, the fact that he'd been allowed to see his surroundings at all merely underlined the fact that his captors had no intention of letting him leave the safe house alive.

Ilya's conversation with Scarlett, muffled by the walls of the van, had confirmed Crocker's fears. The KGB agent with the BBC accent, speaking with such dramatic inflection that he might have been auditioning for the Royal Shakespeare Company, had warned the young woman, *"I know exactly how much is inside, so do my men a favor and don't entertain any notions that might require them to bury a fourth drum."*

At the foot of the stairs, Crocker stopped and waited for his eyes to adjust to the gloom. Ilya shoved him forward.

"Welcome back," said a weak but familiar voice.

"Larry?" Crocker turned toward the support column where he'd left his friend. "Are you still with us?"

"For the moment." Larry sat against the column, his hands still cuffed behind him, his bloodstained face unrecognizable. One eye had swollen shut. The other was just a sliver. Two teeth lay on the ground beside him.

Jennifer occupied the column where Crocker had spent the night. Her distant expression sent a chill, then a surge of anger through him.

What the fuck did they do to her?

Beside her, the fat goon's hands struggled beneath his enormous gut, threading his belt through the loops on his pants.

Crocker's hands clenched into fists.

"It appears," said Ilya, "that you and Ms. Williams will have to share a pillar." He gave Crocker another shove. "Have a seat."

Crocker leaned against the column and slid to the ground.

Ilya tossed a set of keys—Crocker's keys—to Jesse. Jesse caught them and coaxed his oversized frame into a kneeling position beside the couple.

Crocker cocked his head toward Jennifer and whispered, "Are you okay?"

She nodded but didn't speak.

Jesse removed Crocker's left cuff, wrapped it around the narrow column, and refastened it to Crocker's wrist. He tested that the cuffs were secure, then began the laborious process of standing.

"Careful you don't have a heart attack," said Ilya as he took a seat on the bottom step.

Jesse used the support column to steady himself. "Don't worry about me." He took a couple of deep breaths. "How'd it go in the city?"

"Beautifully. I owe Volodya an apology for doubting his plan."

Jesse wiped the sweat from his brow. "Does this mean we dodged the bullet with Las Víboras?"

Ilya leaned back against the steps. "By tomorrow morning, our accounts will be squared, and this nasty debacle will be behind us."

The door at the top of the stairs swung open, pouring light down the steps.

Trooper Haley shouted, "Watch out below!"

Ilya glanced back. "I beg your pard—" He jumped to his feet and stepped to the side as a blue plastic barrel hurtled past.

The barrel reached the bottom of the stairs and rolled across the floor, passing between the support columns and stopping against the back wall.

Jesse laughed. "It's like Donkey Kong."

"Shut up," muttered Ilya. He looked back up the stairs and yelled, "Haley!"

"What?" replied Haley.

"Get down here."

"I have to go back for the other barrel."

"Come here."

The sound of footsteps on the stairs signaled Haley's acquiescence. Crocker saw that the corrupt highway patrolman had taken the time to dress himself before returning with the barrel. He had on civilian clothes but wore both his gun and his badge on his belt.

Haley reached the bottom of the stairs. "What?"

Ilya pointed to the blue barrel lying on its side. "Pick that up, and set it out of the way."

Haley gave a mock salute. "Yes, comrade."

"How many empty drums are there?"

Haley picked up the barrel. "This one and one more."

"Bloody hell. I guess we're going to need the tools. I'd hoped to avoid that mess."

"Want me to get them?" asked Jesse.

Ilya nodded. "Fetch the slag too. I want her to see what lies in store for her if she talks."

"You mean the redhead?" asked Haley.

"Yes, young Ms. Scarlett, our lady of the night."

"She left."

Ilya's face turned ashen. "What do you mean 'she left'?"

"When I was walking back with the barrel, I saw her leaving in that yellow Corvette. She waved, but my hands were full, so I—"

"Goddammit!" yelled Ilya. "Jesse, come with me." He pointed at Haley. "Stay here and watch them."

He sprinted up the stairs. Jesse lumbered after him like an elephant ascending the Alps.

When both men were out of earshot, Haley muttered, "Weird-ass foreigner. It's not my fault somebody left the keys in the car."

"They didn't leave the keys in the car," said Larry, his voice wheezy. "Scarlett knows I keep a spare key inside the gas cap."

Haley snorted. "It would serve them right if that crazy bitch took off with all their money."

All their money, thought Crocker.

A ball of panic swelled in his throat. If Scarlett had all the money, she also had the tracking device. Had Special Agent Eastland's team zeroed in on the safe house, or would they end up following Scarlett?

Through the open basement door, he heard his answer.

"What is that?" asked Haley. He climbed the first two steps and stared up at the door.

"Don't ask me," said Larry. "My ears have been ringing ever since that 'crazy bitch' kicked me in the head."

Crocker felt a sudden surge of confidence. "Come on, Trooper Haley. Surely you've heard a helicopter before."

Haley looked back at the hostages. "What helicopter?"

Crocker grinned. "HRT."

It was a bit of an embellishment. He knew that Special Agent Eastland couldn't have activated the FBI's elite Hostage Rescue Team on such short notice, but he also knew that law enforcement professionals held the initials HRT in the same high regard with which soldiers held the name SEAL Team Six. He wanted to put the fear of God into the corrupt officer.

Haley glanced at the door, then back at Crocker. "Bullshit."

"You're a trained law enforcement professional. Haven't you seen those stacks of hundred-dollar bills with the hidden transmitters inside—the ones they use to track bank robbers?"

"Bullshit," repeated Haley, with less conviction than before. "It's probably one of those Grand Canyon tours or something."

"If it is," rasped Larry, "they're way off course. The Grand Canyon is *east* of the city."

"But if you're so confident," said Crocker, "go check for yourself."

"I—"

Whatever Haley was about to say was cut short by an almost-deafening explosion upstairs.

Somewhere up there a voice called out, "FBI, get down on the ground!"

Another voice yelled, "Show me your hands!"

There was a loud burst of gunfire followed by a heavy thud.

Haley placed a hand on the butt of his gun.

"Is that really the play you want to make?" asked Crocker.

Haley removed his hand from the gun and hesitated.

The clatter of boots shook the floor above.

"Time's almost up," said Crocker.

Haley raised both hands above his head.

Crocker gave an approving nod. "Smart thinking."

The dirty cop waited at the foot of the stairs with his hands in the air. The footsteps grew louder.

"Badge!" yelled Jennifer.

Crocker turned, surprised to hear her speak.

Her eyes were fixed on Haley. "Don't forget to hold up your badge."

As if under some sort of spell, Haley glanced down at the badge clipped beside his holster and grabbed for it.

Two shots rang out from the top of the stairwell.

CHAPTER TWENTY-FOUR

Jennifer barely registered the object as it bounced off a step midway down the stairs and cartwheeled over Trooper Haley's crumpled body. Only when it disintegrated in a deafening explosion did she realize it had been some sort of grenade.

Her eyes closed against the bright flash, but the light remained. She opened her eyes but still saw only white. She briefly considered the possibility that she'd died, but the stench of smoke and the painful ringing in her ears seemed to indicate otherwise.

A few seconds later, her vision began to adjust. The basement took shape. A number of dark figures passed in front of her.

Angels of death or agents of the law?

Her eyes focused on the figures—men in olive-drab uniforms, men with helmets and rifles, men with vests labeled FBI.

Crocker was telling the truth.

One of the FBI agents stopped in front of Crocker and leaned down. His lips moved as if he were speaking—no, shouting—but Jennifer heard only the incessant ringing.

Another agent, this one carrying a bag instead of a rifle, knelt in front of her and flashed a small penlight into her right eye. He watched intently from behind clear goggles, then flashed it into her left eye. When he'd seen whatever he wanted to see, he nodded and spoke words that Jennifer heard but didn't understand. His muffled voice reminded her for some reason of the old Charlie Brown Christmas special.

The agent or medic or whatever he was raised his free hand in an "okay" gesture. He turned toward Crocker, saw that the other agent was now speaking directly into Crocker's ear, and moved on to Larry, who already had two agents kneeling beside him.

As she watched the agent speak into Crocker's ear, Jennifer picked up the word *officer*. The agent pointed toward the foot of the staircase, where another agent was performing CPR on Officer Haley.

Jennifer focused on the agent speaking to Crocker and found that by watching his lips as she listened, she could piece together his words.

"The man with the badge," he continued. "Is he a police officer?"

She shifted her gaze to Crocker's lips.

"Highway patrol," shouted Crocker, much louder than necessary.

He's as deaf as I am.

Crocker continued, "On Dudka's payroll. Said he couldn't go to prison and reached for his gun."

That last bit of unsolicited—and completely fabricated—information seemed to satisfy the agent. He stood and said something to the man performing CPR. The would-be lifesaver continued doing chest compressions but with less grim determination than before.

Jennifer wondered if the agent performing CPR had been the shooter. She felt a moment of sympathy for him, then pushed it away.

The impulse had come on so quickly, the idea so unexpectedly, that she'd acted without thinking. When she saw Haley about to surrender, her thoughts had skipped from the teenage girl with the bruised legs and doll-like eyes to Crocker's account of his fiancée's death. Before she'd realized what she was doing, she'd heard herself yell, *"Badge!"*

Watching the resuscitation effort, she felt a twinge of disappointment that she'd had to settle for the corrupt cop instead of that fat son of a bitch with the silver-tipped belt.

An agent knelt in front of her and studied some sort of digital tablet in his hand. He looked from her to the tablet, then from Crocker to the tablet. He repeated the sequence a couple of times before placing a hand to the head-set microphone jutting from his helmet and saying, "Confirmed. Chappell, Crocker, and Williams have been secured. Dysart is still unaccounted for."

Jennifer felt a tug on the handcuff chain behind her. She glanced over her shoulder to see an agent kneeling there. A moment later, the left cuff sprang open and she was free.

◆ ◆ ◆

Crocker paused on the front porch and turned an ear to the sky, listening just long enough to confirm that a pair of helicopters were circling somewhere nearby. Special Agent Eastland may not have had time to activate Hostage Rescue, but he'd apparently called in every other resource at his disposal.

A pair of armored SWAT trucks sat on what used to be the front lawns of the two safe houses. A black command-and-control vehicle—the bastard child of an RV and a fire truck—occupied most of the street. Based on the number of people running around in tactical gear, it seemed that at least two additional waves of SWAT agents had backed up the air assault team.

Crocker heard the creak of door hinges and glanced back as Jennifer emerged from the house.

She stopped beside him. "Are you going to tell me how you pulled this off?"

"Me?" He watched the unfolding operation. "I'm not the one who slipped a note to the feds."

"Note? You mean *my* note?"

"And all this time I thought I was being smart by staying *out* of Vegas's panties."

Their escort, a behemoth of an FBI agent, glanced back from the front walkway and yelled, "Keep up, you two. You're too exposed out here."

They followed the agent into the street and waited as he pounded on the back door of the large command-and-control vehicle. The door opened at the hand of a smartly dressed woman of perhaps fifty. An FBI badge hung from a chain around her neck.

"Are these our two troublemakers?" she asked.

"Yes, ma'am," replied the agent.

She turned her gaze to Jennifer and Crocker. "Get in here, both of you, before some sniper takes your heads off. I just told the director we've secured two key witnesses, and I'll be damned if I'm going to call back and say, 'Never mind.'"

Something about being called a key witness made Crocker uneasy, but he wasn't about to stand around with his back exposed to fifty miles of desert. He helped Jennifer up the steps and followed her into what appeared to be a small conference room. The SWAT agent remained outside and closed the door behind them.

"Do either of you need medical attention?" asked the woman. "The tac medic obviously cleared you to walk, but I want you to tell me if anything hurts." She looked at Jennifer. "You have blood on your legs. Do you want me to call up front for a paramedic?"

"No," replied Jennifer, "I'm fine."

Crocker glanced at the welts on the back of her legs. "Are you sure?"

She shot him an icy look. "I said I'm fine."

He took a small step to the side, giving her a bit more room, and said, "I guess we're okay for now."

The woman nodded. "Once we get the two of you someplace safe, we'll have you checked out by a doctor, but for now I think you'll live."

Jennifer said, "I appreciate your concern, but who are you?"

The woman smiled politely and extended a hand. "Madelyn Welch, special agent in charge, Las Vegas field office."

After hesitating long enough that the moment threatened to turn awkward, Jennifer accepted the handshake. "Jennifer Williams."

The woman's smile widened. "Yes, Ms. Williams, I know who *you* are. Your note—or, rather, your method of delivery—is destined for a place in FBI history."

"Won't that be fun for my grandkids. Would you mind telling us what the hell is going on?"

"What's going on," said Welch, "is that an agent from our DC office woke me shortly after three this morning and informed me that he needed an immediate tactical response to a hostage situation and that we couldn't involve local authorities."

"You're referring to Special Agent Eastland?" asked Crocker.

"Correct. That was"—she checked her watch—"six hours ago. Six hours that have probably taken six years off my life. This operation was fast and dirty, and a whole lot of people back in DC are waiting to hear whether it was a success."

"I'd call this a success," said Crocker. "Wouldn't you?"

"The jury is still out. And the verdict may depend on how much you can help us. Do either of you know what Dudka's people did with Ms. Dysart?"

"Who?" asked Crocker.

"Kathleen Dysart. We were led to believe she was taken hostage with the two of you and Mr. Chappell."

Crocker shook his head. "It was just the three of us."

Welch turned to Jennifer. "Ms. Williams?"

"Never heard of her."

"All right," said Welch, "I'll double-check that information once Eastland arrives. Were we informed correctly that prior to being kidnapped you successfully negotiated the return of Ashley Thomas, the young woman who was taken from the La Condamine hotel two nights ago?"

"Yeah," said Crocker. "We... uh... negotiated her return. She's safe now."

"And where is she?"

"She's...uh..."

"We're not currently at liberty to say," said Jennifer.

Welch scowled. "We'll revisit that later. What about Dudka himself? Do either of you know where we might find him or the rest of his crew?"

Jennifer shook her head. "I haven't seen him in hours."

"I haven't seen him since we arrived at the house last night," said Crocker. "How many of his thugs did you round up?"

"In the house where we found you, two suspects are dead, and one is in custody. I'm still waiting on a sitrep from the second house."

"What about Ilya Boy...Boya..."

"Boystov," said Welch. "We've tentatively identified the surviving suspect as Ilya Boystov, but we won't know for sure until we process him."

Crocker thought he saw a hint of a smile form at the corners of Jennifer's mouth but dismissed it as his imagination.

Why would she possibly be glad that Ilya is still alive?

He turned his attention back to Welch. "How is it that you've only accounted for three of Dudka's men?"

"At this point, you know as much as—"

A knock at the door shook the vehicle.

"Come in," called Welch.

The behemoth of a SWAT agent poked his head inside. "Ma'am, we've had two significant developments. First, we've discovered more than a dozen women locked up in the second house."

"More than a *dozen*?"

"Fourteen, to be exact. None of them speak English, so information is still sketchy, but it definitely looks like a human-trafficking situation."

"And all these women are alive and well?"

"Yes, ma'am. That's the good news."

"There's bad news?"

"Not so much bad as complicated. The second house also contains a modest-sized drug lab, which means we need to get everyone clear and bring in Hazards Response."

"Okay," said Welch, "get the women into the vans, and do a final sweep of the houses; then lock down the site until THRU arrives."

"Yes, ma'am."

The agent disappeared, closing the door behind him.

"What is this place?" asked Jennifer. "Who builds two suburban-style homes in the middle of nowhere?"

"We're working on that," replied Welch. "Somebody is pulling the county assessor's records as we speak, so—"

"Pyrite Valley Estates," said Crocker.

"Excuse me?"

"Unless I'm mistaken, you came in on Tecopa Road and turned right about a mile before the California state line, correct?"

"That sounds right."

Crocker nodded. "This is Pyrite Valley Estates. Or, rather, that's what it was supposed to be. It's a housing development that went under when the bubble burst. From what I heard, the developers built a couple of model homes but never sold a single lot."

After a moment of silence, Welch said, "That fits. Dudka is heavily invested in legitimate real estate ventures. He could have repurposed this one after it failed."

"Highest and best use," muttered Jennifer.

"I didn't figure it out," said Crocker, "until I saw the houses from the outside." He turned to Jennifer. "That long drive from the Prickly Pear was all for show. We could have been here in seven or eight minutes if they'd taken the back roads."

"This is good," said Welch. "Now that we know he's using his investment properties as safe houses, we can check—"

Another knock interrupted. Welch stepped past Crocker and opened the door.

Special Agent Eastland waited on the first step, ahead of a small line of people. He'd ditched the La Condamine blazer and rolled up his shirtsleeves. Like Welch, he wore an FBI badge on a chain around his neck. Welch waved him inside.

Crocker recognized the next person through the door and smiled. He couldn't remember the last time he'd seen Sheriff Cargill in full uniform. He stepped forward to shake his friend's hand but froze midway as two familiar faces followed the sheriff into the conference room.

Hall and McMahon were dressed exactly as they had been in the cash cage, but instead of private patrol officer IDs, both now wore FBI badges clipped to their jacket pockets.

Seeing Crocker's reaction, Eastland grinned and said, "We had you pretty well covered back at the casino."

Crocker shook his head in disbelief and turned to Sheriff Cargill, who had removed his white Stetson and was using a handkerchief to wipe the sweat from his forehead. "Sheriff, I think you finally have proof that Vladimir Dudka is engaged in criminal activity within Nye County."

"No shit," said the sheriff. "A team of feds is tearing apart the Winter Palace as we speak, and I've put out APBs with every agency from San Diego to Salt Lake City. That son of a bitch is now the most wanted man west of the Rockies." He paused. "Where are Larry and the Dysart woman?"

Before Crocker could answer, Welch said, "Mr. Chappell sustained moderate to severe injuries as the result of an apparent beating. He's conscious and coherent but in need of immediate medical attention. Our tac medic and two others are preparing him for air evac. As for Kathleen Dysart, there seems to be some confusion as to who she is and whether she was involved at all."

"Okay," said the sheriff, "I'll double-check my information on Ms. Dysart. What are your plans to protect Chappell at the hospital?"

"We'll have two agents standing by when he arrives."

"Good. Now, what do you say we get these two out of the line of fire?"

"Eastland," said Welch, "do we have a short-term witness protection plan?"

"Yes, ma'am," replied Eastland. "The sheriff and I will take Mr. Crocker and Ms. Williams to the sheriff's station in Tonopah and wait there for the marshals."

Welch nodded. "Good. As soon as I hear back from the AG's office, we'll get the ball rolling with WITSEC and—"

Two quick knocks interrupted.

Eastland turned and opened the door. A female agent in full SWAT gear squeezed into the small conference room.

"What do you have for me?" asked Welch.

The SWAT agent held up a clear plastic bag containing what appeared to be a stack of hundred-dollar bills wrapped in a La Condamine band. "Based on our preliminary search, this is the only sign of the money taken from the casino."

Welch took the bag. "Is this—"

"Yes, ma'am, that's the decoy stack containing the transmitter."

Welch turned to Eastland. "What are we looking at here? Did Dudka spot the tracking device and bug out with the cash?"

"It wasn't Dudka," interjected Jennifer.

"Excuse me?"

"Dudka hasn't been here in a while. I'm not sure how long, but he left sometime last night. Scarlett has the money."

"Scarlett?" asked Eastland.

"One of the girls from the Prickly Pear Ranch," explained Crocker. "She's the one who turned us over to Dudka."

"Hang on a second." The sheriff pulled a notepad from his breast pocket, flipped a couple of pages, and studied something written there. "There it is: 'works under the name Scarlett.' This Scarlett woman is our mysterious Ms. Dysart."

"Okay," said Welch, "that's one mystery solved." She turned to Crocker. "And you're fairly certain this Dysart woman is one of the perpetrators, not one of the victims?"

"If we're talking about Scarlett, she's definitely not a victim."

"And you believe she has the money—could she be taking it to Dudka?"

"Hard to say. She was having an affair with one of Dudka's men, so it's possible. But I wouldn't describe her as loyal, so it's just as likely she's headed for the Mexican border."

"Hang on," said Eastland, "how did she find the transmitter so fast?"

"Didn't you tell me that banks use this type of tracking device to catch robbers?" asked Crocker.

"That's right."

"Well, as luck would have it, our young Ms. Scarlett is a former bank teller and a veritable fount of information about bundled cash."

Welch sighed. "Okay, Sheriff, that's one more APB you need to put out. Do we know anything else about this woman that might help us catch her?"

"Yeah," replied Jennifer. "We know what she's driving."

♦ ♦ ♦

The developers of Pyrite Valley Estates had put in streets and street signs but no houses. Jennifer watched from the backseat as the patrol car passed the intersection of Prospectors Place and Silver Lane.

In front of her, Sheriff Cargill steered with his left hand and operated the police radio with his right. "No," he said into the microphone, "if it's not registered to Lawrence Chappell or Prickly Pear Inc., hold off on the plate number for now, and issue the APB as 'late-model yellow Corvette.'"

A woman's voice replied, "Copy that, Sheriff. We're on it."

The sheriff moved to hang up the microphone, hesitated, and raised it again. "One more thing. Get on the horn to EMS, and tell them to send a heavy-lift gurney over to the scene. Apparently, one of the deceased suspects is a big fella."

"Ten-four," replied the woman.

Once again, Jennifer fought to suppress a smile.

Burn in hell, you fat fuck.

Riding shotgun, Special Agent Eastland held a cell phone to his ear and carried on his own conversation. "No," he said, "we want the marshals to run it through WITSEC." His free hand rubbed his temple as he listened. "If I thought we could handle it internally, I wouldn't have... Yes, but the information we do have points to an international crime syndicate, which means this could stretch on for months or even years. That puts it outside the purview of the Bureau."

Jennifer leaned to her right and whispered in Crocker's ear, "What is he talking about?"

Crocker held a finger to his lips and waved her away.

Eastland continued, "Okay.... Thank you.... Yes, have the preliminaries faxed to the Nye County sheriff's station in Tonopah, Nevada. I'll follow up when we get there.... Understood. Thanks." He ended the call.

Crocker leaned forward and rested his forearm against the steel mesh divider. "What exactly did you mean by 'months or even years'?"

"That's a worst-case scenario," replied Eastland. "We'll have a more accurate projection once the facts are in. Right now we're simply covering all the bases."

"But if you're having the Justice Department clear us for witness relocation, you must think it's pretty serious."

"Relocation?" asked Jennifer. "As in new identities? As in no contact with friends or family?"

Sheriff Cargill glanced back and, in a conciliatory tone that bordered on condescending, said, "Don't start assuming the worst, Ms. Williams."

"Why not?" asked Jennifer. "The FBI clearly is." She turned to Eastland. "Do we at least get a say in this?"

"She's right," said Crocker. "This is something we need to discuss."

"And we will," said Eastland, "but not now. Right now it's a safe bet that Dudka's gang is out there with orders to clean house—to hunt down and kill any outsiders who know about his operation. If you want to have a heart-to-heart about your future, we can do that, but we're going to wait until you're safely beyond Dudka's reach. Until then, it's premature to assume you *have* a future."

Kill any outsiders who know about his operation? thought Jennifer.

She leaned forward, grabbed the steel mesh with both hands, and asked, "What about Vegas?"

"It's too risky," said Eastland. "Dudka's men could be waiting for us to take you back into the city. You'll be safer in Tonopah."

"Not *Las* Vegas," said Crocker. "She means *Vegas*—Megan Burnett— the girl who found Jennifer's note. She's in danger too."

"Not possible," said the sheriff. "I picked up that note personally and interviewed Ms. Burnett myself. Not even my own deputies know she's involved."

"Not for passing the note," snapped Jennifer, "for helping us rescue Ashley."

Eastland turned to face her. "What the hell are you talking about?"

"I knew it," said the sheriff. "'Negotiated' her return, my ass."

"We did negotiate her return," said Crocker. "We arranged to exchange the seized money for her."

"Money you didn't have," said the sheriff. "Where I'm from, we call that a con, not a negotiation."

"Whatever you call it, it worked. We got Ashley, and three of Dudka's guys got pinched."

"No wonder he has such a hard-on for the two of you," said Eastland. "And you're saying Ms. Burnett was part of this scheme?"

"She and Scarlett both," replied Jennifer.

"Christ on a cracker," said the sheriff. "You could have mentioned this sooner."

"What's done is done," said Eastland. "Where can we find Ms. Burnett? I'll send somebody to pick her up."

"Probably at the Pear," replied Crocker.

"Good," said the sheriff. "I've already dispatched a unit there to watch for this Scarlett woman. I'll tell my deputy to bring in Ms. Burnett." He grabbed the radio microphone. "Unit twenty-three, this is Sheriff Cargill. What is your ETA to the Prickly Pear Ranch?"

After a short pause, a man's voice came back, "Sheriff, this is unit twenty-three. I'm a little more than twenty minutes out."

"Twenty minutes!" exclaimed Jennifer. She turned to Crocker. "Didn't you say we're closer than that?"

"She's right," he said. "We could take Camellia Road and be there in less than ten."

"Don't ask me," said the sheriff. "I'm just the chauffeur. Ask the man with jurisdiction."

Eastland was already shaking his head. "Nothing doing. We're taking you two straight to Tonopah. No detours."

"We're not under arrest, are we?" asked Jennifer. "We still have some say in what we do and where we go, don't we?"

"You're not under *arrest*," conceded Eastland, "but—"

"But nothing," said Jennifer. "If you want my help, we're going to pick up Vegas."

"Ms. Williams, your friend will be fine for another ten minutes."

"Then we'll be fine going to get her."

"I'm with Jennifer," said Crocker. "We owe Vegas too much to leave her unprotected for even five minutes. Besides, my only change of clothes is at the Pear. This suit needs to be burned."

"That's two to one for going to get her," said Jennifer. "And I'll borrow a change of clothes while we're there. My dress is ready to join Crocker's suit in the incinerator."

"This isn't a democracy," said Eastland, "and nobody is stopping for clothes." He turned and faced forward. "We're going straight to Tonopah, no stops."

"Don't turn your back on me!" exclaimed Jennifer. "I'm not some child who—"

The car slowed.

"What's going on?" asked Eastland, glancing around.

They were on empty desert blacktop, a hundred yards past the last of the phantom street signs.

Sheriff Cargill turned the wheel hard left. "If I have to listen to this for the next three hours, I'll kill both of you myself." He accelerated into a U-turn and lifted the radio mic. "Dispatch, this is the sheriff. I'm approximately ten minutes out from the Prickly Pear Ranch and will advise unit twenty-three when I arrive."

CHAPTER TWENTY-FIVE

As Crocker had expected, the midmorning lull was in full effect when Sheriff Cargill's car turned under the large neon cactus. Only a handful of vehicles dotted the Prickly Pear parking lot.

"Go slow," said Eastland. "Circle around back so that we can check for that yellow Corvette."

The sheriff narrowed his eyes at the FBI agent. "This ain't my first rodeo, you know."

The car crept past the building and turned onto the back drive. Three of the guest cabins had vehicles parked in front, but there was no sign of the Corvette. The patrol car rolled past Larry's private cabin and the ancient green Land Rover.

"Satisfied?" asked the sheriff.

"Okay," said Eastland. "Pull around front and park near the entrance."

Sheriff Cargill completed the loop and parked in a fire lane. "You three wait here while I check it out." He turned to Eastland. "I'm leaving the keys. If I radio out and say 'go,' you go."

"You won't get any argument from me."

The sheriff grabbed the microphone from beneath the dash. "Unit twenty-three, this is Sheriff Cargill. I'm at the Prickly Pear Ranch. What is your ETA?"

A moment later, the same male voice as before came back, "Sheriff, this is unit twenty-three. ETA is less than ten minutes."

"Copy that. There is no sign of the yellow Corvette in the parking lot. I'm going to step inside and speak to the front desk attendant. Stand by."

"Ten-four," replied unit 23.

The sheriff climbed out of the vehicle and stood in the V of the open door, scanning his surroundings. The desert wind whistled through the opening. After two 360-degree scans, he switched on the radio on his belt and shut the door. He walked in a wide arc, approaching the entrance from the side.

Crocker wondered if perhaps they should have listened to Eastland and stayed on the road.

The sheriff stopped and placed a hand on the butt of his pistol before yanking open the windowless door and stepping inside.

Eastland turned toward the backseat. "I understand your desire to help your friend, but this is an unnecessary risk."

"Duly noted," said Crocker.

The threesome waited in silence.

A minute later, Sheriff Cargill reemerged, his gait more relaxed, and made his way to the passenger side of the car.

He opened Crocker's door. "It's clear. The bouncer says Scarlett hasn't been in since sometime yesterday evening."

"Did you locate Ms. Burnett?" asked Eastland.

"She's waiting in the front office with Larry's assistant, Dottie. I haven't told them what's going on. They're both pretty shaken up, so I thought it might be better if they see Crocker and Ms. Williams first."

"Fine." Eastland opened his door. "Let's make this quick."

◆ ◆ ◆

Jennifer hesitated, unsure whether the young woman seated next to Dottie on the office couch was Vegas. She wore a UNLV T-shirt and blue jeans and looked to be about seventeen. A baseball cap partially obscured a make-up-free face and eyes puffy from crying. For a moment, Jennifer thought the girl might be someone else—perhaps Dottie's daughter—but when the young woman spotted the visitors in the doorway, the smile that spread across her face was unmistakably that of Megan "Vegas" Burnett.

Vegas bounded across the room and wrapped an arm around each of her friends. "We've been so worried. We've just been waiting here for hours, not hearing anything. I must have peed like twenty times. Are you okay?"

"Thanks to you," said Jennifer. "If you hadn't found that card—"

"Oh, my God!" Vegas took a step back. "Talk about a surprise! I tried on those panties you gave me, and suddenly something was…you know… ringing the doorbell. I thought maybe I'd missed a tag, but it was that card stuffed in the gusset lining."

"I didn't have much time. I had to improvise."

"Well, it worked. That corner you folded up was quite the attention getter."

To Jennifer's amusement, Crocker looked a little embarrassed.

Vegas didn't seem to notice. "Anyway, I'm really glad you're safe, and I want you both to know that—" She cast a quick glance at the open door before whispering, "I want you to know that I didn't tell them anything about last night. I just—"

"It's okay," said Crocker. "You did great." He leaned in and kissed her on the cheek.

Vegas blushed.

Watching from the couch, Dottie asked, "Matt, where are Larry and Scarlett?"

Vegas's expression changed to one of concern. "Aren't they with you?"

"Larry had to be taken to the hospital," said Crocker. "He's hurt, but he's going to be okay. When we left him, he was sitting up and talking, and he had a whole team of paramedics checking him out, so I'm sure he's going to be just fine."

"Which hospital?" asked Dottie.

Through the open door, Sheriff Cargill replied, "They're taking him into the city. Probably UMC."

Dottie jumped to her feet. "I need to get there."

The sheriff stepped into the room. "Wait a few minutes, and I'll have one of my deputies drive you."

"No, I need to go now."

"Dottie, I can't have you haulin' ass down 160, endangering yourself and everyone else in Southern Nevada. I have a unit on its way. It should be here in five minutes."

"There's no reason—"

"Please don't argue with me. Go gather some of Larry's things—whatever you think he might need—and my deputy will be here by the time you get back."

Dottie sighed. "Okay." Her voice trembled. "Thank you." She squeezed past the congregation and exited toward the lobby.

The sheriff stepped back into the short hallway that separated the office from the lobby and watched through the beaded curtain as she hurried away. When he seemed satisfied that she was doing as he'd asked, he stepped back into the office and closed the door behind him.

He faced Vegas. "Ms. Burnett, we have a bit of a problem."

"What kind of problem?" she asked.

"You, Ms. Williams, and Mr. Crocker are witnesses to criminal activity of a conspiratorial nature. The FBI believes, and I concur, that your lives may be in danger."

"But I haven't witnessed anything. I—"

The sheriff raised a hand. "What you have or haven't witnessed isn't nearly as important as what the perpetrators think you've witnessed, and that's something we can't know for sure. Right now we need to get all three of you someplace more secure, so I'm going to ask that you quickly grab whatever you might need for an overnight trip and help Ms. Williams find a change of clothes. We're leaving here in five minutes."

Vegas glanced around as if getting her bearings. She turned to Jennifer. "Okay, let's go to my room. I'll find you something to wear and grab my things." She looked at Crocker. "Matt, the clothes you had on yesterday are in a grocery sack under Larry's desk." She pointed to the desk. "Dottie washed them for you."

Crocker nodded. "Thanks."

The young woman grabbed Jennifer by the hand. "Follow me."

"Hang on," said the sheriff. "I'm going with you." He opened the door and glanced back at Crocker. "Agent Eastland is out in the lobby if you need anything. We'll meet you back here in five minutes."

"Go," said Crocker. "I'll be ready."

The sheriff turned and exited. Vegas followed, dragging Jennifer with her.

As Vegas pulled her out of the room, Jennifer glanced back at Crocker and said, "See you in five, I guess."

She followed Vegas down the short hallway, through the beaded curtain, and out into the lobby. Special Agent Eastland sat at the reception desk, engrossed in a phone call.

"Absolutely not," he said. "Ilya Boystov was trained by the KGB—nobody is to attempt an interrogation until we get him back to DC. All I want is the information from his cell phone. Look for anything that might point us to Vladimir Dudka."

Vegas led Jennifer around the corner, past the shoe wall, and down the main corridor. Sheriff Cargill followed, staying within arm's reach. When they got to the end of the main hall, they turned left down a much narrower hallway.

"This is the back of the house," explained Vegas. "No customers allowed. My room is right down here."

"Does Scarlett have a room back here?" asked the sheriff.

"At the very end of the hall," replied Vegas. "But she stays in Larry's cabin most of the time." She glanced back at Jennifer. "Did Scarlett go with Larry to the hospital? Should I grab some things for her too?"

"Hon," said Jennifer, "there is something you need to know."

The young woman stopped in front of a door labeled VEGAS in glittery gold letters. "Is she okay? She's not..."

"No, she's not hurt or anything like that." Jennifer looked to the sheriff, unsure if she should continue.

He nodded.

Jennifer sighed and met Vegas's gaze. "It was Scarlett who turned us over to Dudka and told him that Matt could rob the tournament. She's also the one who beat up Larry."

Vegas looked confused. "But Larry is huge. How—"

"He was handcuffed to a post," interjected the sheriff.

Vegas stared at the ground. After a few seconds, she looked up at Jennifer and said, "Scarlett can be a grade-A bitch sometimes."

Jennifer smiled. "You can say that again."

Sheriff Cargill seemed less amused. "You don't have any idea where we might find her, do you?"

Vegas shook her head. "If she's not here, I don't know where she'd be."

"That's all right—we'll find her. For now, let's worry about getting your things together and getting out of here."

Vegas pointed to her moniker on the door. "This is me." She reached for the knob.

The sheriff grabbed her hand and gently removed it from the knob. "I'll get it. Do me a favor and take two steps back."

Vegas eyed him suspiciously but complied. Jennifer stepped back also.

The sheriff moved to the side of the door and drew his pistol. His left hand reached for the knob as his right held the gun tight against the side of his chest. He shoved the door open with brutal force and took a quick step back, pointing the gun into the room. He moved slowly from one side of the doorway to the other, scanning the room. When he'd finished the scan, he moved quickly into the room, glancing left and right as he did. He pivoted slowly, giving the room a quick 360-degree scan.

"Okay." He stepped back outside. "Whatever you ladies need to do, you have three minutes. I'll wait out here."

Vegas led Jennifer into the room and shut the door behind them. Aside from the strong odor of scented body oils, the living space was indistinguishable from a college dorm room.

The twin bed was a tangle of sheets and blankets. Beneath the room's only window, a small desk had been turned into a makeshift sewing table, complete with scraps of fabric, bobbins of thread, and a high-tech sewing machine.

"I made the curtains myself," said Vegas with a hint of pride.

Jennifer noted the gaudy window treatment. "I like it."

Vegas smiled.

"Do you live here all the time?" asked Jennifer.

"Yep. Some of the other full-timers have apartments in town, but I'm saving my money until I can afford a real house."

Jennifer turned in place, surveying the room. Half the dresser drawers were open, and half of those had articles of clothing hanging out of them. Posters for famous Broadway musicals adorned the cheap plywood armoire beside the door.

She wanted to ask if Vegas had ever been to Broadway but thought better of it. "Where is the bathroom?"

"We have a community bathroom at the end of the..." Vegas's words trailed off.

Jennifer glanced back to see what had distracted her. Vegas stood with a hand over her mouth, staring at the backs of Jennifer's legs.

Jennifer did a quick about-face, hiding the abrasions from view. "It looks worse than it is."

Vegas nodded and lowered the hand from her mouth. "I was going to see if you could fit into a pair of my jeans, but..."

"But that might not be the most comfortable choice," agreed Jennifer.

Vegas regained her composure and walked to the dresser. "Don't worry"—she opened a drawer—"I can dress anybody."

♦ ♦ ♦

For a moment, Crocker's sleep-deprived mind insisted he'd been stung by a large scorpion hiding in the toe of his shoe. Then he realized that whatever he'd felt had been more surprising than painful. Something stuffed inside the shoe had poked him between the toes.

He turned over the shoe and shook it. A key fell onto Larry's desk. Crocker picked it up and stared at the Enterprise Rent-A-Car key chain, trying to recall where he'd seen it.

Oh, right.

Jennifer's rented Chevy Traverse—or, rather, her dead boss's rented Chevy Traverse—was still collecting dust in the parking lot.

He dropped the key into the pocket of his cargo shorts and finished putting on his shoes. Wearing clean clothes felt good, but not as good as a shower would. Unfortunately, that was going to have to wait until they got to Tonopah.

He considered that he might be able to grab a few hours of sleep during the drive, assuming of course that Vegas didn't talk the whole way.

And assuming that Dudka's men don't ambush us in the middle of the desert.

With that unpleasant thought rattling around his head, he opened the top drawer of Larry's desk and rummaged through it until he found a white pill bottle.

According to Larry, his ubiquitous bottles of caffeine pills were a weak but necessary substitute for a decades-long cocaine habit that had almost killed him in the late nineties. Crocker dry-swallowed two pills and pocketed the bottle.

Better tired than dead. Better wired than tired.

He closed the drawer and reached under the desk, searching for the hidden shelf. He felt the shelf but not what he was looking for. He peeked under the desk.

Damn. Must be in the cabin.

He could think of a couple of places where Larry's .357 Magnum might be hiding, but he doubted he'd get a chance to look for it. Special Agent Eastland would almost certainly pooh-pooh the notion of allowing a protected witness to be armed.

Sheriff Cargill, on the other hand...

Having taught dozens of Nye County deputies to shoot, Crocker didn't think it would be unreasonable to ask the sheriff to trust him with a sidearm.

Borrowing one of the department's weapons was out of the question, but perhaps he could borrow one from the sheriff's personal collection.

As he made his way to the lobby, Crocker mentally rehearsed the case he'd plead to the sheriff. He stepped through the beaded curtain and found Eastland sitting at the receptionist's desk, talking on the phone.

"Is that a town?" asked Eastland. "I've never heard of it. What's it near?"

Crocker whispered, "I'm going to find the sheriff."

Eastland shook his head and covered the phone. "Not by yourself. Hang on."

So much for getting the sheriff alone.

Eastland uncovered the phone. "Okay, cross-reference known associates and real estate holdings for anything within fifty miles of this Kayenta place. I'll call you when we're back on the road." He hung up and pocketed the phone.

"Kayenta, Arizona?" asked Crocker.

"Yeah. You know it?"

"Sure, it's a little hole-in-the-wall just south of the Utah border. Last stop before Monument Valley. What's the connection?"

"That's what we're trying to figure out. Fifteen minutes before the raid, Ilya Boystov placed a call to a prepaid cell phone. The call connected through a tower outside of Kayenta. We're hoping it might point us to Dudka."

Crocker shook his head. "There's nothing in Kayenta but some fast-food joints and a few overpriced hotels. The only reason I know it is that it's one of the few places to eat between here and...*Shit!*"

CHAPTER TWENTY-SIX

Jennifer treated yoga pants the same way she treated swimsuits and snow boots: They had a place in her wardrobe but weren't for everyday wear. This was a guideline that had served her well and one that she was now breaking.

Because she shared neither Vegas's thin-waisted, broad-chested physique nor the young woman's provocative taste in fashion, Jennifer had accepted the offer of black yoga pants and a long T-shirt. A tank top served as a passable substitute for a bra, and the stretch pants doubled as a compression bandage to soothe her battered legs.

She studied the ensemble in the full-length mirror hanging on the door. With the addition of a belt and some leg warmers, the outfit would have been a big hit in junior high. Across the front of the pink shirt, glitter spelled out WHAT HAPPENS IN VEGAS STAYS IN VEGAS.

"Is this a reference to your nickname?" she asked, pointing to the slogan.

Vegas looked up from stuffing toiletries into the paisley diaper bag. "Oh, yeah. That was a gift from a customer."

"That's sweet, I guess."

Vegas snatched a leopard-print bra from the floor and crammed it into the bag. "Nah, it was meant as a sick joke. He was always bugging me to let him party without a condom."

"What?" Jennifer reread the shirt. "Eww! That's disgusting."

"Yeah. Dottie finally told him not to come back."

"Why did you keep the shirt?"

Vegas shrugged. "It's good for sleeping in. Besides, I won't be a whore forever. Someday I'll have a job where people call me Ms. Burnett and don't concern themselves with what happens *in* me. Then it'll just be a shirt."

Jennifer smiled. "Any idea what that job might be?"

"Who knows. Maybe I'll sell real estate like you."

"That's kind of a lateral move if you ask me."

Vegas giggled. "Okay, maybe I'll be a shooting instructor or a sheriff's deputy."

"Speaking of the sheriff," said Jennifer, "he's going to come drag us out of here any second." She gave the outfit one last look. Her gaze settled on her bare feet. "I need shoes."

Vegas glanced up from the bag. "Your feet look a lot bigger than mine, but I think I have a pair of flip-flops on the other side of the bed."

The space between the bed and the wall was littered with odds and ends: a soda can sitting atop a stack of gossip magazines, an open bag of potato chips, a teddy bear, a large black garbage bag containing God knew what, a—

What the hell?

Thinking she must be mistaken, she pushed the garbage bag out of the way for a better look. She wasn't mistaken—it was Tom's skydiving rig.

"What are you doing with this?" She lifted the rig onto the bed. A sewing needle hung on a black thread dangling from one of the flaps. "Are you trying to fix it for Tom?"

"What?" Vegas joined Jennifer beside the bed. "Is that his parachute? Where—"

"Shhhh," hissed a soft voice from the other side of the room.

Jennifer turned toward the voice.

One of the doors of the armoire stood slightly ajar. From the dark interior emerged the barrel of a gun.

◆ ◆ ◆

Crocker dropped the pen on the scratch paper and stared across the reception desk at Special Agent Eastland. "If I'm right, we have about an hour until Dudka and his men reach Cortez, which might give Cortez PD just enough time to set up an intercept."

"That's *if* you're right," said Eastland.

"Well, *if* I am, we'd better act fast, because we have no way to get hold of Tom and Ashley to warn them."

◆ ◆ ◆

The hinges squeaked in protest as the armoire door opened. Inside, among the wigged mannequin heads and sequined costumes, crouched a woman in a familiar pink jogging suit.

Scarlett's hair was now jet black, but the hatred in her eyes hadn't changed.

"Hey," exclaimed Vegas, "that's my wig!"

Scarlett pointed the revolver at her and whispered, "Bitch, if that cop comes in here, I'm going to shoot all three of you."

The abrasions on the back of Jennifer's legs began to throb.

Scarlett kept the gun trained on the two women as she climbed out of the armoire. When her feet were on solid ground, she looked at Jennifer and said, "Get away from my money."

Jennifer felt feverish. Through clenched teeth, she asked, "What money?"

Scarlett pointed to the skydiving rig. "That money."

Jennifer stared at the rig but saw only the memory of Jesse's silver-tipped belt. A sharp pain in her hands snapped her out of it. She unclenched her fists and saw a thin red line across each palm, where her fingernails had torn into the flesh.

"Move it!" snapped Scarlett, struggling to keep her voice down.

Jennifer moved to the side and leaned against the makeshift sewing table.

Scarlett turned to Vegas. "Okay, you're going to finish this for me."

"Finish what?"

"Grab that black garbage bag beside the bed."

Vegas moved to the side of the bed and located the bag. "What is it?" She picked up the bag and looked inside. "Holy crap! How much is this?"

"Three hundred and fifty thousand," replied Scarlett. "You're going to sew it into Tom's parachute rig."

"What? Why?"

"Don't worry about why; just do it. I'd have been done and gone by now if you and your cop friend hadn't interrupted me."

"I don't know anything about sewing something like this. How am I—"

"Christ, bitch, it's not that tough. I already put most of the money in the part where the missing parachute went. All you need to do is take out the other parachute, put the rest of the money in there, and sew it shut."

Vegas stared at the rig. "But...I don't..." She looked up at Scarlett. "Did you really hurt Larry?"

Scarlett's face flushed red, but whatever brewed inside her was preempted by a loud knock at the door.

From the hallway, Sheriff Cargill yelled, "Wrap it up, ladies. We gotta roll."

Scarlett took a step toward Vegas and whispered, "Stall him."

Vegas scowled at Scarlett and shouted, "We're not dressed. Just give us a few more minutes."

"I'll give you two minutes," replied the sheriff. "Then I'm coming in."

Scarlett nudged Vegas with the barrel of the gun. "Get over there and open the window."

"The window?"

"Yeah." Scarlett snatched the skydiving rig from the bed. "We're leaving."

Jennifer stepped aside to let Vegas onto the desk. Vegas crawled over the sewing machine and flipped the window latch.

Scarlett slipped her left arm through the rig's left shoulder strap.

"How exactly do you see this working?" asked Jennifer.

Scarlett switched the gun to her left hand. "Shut up." She slipped her right arm through the other shoulder strap, then returned the gun to that hand. "You don't need to know how it's going to work."

"What I mean is, do you plan on going out first and trusting Vegas and me to follow, or do you plan on going out last and trusting Vegas and me to wait for you?"

Scarlett wore the rig like a backpack, with the leg straps dangling free behind her. She stared at Jennifer.

"Or," continued Jennifer, "you could try having one of us climb out before you and the other after you, but then you'd have to cover both inside and outside, and you only have one gun."

"Shut up," said Scarlett. "Let me think a minute."

"Got it!" exclaimed Vegas. The window slid up with a loud rattle.

"Better figure it out quick," said Jennifer, "before the sheriff comes in to find out what that was." She saw Scarlett's jawline become more pronounced and knew she was getting to her. "I suppose you could just shoot us, but the sheriff would probably be in here before you got off the second shot." She saw Scarlett's left hand tighten into a fist and knew she had her on the ropes. "Maybe you'd better just make a run for it. Forget about us. Try to get a head start on the sheriff."

Scarlett's eyes narrowed. A shallow grin formed at the corners of her mouth.

Shit. What did I miss?

Scarlett pointed the gun at Jennifer's face and cocked the hammer.

Jennifer swallowed hard. "Scarlett, I—"

Scarlett raised a finger to her lips.

Out of the corner of her eye, Jennifer saw Vegas frozen atop the desk.

Scarlett lowered the finger and screamed, "Help, Sheriff! Hurry!"

As the doorknob turned, Scarlett pivoted away from Jennifer and fired three quick shots through the door.

For the second time in the past hour, Jennifer found her hearing replaced with a painful ringing. She was still staring at the three holes in the door when Scarlett turned and pointed the gun at her head. Her field of vision narrowed until only the gun and Scarlett's grinning face remained. She wanted to lunge for the gun, to take it away and beat that evil grin into a bloody mash of teeth and bone. But Scarlett had the drop on her.

Then the evil grin was gone, replaced by the blur of a white sneaker as Vegas's foot connected with Scarlett's face. Scarlett went flying backward—wig, gun, and all.

Instinct took over, and Jennifer's legs propelled her toward the door. She grabbed the knob, yanked open the door, and stepped out into a trail of blood. She slipped and crashed into the far wall.

She fell to the floor and pivoted back toward the room, certain that Scarlett was about to put a bullet in her back. She saw only Vegas, still standing on the desk.

"Come on!" screamed Jennifer. "Run!"

Vegas covered half the length of the room in a single bound. She was one step from the door when her gray UNLV shirt disintegrated in a plume of red. She fell face-first, with one outstretched hand extending into the hallway.

Jennifer reached for the hand but felt herself yanked clear of the doorway just as the doorjamb exploded in a cloud of splinters. She looked back and saw Sheriff Cargill lying on the floor, pulling her with his left arm—the one not soaked in blood.

CHAPTER TWENTY-SEVEN

The burnt smell of smokeless powder reached Crocker's nostrils as he neared the end of the main hallway. Somewhere behind him, Special Agent Eastland shouted at him to stay back, but Crocker wasn't about to slow down and wait for someone else, even an FBI agent, to go first.

He knew better than to rush headlong toward the sound of gunfire. A lifetime of training told him to hang back, to clear the corners, to advance with caution. He'd spent years warning students to fight the initial surge of adrenaline, to go slow, to *slice the pie*. All of that was well and good in the academy's shoot house or on a SWAT raid, but this was personal.

He rounded the corner at a dead run and saw Sheriff Cargill, soaked in blood, lying on the floor with his head propped against the wall. Crocker slid to a stop at the sheriff's side and reached to take the pistol from the injured man's one good hand.

The sheriff shook his head and pulled the gun away. "It's over. Go help her." He nodded at the open doorway across the hall.

Crocker turned and looked into the room.

Just inside the doorway, Jennifer—wearing a pink T-shirt splattered with drops of red—knelt over Vegas, pressing down on the girl's blood-soaked chest.

Crocker stood and approached the doorway.

Jennifer looked up and, speaking in rapid-fire bursts, said, "I think she's okay—I think it missed her heart—I think she's going to be okay."

One look told Crocker that Vegas was not okay. The logo on her shirt had vanished beneath a pool of blood. The veins on her neck and head bulged as if they might burst through her skin. Her eyes were open but unfocused, and her breathing was shallow and rapid.

"I just need to stop the bleeding," said Jennifer, still speaking in staccato bursts. "I can't stop the bleeding—I think she'll be all right if I can stop the bleeding, but I can't stop the bleeding—I need a towel or something—all I could find was this shirt."

In Jennifer's hand was a bloody rag that might once have been a shirt.

"Tampons," said Crocker. "You need to stick a tampon in the wound."

Behind Crocker, a voice called, "Officer down. Officer down at the Prickly Pear Ranch."

He glanced over his shoulder and saw Eastland using the radio attached to the sheriff's belt.

"On the dresser," said Jennifer. "Look in the diaper bag on the dresser— she has tampons in the diaper bag on the dresser."

Crocker stepped around Vegas's outstretched body and walked to the dresser. Scraps of fabric and bits of thread danced in the breeze from the open window. He grabbed the bag and unzipped it.

"Side pocket," said Jennifer. "Check the side pocket—she has tampons in the side pocket."

Crocker sat beside Jennifer, dug through the items in the side pocket— condoms, makeup, the cell phone he'd used at the Stratosphere—and finally pulled out a tampon.

Vegas choked and coughed up a little blood.

Crocker unwrapped the tampon. "Move your hands."

Jennifer didn't move.

"*Jennifer*," he said, "you have to move so that I can get to the wound."

Jennifer nodded and pulled her hands away.

Crocker moved the applicator toward the wound and froze.

"What's wrong?" asked Jennifer.

"This is an exit wound."

"Scarlett shot her in the back."

"Larry's three fifty-seven," muttered Crocker. He laid the tampon on the ground.

"What are you doing?"

"Just keep pressure on it."

"What?"

"The bullet passed all the way through. I can't plug it."

Jennifer scowled and placed the bloody rag over the wound again.

Vegas choked again and tried to say something.

"What's that, honey?" asked Jennifer.

Vegas pointed to the bag and mumbled something.

Jennifer leaned in close. "Tell me what you want."

Crocker heard Vegas's raspy whisper but couldn't decipher it. "What is she saying?"

"She's asking for her phone." Jennifer smiled unconvincingly at the young woman. "Don't worry, hon. We'll bring it to the hospital for you."

Crocker pulled the phone from the side pocket of the diaper bag and offered it to Jennifer. "Give it to her if she wants it."

Jennifer shot him a deadly look. "We have to stop the bleeding."

"We will." He pressed the phone into Jennifer's hand. "Ask her who she wants to call. I need to check on the sheriff."

Eastland was perfectly capable of tending to the sheriff, but Crocker couldn't bring himself to sit and watch Vegas—Vegas who'd giggled like a little kid after firing a gun for the first time, Vegas whose schoolgirl crush he'd dodged for nearly two years—die on the floor of her shitty brothel dorm room.

He leaned forward and kissed her on the forehead. "Make your phone call, kiddo. I'll check on you in a few minutes."

She gave a gentle nod, barely discernible from the tremors that had taken hold of her.

Crocker stepped into the hallway and knelt beside Eastland, who was applying pressure to a bullet wound in the sheriff's hip. The sheriff was using his left hand to put pressure on a bullet wound—clearly the source of most of the blood—in his right arm. Through a hole in the sheriff's shirt, Crocker saw the shiny copper jacket of a bullet trapped in a bulletproof vest.

He pointed to the trapped bullet. "Good thing you're wearing your Kevlar."

The sheriff nodded. "How's the girl?"

Crocker shook his head and wiped his eyes.

"Goddammit," said the sheriff. He turned his head to the side, breaking eye contact. "I should have checked the room more carefully. I—"

"Crocker!" screamed Jennifer. "Help!"

He turned and stepped back into the room.

"She's not responding," said Jennifer. "I can't tell if she's breathing—she's not responding—I can't...she..."

Crocker knelt beside her. Vegas's eyes were still open, but the life had gone from them. He placed an ear on her bloody chest. He didn't hear a heartbeat. He did, however, hear a woman's voice, faint and distorted, saying, "Megan, honey, is that you? Are you there?" The cell phone lay on the ground beside Vegas's head. He picked it up. The text on the screen said MOM.

Jennifer whispered, "I just dialed it."

He pressed the disconnect button and laid the phone beside its owner.

From the hallway, a man yelled, "Out of the way! Let me through."

Crocker looked back and saw a sheriff's deputy—one of the few he didn't know—pushing his way through the door.

Unit 23 had arrived.

Crocker placed a hand on Jennifer's shoulder and said, "We need to let the deputy take over."

She shot him the same deadly look as before. "No, I'm not—"

"The deputy knows what he's doing. You and I need to go wait for the ambulance so that we can show the paramedics how to get back here."

Without waiting for her to reply, he took her by the shoulders, stood her up, and pointed her into the hallway.

Jennifer stopped beside the sheriff. "Are you okay?"

"I'll live," he replied.

"I shouldn't have made you bring us here. I—"

"Stop it. There ain't no one to blame but the person who pulled the trigger."

"He's right," said Eastland.

Jennifer nodded as if she understood, but Crocker knew she'd require a lot more convincing. A therapist had once told him that no emotion is more persuasive than guilt.

"Come on," he said. "Let's go flag down those paramedics." He put an arm around Jennifer. "Bill, do you want me to call Jim?"

The sheriff shook his head. "I'll get one of my deputies to call him before I'm loaded into the ambulance. That way, he can hear my voice and know I'm okay."

Crocker nodded and led Jennifer down the hall.

Most of the doors that lined the hallway stood open, occupied by young women wearing nightgowns or wrapped in bedsheets. They were obviously curious about what was happening but streetwise enough not to get involved.

As Crocker and Jennifer rounded the corner into the main hallway, a woman behind them let out a despondent scream. Crocker wasn't certain, but he thought it sounded like Dottie. He didn't have the nerve to go back and check.

Jennifer stopped at the end of the main hallway, in front of the shoe wall. When she didn't say anything, Crocker asked, "Are you okay?"

He immediately regretted the question. Nobody was okay. Rather than press the issue, he joined her in staring at the rows of shoes. Because only a handful of the Prickly Pear's working girls were with clients at this early hour, most of the shoes were what Jennifer had referred to as *hooker pumps*.

Jennifer grabbed a pair of purple sneakers hiding among the foot-contorting stilettos and checked the size. Without a word, she sat on the floor and put on the shoes, sans socks. When she'd finished lacing up the shoes, she stood and walked to the door, not once looking back to see if Crocker was following.

He caught up to her in the parking lot, where she'd taken a seat on the bumper of Sheriff Cargill's patrol car. She stared in the direction of the faintly audible sirens. He stood beside her and watched for the not-yet-visible flashing lights.

Without taking her eyes off the road, Jennifer said, "She was hiding in the armoire."

"What?"

"Scarlett. She was hiding in Vegas's big wooden wardrobe. She had a gun."

Crocker thought, *No shit she had a gun,* but had the good sense not to say it.

Jennifer continued, "She shot the sheriff through the door. She was about to shoot me, but Vegas kicked her, and..."

Crocker took a seat on the bumper and wrapped an arm around Jennifer. "Vegas liked you. Wherever she is, she's happy you're okay."

Jennifer's voice cracked as she said, *"Everyone* would be okay if it weren't for me."

"If you keep blaming yourself, the guilt will eat you up inside."

"But if I hadn't made the sheriff—"

"You didn't make the sheriff do anything. He was in favor of coming here. So was I. How could any of us have known Scarlett would be hiding in Vegas's room? What possible reason—"

"She was using Vegas's sewing stuff. She hid in the wardrobe when she heard us coming."

"Sewing?"

Jennifer nodded. "She sewed most of the stolen money into the empty compartment in Tom's parachute rig."

"What the hell for?"

"Hide it, I guess."

"If you want to hide eight hundred thousand dollars, you sew it into a stuffed animal or the lining of a suitcase. Why would she..."

He stood and looked toward the dry lake bed. A faint cloud of dust hung over the dirt road.

"What is it?" asked Jennifer.

"There is only one place around here where walking around with a parachute would look natural."

"The skydiving tournament?"

"She can't take a commercial flight—she's a fugitive. Lucky for her, we showed her a way around that."

"But that only worked because Tom has friends there. Scarlett doesn't."

Crocker walked around the left side of the car. "A woman with almost a million in cash can make friends fast."

"Six hundred grand." Jennifer stood and walked around the other side of the car. "The rest of the money is still in Vegas's room."

"Six hundred thousand dollars and a three fifty-seven revolver can be pretty damned persuasive." He tried the driver-side door but found it locked. "Shit."

"What do you need?"

"Police radio. Come on, we need to tell Agent Eastland and the sheriff."

As he turned toward the building, he spied a familiar Chevy Traverse parked twenty yards away.

He stuck his hand into his pocket and pulled out the key. "Change of plans. You go tell the sheriff and Eastland. I'm going after—"

The sound of smashing glass obscured his words. He turned back toward the sheriff's car.

Jennifer stood beside the front passenger-side door, staring through the opening where there had previously been a window.

She looked up at Crocker. "I found a rock."

CHAPTER TWENTY-EIGHT

The unpaved road between the Prickly Pear and the dry lake bed was no less bumpy in Bryan's rental car than it had been in the limo, but the nausea Jennifer had felt the night before was now held at bay by seething hatred.

Crocker's radio call from the sheriff's car had lasted less than five seconds: *"Sheriff, this is Crocker. Scarlett is headed to the dry lake bed. We're going after her."* They hadn't waited for a reply.

Jennifer spied the white fence post and recalled Vegas's giggly voice proclaiming, *"Welcome to California."* The memory of how much the young woman had enjoyed the excitement the night before brought tears to her eyes.

She glanced at Crocker. "How do we find Scarlett?"

He swerved to avoid a small boulder. "We ask around."

"Ask if anyone at the skydiving tournament has seen a girl carrying a parachute?"

"A pretty redhead." He eased off the gas as the car reached the top of the hill. "People always remember pretty redheads."

"That won't work—she's wearing a black wig she stole from Vegas."

Crocker sighed. "We'll find her. A parachute and a wig aren't enough to make a girl like Scarlett blend in."

As the car crested the final hill, the skydivers' tent city came into view a couple hundred yards ahead.

"There must be at least two thousand people down there," said Jennifer.

"We'll find her."

"And when we do?"

Crocker slowed the car as it approached the first cluster of tents. "Sorry, Jennifer, but I'm fresh out of plans. We're just going to have to improvise." He brought the car to a crawl as the road became thick with pedestrians. "You watch right. I'll watch left. My guess is she'll be somewhere near the planes, so—"

"There!" exclaimed Jennifer.

Parked side by side between a pair of tents were Larry's yellow Corvette and the ancient green Land Rover.

Crocker mashed on the brake, bringing the car to a sudden stop. "That's why we didn't see the Vette in the parking lot. She must have parked it here and hitched..."

Jennifer was out of the car before Crocker could finish his sentence. She scanned the area for a black wig and pink jogging suit. She heard Crocker's footsteps, then felt his hand on her shoulder.

"Stay back," he said.

He approached the Land Rover in a crouch and peered through the rear window. He worked his way around to the front, checking each window as he moved.

Jennifer watched his surreptitious movements and thought, *He knows he doesn't have a gun, right?*

When he reached the front, he spun and moved to the Corvette, still crouching. After a quick peek through the passenger-side window, he straightened himself and shook his head.

A few yards from the cars, three middle-aged men sat in lawn chairs in front of a trio of tents, watching Crocker with expressions of amused curiosity.

"Hi there." Jennifer waved and walked toward them. "Did any of you happen to see the woman who got out of that Land Rover?"

"Sure," said the man in the middle. "Pretty little thing dressed all in pink. Sped up here about five minutes ago, jumped out, grabbed her rig, and ran off toward the runway like she was afraid she was going to miss her load."

Crocker joined Jennifer beside the men. "Her load?"

"You know, like she was going to miss her jump, like the plane was going to take off without her."

"And where would someone go to get on a plane, or a load or whatever?" asked Jennifer.

The man chuckled. "You folks aren't jumpers, are you?"

"No," said Crocker, "We're—"

"We're trying to warn her," said Jennifer. "We think there might be something wrong with her parachute."

The man frowned as if this were an odd concern. "Well, if you need to get hold of her, you can page her from the manifest desk. That's where people go to sign up for loads." He pointed toward a large blue tent near the runway. "But there's no need to rush. FAA has us shut down until further notice."

"No planes are flying?" asked Crocker.

One of the man's friends, an aging-biker type with tattoos and a long beard, said, "Nah, the goddamned feds suspended our NOTAM just before nine this morning. Said the airspace was closed due to a police pursuit."

Crocker glanced at the blue tent, then back at the three men. "Does one of you have a pocketknife I can borrow for just a second?"

The aging biker dug into the front pocket of his blue jeans. Without saying a word, he pulled out a large folding knife and tossed it to Crocker.

Crocker reached out and caught the knife.

"Careful," said the man. "It's sharp."

Crocker nodded and turned to Jennifer. "Head over to the manifest tent, and try to get them to make some sort of public address. Make it so she can't hide."

"What are you going to do?"

"I'm going to make it so she can't run." He turned and walked toward the cars.

"J. D.," said the first man, "don't you think maybe you should have asked why he wanted to borrow a knife?"

Jennifer and the three men watched as Crocker knelt and plunged the knife into one of the Corvette's rear tires.

"Yep," said the biker, "definitely should have asked."

♦ ♦ ♦

The faint scent of sweat and nylon hung in the air beneath the big blue manifest tent. A patchwork of tarps created a floor on which a half-dozen men and women packed parachutes. Jennifer stepped over stretched lines and around colorful bundles of canopy, making her way to the left side of the packing area, where the tent abutted a mobile office trailer outfitted with three service windows. She was two steps from the trailer when the first window slid open.

A plump young woman poked out her head, scowled, and said, "There is still no news. As soon as we hear something, we'll make an announcement."

"What?" asked Jennifer.

"Weren't you going to ask when we'll be flying?"

"No, I need you to make an announcement."

"All right." The woman reached for a pad and pen. "Who do you want to page?"

"I don't want you to page her. I want you to warn people about her."

The woman set down the pen. "If you think someone is being unsafe, ask the organizers to have a talk with her. We don't air dirty laundry over the PA." She reached to close the window.

Jennifer blocked the sliding window. "There is a murderer running around here with a gun."

"Is this a gag?"

"Bitch, look at the red spots on my shirt. Do I look like I'm joking? You're aware that your flights are grounded because of a police pursuit, right?"

The woman stared at Jennifer for a long moment. "Listen, I've never seen you before, so unless you can show me a badge, I'm not announcing to the whole drop zone that there is a killer on the loose. If you like, I'll try to find our director of security, and you can—"

A man appeared beside the woman. "Sorry to interrupt," he said, "but the pilot from Lone Star Skydiving is asking if he's okay to taxi to the fuel tanks."

"Now?" asked the woman. "He's going to have to pump it himself—we released the fuel crew until the flight restriction is lifted."

Jennifer recalled the plane with the Texas flag on the tail. "Brent!"

The man and woman both stared at her.

Struggling to keep her voice steady, Jennifer said, "The pilot from Lone Star Skydiving is named Brent. He knows me. He can vouch for me."

The man gave the woman a bewildered glance.

Jennifer took her hand off the window and, mustering as much calm as she could, said, "Tell Brent that Tom's friend Jennifer says you're in danger. Ask if you should take me seriously."

"Is she for real?" asked the man.

The woman sighed. "I don't know. Tell Brent he's responsible for self-reporting how much fuel he pumps." She glanced at Jennifer. "And ask him if he has any idea what this woman is talking about."

The man walked away, shaking his head in either confusion or disbelief.

"Wait here," said the woman. She closed the window and disappeared into the back of the trailer, leaving Jennifer staring at her own reflection in the dirty glass.

Jennifer saw that her hair had taken on an escaped-mental-patient quality that couldn't be helping her case. She gathered it into a ponytail while scanning for anything to use as a hair tie.

"Need a pull-up cord?" asked a soft female voice.

Jennifer turned and, for one terrifying moment, thought she was staring at Vegas's ghost.

"Are you okay?" asked the girl. She was maybe eighteen or nineteen and had the same platinum blond hair as Vegas but otherwise bore little resemblance to the recently departed.

"You startled me," said Jennifer.

"Sorry." The girl gave an apologetic smile that again reminded Jennifer of Vegas. "I saw you messing with your hair and figured you were looking for a pull-up cord."

"A pull-up cord?"

"To tie your hair."

"Okay, sure." Jennifer had no idea what a pull-up cord was. "Do you have one?"

The girl knelt and pulled a foot-long length of purple ribbon from the skydiving rig lying at her feet. "Here you go." She held out the ribbon to Jennifer. "I'm done with it."

Jennifer took the ribbon. "Thanks."

As she turned away from the girl, the fleeting resemblance to Vegas struck her one last time. She looked for the girl's reflection in the dirty glass, half expecting it not to be there, but once again saw a girl who, aside from her hair, looked almost nothing like Vegas. She watched the girl pick up the skydiving rig and walk away.

Using the dirty glass as a mirror, Jennifer tied the ribbon around her ratty ponytail. As she gave the bow a final tug, a dark silhouette enveloped her reflection. She spun, prepared for the worst, but found only Crocker standing behind her.

"Sorry," he said. "Are they going to make an announcement?"

Jennifer took a breath. "They're asking Tom's friend Brent, the pilot, to vouch for me."

Crocker nodded. "It may be a moot point. In five minutes this place will be crawling with deputies."

Jennifer heard the window slide open and turned to face the uncooperative woman. "Well? What did Brent say?"

The woman looked annoyed. "He said to meet him over by the fuel tanks and explain the situation to him. If he thinks it's serious enough, he'll relay the message to me."

"Serious enough!" exclaimed Jennifer. "You get that we're talking about a—"

Crocker placed a hand on her waist. "Come on. We may need Brent's help anyway."

"For what?"

Crocker was already dragging her away from the window. "I'll explain it to both of you at once."

"Wait until he shuts off the propellers," called the woman. "We don't need a couple of spectators getting their heads chopped off."

◆ ◆ ◆

The midmorning sun baked the fuel-splattered portable tanks, making the area reek like a kerosene-diesel cocktail. After a couple of minutes of inhaling the fumes, Crocker understood why the refueling area was located at the far end of the runway, at least two hundred yards from the nearest campsites.

As the twin-engine plane with the Texas flag on its tail turned off the runway and taxied toward the tanks, Crocker chanced another quick glance at Jennifer. He knew his glances were growing increasingly less subtle, but he still wasn't sure whether the look in her eyes was grief, anger, or a complete departure from reality. Whatever it was, it was unnerving. He gripped her hand a bit tighter, worried that she might inadvertently walk headlong into a spinning propeller.

The plane rolled forward and made a hard left turn, stopping with its right wingtip just a few feet from the foul-smelling tanks. The propellers slowed to an idle but continued spinning.

"Is he going to shut down?" asked Jennifer.

"I don't know."

"Can he refuel with the engines running?"

"I don't know." Crocker glanced around, but there was nobody to ask. He opened his mouth to tell Jennifer to stay put but thought better of leaving her alone. Instead, he said, "Stay with me."

Leading her by the hand, he cut a wide path around the tail of the plane and approached the large Plexiglas door behind the left wing. The wind and noise from the idling engines were surprisingly violent. He knocked on the door.

They waited but saw no sign of Brent.

Jennifer pounded twice more and screamed, "Brent! We need to talk to you!"

There was no reply.

Crocker studied the clear door for a moment. There was no handle, but he remembered seeing Brent slide it straight up. He placed his hands on the smooth plastic and pushed upward. It moved about an inch, exposing the bottom edge of the door.

"Give me a hand!" he shouted.

Jennifer pushed on the exposed edge of the door. It slid upward until the gap at the bottom was a couple of feet high.

"Good enough!" He bent over and made a stirrup with his hands. "Climb up!"

Jennifer placed one foot in his hands and pulled herself up into the plane, crawling through the small opening they'd created.

Crocker hoisted himself up and squeezed through the gap, into the narrow fuselage. He crouched beside Jennifer and inspected their surroundings. The main cabin was devoid of seats but had two rows of seat belts bolted directly to the floor. Through the archway in the front bulkhead, he could see the cockpit controls but not the pilot.

"Brent," he called, "you up there?"

From the pilot's seat, Brent poked his head out and hollered, "Shut the door and come up here."

Crocker was grateful to find a handle on this side of the door. He pulled it shut and followed Jennifer to the front of the plane.

"Brent," he said as they reached the bulkhead, "we have a bit of a situation."

"No shit," replied Brent.

A .357 revolver peeked out from the copilot's seat.

Scarlett, still wearing the black wig, leaned out behind the revolver and said, "Throw me your gun."

Brent glanced back from the pilot's seat and said, "I woulda warned you if I coulda, but she had the drop on me."

Crocker nodded that he understood.

"Your gun," repeated Scarlett. "Now!"

"We're not armed," replied Jennifer.

"Bullshit."

"It's true," said Crocker. "I'm all out of guns. I was looking for that one in Larry's office when…"

"When you shot Vegas," said Jennifer, glaring at Scarlett.

Scarlett locked eyes with Jennifer. "That was your fault, you know. If you'd just done as I said, I wouldn't have had to—"

"Wouldn't have had to what?" Jennifer took a step forward. "Wouldn't have had to shoot your friend in the back as she was running away?"

Scarlett pointed the gun at Jennifer and cocked the hammer. "Take one more step. I dare you."

Crocker raised an arm to block Jennifer from advancing. Still staring at Scarlett, he said, "Whatever you're planning, it's not going to work. The FBI wants you for murder, kidnapping, and, if I were to guess, a whole host of conspiracy charges. By now every county and municipal law enforcement agency west of the Mississippi has your picture. Kathleen Dysart is officially one of the most wanted fugitives in America."

Scarlett flinched at the mention of her real name but quickly recovered. She offered an unconvincing smile. "I guess it's a good thing I can afford to live abroad." She patted something between her legs.

Crocker leaned forward and saw Tom's skydiving rig sitting on her lap. He laughed. "Live abroad? If this plane takes off, the FBI will be right behind you. This whole area is a no-fly zone."

Scarlett shook her head. "Not according to the pilot."

Crocker turned to Brent. "What does she mean?"

Brent sighed. "The temporary flight restrictions overlap a small portion of the drop zone, so the FAA halted all skydiving operations, but the runway itself is technically outside the restricted area."

Crocker scowled. "Why would you tell her that?"

"At the time, she wasn't pointing a gun at me."

"See," said Scarlett, "we can still take off."

"We?" asked Jennifer.

"I'm not leaving you here to call the FBI on me."

Jennifer's face was turning red. "And where do you think *we* are headed? How far do you think an old skydiving plane and six hundred thousand dollars can take you?"

"If this plane is as fast as Brent says, we can be in Baja in less than an hour."

"*Mexico?* That's your big plan?"

"It's an awesome plan." Scarlett's tone was indignant. "The FBI has no jurisdiction in Mexico. I have a friend who's been down there since she was indicted for selling ecstasy. She turns tricks at this dive bar in Ensenada. I'm going to buy the bar, take a piece of the action from all the girls working there, and spend my days drinking piña coladas on the beach."

Jennifer turned to Crocker. "Is this what you meant by 'street smart'?"

Not wanting to piss off the woman with the gun, Crocker didn't respond.

"Fuckin' right I'm street smart," said Scarlett. "You wouldn't have thought of this plan."

"True," said Jennifer. "My plan wouldn't be full of holes."

"Bullshit. What holes?"

"For one thing, foreigners can't own property on the Mexican coast."

"What?"

"You can't buy a bar in Ensenada. Also, Mexico has an extradition treaty with the United States. The FBI might not bother tracking down a hooker who sold some ecstasy, but you can bet your perky ass they'll track down one who kidnapped and murdered people."

Scarlett hesitated, then said, "I'll buy a new identity."

"You think it's that easy, huh? Just buy a whole new identity? So let me get this straight. You kill off Brent and Crocker and me and—"

"Is this your idea of helping?" asked Brent.

Jennifer continued, "After you kill off the three people who know about your plan, you—what—walk around the streets of Mexico, asking if anybody sells identities?"

Crocker wasn't sure where this was going, but he hoped Jennifer did.

"Of course," continued Jennifer, "that's assuming you don't get shot down crossing into Mexico. Brent, correct me if I'm wrong, but don't you need to file a flight plan or something before crossing international borders?"

"Uh... Yeah," said Brent, clearly uneasy. "Foreign governments generally frown on planes entering their airspace unannounced."

Scarlett was visibly frustrated. "Can't you fly under their radar or something?"

Brent swallowed. "Well, umm...I..."

"It doesn't matter if he can or not," said Jennifer.

"Why not?" snapped Scarlett.

"Listen."

"What? Just say what you have to say."

"No, I mean really *listen*. Can you hear them?"

"Hear what? There's nothing to hear but the fucking engines."

"If you listen carefully, you can hear the sirens on the sheriff's cars driving down the dirt path from the Pear. Before Crocker and I left, he radioed and told them you were headed this way."

Scarlett stood and looked out Brent's window. "Shit!"

Crocker leaned through the opening in the bulkhead and looked for himself. Three Nye County sheriff's vehicles led a procession of FBI vehicles down the hill that separated the lake bed from the Pear.

Jennifer leaned in beside him. "Have you ever seen that many cop cars, Scarlett? I know I haven't."

Scarlett turned and pressed the gun into Jennifer's chest. "Back up! Both of you!"

Crocker put an arm around Jennifer's waist and walked backward, dragging her toward the tail of the plane.

"Go ahead and shoot us," said Jennifer. "You're on such a roll, why not make it an interstate killing spree? Maybe you'll get the death penalty."

"That's far enough," said Scarlett. "Both of you put your hands up and stand aside."

Crocker and Jennifer complied.

Scarlett pulled the gun tight to her chest and eased past the pair, giving them as wide a berth as the narrow fuselage would allow.

She remembers her training, thought Crocker.

When she was safely past them, she hurried to the Plexiglas door and stared outside.

Police sirens shouted to be heard over the hum of the idling engines.

Scarlett pointed her gun toward the cockpit. "Take off!"

"Where do you want to go?" asked Brent.

"Mexico. Anywhere. I don't care. Just take off!"

Brent glanced at Crocker as if looking for advice.

Standing there with his hands up, Crocker simply shrugged.

"Okay," said Brent, "the lady with the gun gets her way." He turned back toward the controls and hollered, "Everyone take a seat." As he put on his flight headset, he added, "Find a seat belt if you can. We're taking off downwind, so this could get ugly."

Crocker watched Scarlett, hoping she might drop her guard in her rush to get back to the cockpit. But instead of moving back toward the front of the plane, she lowered herself to the ground and grabbed the seat belt nearest the door. Using one hand, she fastened the belt around her waist. The other hand kept Larry's .357 revolver pointed in the direction of her three hostages.

The whine of the engines grew louder, and the plane lurched forward, causing Crocker and Jennifer to stumble.

Crocker grabbed Jennifer by the waist and pointed her toward the copilot's seat. "Sit next to Brent. I'll sit back here."

Jennifer ducked through the archway, into the tiny cockpit.

As the plane turned down the runway and accelerated, Crocker lowered himself against the bulkhead behind Brent's seat. He glanced over his left shoulder and saw Jennifer sitting in the copilot's seat, pulling a pair of shoulder straps down over her head.

He felt behind him and found a seat belt bolted to the floor. He quickly fastened it around his waist.

Back by the door, Scarlett kept the gun pointed in his direction.

He felt the wheels lift off and glanced out the small round window to his right. On the ground, the convoy of sheriff and FBI vehicles snaked its way through the tent city.

♦ ♦ ♦

Jennifer felt a tap on her shoulder and glanced over at Brent.

He pointed to a headset hanging near her right knee.

She grabbed it and put it on.

Before she'd had a chance to adjust the fit, he asked, "Can you hear me?"

"Loud and clear," she replied.

"I expect your young friend will make her way back up here as soon as I level out, so do what I say, and don't ask any questions."

"Roger." As soon as the word was out of her mouth, Jennifer wondered why she hadn't just said *okay*. Wearing a headset apparently made her want to talk like Iceman.

"Reach under your seat," he said. "There is an iPad under there."

Jennifer leaned forward and moved Tom's parachute rig to the side.

"Careful not to hit the yoke or the pedals," added Brent.

Jennifer found the iPad, sat up, and turned toward the pilot's seat.

"Don't hand it to me!" he snapped.

Jennifer recoiled.

Brent cast a quick glance over his shoulder. "She can't see our seats, but she can see if we pass anything between them."

Jennifer nodded and looked at the tablet in her hands. "What do you want me to do with this?"

"Turn it on and open the Flight Planner app."

Jennifer pressed the power button and risked her own glance back while it booted. Scarlett had the gun pointed at Crocker, who was staring out the window to his right. Jennifer contemplated trying to get his attention but decided against it.

"Okay," said Brent, "it's the icon on the top left."

Jennifer looked down and saw that the iPad had booted. She opened the app. "Now what?"

"Click on 'Monitor Flight' and then 'Set Waypoint.'"

Jennifer located the appropriate tabs. "Done."

"Type in 'Indian Springs.'"

She typed the name and pressed SEARCH. "Okay, it says, 'Creech AFB,' and then, in parentheses, 'INS.' Is that what you want?"

"Yes. Press 'Confirm' and tell me what my bearing should be."

Jennifer pressed CONFIRM. "It's showing me a map with a path drawn on it."

"Look at the information at the bottom of the screen. You should see the letters BRG followed by a three-digit number. What is the number?"

Jennifer scanned to the bottom of the page. "It says zero three four."

"Okay, stick the pad back under your seat before I start my turn."

Jennifer nudged Tom's parachute out of the way again and slid the tablet under her seat. When the tablet was stowed, she glanced back over her shoulder.

Neither Crocker nor Scarlett had moved.

The plane banked slowly to the right, and Jennifer saw Las Vegas in the distance.

"What is Creech AFB?" she asked.

"Creech Air Force Base. It's the command center for the U.S. military's drone operations around the world."

"Why would we want to go there?"

"Because it's restricted airspace. If we get too close, Nellis will deploy a couple of fighter jets to escort us down."

"Escort us down or shoot us down?" Jennifer already didn't like this plan.

"As long as we do as they say, they'll just escort us."

"And if the crazy hooker with a gun refuses to do as they say, where does that leave us?"

Brent didn't answer.

Jennifer shot him a sideways glance. "You need a better plan."

CHAPTER TWENTY-NINE

As the plane leveled out of its turn, Crocker glimpsed the peak of Mount Charleston off the right wingtip and wondered what Brent was up to. Scarlett might have been naïve about the logistics of flying to Mexico, but she was smart enough to realize the plane was flying in the opposite direction.

As far as he could recall, there was nothing north of Mount Charleston except hundreds of miles of empty desert and a few military testing sites.

The plane was still climbing but not as steeply as before. Scarlett glanced from the Plexiglas door to the row of windows on the opposite side of the plane.

"Hey!" she yelled over the engine noise. "Why are we heading north?"

Crocker shrugged.

She pointed the gun toward the cockpit. "Ask them!"

He looked back over his left shoulder and waved to get Jennifer's attention. She leaned toward him and pulled the headset away from her ear.

He cocked a thumb in Scarlett's direction. "She wants to know why we're heading north."

Jennifer replied, "We've been ordered to land."

"What?"

"Something about us flying too close to Creech Air Force Base while the FBI's flight restrictions are still in place. They think we might be a threat to national security."

"Threat to national security? What does that mean?"

From the back of the plane, Scarlett shouted, "What are you talking about?"

Crocker hoped she wasn't about to shoot the messenger. "The air force is telling us we have to land. They're saying we're a threat to national security."

"Land?" she screamed. "We are *not* landing!"

She unbuckled her seat belt and stood with the gun against her side, pointed at Crocker. She took a couple of steps toward him but stopped before she was within reach.

"Hey, pilot!" she screamed. "Brent!"

Brent turned and glanced back through the bulkhead archway.

Scarlett pointed the gun at him and yelled, "If you land this plane, I'll kill all three of you."

"If we don't," he said, "the air force will kill all *four* of us. Nellis Air Force Base is sending a pair of F-16s to intercept us. We've been ordered to land at the North Las Vegas airport, or they'll shoot us down."

"No!"

She looked as though she might take another step toward the cockpit.

Crocker readied himself to grab the gun.

Scarlett glanced at him and, as if reading his mind, took a step back. She glanced out the window to her left. "Land someplace else, someplace close, before the air force planes get here."

"Wake up!" yelled Jennifer. "They're tracking our plane. No matter where we land, local police are going to be waiting for us. You have two choices—land and get arrested or stay in the air and get blown up by a missile."

Scarlett responded with an earsplitting scream that might have been directed at Jennifer or the situation or some combination of the two.

"Scream all you want," said Brent, "but I'm landing at North Las Vegas. I'd rather take my chances with that revolver than with an AMRAAM missile."

The plane banked slowly to the right, turning toward North Las Vegas. Scarlett took another step back and glanced nervously from window to window.

"Just turn yourself in," said Crocker. "Fighting the inevitable is only going to make things worse."

"Worse?" she screamed. "As in I might get the electric chair instead of the gas chamber?"

Crocker considered pointing out that Nevada used lethal injection to execute prisoners but thought better of it. Instead, he said, "Nevada isn't big on the death penalty. They haven't executed anybody in years."

Scarlett shook her head. "I'm not landing!" She turned and looked out the Plexiglas door.

"I have an idea," said Jennifer.

Scarlett turned back toward the cockpit.

"When the police storm the plane," continued Jennifer, "you just offer them some of that 'special attention' that got you and Vegas off the hook when you went to buy drugs with your buddy Stinky."

Scarlett's face turned red.

"Blow jobs alone might not be enough." Jennifer reached for something near her feet. "But blow jobs and six hundred thousand in cash might be." She tossed Tom's skydiving rig through the archway. It landed at Scarlett's feet.

Scarlett stared down at the skydiving rig for a long time.

Crocker quietly unbuckled his seat belt and prepared to rush her if she raised the gun toward Jennifer. He was certain that some sort of outburst was coming. But when Scarlett looked up, the anger was gone from her face.

She reached down and picked up the skydiving rig. "This thing still works, right?"

"What?" asked Crocker.

"Tom said there's still one parachute left in this thing. Brent, would it still work?"

She can't be serious, thought Crocker.

Brent turned to look at the rig. "That depends on what you did to it when you were stuffing it full of cash."

"I just sewed these top flaps shut"—she pointed to her handiwork—"the ones where the other parachute went."

Brent stared at the tangle of nylon straps and steel buckles. "If you didn't modify the bottom flaps, it would probably work, but I wouldn't bet my life on it."

"How do I use it?"

"Use it? You want me to give you a skydiving lesson while I'm flying the plane?"

"I don't need to know how to do backflips. Just tell me how to put it on and make it open."

Crocker's first instinct was to try to talk her out of it. Then he thought about the fighter jets and the sound of Larry's labored breathing on the basement floor and the voice on the phone saying, *"Megan, honey, is that you?"* and decided this was as good a solution as any.

◆ ◆ ◆

By the time Brent had talked Scarlett through the process of putting on the skydiving rig and explained how to deploy the parachute, Las Vegas was close enough to fill most of the front windshield.

Jennifer turned around and yelled, "If you don't want to land in a housing development, you'd better go now."

With the skydiving harness cinched around her pink tracksuit and the gun in her hand, Scarlett looked like a dark-haired Barbie doll that had gotten its accessories mixed up with a G.I. Joe's.

She stared out the Plexiglas door. "Where are the jets?"

Jennifer pretended to check. "I see a plane in the distance. I'm not sure if it's a fighter or an airliner. If you go now, you'll be long gone before it's close enough to matter."

Scarlett knelt and examined the door.

"Just pull it straight up," said Crocker.

She grabbed the handle with her left hand and gave a halfhearted tug. The door didn't budge.

"With both hands," added Crocker.

She shook her head and stood. "Jennifer, you do it."

"What?" asked Jennifer.

"I'm not putting down the gun. Get back here and open the door for me." Crocker rose to his feet. "I'll do it."

Scarlett pointed the gun at him. "Sit down. Jennifer can do it."

This wasn't part of the plan, thought Jennifer.

Tricking Scarlett into jumping had been her idea, but she had little desire to open an airplane door in flight and zero desire to do so at gunpoint.

"Now!" yelled Scarlett. "Before the jets get here!"

Jennifer took a deep breath and reassured herself that this would all be over once Scarlett was out of the plane. She fumbled with the seat belt buckle, trying to figure out how to release the four-point restraint. Brent reached across and unbuckled it for her. She nodded in appreciation and climbed out of the seat.

Crocker's eyes reflected Jennifer's own deep concern as she stepped past him. She forced a reassuring smile and made her way to the back of the plane.

Scarlett peered out through the Plexiglas. "Where are we?"

"Damned if I know," said Jennifer. "All I know is that in another couple of minutes, we're going to be over the city."

"We're following Highway 95," said Crocker, staring out the window to his right. "It looks like we're about a mile from that big golf resort on the outskirts of town."

"Perfect." Scarlett's voice trembled. "I'm great with golfers."

"So you should have no trouble finding a ride," said Jennifer.

Scarlett's eyes did not project the determination of a woman prepared to jump out of an airplane.

Maybe encouragement is the wrong approach.

Jennifer let out an exasperated sigh. "So do you really want me to open the door, or can we dispense with this charade and let Brent land the plane?"

Scarlett's eyes widened.

Jennifer continued, "Because you and I both know you're not the jump-out-of-an-airplane type." She hesitated. "You're more the shoot-a-friend-in-the-back type."

The surprise in Scarlett's eyes turned to anger. She pointed the gun at Jennifer's chest and said, "Open it."

Finally! thought Jennifer as she knelt.

She slipped her fingers under the thin handle and pulled upward with all her strength. The door slid open.

The sudden rush of cold and noise took her breath away. She looked at the ground several thousand feet below and felt the world start to spin. She took a quick step back and closed her eyes until the feeling passed. When she opened them, she saw Scarlett frozen in place. The black wig flapped in the wind, revealing occasional flashes of red.

"Okay," yelled Jennifer, "prove me wrong."

Scarlett took a slow step forward, shifted the gun to her left hand, and used her right to hold on to the door frame. She stared out at the same view that had made Jennifer dizzy.

Jennifer saw that the plane was already past the golf course. They'd be over the city in less than a minute. She contemplated trying to shove Scarlett from behind but recalled from childhood that trying to push someone into a swimming pool was a great way to end up in the pool yourself.

Time was running out. The bluff wouldn't work if Scarlett chose to land with the plane—she'd see that there were no jets and no police officers and order Brent to take off again.

In desperation, Jennifer yelled, "What are you waiting for? Don't tell me you're worried karma might be a bigger bitch than you are."

Scarlett turned from the door.

As soon as Jennifer saw the young woman's eyes, she knew she'd taken it too far. She fixated on the gun and didn't see Scarlett's other hand until it had grabbed hold of her blood-splattered WHAT HAPPENS IN VEGAS T-shirt.

Scarlett pulled Jennifer toward the door. "I think you should come with me!"

Jennifer clawed at Scarlett's wrist and leaned back, straining against the pull. In her peripheral vision, she saw Crocker jump to his feet and move toward them.

Scarlett pointed the gun at him and laughed.

He stopped where he was.

Scarlett put all her weight into dragging Jennifer toward the door.

Jennifer's feet struggled for purchase on the carpeted floor. Her foot slipped on a seat belt buckle and slid out from under her. She landed on her butt.

Scarlett's grip on the T-shirt held tight.

Jennifer began sliding feet-first toward the open door. She grabbed the seat belt with one hand and hung on with every ounce of strength she could muster, praying that the shirt's stitching would give out before her arms did. She dug the fingers of her free hand into Scarlett's wrist, with no discernible effect.

"Let her go!" yelled Crocker. "Jump before it's too late!"

Still pointing the gun at him, Scarlett replied, "You're like a bad-luck charm, Matt. First your fiancée, then Vegas, and now this uptight..."

The words faded to noise as Jennifer's gaze landed on a red, pillow-shaped handle attached to Scarlett's harness.

An image of Tom standing on the runway in his boxer shorts flashed through her mind.

She released Scarlett's wrist and grabbed the handle. It made a ripping noise as it pulled free of the harness. Two yellow cables trailed behind it.

Scarlett went silent. Her eyes widened.

Jennifer yelled, "You want to jump now, bitch, be my guest."

Scarlett released Jennifer's shirt and grabbed the handle. "What is this?"

"Karma!" Jennifer's foot found the crotch of Scarlett's velour tracksuit.

Scarlett tumbled backward through the door. The black wig flew away first. The rest of her followed, disappearing in a pink blur.

◆ ◆ ◆

As soon as Scarlett grabbed the red handle from Jennifer, Crocker rushed for the gun. Another half second and he would have had it. Instead, he got there just in time to see Scarlett fly out the door—gun, wig, pink tracksuit, and all—and cartwheel beneath the tail of the plane.

She fell for three or four seconds before the parachute deployed. Then she continued falling, away from the parachute.

Crocker stared at the spot where he'd lost sight of her, until the Plexiglas door slid shut in front of him. He hadn't even noticed Jennifer standing to close it.

"What was that?" he asked. "That thing you pulled."

She stared out the door. "Cutaway handle. Tom pointed it out."

"So that's why..." He searched for the right words.

Jennifer met his gaze. "That's why the only way Scarlett is getting a lift from a golfer is if he happens to have a snow shovel and some Hefty bags in his cart."

Crocker stood dumbfounded as she casually adjusted her stretched-out T-shirt.

From the front of the plane, Brent yelled back, "Did she jump?"

Crocker walked to the cockpit and leaned through the opening in the bulkhead. "You didn't see?"

"No, once the door came open, I had to focus on keeping us straight and level. What was all the yelling about?"

Jennifer leaned in beside Crocker. "Scarlett was having second thoughts. But she finally jumped."

"Good. Did her chute open?"

Crocker exchanged a look with Jennifer. "Uh, yeah, I'm pretty sure I saw it open."

Brent nodded. "Now she's the cops' problem. Let's get back to the drop zone."

"The drop zone? I thought we had to land at North Las Vegas."

"Nah, that crap about the air force ordering us to land was just a bluff to get her out of the plane."

Crocker turned to Jennifer. "Did you know about this?"

"Know about it?" She looked as though she were suppressing a smile. "It was my idea."

"And it was a damn sight better than what I had in mind," said Brent.

Crocker shook his head in amazement.

"Now," said Brent, "if you don't mind, I need to let air traffic control know what we're doing up here and figure out the safest route back to the lake bed."

"Wait," said Crocker. "Instead of returning to the lake bed, could you get us to Cortez, where you dropped off Tom and Ashley?"

Brent hesitated as if waiting for a punch line. "You want me to fly you to *Colorado?*"

"Why?" asked Jennifer.

"Because Dudka and his men are going after Tom and Ashley."

Jennifer gasped. "Right now?"

Crocker nodded. "The FBI checked Ilya's cell phone records, and it looks like Dudka and his men could be as close as…" He looked at the digital clock on the plane's console. "They could be within ninety minutes of my place."

"Hell," said Brent, "it would take us almost that long just to get to Cortez. Even if you had a car waiting at the airport, that puts you at least an hour behind them. What do you hope to accomplish?"

"Maybe nothing, but I damned sure won't be able to help if I'm eight hundred miles away."

Jennifer turned to Brent. "Do we have enough fuel to get there?"

He glanced down at his gauges. "We don't have as much cushion as I'd like, but it's doable."

"Then let's go," she said.

Brent sighed. "Copy that." He depressed a button on the yoke. "Las Vegas approach, King Air five one one Bravo Foxtrot. Request."

Crocker placed a hand on Jennifer's shoulder. She took it in her own hand and squeezed.

Brent depressed the button again. "King Air five one one Bravo Foxtrot is a Beech Bravo niner zero at one two thousand, seven miles northwest of North Las Vegas—Victor Golf Tango—en route to Colorado. Request flight following."

He adjusted a dial on the console and turned to Crocker. "Okay, we're looking at—best guess—an hour and a quarter until wheels down."

"Do you have a cell phone?" asked Crocker.

"I thought there was no cell service at your place."

"There isn't. I need to confirm that police are on their way."

Brent pulled a phone from under the seat, pressed the power button, and handed it to Crocker. "If I get a fine from the FCC, I'm billing Tom for it."

Crocker pulled Sheriff Cargill's crumpled business card from his pocket. He dialed the number for SA Bruce Eastland and waited.

After one ring, Special Agent Eastland answered, "Eastland. Who is this?"

"It's Crocker. What's the status of the police response to my cabin in Colorado?"

"Christ!" exclaimed Eastland. "Where are you? Tell me you're not in that skydiving plane that took off from the lake bed."

"We're on the plane. One of Tom Blackwell's friends is flying us to Colorado. How far out are the cops?"

"So Kathleen Dysart—er, Scarlett—isn't with you?"

"Uh…" *One thing at a time*, thought Crocker. "No, she's not. It's just Jennifer, the pilot, and me."

"Christ, man, we were afraid we were dealing with some sort of hostage situation. We have agents coordinating with the FAA as I speak."

"It's complicated, but I'll explain it all once we know Tom and Ashley are safe. Where are the cops?"

"We're working on it," said Eastland. "Several agencies are activating their SWAT teams as we speak."

"SWAT teams?" yelled Crocker. "Dudka's men could be there in less than an hour and a half!"

"I'm aware of the timeline, but we're talking about an unknown number of heavily armed killers. No agency is willing to send anything short of a fully equipped tactical unit."

"Just have somebody pick up Tom and Ashley and get them out of there."

"Your house is too damned remote. Nobody has a patrol that can get there in less than an hour, and you said yourself it takes twenty-five to thirty minutes to get back to the highway. They're not going to risk running into a vanload of Russian mercenaries on a one-lane dirt road."

"Goddammit!" said Crocker. "How far out are the tactical teams?"

"As we speak, the police departments in Durango, Cortez, Telluride, and Silverton are all activating their teams, as are the La Plata and Dolores County sheriff's departments. Cortez is closest—they say they can be there in less than an hour and twenty minutes, once the team is assembled."

"And how long will that be?"

"Probably another thirty to forty-five minutes."

"Are you fucking kidding me?"

"The Bureau's Denver team will be on a chopper within the next twenty to thirty minutes, but they're looking at a ninety-minute flight time."

"So you don't have anybody who is likely to get there *before* Dudka's men? What about a roadblock?"

"A roadblock still requires a SWAT team. Nobody is going to send a couple of patrol officers to get gunned down by a KGB death squad."

"Fuck," said Crocker. "Okay, keep working on it. I'm going to try to figure out something else."

He hung up the phone and realized that both Jennifer and Brent were staring at him. "It's not looking good."

"We heard," said Jennifer.

"I could try buzzing the house," said Brent. "Maybe we could get Tom or Ashley's attention and prompt them to run up that hill where you said they could get cell service."

"Perhaps," said Crocker, not liking the idea of watching helplessly from an airplane as Tom and Ashley got ambushed by Dudka's goons.

An idea struck him. "Do you have any more parachutes?"

"Fresh out," said Brent. "And even if I did, trying to use them at that altitude in mountainous terrain would be suicide."

"What does the altitude have to do with it?"

"Same reason you can't fly a helicopter to the top of Mount Everest—the air is too thin. Rotor blades and parachutes need dense air to work."

"Well, I know helicopters work at my place. The Forest Service uses them for— That's it!" He dialed 411 on the phone.

"Who are you calling?" asked Jennifer.

Crocker held up a hand to silence her.

An electronic voice on the other end of the line said, "Directory assistance. Say a city and state."

"Durango, Colorado."

"Please say the name of the business you want."

"United States Forest Service."

"Connecting."

After two rings, a woman answered, "San Juan Public Lands Center. How may I direct your call?"

"I need the forest fire management officer."

"Please hold."

The phone rang twice, and a woman answered, "Allison Bensimon, forest fire management."

"Allison, it's Crocker. How quickly could you get a helicopter out to my place?"

"Crocker? What's going on? Are you in trouble?"

"It's not me. It's the kids you dropped off the rental car for. We need to get them out of my house fast."

Allison was silent for a moment, then said, "Does this have anything to do with the call we just got from the Durango police?"

"The police called?"

"They wanted to know if we could use our helitack choppers to transport SWAT officers into San Juan. But our helitack crew has both of our choppers down in New Mexico, helping out with the fires at Gila."

"So you don't have anything?"

"Nothing that's ready to go. I could call over to Mesa Verde and ask if the park's 206 is available, but it'll take them thirty or forty-five minutes to get their pilot to the pad, do the preflight, and get airborne."

"And how long to get out to my place?"

"I don't know. Maybe fifteen minutes."

Cutting it too close, thought Crocker. He couldn't ask the pilot to risk walking into an ambush.

"What about Cortez?" he asked. "Could you have it meet me at Cortez Muni and take me out there?"

"I'd have to lie on the paperwork and say you have an official purpose for being on the flight."

"I hate to ask you to do this, but lie on the paperwork. Put both my name and Jennifer Williams."

"Who is Jennifer Williams?"

"I wouldn't even know where to start. Please just make this happen. Ms. Williams and I will meet the pilot at Cortez in one hour. Tell him to keep the engine running."

CHAPTER THIRTY

The helicopter pilot turned out to be a *her*, not a *him*, but she did keep the engine running. Brent's plane pulled to a stop fifteen yards from the helipad, and Jennifer and Crocker sprinted from the plane to the pad, where the young pilot—dressed in a military-style flight suit and helmet—met them and instructed them to approach the helicopter from the side and stay clear of the tail rotor. A minute later, they were in the air.

Jennifer didn't enjoy her first helicopter flight nearly as much as she'd always thought she would. She had other things on her mind.

She didn't think of Crocker's plan as foolish, but it certainly wasn't foolproof. He seemed certain that Dudka's men wouldn't risk speeding and, therefore, couldn't reach the house before 10:50 a.m. The helicopter would touch down at approximately 10:55, which meant Dudka and his men might already be there, but only if they'd driven the last three hours without stopping.

Crocker didn't think they'd drive straight through. He predicted they'd fill up with gas in Cortez, in case they had to make a quick getaway, and stop again after leaving Cortez, to put on their gear and review their plan of attack.

Jennifer thought this sounded like hopeful speculation, but she didn't say so. He seemed confident, though not so confident as to have the helicopter land directly in front of his house.

At Crocker's request, the helicopter stayed out of sight of the house and approached through a nearby valley. It set down in a clearing a quarter mile south of their destination.

The rotor blades slowed to a stop, and, for the first time in almost two hours, Jennifer's hearing wasn't under assault from aircraft engines.

The pilot opened the helicopter's large sliding door, and Jennifer followed Crocker out into a setting that, compared to the Nevada desert, might have been another planet.

The valley was bordered on either side by tall evergreens. Aside from the calls of a few birds, the only sound was the babbling of a nearby stream. The air smelled of pine and moss—and a hint of helicopter exhaust.

The pilot removed her helmet and ran a hand through the short, dark hair underneath. "Allison was pretty vague about what's going on, so I'm just going to ask you two point-blank: Am I safe here?"

Jennifer turned to Crocker and waited for a reply.

He gave a less-than-reassuring nod. "More or less." He pointed to a footpath running up the left side of the valley. "But if you see trouble coming down that trail, go ahead and take off."

The pilot frowned. "What would trouble look like?"

"Men with guns."

"Fuck."

"Yeah," said Jennifer, "it's been that kind of week."

◆ ◆ ◆

After months in the desert, Crocker's body was no longer acclimated to this altitude. The two-hundred-yard run up the side of the valley had left him panting for air. Behind him, Jennifer leaned against a tree, trying to catch her breath.

"Can...you...see...anything?" she gasped.

The house itself was hidden by the trees, but he could see where the dirt road rounded the hill and turned toward his driveway. The ground was bone dry, which meant that if anyone had driven that road in the past five minutes, a cloud of dust would still be visible.

"I think we beat them," he said. "You ready?"

Jennifer joined him at the ridge, still panting. "How much farther?"

"We're halfway there. It's downhill from here."

"Can you see the house?"

"Not from here, but that bend in the road is where I plan to pin down Dudka's men. It's clearly visible from the guest bedrooms on the second floor."

"How far from the house?"

"Almost eight hundred yards. It's a difficult shot but doable. I'll keep them busy dodging three-oh-eight rounds until SWAT arrives. With any luck, you'll be back at the chopper before the shooting starts. C'mon."

He took off down the wooded path, accelerating to a fast run, then slowing a bit as he reminded himself that the downhill part of a hike is always the most dangerous.

The sound of feet shuffling behind him told him Jennifer was keeping pace.

The previous August he could have run this path blindfolded, but the intervening months had taken a toll on both his recollection of the trail and the trail itself.

I should warn—

Jennifer screamed.

Crocker glanced back in time to see her hit the ground, hard. She tumbled and came to a stop a couple of yards behind him.

He spun and hurried to her side. "You okay?"

She shook her head and, through gritted teeth, said, "Ankle... Twisted my ankle.... Damned rock rolled right out from under me."

"It's my fault. I should have warned you." He knelt to check her ankle. "The winter ice dislodges the rocks."

"Help me up," she said. "We have to keep going."

He gave her his hand and helped her to her feet. "Can you put weight on it?"

She tried and winced. "Yeah, but it's not fun."

"Take a couple of steps."

She hobbled forward. "You go on. I'll catch up."

He considered his options. Sending her back to the chopper wouldn't work—he needed her to show Tom and Ashley the path. He could wait for her to catch up, but that would delay Tom and Ashley's departure.

"Raise your right arm," he said.

"What?"

"I'll get you to the house. Tom and Ashley can help you back to the chopper. Raise your arm."

Jennifer complied. Crocker grabbed the arm, knelt, and hoisted her into the fireman's carry he'd learned in the marines.

With Jennifer slung over his shoulders, he ran.

♦ ♦ ♦

Jennifer saw the two-story log cabin the moment they cleared the trees. Riding sideways on Crocker's shoulders prevented her from studying it in detail, but it was every bit as big as he'd described.

His heavy breathing was growing wheezy, but he didn't break stride until they reached the porch. He struggled up the steps and set her in a rustic porch swing.

She grabbed one of the chains supporting the swing and pulled herself to her feet as he hurried to the front door.

"Tom!" Crocker pounded on the door and sucked in another wheezing breath. "Ashley!" He kept pounding. "Tom...Ash..." His voice trailed off as he gasped for air.

"Tom!" screamed Jennifer. "Ashley! Open the—"

The door opened.

Tom, dressed only in a pair of boxer briefs, held a silver revolver at his side. "Christ, y'all just about scared us half to death. How'd you get here?"

"Where is Ashley?" asked Jennifer. "We have to get out of here, *now*."

"She's upstairs. What's going on?"

Crocker opened his mouth, but only a guttural wheeze emerged.

Jennifer hobbled toward the door. "We'll explain while you get dressed. Where'd you get that gun?"

In a strangled half-whisper, Crocker said, "Not... real." He sucked in another breath. "Prop."

Jennifer placed a hand on his back and led him into the house.

Tom shut the door behind them. "The gun was mounted on the wall. Are you two okay?"

Jennifer leaned against a table for support. "We could be better. I sprained my ankle, and I think he's having an asthma attack."

Crocker nodded and stumbled toward a large sofa.

Jennifer surveyed the high-ceilinged living room. It struck her as the type of place Teddy Roosevelt would have hung out. Native American art adorned the walls. A painting of a herd of elk hung above the stone fireplace.

Crocker collapsed onto the sofa.

Jennifer hobbled toward him. "Do you have a rescue inhaler?"

He nodded again. "Master"—he struggled for a breath of air—"bathroom."

"Jennifer!" Ashley stood on the second-floor landing atop the large staircase. Her hair suggested she'd just crawled out of bed. She wore a thigh-length Denver Broncos jersey and tube socks. "How did you get here?"

"Get dressed," said Jennifer. "Dudka and his men will be here any minute."

Ashley's eyes widened. She nodded and turned away.

"Wait!" called Jennifer.

Ashley turned back.

"Do you know where the master bedroom is?"

"Up here. Do you want to follow me?"

Jennifer sighed and hopped toward the stairway on one foot.

"Are you okay?"

Jennifer grabbed the banister at the foot of the stairs. "Nothing is okay." She put her weight on the banister and hopped up one step at a time.

Ashley rushed to meet her. "Here, let me help you."

Jennifer wrapped an arm around Ashley's neck and hobbled up the remaining steps.

When they came to the hallway at the top, Ashley said, "Almost there. First door on the right."

They reached the door and shuffled inside. Jennifer saw the unmade bed, paused only a moment to process that it appeared to have been shared, and then collapsed onto it.

"What's going on?" asked Ashley.

"Too many things to list. Check the bathroom for a rescue inhaler. Crocker is having an asthma attack."

Without a word, Ashley turned and disappeared through the bathroom door.

Jennifer heard cabinets being opened and drawers being rummaged. She lifted her injured leg onto the bed and saw that the ankle was starting to swell. She grabbed the corner of the bedsheet and pulled until it ripped. She tore a six-foot strip and began wrapping her ankle.

"Found it!" Ashley emerged from the bathroom carrying a plastic inhaler like the ones Jennifer had seen kids use in elementary school. "Want me to take it to Crocker?"

"Yes. Then get your ass up here and get dressed. We have to go."

Ashley was gone for only a few seconds. She reentered the room at a run and skidded to a stop in front of a dresser on which sat three Walmart shopping bags.

"I tossed the inhaler down to Tom." She dug into one of the bags. "Let me grab some clothes; then I'll help you to the car. I can change on the road."

"We can't take the road," said Jennifer, still wrapping her ankle. "We have to hike out of here."

Ashley stopped. "You and Crocker don't seem in much shape to hike."

"Crocker isn't coming. He has a hunting rifle in a safe downstairs. He's going to assume a sniper position and hold off Dudka's men."

"From how far away?"

Jennifer threaded the bandage back through the wraps. "I don't know. A long way." She tied off the loose end. "I think he said eight hundred yards."

"Is that still going to work?"

"What do you mean?"

"Well, I'm no sniper, but I grew up around enough hunters to know that you have to control your breathing to make the long shots. Can Crocker control his breathing if he just had an asthma attack?"

Jennifer didn't know the answer to that question, so she focused on what she did know. "This place will be crawling with SWAT teams in twenty minutes. With any luck, they'll arrive before Dudka's men do. Now get dressed."

◆ ◆ ◆

Although the makeshift bandage had eased the pain in Jennifer's ankle, she clung to Ashley's arm and avoided putting much weight on the afflicted leg as they descended the stairs. There was no time for another mishap.

Ashley had taken less than two minutes to dress in a Denver Nuggets sweatshirt, lightweight cargo pants, and cheap hiking boots that still had tags dangling from the laces. In her free arm she carried a grocery sack stuffed with Tom's clothes.

At the foot of the stairs, Jennifer let go and hurried toward Crocker as fast as her swollen ankle would carry her.

Ashley tossed the sack to Tom. "Get dressed. We don't have much time."

Crocker lay on the couch, breathing normally but sound asleep.

"Jesus!" said Jennifer. "What happened?"

Tom replied, "After he used the inhaler, he kind of relaxed and then—I don't know—I guess he passed out or something. I've been trying to wake him, but he's out cold."

"What now?" asked Ashley.

"I don't know." Jennifer racked her brain for a new plan. "Just give me a minute."

"Where is that rifle you mentioned?"

"It's in the safe, but Crocker has the combination."

Tom pulled on his shorts. "I'll get some water to splash on his face." Still barefoot and shirtless, he turned and ran down the first-floor hallway.

"How much time do we have?" asked Ashley.

"I don't know. Dudka's men could have been here fifteen minutes ago."

"Maybe they took a turn too fast and drove off that nightmare of a road."

"If only," said Jennifer. "Wait, what do you mean by 'nightmare'?"

"I mean I don't know how this place ever operated as a bed-and-breakfast. They must have lost a carload of customers a week."

"Is it narrow?"

"More like a horse trail than a road."

"Where is your rental car?"

"Out back. What do you have in mind?"

"If I can use your car to block the road, Dudka's men will have to proceed on foot. That should buy you three enough time to get back to the helicopter."

"There's a helicopter?" asked Tom as he arrived with a glass of water.

"Wake Crocker," said Jennifer. "He'll show you the way."

"You show the way," said Ashley. "I'll block the road. You can't possibly get back here on that ankle."

"Neither of us will have time to get back here. But it's going to take two people to help Crocker up that path, and I won't be any help on this ankle."

"So let's all four make a run for it."

Jennifer shook her head. "We'd move too slow. Dudka's men could arrive before we reached the tree line; then we'd be fucked."

"So you're going on a suicide mission?"

"I'll block the road and hide in the trees until the police arrive. Dudka's guys aren't going to stop to search the forest."

Ashley looked as though she was considering another protest, but the debate was cut short by the sound of splashing water.

◆ ◆ ◆

Jennifer focused on keeping the worn-out Jeep Grand Cherokee centered between the trees to her right and the steep embankment to her left. Her speed was beyond reckless, but she was past the point of worrying about dying in a car crash.

As she neared the first bend in the road, she risked a glance down the embankment, saw a shallow creek a hundred feet below, and made a snap decision: She would not be abandoning the car and hiding in the trees.

She let off the gas and eased on the brake. The road ahead made a sharp turn to the right, following the creek. She slowed to a stop twenty yards short of the turn and surveyed her surroundings.

Ashley hadn't exaggerated the narrowness of the road. It reminded Jennifer of riding mules along the North Rim of the Grand Canyon with her parents when she was twelve. Her inner Realtor wondered if the developers who'd defaulted on this land had failed to factor the cost of road construction into their plans.

She rolled down the windows and listened. The only sound was her own car engine. She stared at the point where the road disappeared around the bend and marveled that she could feel so much fear in a place so inherently peaceful.

Seat belt!

She pulled the belt across her chest and buckled it. Then she grabbed the steering wheel at ten and two, remembered the airbag, and moved her hands to nine and three.

The replica revolver lay on the seat next to her—Tom's idea of a backup plan. It was a bluff, but it might be better than nothing.

When she'd left the house, Tom and Ashley had been trying to coax the safe combination out of Crocker, who'd seemed only vaguely aware of what was happening. Jennifer hadn't seen any benefit in waiting around to retrieve a gun she didn't know how to use. At least she couldn't hurt herself with a replica.

She glanced at the mountain peaks in the distance and wondered how it was possible that only a day had passed since she'd stood in Crocker's trailer, listening to him describe this place.

Stay focused.

Her hands tightened around the steering wheel.

What is taking them so long? Did they stop to eat?

She imagined Dudka's van blocking a drive-thru line as a half-dozen hit men sorted out their orders.

Maybe they heard about the FBI raid and turned around.

The dashboard clock read eleven fifteen. The police would arrive at any minute. Jennifer loosened her grip on the steering wheel and allowed herself to hope that the danger had passed.

Then she heard the crunch of tires on gravel.

She glanced again at the clock and realized she had no way of knowing if she was hearing one of Dudka's vans or a SWAT vehicle. She eased her foot off the brake and let the Jeep crawl forward.

Ahead of her, a white van nosed around the bend.

She wasn't sure if she was looking at one of Dudka's vehicles or a small-town police van, until she saw the driver. Scarlett's favorite client, Sasha, was behind the wheel.

Jennifer pressed the accelerator to the floor and steered toward the van.

Sasha's eyes widened at the sight of the oncoming vehicle.

The Jeep struck the van's left front quarter panel. Jennifer's vision went momentarily dark, then totally white.

She gasped for air and watched the world reappear as the airbag deflated. The collision had stopped the Jeep in its tracks. The van was nowhere to be seen.

A cloud of dust hung over the road. Through the ringing in her ears, Jennifer heard a staccato series of crunches that could only be the van rolling down the embankment.

The Jeep started forward at idle speed. Without thinking, she threw the transmission into park, grinding the gears and bringing the vehicle to an abrupt halt.

Part of her wondered how many men had been in the van, but she couldn't bring herself to care. She was too dazed to feel anything beyond a vague sense of surprise that her plan had worked.

She tasted something warm and salty and realized that her nose was dripping blood. A quick dab with the tail of her WHAT HAPPENS IN VEGAS T-shirt only succeeded in smearing the blood. She needed cotton balls or gauze to stem the flow.

Every aching muscle in her body told her to wait there for the SWAT medics, who would have cotton balls and gauze aplenty. But the thought of her friends flying away and leaving her alone was suddenly more than she could bear.

Steam hissed from beneath the Jeep's crumpled hood, but the engine still hummed with life. Jennifer threw the vehicle into reverse and backed up the road. She drove slowly, now very aware of the perils of the narrow path.

She ignored the blood dripping down her chin and focused on keeping the cabin centered in the Jeep's rear window. As Crocker's two-story dream home grew closer, she felt an overwhelming desire to spend a whole day just sitting on the porch swing, doing nothing but rocking and listening to the birds.

A loud pop shattered her fantasy. The car jerked toward the trees. Jennifer corrected the wheel and stepped on the brake. Her heart raced as the car came to a stop.

Blowout. The crash caused a blowout.

She shifted into park and looked back at the house, no more than a hundred yards away.

Something struck the front windshield. She turned forward to find a fog of cracked glass. The myriad of tiny fractures led to a small hole just below the rearview mirror.

A second bullet tore through the glass and whistled past her head. She fumbled with the seat belt and rolled onto the floorboard as two more shots crashed through the windshield. Peering over the edge of the seat, she saw a golf-ball-size hole in the laminated glass.

Stay or go? Stay or go?

She had no idea how many men were firing at her, no idea how far away the SWAT teams were.

Two more shots pierced the windshield. The second sliced the steering wheel.

Fuck it.

She lunged for the passenger-side door, opened it, and dove behind a tree as a shot impacted the open door behind her.

She crouched behind the tree and looked back at the car. The windshield was a spiderweb of cracks. Light streamed through a hole in the open door. The prop pistol lay on the passenger-side floorboard, where it had landed after her collision with the van.

Some backup plan.

She crouched as tightly as she could and prayed for a helicopter filled with FBI agents to descend into Crocker's front yard at that very moment.

She listened for the sound of rotor blades but heard only the dinging of the Jeep's door alarm.

She crouched and waited, unable to process the passage of time, not sure if minutes had passed or just seconds. She waited and listened for the sounds of rescue. What she finally heard was footsteps.

SWAT team, she told herself. *It's a SWAT team. They've had more than enough time to—*

"*Dobryĭ den'*, Miss Williams," said a familiar voice.

Jennifer turned toward the trees. Ten feet away stood Vladimir Dudka, half concealed behind an aspen, staring at her through the scope of a rifle.

"Your hands," he ordered. "Show them to me."

She complied.

He peeked around the rifle scope. "You have a gun?"

"In the car." She didn't see any point in telling him it was just a wall decoration.

Dudka stepped out from behind the tree, wearing camouflage fatigues that resembled an earth-toned Jackson Pollock painting, and sidled left until he could see into the car.

"Good," he said. "Lie on your belly."

Jennifer leaned down, placed her forearms on the ground, and crawled forward into a prone position.

"Now interlock your fingers behind your head."

She kept her eyes fixed on him as she complied.

He lowered the rifle and walked toward her. "Ramming my men off the road was a bold move." He continued past her, toward the Jeep. "Sasha reports that there are a couple of broken bones but that the majority of my soldiers will be joining us shortly."

Fuuuuuuck!

He paused at the road, raised the rifle, and scanned in both directions before approaching the car. He checked the backseat, then lowered the rifle and knelt beside the open door.

"A Colt Peacemaker." He picked up the gun. "What an odd—and uniquely American—choice for a defensive weapon."

"Crocker had it lying around."

Dudka tucked the gun into the waistband of his pants and walked toward Jennifer. "And where *is* Matthew?" His boots stopped just inches from her face. "Until I saw you dive out of this car, I was under the impression that both you and Mr. Crocker were still enjoying my hospitality back in Pahrump. But I have to assume that if you're here, he is too."

"You just missed him."

Dudka placed the toe of his boot on the side of her face. "Has he perhaps taken up a sniper position somewhere above the cabin?"

"Your guess is as good as mine."

Dudka added a bit of pressure with his boot. "I was prepared for the possibility of snipers watching the road. That's why my men waited for me to climb this godforsaken hill and take up a countersniper perch." He pressed down harder. "But instead of sniper fire, I heard a car crash."

Jennifer ignored the pain in her face and tried to think of anything that might keep Dudka busy until help arrived. "Would it help if I said I was sorry?"

"Oh, don't apologize." He pressed even harder. "I admire someone who can—what is the term?—oh yes, 'think outside the box.'"

"You should come to one of my firm's motivational seminars. They're all about thinking outside the box."

"Is that so?" He pressed harder.

"I don't care for them much myself." Her mouth caught dirt and leaves as she spoke. "There's one coming up next month that I'm really dreading."

He took his foot off her face and knelt beside her. "Don't worry, Ms. Williams, you won't be attending."

She felt the gun barrel press against her ear and blurted, "I can show you where the others are!"

"The others?"

"They're hiding. I can—"

"We'll find them without you."

The sound of a hammer cocking hit Jennifer like a punch to the stomach. Dudka whispered, *"Do svidaniya, sladkaya."*

Jennifer opened her mouth to protest but was preempted by the loudest click she'd ever heard.

She looked up and saw that Dudka—crouched so close his knee was almost touching her cheek—was holding the prop pistol he'd taken from the Jeep. He scowled at the gun and tossed it to the side.

Jennifer raised her right hand into a fist and brought it down in a hammer blow to the crotch of his camouflage pants. He gasped and tumbled backward.

She jumped to her feet.

On the ground, Dudka reached for a black handgun holstered on his hip.

Jennifer ignored the pain in her ankle and sprinted for the road. She curved her path around the Jeep, trying to keep it between her and the gun—the *real* gun—in Dudka's hand. She reached the other side of the narrow road and skidded to a stop.

The embankment was not too steep to climb down, but it was definitely too steep to run down. She dropped to her butt and tried to slide, but the rocky ground kept her from picking up any speed.

She heard footsteps just behind her and turned to see Dudka standing at the edge of the road, less than ten feet away.

He raised the pistol and took aim. *"Glupaya suka."*

The gun seemed to discharge twice. The first shot shook Dudka's whole body, and the second sent up a spray of rocks a few inches to Jennifer's right.

Dudka collapsed face-first onto the rocky slope.

Jennifer watched his motionless body for several seconds before noticing a small, bloody hole hiding in the camouflage pattern of his shirt, just below his left shoulder blade.

Crocker!

She scrambled back up to the road. As she reached the top, she stood and yelled, "Crocker!"

But it wasn't Crocker standing thirty yards down the road, holding the rifle.

Ashley lowered the gun and slipped her left arm through the sling.

Jennifer swallowed her surprise and gave a slow wave. Ashley waved back—the same enthusiastic wave she'd given two days before in the bar at La Condamine. Before Jennifer could say anything, her young friend broke into a run.

Jennifer opened her arms and caught Ashley in an embrace. "What happened to going to the helicopter?"

"We were halfway up the hill when we heard a crash. I had the rifle, so I just came running."

Ashley let go of Jennifer and stared down the rocky slope at Dudka's body.

Jennifer placed a hand on her friend's shoulder. "You okay?"

"Yeah." The young woman turned away from the embankment. "Now I remember why I never liked hunting."

Jennifer nodded as if this made perfect sense. "We need to get back to the house. Dudka's men rolled to the bottom of the ravine, but they're still alive."

"I think these guys can handle them." Ashley nodded at something over Jennifer's shoulder.

Jennifer turned to see a convoy of vehicles with red and blue flashing lights coming around the bend. "Oh, thank God." She glanced back at Ashley. "Maybe you should put down that gun."

"Oh." Ashley glanced at the rifle. "Oh yeah." She dropped it to the ground and began waving to the SWAT vehicles.

Jennifer waved too.

After a few seconds of waving, Ashley leaned over and said, "Did you hear me say, 'Smile, you son of a bitch'?"

Jennifer stopped waiving. "What? Like in *Jaws*?"

"Uh-huh. Right before I shot him, I said, 'Smile, you son of a bitch.'"

"Seriously?"

"Nah, but I should have. That would have been cool."

EPILOGUE

When the hot water finally ran cold, Jennifer decided it was time to get out of the shower. She couldn't swear that this had been the longest shower of her life, but it had certainly followed the longest sleep of her life.

Aside from occasional trips to the bathroom and a short visit from Crocker, who'd brought her a cream cheese bagel sometime the previous afternoon, she'd slept for the better part of thirty hours.

Now she was moderately rested and completely famished and eager to see if the sunrise view from Crocker's back porch lived up to the photo she'd seen in his trailer. She wrapped her hair in a towel, slipped on the ankle brace the paramedics had given her, and donned a white robe with ARROWHEAD BUTTE B&B embroidered across the back.

The second-floor hallway was still dark. She paused outside the master bedroom and considered the possibility that Crocker would prefer a few more hours of sleep over getting up at five thirty to see the sunrise.

She was on the verge of turning back toward her room when inspiration struck. She would slip into bed with him and coax him awake in a way he couldn't object to.

She eased open his door, stepped quietly inside, and gasped at the sight of Ashley's blond curls bouncing rhythmically above her toned, arched back as a pair of strong, masculine hands gripped her perfectly round ass.

Ashley screamed and rolled to the side, covering herself with the blanket as she did.

Tom covered himself with the sheet and yelled, "Jennifer, what the hell?"

Jennifer averted her eyes. "I'm sorry! I'm sorry! I was looking for Crocker." Pulling the door shut, she added, "I'm really so sorry."

◆ ◆ ◆

She found Crocker on the back porch, drinking coffee with Special Agent Eastland. The sun was just beginning to crest the mountaintops.

Crocker looked up and smiled. "Morning, sleepyhead. In case you're wondering, it's Sunday. You slept through Saturday."

"Apparently that's not the only thing I slept through. When did you get here, Agent Eastland?"

"Call me Bruce." He stood and motioned for her to take his seat next to Crocker. "I got in last night."

Jennifer accepted the seat. "Thank you."

Eastland pulled up a chair across from them. "I'd hoped to convince you all to come straight into protective custody, but Crocker was quite insistent that I not wake you."

Jennifer smiled at Crocker. "Smart man."

Crocker returned the smile. "Bruce brought some good news."

"Oh?"

Eastland nodded. "It looks like both Sheriff Cargill and Larry Chappell are going to be okay. I got word just before I arrived that the sheriff came through his second surgery with no complications. His prognosis is good."

"And Larry's?"

"He's going to be eating through a straw for a while—they had to wire his jaw shut—but he'll recover."

Jennifer took a deep breath. "Good. I'm not sure I could stand to lose anyone else right now."

"Me either," said Eastland. "That's why I'd like to put you and your friends in safe houses until we confirm that Dudka's organization is permanently out of commission."

Jennifer turned to Crocker. "What do you think?"

He set down his coffee cup. "You need to do what's right for you, but I'm going to stay right here. Dudka is dead and Ilya is in jail, and I'll be damned if I'm going to let any of their half-witted minions scare me away from my home."

Jennifer took in her surroundings. "I guess that works here, but my apartment in Dallas is a little more vulnerable."

Crocker looked surprised. "I meant that you should stay too—I mean, if you want to—until the FBI figures out whether the threat has passed." Before Jennifer could reply, he added, "And there is plenty of room if Tom and Ashley want to stay."

Jennifer giggled.

"What did I say?"

She smiled and shook her head. "Nothing. I just didn't realize you'd let them keep the master bedroom."

"Oh?" A look of realization passed over his face. "Oh! Sorry about that. They haven't come out long enough for me to ask them to switch rooms."

Eastland looked a bit confused.

Jennifer smiled again. "Don't sweat it. It was the best surprise I've had all week."

AUTHOR'S NOTE & ACKNOWLEDGMENTS

The writing of this novel involved a great deal of research; however, I must confess to taking some creative license. Virtually all the details regarding casino security, at both the fictional La Condamine and the real Stratosphere (StratosphereHotel.com), are the product of my imagination. As much as I enjoyed researching real casino security and real casino robberies, I wanted to be sure I didn't create a how-to guide for real criminals.

My portrayal of human trafficking is also highly fictionalized. Although human trafficking is a real problem in the United States and throughout the world (PolarisProject.org/Human-Trafficking), real human trafficking typically involves the exploitation of vulnerable adults or children and hardly ever involves kidnapping by a stranger.

The town of Pahrump (VisitPahrump.com) is very real; however, it is not—as Al disparagingly calls it—a "shithole," and it is not (to the best of my knowledge) plagued by organized crime.

There really is a world-famous shooting school outside Pahrump. Front Sight Firearms Training Institute (FrontSight.com), one of the world's largest private shooting schools, served as the inspiration for the fictional First Shot Shooting Academy.

The Prickly Pear Ranch is fictional, though it would fit right in with the real brothels located along Pahrump's Homestead Road, which does turn into a dirt road and cross the California border (as Mesquite Valley Road) before running into a dry lake bed. To the best of my knowledge, nobody has ever hosted a skydiving tournament at the lake bed; however, skydiving is a regular part of the annual Burning Man festival, which is held on a dry lake bed in northwest Nevada.

This novel would not have been possible without the support and encouragement of my parents, to whom it is dedicated. I also owe a great deal of gratitude to my ex-wife, Anna, and my friends Daniel and Madison, who—along with my parents—offered their input on early drafts and helped me avoid countless missteps.